THE NOORIABAD FILE

THE
NOORIABAD
FILE

Geoffrey Watson

CHARLES SCRIBNER'S SONS
NEW YORK

Copyright © 1979 Geoffrey Watson

Library of Congress Cataloging in Publication Data

Watson, Geoffrey, 1942-
The Nooriabad file.

I. Title.
PZ4.W33883No [PR6073.A862] 823′.9′14 79-19637
ISBN 0-684-16292-X

First American edition published 1979. Printed in the
United States of America.

1 3 5 7 9 11 13 15 17 19 O/C 20 18 16 14 12 10 8 6 4 2

For Ylva and Dennis and
especially Zelda, without
any of whom it would not
have been possible

THE NOORIABAD FILE

MIKE

One

Now that it's all over, I have given myself indefinite sick-leave. The wound in my groin is healing; it's not there that the trouble lies. But as I watch my hands shake, picking up a spoon, lighting a cigarette, I feel as though I have lived through months of tension. It is only the clarity of my recollection of that Friday afternoon which reminds me that it is – unbelievably – no more than two weeks ago that it all began.

Fate plants clues to an impending catastrophe, if only we could find them. And the fact that I can't does not prove that they were not there, but merely that I have not yet found out how to look for them in the right way; that I perhaps need a telescope instead of a microscope, or a different developer for the invisible ink.

I don't mean anything as easy as a remark I paid too little attention to at the time, or something I should have known which just slipped my memory. I mean something more metaphysical than that. Cheerful Jack Kennedy, waving from the back of an open limousine on a bright November afternoon in Dallas, the shadows flashing across his face as his convoy approaches the underpass, stoops for a moment to murmur something to his wife.

A busy London street scene: the Cockney wit of the extras not dulled for a moment by the stacked sandbags, the A.R.P. armbands and the blackout curtains, while a few minutes away in Peenemünde the reeds under the launching ramps are still scorched and smouldering. The hayricks and tractors beside the motorway and your baby on the back seat waving at the village children on the bridge just before the guard-rail buckles and – gracefully, smoothly – a semi-articulated low loader with a Caterpillar tractor somersaults like a ballet-dancer of monstrous proportions into your path . . .

Whenever I think I am about to grasp the suspicious element in the innocence of certain scenes, it slips away again. Perhaps I'm just in no state to think about it right now.

They called me a whiz-kid, they thought that I could work miracles for them – the first actuarian consultant under forty to be on the Secretary-General's list of private telephone numbers. But when it came to the crunch, I'll bet they all wished they had had James Bond around. As it was, they had only me, and even if they all seem satisfied with the outcome, I'm the one who is left with hands so shaky that I can't light a cigarette from the one before.

Not that it was a Friday afternoon like any other, that's not what I mean at all. There was certainly a sense of unpleasant anticipation feeding the embryonic migraine headache just behind my right eyebrow as the train pulled in to Terontola. But it was more anticipation of the next few weeks of very unpleasant, very hard work, the careers which would suffer, the lives which would be ruined. And the knowledge that I was going to bring a lot of trouble to my friend and client, Bob Harding, because what I had uncovered on his mandate was even more explosive than he had thought.

It was a golden September evening which made the tired houses and shops of Terontola look marginally less ugly than usual. The real, old Terontola is still a collection of Tuscan stone farmhouses among the vineyards and olive groves overlooking Lake Trasimene a couple of miles down the hill, where the waters ran red when Hannibal slaughtered thirty thousand Roman soldiers.

2

But the main railway line from Rome to Milan and points north (from Rome to Europe, some of the less kindly exiles in the Eternal Trashheap said) had attracted hideous prefabricated factories and garish supermarkets down to the plain. The international expresses would never have deigned to slow down for such an insignificant place if were it not that here the branch line for Perugia and Assisi and the other main line down the Adriatic coast joined up, and so the service was surprisingly good.

I offered my newspaper to a businessman who was making no move to leave the carriage, and we joked for a moment over the fact that the news was becoming increasingly monotonous and predictable. Gunfight outside a Milan jeweller's; a strike at Rome airport (which had that morning delayed my incoming flight from Koristan for an hour and a half); ultra-left terrorists in Western Germany failing to kidnap a sleepy judge in a linen nightshirt and killing him as they escaped the police net; thirteen army captains sentenced to death in Uganda. Business as usual.

I trotted out the only joke I have ever coined in Italian, the one about *Santo Sciopero* (St Strike) having the most feast days in the Italian calendar, and got the usual embarrassed laugh in reply. There were not many *stranieri* bold enough to make fun of a malaise of which even native Italians were becoming ashamed. That damned strike almost cost me more than merely a sticky hour and a half in the chaos of Fiumicino airport, waiting for my baggage and customs clearance; it nearly cost me my life.

As it was, all I knew as I clambered down on to the platform at Terontola was that the delay had made me too late to talk to Cyril Mkara that week, for the Ghanaian Chief Executive of I.D.A., the International Development Agency of the U.N., which employed Wharton in Koristan, had had to leave for Stockholm. With the critical evidence against Wharton in my briefcase and some even more critical questions in my head, I had not dared to make the frightening extent of my discoveries clear to 'Black Jack' Mkara in my telex requesting an appointment. I reckoned that he had assumed it was a routine matter which could wait, and had left a message with his secretary re-timing our meeting for Monday morning.

Was it coincidence that I was near my retreat in the Tuscan mountains with a weekend on my hands? Whatever I did not realize at the time (and it would be downright dishonest to pretend now that I was on the alert), I was at least aware enough of the need for security to think of somewhere to stash the incriminating document which had made me feel all the way from Nooriabad as though my briefcase was bleeping loudly and flashing red lights. If I had gone any further than that, I would probably have jeered at myself ... I mean, really: an unobtrusive, blond, bespectacled junior-executive type in a lightweight linen suit, thinking the Kung Fu Brothers were shadowing him across Rome!

I had taken a taxi to the American Express office by the Spanish Steps and sent in my card to Jim Hawthorne. He had me ushered into his air-conditioned office, past the long-haired, backpack-toting freaks and the blue-rinsed grandmas from Arkansas queuing resignedly at all the counters.

'Mike, you look worried. What can I do for you?'

'I'm afraid it's probably not strictly legal, Jim, but I need to put something in a vault for a few days and all the regular banks are closed.'

'Hell, that's no problem,' he said, while his bushy eyebrows crawled up his forehead. 'You're a regular card-carrying member of the Amexco party, and I guess you're entitled to a service or two, the amount of turnover you bring me.'

I showed him the plain manilla envelope with the high-explosive contents, and he turned the papers face down and rifled through them as a formality, carefully looking ten centimetres off to the right. 'Sure as hell no plastic bombs in there,' he grinned, but the grin faded as he saw what I was writing on the envelope.

'There's another one, Jim,' I said apologetically, and gave him the photocopies, which he went through with slightly more difficulty in keeping his eyes away. It was not every day he was asked to look after an envelope to be sent 'For your eyes only' to the Secretary-General of the United Nations if not picked up personally by the depositor within five days.

The second envelope was only addressed to my partner in Geneva, but that didn't make him look any happier.

'Hell, Mike,' he said again, 'we don't have the machinery for top-secret dispatches to the U.N., you know that. Not that I expect anything will stop you picking it up, but if you don't, how

4

in the name of God do you think I can get this to New York? Amexco doesn't run a diplomatic courier service.'

'I know that, Jim. It isn't going to come to that. But where else do you expect me to go at five p.m. on a Friday in Rome? The banks are closed, there isn't an embassy I would trust within spitting distance of this stuff. And even if there were there wouldn't be an officer available this side of Elba by now. You ought to know what their weekends are like; you did it yourself for long enough.'

Jim shrugged and stood up. I was sorry to put him in this position, but I would feel better with that material behind eight inches of armour plating.

'The cashier will give you a receipt,' he said, and added, more as a formality than as a question, 'Do you want to see this deposited?' His smooth gait faltered for a second when I said yes. We watched together in silence as the chief cashier's back politely blocked off the view to the dials he manipulated, and when the steel door sighed back into place and the oiled tumblers gave a heavy satisfying *click* I was surprised to hear myself exhale with relief.

I could feel the comfort of Jim Hawthorne's firm handshake as I crossed the road from Terontola station and pushed aside the strips of coloured plastic serving as a fly-curtain at the front door of the bar. The coffee I ordered was almost a ritualistic offering, and the sweet black liquid, *corretto* with a shot of Stravecchio brandy, put me back on my feet better than a Swedish massage.

In the five years since I had married Sophie and thus acquired, apart from a marvellous wife, the keys to her Tuscan retreat, I had spent two weekends out of every four here. And whether I had come by train or by car, the coffee at the bar opposite the station had always marked the line which divided Geneva, my partner Sam, my secretary Christine and the staccato clicking of the IBM printer, from idyllic seclusion, *vino santo* with old Giorgio in the village shop, and coming down into Olmo on a Saturday morning to wander through the stalls of the weekly market.

Never, up till now, had I brought work with me which I could not shrug off at the door of the bar, and Rita behind the counter sensed the difference in a moment.

'Molto preoccupato stasera, eh dottore?'

She frowned as she polished the counter, even though it was already spotless, and her two chins wagged as she nodded to herself, confirming her rhetorical question. It did not escape me that this was the first time in five years that she had asked me anything remotely personal; by her lights, that is. To ask after the family, even in great detail, was not being personal, for the family is public property, and the community has a right to know about it. But she was right. I was still worried, and it must have shown on my face.

Aware that I was, as usual, drinking too much coffee, I sipped the pungent, warming liquid and lied as I watched her performing the age-old rituals of the village bar.

'Moh, niente d'importanza, Rita. It's just Rome that gets me down at this time of year. A glass of wine and some sausages over the fire and I'll be as right as rain.'

Rita recognized the lie as a friendly formula, and her jet-black eyebrows scarcely twitched in acknowledgement. As far as she or anyone else in Terontola could guess, I never went any further than Rome on the early morning train. Indeed, as far as old Giorgio in the village an hour's drive away was concerned, I don't think he imagined I went any further than Terontola.

'La bambina com'è, dottore?'

'Grazie, Rita, Caterina is much better. The doctors are quite satisfied with her progress and Sofia will be bringing her down this week.'

I had long before conceded to the habit of Italianizing names, which in Sophie's case was quite easy. Katrina, of course, became Caterina and won an extra syllable, while those who didn't call me 'dottore' made Michele out of my own name.

Rita, as a matter of fact, had started this dottore business, because she saved up my private mail for me and read the title on the envelopes. But up in the hills they called me Michele, in the pleasant, natural way which many foreigners at first mistake for over-familiarity.

I glanced through my mail while Rita made me my second coffee, and stuffed it all, unopened, into my briefcase which now, without that manilla envelope inside, looked so innocent it was hard to imagine that I had clutched it tightly a quarter of the way across the world.

I had to ask Rita how much her husband had paid for the

6

servicing of the jeep. There was no way she would have had the tactlessness to remind me of the debt, and she apologized for the amount he had scrawled on a sheet off the waiter's block.

'But it's the petrol that costs so much, dottore. Look, he's charged only six thousand for everything else.'

Poor Rita, I thought, how do you ever make a living? Still asking only three hundred lire for a coffee laced with brandy, and your crippled husband taking six thousand for two hours' work, including all his material as usual. I counted out the change and Rita gave me a hundred and fifty back in the crumpled, grubby scrip which has almost become legal currency in confused, catastrophic Italy. I could not have offered a tip; she would not have understood what I meant if I had.

It was still warm enough to drive up the hill with the hood off the jeep, but even the wind in my hair and the welcoming shape of the approaching mountain as I swung up under the massive walls of Olmo didn't cheer me up overmuch.

It was proven beyond any doubt that Wharton was as guilty as hell. My stop-over in Rome had served no further purpose than to back up my report with figures out of the I.D.A. files; figures which none of the bird-brained, chattering, three-year-contract assistants at Head Office had recognized as adding up – or perhaps subtracting – to disaster.

To be fair, I told myself, even Bob Harding who had called me in from his desk overlooking the river in New York hadn't seen it, otherwise he wouldn't be budgeting my by no means modest fee for the investigation. But the case was watertight, there was no doubt left in my mind. I even remembered where to find one or two figures which had puzzled me while doing the preliminary desk research in Rome before going to Nooriabad three weeks earlier.

I started to overtake an ancient truck loaded with tree-trunks, grinding up the steep curves, and had to pull back, my heart thumping, as two eerie figures in black leather and science-fiction helmets with darkened visors snarled towards me on heavy motor cycles. Since the crash, which had left me, by a miracle, physically unhurt while breaking both Sophie's legs and covering the baby with burns, I hated driving more and more.

The truck safely negotiated, my thoughts turned back to my report. On the flight back from Nooriabad I had made use of the

7

privacy of the first-class cabin to write the draft of it, or at least of the succinct, fifteen-page summary which was going to cost Charles Wharton his neck. There were now only the figures to add. I would spend the weekend editing the summary and typing up the sordid, distasteful business in two numbered copies. Although I trusted my secretary implicitly, I did not feel authorized to let Christine see the evidence.

I would not need the incriminating documents I had left in Jim Hawthorne's safe. The most important figures I had already used in my draft, and I knew my way around the material well enough now, so that if I decided to quote any others, I could safely write the text and leave a space to copy in the exact figure on Monday.

Wharton was due in Rome the following Sunday in any case for the annual co-ordination conference of I.D.A. Asian Mission Chiefs. This was one of the most important conferences on the U.N. calendar, for I.D.A. was the body which supervised and correlated all development programmes, whether U.N. or otherwise, in every field: agriculture, population control, emergency nutrition – all sectors in which vast sums of money were changing hands. Until the conference, I had a week to work out exactly how many thousands of tons of rice, how many tractors, how much building material, how much specialized machinery – *how many millions of dollars* – were involved. Wharton's confession had been comprehensive, but I needed cold figures.

I thought about this illegal flow of material and money, all intended for projects aimed at helping a people out of its mediaeval rut and giving it twentieth-century opportunities to develop, and which Charles Wharton had appropriated. Where had it gone, I was wondering. Who had been his accomplices? Theft on such a scale was possible only with active government connivance, and top-level government at that.

And this, too, was going to be the major problem during the coming days. How many other people were likely to know about it? It was all going to revolve around that, I could smell it already.

It gave me no satisfaction at all to know that Cyril Mkara was going to spend a far more unpleasant week than I. A phone call from New York on Tuesday or Wednesday would cancel every engagement in his book, except a flight from Fiumicino to

J.F.K., and he would spend the rest of the week wondering whether I.D.A. could handle this internally before the shit hit the fan. My recommendation was going to be to cable Wharton to come early to the conference and to have Mkara carpet him the next weekend.

The encounter would not be pleasant for anybody involved. The Ghanaian Chief Executive of the I.D.A., beneath his courteous exterior, was a hard and unpopular man. He was rumoured to have got his post through brilliant and ruthless string-pulling, and finally to have clinched it by something little short of blackmail at the U.N. And from what I knew of him it was clear that he would resent any investigation into his tightly run little world. Especially, it had been hinted to me, by whites.

But in my profession I had had a lot to do with hard, unpopular men. I often found out that they were most unpopular where there were axes to grind, where their efficiency would endanger the cosy world of some bumbling bureaucrat. I learned early in my career to treat hints carefully and to evaluate the interests of the hinter, for rumours often seemed to generate almost by spontaneous combustion where there was a foothold for unpopularity.

In my experience, Cyril Mkara was hard-working, tirelessly efficient and – where it did not concern his personal interests – scrupulously fair. During the course of my contacts with I.D.A., I treated with especial caution those who, because of his reputation for 'chopping' or sacking inefficient officers, called him 'Black Jack'.

The wheels of the jeep grated on a gravel curve, and I noticed that I was developing a fully-blown migraine despite the two tablets I had taken on the train, and two before that in Rome. I tried to remember whether there was a stock of Veganin in the house.

Normally we prepared a shopping-list on Sunday nights and dropped it in to the village shop on the way down to Rome, picking up the supplies the next Friday evening, already packed in plastic carrier bags. But on our last visit Sophie had been about to leave for England, and I had known that the Koristan trip might develop in unexpected ways for me, so we had stocked up in the village on Sunday morning.

I turned up the track towards the house without needing to

pass through the village at all. As the road got steeper, occasionally disappearing where great outcrops of bedrock slashed down through the woods, the sun was retiring gracefully into a Raphael glory of pink and blue. I pulled my fur collar up around my neck and resisted a fuzzy impulse to look for cherubim among the clouds.

It did not cross my mind that nobody in the village had the slightest idea that I was there that evening . . . or that it would matter.

Two

There is a point on the track where I often stopped to admire the view. My work takes me pretty well all over the world, and occasionally to some fairly spectacular places, but for sheer pastoral tranquillity Tuscany is my favourite landscape. I stopped the jeep and turned off the engine at this familiar corner where the track rounds a bluff and emerges from the trees for a few yards before plunging back into the darkest part of the wood and the steepest climb up to the house.

The woodland makes a dense carpet here, falling quite steeply away at first, but soon becoming a gently rolling succession of smaller and smaller mountains, until in the distance on a clear day you can see the wide plain of Val di Chiana between two hill-tops. And if you know exactly where to look (it took me two years to discover it), you can just make out the mediaeval fortress which crowns the hill of Olmo.

I lit a cigarette and sat on the bonnet of the jeep, listening to the cracking and pinging of the cooling metal while the shadows deepened. For five minutes or more, the I.D.A., Rome, New York and Koristan faded from my mind. As often happened when I stopped at this tranquil spot, I reflected how lucky I was to be here and to have the leisure to enjoy it and how lucky I was to have Sophie.

We met because her brother Burt, who was a successful young

doctor, had been recommended to me by a client when the migraine attacks, which I got in moments of strain, were becoming so frequent that they were leaving me virtually no pleasure in life. Burt was an American-born, naturalized British citizen. He was very fond of his family and had brought his parents across from New Jersey to spend their retirement years with him in Surrey. We became quite good friends during the course of the treatment, and one evening he invited me to join him for the private view of his sister's exhibition of lithographs and etchings in Chelsea.

I hadn't even known he had a sister and, orientating my imagination on Burt's solid form, I had been totally unprepared for the tall, slender, amber-eyed girl to whom he introduced me. Sophie had high cheekbones and a faintly oriental configuration of features which I did not at first find very attractive. But her long red hair shone like Cornish gold and there were depths to her eyes that I have not fathomed to this day.

It wasn't until I read the appreciation of her work in the next week's *Sunday Times* colour supplement that I realized that she was already an established name in her field. I never imagined that this exotic artist would notice or remember a shy, retiring guest at her exhibition, but when we bumped into each other in Oxford Street ten days later she seemed delighted, and we lunched together in Soho. To my surprise she turned out to be an extremely practical-minded girl, despite what I still took to be a rather extravagant profession.

What she thought of me I did not find out until two weeks later. I had plucked up the courage to ask her to come to a show in the West End. In a quiet coffee-bar afterwards she confessed that she had imagined an actuarian consultant to be a grey man with a grey job, and when Burt had said he would bring me to her inauguration party she had been terribly worried as to what she should talk about to her brother's friend. This particular worry seemed to be solved, for we talked until the bar closed, and at one point we found we were holding hands lightly. We each revised our ideas on the other.

So much so, in fact, that we soon became inseparable, and after six months it had been Sophie who suggested that we marry. 'I really just want to come and live with you,' she said, 'but I think my mother and father would prefer it if we did it properly.'

The country retreat in Tuscany had kept our spare time occupied during the first year and a half of our marriage, and we had set ourselves the aim of renovating it completely before having a child. We kept to the plan, and after Katrina was born a year ago we had spent a lot of the winter in the house. The crash on the motorway to Surrey in the spring, as we were driving out to visit Burt and his wife for the weekend, had shattered our idyllic lives, but bodies and minds were healing fast. We were already over the worst of it, apart from the nightmares which sometimes depressed me.

Suddenly I realized that I was shivering in the cool mountain air. Imperceptibly, the sunset had progressed from one chromatic composition to another more poignant still. It was the last peaceful moment I was to enjoy for ten days. Stubbing the cigarette out carefully – forest fires are a constant danger in the Tuscan hills – I climbed heavily back behind the wheel. Even before I reached for the starter, something odd about the angle of the vehicle made me pause, and a tentative pull on the steering-wheel confirmed my suspicion. In fact, at the back of my mind I had been registering a strange, soft, asymmetrical feel to the steering for some time, but only now that my attention had returned to more immediate problems did I realize what was the matter.

Cursing wearily, I clambered back over the side and examined a definitely flat front tyre. The steep slope didn't worry me too much, as I had faith in the jeep's brakes, and there were plenty of stones to chock the wheels, but the track was quite simply too narrow to work on. I would have to run the jeep at least a hundred yards in one direction or the other until I came to a wide enough place, and then work in the gathering darkness in the reflected light of the headlamps. I never left loose, tempting objects like torches in the open vehicle when it stood in Terontola unattended all week.

I resisted the impulse to give the lame vehicle a petulant kick and decided to go the last kilometre or so on foot. I had only a briefcase to carry, and nobody, except me and my guests, used the track. I could fix it tomorrow, or even telephone for Giorgio's son to come up from the village if I was not feeling better.

Taking my briefcase from the back of the jeep, I set out up the track into the shadows which were already making walking tricky on the rough terrain. My shoes made virtually no sound on the thick carpet of pine-needles. Perhaps this is why I didn't see Klaus until I almost bumped into him.

Of course, I didn't know then that he was called Klaus. I just saw an unfamiliar figure standing in the shadow of a pine, and for a fleeting moment something indefinable about his stance, an interrupted half-movement, perhaps, gave me the impression he was trying to decide whether to turn and hide.

I, too, stopped for a second in surprise, as it was years since I had met anyone crossing this country, too remote even for the most dedicated huntsmen.

But in rural Italy there is no way one may pass a stranger with only a curt 'Good evening'. Like Tuaregs meeting in the pathless desert, Italian countrymen will observe a courteous ritual of greeting, which has an almost obligatory character the further one is from inhabited regions. Fighting down a guilty impatience to get home and sit down, I nodded politely to the stranger and said in the local dialect, 'Buona.'

'Buon giorno,' he replied, and I knew at once that he was German.

In Tuscany, *buon giorno* becomes *buona sera* as early as lunch-time, and he gave the characteristic hard, almost *ch* sound to the soft *g* which does not exist in German.

By nature I am not an isolationist, even though I enjoy my weekend solitude. But a prolonged conversation now would make an invitation for at least a drink, if not dinner, almost de rigueur. And there had never been a less suitable occasion for unexpected guests, with the house dusty, Sophie away in London, my head throbbing and a lot of highly confidential work to do.

In a blessed moment of instinctive self-protection I replied in English, not letting on that I spoke well-nigh perfect German, for I had grown up in Hamburg.

'I hope I'm not blocking your road. I've had to leave my jeep down there with a flat tyre.' I gestured vaguely back the way I had come and he seemed in the dim light to jump nervously at the movement.

'*Ach*, I see,' he said, although for a moment I had no idea what he had seen. Of course, that was it: because of my silent approach, he had been as surprised as I was by our encounter. 'Perhaps I can help you?' His English, although heavily accented, was fluent.

'No, thanks all the same. It will be hard work, and I decided to leave it till the morning. Unless, of course, you need to get past?'

'Er, no, no,' he stammered, and the same thought obviously occurred to each of us at the same time. Since he offered no explanation, I looked at him coolly in the twilight and said, 'Then how did you get up here without a car?'

As the silence lengthened, my irritation turned to dismay. Sophie and I had often discussed the possibility of the house being burgled; it was a tempting target, often uninhabited for days or weeks, and owned by foreigners who would automatically be assumed to be wealthy. Indeed, by the standards of our neighbours we certainly were well off. Not that they would dream of picking even a single fig on our property, but there were gangs which specialized in this sort of job from the towns nearby and even from Rome or Florence, so why not from abroad?

We had spent a lot of money on renovating the house and clearing the land, and it hadn't left much over for Chagalls and Ming vases. There were irreplaceable objects that we loved, but nothing that would interest a burglar much. We had long before decided that the best attitude would be 'Help yourself, cut the phone wires if you must, and go, but don't wave guns around.'

It had all seemed so easy and obvious when we sat discussing it in front of the fire. But now I was tired and irritable and waves of nausea were passing over me.

'I'm afraid I'm not feeling very well,' I said, since he made no attempt to answer my question. 'Have a good walk home. I shall have to go.'

As I made a move to go on up the path, he took half a step towards me and pulled out a revolver. 'Dr Ellis, you will have to come with me.' He was calmer now that the indecision had been resolved, for better or worse.

Nobody had ever pointed a gun at me in my life before, and it must have shown as I said, 'Put that bloody silly thing away. Who the hell do you think you are? You must be off your head.'

But he had taken the initiative now and was not about to lose it again. He moved to where he could push the thing quite hard into my ribs, and I grunted with pain. I had automatically held my arms out like a scarecrow, my briefcase dangling incongruously from the hand furthest from him.

'All right, all right,' I said. 'I'm sick and I'm tired and I'm not going to attack someone twice my size and half my age carrying a pistol. Now tell me what you want, but please let us talk about it in the house.'

Again the initiative seemed to have changed hands, but I felt that I had managed to do it without letting him lose face. And indeed he made no move to stop me as I set off slowly up the track, but fell in behind.

The track got steeper towards the house, and the woods on each side were thick, mainly pines and firs, with some cedars and occasional oaks. There was thick underbrush, but nowhere to run and hide. I could see two things from the state of the surface, even in this light: it had rained during the past week, but dried out again, and there had been a lot of traffic.

This surprised me, because the track led only to the house and served nobody else's property. The land was not regarded as good hunting country, and so we were the only people to use the road at all. We and our visitors.

After a few minutes we passed Sophie's studio, once a barn but now comfortably renovated. Her atelier was on the top floor with plenty of light from the new skylights and her print-shop on the ground floor. Here the presses and acid-baths were installed, and there was a fully equipped darkroom.

It was more than a hundred metres to the house, and we walked in silence while I tried to recall what I had read in detective and spy stories about outwitting a better-armed assailant. True, this was contrary to my 'help-yourself' policy, but at this stage I felt I was still playing it by ear, and that I should at least be prepared to make the best of any opportunity which cropped up. The thief had also demonstrated some uncertainty for a while, which increased my confidence and confirmed my decision to keep an eye open for chances.

However, when we arrived in front of my house, which looked intact, his actions deflated any small hopes I had begun to entertain. Pushing me roughly aside with his revolver, he felt in his pocket and took out a key. Without allowing his eyes to leave me, he fumbled the key into the latch, knocked three times, then once, and opened the door.

'Ich bin's, Klaus. Der Typ ist gekommen, dem das Haus gehört,' he called into the hallway. And then to me, 'Inside, please!'

As I stepped over the threshold – my threshold – the light went on. 'Mach's aus, Du Idiot!' said Klaus in an angry snarl as he pushed me in and shut the door behind us, 'es wäre besser, wenn er uns nicht sieht.'

He was quite right, I thought; it would have been better for them if I hadn't been able to recognize them. And for me, possibly.

It was not yet dark, but I now realized that in the shadows of the woods outside I had seen no more than the vague outlines of the first man's face. Blessing my luck at not having spoken to Klaus in German, I decided to continue to have no idea of what they were talking about.

The second man had already moved towards me away from the light switch, and it was now clearly too late to put on masks or other means of concealment ... Nylon stockings, I thought, as a brief memory of the obscenely smooth heads of some bank robbers in a film came into my mind.

I found myself between the two men who were obviously brothers. Each had shoulder-length, well-kept hair and a bushy moustache, which made the family resemblance even more obvious. They were in their late twenties and looked like any two anonymous students in any north European university town, except for one detail. Both wore heavy black leather trousers, but while Klaus wore what, in the first confused impression, I took for jackboots, his brother was in stockinged feet. An incongruously white big toe emerged from a hole in one sock.

But it was something else which made me drop my briefcase in shock and raise my arms again. Klaus's brother was carrying a small machine-gun.

Three

He saw me gape at this unexpected item of military hardware, and smiled a little. Then, with a self-deprecatory shrug, he put it away on a shelf – but, I noticed, not before he had glanced at Klaus to make sure he was still pointing his pistol at me.

A kaleidoscope of questions made me almost dizzy. Do burglars run to machine-guns nowadays? Even small ones? Do they carry firearms at all? Shouldn't the house be in some kind of ransacked turmoil? Where the hell were the Veganin?

While Klaus was apparently sometimes indecisive and might have been outwitted by a younger or less sick man, his brother radiated confidence. He also spoke far better English. 'We're very sorry to cause you this inconvenience, Dr Ellis. You see, you rather surprised us, arriving on foot like that.'

He smiled again, reassuringly, and I thought, you're not going to smooth-talk me, you bastard, not with that machine-gun on the shelf. Of course, it was unthinkable that anyone should come up the eight kilometres of track without a vehicle, and they had probably been convinced they would have ample warning of anyone's arrival.

Again the momentum was lost for a moment as we all three tried to decide what to do next.

'Look, I don't know who you are or what the hell you want, but before we do anything else, for God's sake let me have a couple of Veganin.'

Klaus and his brother looked at me blankly.

'Veganin, tablets, medicine. I have the most terrible migraine headache and I shall probably faint very soon. They are in the bathroom.'

I made a tentative movement towards the staircase, but Klaus's gun jerked convulsively and I froze mid-step. His brother had tensed for a moment too, but as I stopped and looked at Klaus and wearily spread my arms again he relaxed.

'My dear Dr Ellis, there is no need to raise your hands. Please take off your coat slowly and sit down. I shall bring you your tablets. Just please avoid sudden movements.'

'Who the hell are you to invite me to take off my coat and sit down? This is my house and just because you are waving those guns around you don't have to be insolent as well!'

I could not see Klaus, who was now behind me, but there was no flicker of reaction from his brother. He didn't scream at me, 'You filthy English *Schwein!*' his face contorted with fury, nor did he spread his hands apologetically and say, 'A thousand pardons, sir, we may be robbers but we are chentlemen.'

He just looked at me hard for a few long moments while my stomach knotted with fear and I thought, now I've done it, why can't I keep my big mouth shut?

He turned back from the stairs and spoke in a neutral voice with no trace of threat or violence, just rather slowly as though he was thinking it out while he was speaking. I didn't realize for some time that he was also speaking for Klaus's benefit.

'You must realize, Dr Ellis, that you are completely in our hands. No one would hear a shot up here, and we can disappear at once. Your arrival now makes things as difficult for us as they are for you. We have no wish whatever to harm you, but we shall not hesitate to do so if you try to harm us. We shall go soon, but until then you will have to obey us perfectly. My . . .' he hesitated for a second, 'My friend and I shall decide the best thing to do and then we shall go. Until then you will please regard yourself as a prisoner. I shall now get you your medicine. What was the mark, the brand, again, please?'

'Veganin. In a blue and white pack in the medicine chest over the wash-basin.' My voice had escaped from my control, as the truth of what he was saying became clear to me.

As he went up the stairs I took my coat off, leaving the brief-case under the coat-rack and staying carefully away from the shelf where the machine-gun was.

I went over to the living-room door and turned to ask Klaus whether I might go in there. He spoke before I could.

'Go in very slowly, open the door big and leave it open.'

He followed me closely into the room with his gun about two feet from my spine. I remembered reading in a thriller that the traditional gun-in-the-back method is wrong because the prisoner can turn and knock it aside too easily. I wondered whether Klaus knew this too.

The living room was in as chaotic a state as I had imagined, but as I sat down in front of the hearth, where no fire was lit, I realized that this was not the type of chaos I had expected. Drawers and cupboards had not been rifled, nor had pictures been torn from the walls.

It was the disorder left by sloppy living. Dirty crockery was all over the table, the ashtrays were overflowing, a bottle of red wine had been overturned in a corner and the spilled contents mopped up with newspaper which was still lying there. Items of clothing were everywhere, and a sleeping-bag and a blanket were in an untidy heap under the window. The shutters were closed and the smell of stale tobacco smoke was unbearably strong, even though I smoke quite heavily myself.

'Can I open a window? It smells like a bar in here.'

'I'm afraid not,' said the second man from the doorway. He had returned silently and came to me with the Veganin pack and a tooth-glass of cold water. 'We cannot risk anyone seeing the lights.'

'But nobody can see the lights anyway,' I protested.

'That is what I thought, but I want to be quite sure.'

'You have been living like pigs here. I cannot imagine how two civilized people can make such a revolting mess. Please decide quickly what to do and then go. I shall not follow you, I cannot follow you. My car is broken down and is blocking the road about a kilometre away.'

Klaus and his brother exchanged glances. I took the tablets and leaned my head back with my eyes closed. Klaus spoke in German and I did my best to reproduce the look of someone taking not the slightest interest in a conversation which he cannot understand. I screwed up my eyes and massaged my forehead with my finger-tips. This small pretence was my only advantage at the moment, and I hung on to it like a lifeline.

'Get upstairs, take everything out of the child's bedroom and put in a mattress. And a bucket. Check that the padlock on the window shutters is properly closed and that the key isn't on top of the window or the door or somewhere. And check that the lock on the door works and the key is outside. And put in a blanket and a clean sheet. I think that's all. We'll have to lock him in there until the others come back.'

It took me an immense effort not to groan out loud. I mechanically continued massaging my forehead and screwed up my whole face in pain while I tried not to show that I had understood. *Die Anderen,* the others. It was terrible, terrible.

I heard Klaus leave the room.

'Dr Ellis, wo ist Ihre Frau?'

I looked at him blankly. 'What are you talking about?'

'I wish to know, where is your wife? I think you had better tell us the truth. We wish to avoid violence, and it is therefore better that we do not have any more unpleasant surprises.'

He gave me time to think, because he knew I would realize he was right. I did. It could turn into a tragedy if Sophie walked in on this and somebody panicked.

'She is in England with our daughter. I do not expect her back before Tuesday, if then.'

'I hope that is not just a trick to make us leave quickly.'

My God, I thought, they can't be considering staying that long! A new thought occurred to me.

'How did you know my name?'

'That was a rather foolish question. There is a lot of your correspondence in that desk over there.'

'Why did you choose me? I am not a rich man; there are far richer people in this area you could rob, even if there is more risk involved nearer the towns.'

'Dr Ellis, I am asking the questions and you are answering them. It is for your own good in the end.'

Yes, I thought; that's what they always say, cops or robbers. But perhaps he saw that I had answered my own question, because he spoke again.

'We did not choose you. We chose your house, and we do not wish to rob you. We have made enough money already from a bank raid in Naples, and we wish only to hide for a few days.'

On the run. Of course, that was it. But why should Germans raid a bank in Naples? And only then I remembered, and this time I could not control my face any more than if I had heard him say, I shall shoot you now.

I opened my eyes and saw that he was watching me. When had it been, Wednesday or Thursday? And how many of them had there been? Five? Six? How many did the police kill? I had not read that newspaper article closely; as I had said to the business-man in my compartment, it's always the same nowadays, business as usual. My eyes strayed automatically to the pile of newspapers on the dinner table, and I noticed now that there was an Italian–English dictionary lying open near them. I looked back at him. He was smiling slightly.

'You didn't raid a bank in Naples. You shot a judge in Berlin.'

I didn't see a muscle move in his face, but I was no longer sure that he was smiling.

'Yes.' He hesitated, as though about to add, an unfortunate error, or perhaps an enemy of the people, or a fascist pig, but he said nothing for a moment.

'In fact, we didn't. When I said "yes", I meant that you have realized who we are. It was a police bullet that killed Hans Siebert. That makes no difference at all now. Except that nobody will believe us, so they want us for homicide as well as kidnapping.'

There was really nothing I could say. Of course I deplored violence, of course I was outraged at political or other kidnapping. But there were such things which, for reasons of upbringing or profession or perhaps just personal interest, horrified me far more. Kidnapping and political ransom was something far away from my world, something to which the distance and the dulling effect of frequent and detailed press coverage had inured me, until the TV news report on a spectacular crime was no more than a rather less exciting version of the play that followed it.

For a crazy moment my thoughts wandered from Berlin to Nooriabad. Less spectacular, perhaps, but was Wharton's crime not just as sordid? How many thousands of nomads died when the crops failed and the last scrawny chicken was killed; and still the rice did not arrive? Wharton, whose job had been to combat the natural, local tendency to channel everything into the wrong pocket, and who instead had seen his job as choosing pockets. This was my world; I had nothing to do with kidnappers and judge-shooters.

Except that I did. One of them was sitting in my living room now, pointing a pistol loosely in my direction and planning to lock me into Katrina's room with a mattress and a bucket. This was more real than any bureaucratic foul-up which would be solved by moving a crooked man to a minor station and quietly retiring him with a pension.

As I wearily closed my eyes again, the phone rang.

Four

Footsteps crashed on the stairs and Klaus came into the room in a hurry. Again and again the bell shattered the tense silence while Klaus and I both looked questioningly at his brother, who was looking at no one, but calmly deciding how to handle the call. It was rapidly becoming obvious that he was not only the coolest person present, but also that his authority was accepted and deserved.

The bell rang again. He got off the table where he had been sitting and without his eyes leaving for a moment picked up the receiver with one hand and held the other – the one with the gun in it – poised over the receiver rest. If I drew a breath to shout he could cut the connection and apologize later for a fault on the line if the caller should ring back.

'Pronto?'

The call must have been from near by, because the non-Italian intonation of the reply was clearly audible across the room.

'Dr Ellis?'

'No, I am a colleague of Dr Ellis. Can I take a message?'

Hesitantly the caller asked, 'Jens?'

Jens's face relaxed and he switched into German. His hand drifted away from the phone, but the gun was still pointed in my general direction and his eyes were on mine.

'Ja, was ist denn los, Ulli?'

Now the caller spoke fast and I could no longer make out every word; but from the intelligible snatches and Jens's replies it was obvious that Ulli was one of 'the others' who had been coming back, had found the disabled jeep on the track, and had returned to a call-box to investigate the situation from a safe distance.

'It's okay,' said Jens, 'Ellis came back but we captured him. Can you get past the jeep on the bikes?'

The bikes! The black leather trousers and the jackboots. And the two eerie figures on the road from Olmo. But the information I had was meagre. I still had no more than three first names and a minimum number of four people. With an effort I tried this time to mime an eavesdropper who understands nothing but is anxious to know what is happening; if this goes on much longer I can write exercise books for drama schools. I thought.

'How did you get on?' Jens was asking.

The reply mentioned *Zeitungen,* an *Anruf* (this one in detail), and something about penicillin. So one of them was wounded? They had gone to pick up newspapers to follow the manhunt and to call someone about where to go on next? Or was that just worthless guesswork on the basis of too little information?

'All right, get up here fast.' Jens's voice was not brusque, just authoritative. He was used to making the decisions and having them obeyed. 'Hold on a minute.'

To my surprise he said to me in English, 'Dr Ellis, you may be a prisoner for a day or two, and we shall be leaving the house as little as possible. Is there anything urgent you require, medicines, cigarettes, anything?'

My thinking was nothing like as fast as his. I realized this might be turned into an opportunity to get them to give themselves away somehow, but all I could manage off the cuff was, 'You might pick up my mail at the village shop.'

Without a trace of inflection Jens said, 'I'm afraid that won't be possible. Schon gut, Ulli. Komm mal 'raus jetzt.' He hung up and gave me a tight smile. 'You must realize, Dr Ellis, that we are professionals. If you co-operate with us, you will come to no harm and we will be gone sooner and with less inconvenience. If you insist on struggling, we shall be obliged to make life unpleasant for you.'

This young man was not being melodramatic; he was not making sadistic threats. He said exactly what he meant, of this I was sure, and meant in this case simply that he would have to tie and gag me, or something similar. His attitude was reasonable and considerate, but firm. It was calculated to win my co-operation.

Yet in his literal, linear thinking was hidden a trap of which he seemed unaware: since the logical reaction to his reasonableness was my co-operation, this was exactly what he would expect and be looking for. I was already at a hopeless disadvantage, and would only risk unpleasantness if I continued to try to outwit him.

But the urge was in me, perhaps because wherever there is a challenge a man will try to pit himself against it. And I noticed

23

that the Veganin were already taking effect, despite (or perhaps because of) the drama of the situation.

He did not wait for my reply, but asked Klaus, 'Is the room ready?'

Klaus nodded and Jens turned again to me.

'Dr Ellis, will you please go up to your child's room and permit us to shut you up there for a short while. We shall prepare some food and bring you some of it. Is there anything else you require?'

There was little point in making difficulties by pointing out that it was my own property that they were offering me. At this stage, there was no alternative but to play along, but I was not going to make a weak showing.

'Yes, I would like some of the wine out of the pantry – give me a bottle and a glass – and these newspapers.' I picked up the pile of papers on the dinner table and tucked them under my arm with what I hoped was a businesslike, natural movement. To my surprise, there was no objection from either jailer, and I went up the stairs feeling I had won a point.

Katrina's room was more or less as I had expected it would be; everything removed to leave it clear and easy to survey. A camp bed from the guest room stood against the wall opposite the door, with a mattress and a tidy pile of folded bedclothes. Behind the door was a bucket and a roll of toilet paper. The padlock on the inside of the shutters was closed, and I cursed my own perfectionism for a fleeting moment as I remembered screwing the hasp to the frames in such a way as to leave the screws visible only when the whole device was open.

'And I shall need some hangers and a chair for my clothes,' I told Klaus. 'And what are you cooking for dinner?'

The bemused look on his face would at any other time have made us burst out laughing.

'I ... I have no idea,' he said. 'I shall see what is in the kitchen.'

He retreated and locked the door behind him. I heard him try to turn the key twice, but it was not a double-throw lock and he had to be content with one turn. This door was the weak point in their defences, and I would have to watch for escape opportunities every time it opened or closed.

Listening to his footsteps descending the stairs, I sat down with my head in my hands and breathed deeply for a while in order to relax. I had taken it rather well, I thought, and then corrected myself: I had been very lucky. These were extraordinarily well-mannered terrorists. Perhaps there did exist the gentlemen criminals I had always scoffed at in the movies? Perhaps, as Jens had said, I only needed to co-operate and all would turn out well?

Somehow I fancied this was not the case. Jens's politeness and calm served some purpose which would ultimately not be for my benefit, of that I was sure. And sometimes I had had a fleeting impression, too brief to nail down, that he was constantly having to remind himself to be cool, to hold himself in check. This must have some vital significance, I reasoned: perhaps they had orders from somebody else to treat me with care? I had not enough evidence to work on.

So where did that leave me? Alone against four, and at least two of them well-armed and athletic, ten years my junior. I am a methodical man – perhaps as a result of professional training – and used to trying to split the most complex situations down into their components before beginning to look for solutions. There are so many small points you might otherwise overlook, which later turn out to have been important, often deliberately played down by somebody with ulterior motives. But try as I would, I could sift very little to my advantage out of this situation, except perhaps for my fluent knowledge of German.

I am not tall, and although I have not yet completely gone to seed, years of sedentary work have left me in no shape for physical mayhem. All in all, and especially in view of their superior firepower, I knew that my only chance of turning the tables lay in outwitting them somehow. Part of that policy must consist of letting them think that their arguments in favour of reasonableness and co-operation had convinced me. Reviewing my behaviour thus far, I felt I could be satisfied with the impression I had probably made: outraged at first, and reluctantly growing meeker.

And any action I did decide to take, I told myself firmly, must fulfil two conditions: it must be soon and sure. Soon, while they were still taken off-balance by my arrival, and sure because they would not be likely to give me a second chance if I botched the first. My docile cover would be blown, and Jens's threats of unpleasantness might well turn out to be bitter truth.

I took off my jacket, made a mental note to ask for some jeans and a sweater to change into, and wished I hadn't left my suitcase with all my toilet gear and a change of clothes at the airport. It had seemed at the time that I would be flying out again Saturday noon at the latest, and even when I found out that Mkara had left and I was stuck until Monday, there had been no need to bring anything with me to the house.

But there was something in that suitcase I wished I had with me now. A photo of Sophie and Katrina.

Standing up and looking around the bare room, I started taking stock of my assets, but I hadn't got very far before I was aware of a new sound in the night.

Two powerful motor bikes were coming up the last stretch of the track and stopping in front of the house.

Five

I strained my ears and closed my eyes in that involuntary gesture of the listener, which serves to sharpen one sense when another is turned off. I could hear Bach on the cassette-player: the Second Brandenburg Concerto. Knowing the house as I did, with all its particular squeaks and cracks and gravel patches, I could quite easily follow the action.

Although I pressed my ears to the door panel, I heard not a word as the door was opened for them and they stepped inside in heavy boots.

I could well imagine that they were let in by someone with his finger to his lips and an explanatory pointing up the stairs. I heard the rustle of packages changing hands, the ripping sound of heavy zip fasteners being opened, and then the door to the dining room opened and closed and I was cut off.

Katrina's room was over the kitchen and the master bedroom next door was over the dining room, so that there was no way I could overhear the conversation below. I lay on the floor and pressed my ear to the old red tiles, and even held the other ear closed, but all I could make out was a distant murmur and the roaring of my blood.

I was about to get up and start my stocktaking over again when a movement below made me stop and stealthily spread myself more comfortably on the floor.

'Was gibt's denn hier zu essen?' It was Klaus's voice. My inquiries about the evening's menu were obviously having some result.

Nobody seemed disposed to help him, for the other voices, although slightly louder now due to the open door downstairs, remained unintelligible.

'I'll do the sausages with some fried onions and boiled potatoes,' announced Klaus, but his suggestion met with disapproving groans and apparently some counter-suggestions, for he replied, 'You will have to do that, because you don't like the way I do it.'

Suddenly one of the voices detached itself from the background and approached under me, and the last part of a sentence about putting a lot of fuel into the bikes was audible. It was a new voice, a musical bass with mellow, warm intonation; more like Santa Claus than a terrorist.

'Du, Hartmut,' said Klaus (and I added another name to my pitiful list of facts), 'gib mir das lange Messer.' I tried to picture Hartmut handing him the knife, handle first, but gave it up as pointless. 'Wie geht's dem Bernd?'

My right ear would have pricked up if it had not been firmly pressed to the tiles. Jens and Klaus, Ulli and Hartmut; it sounded like a cheerful harmless student group on holiday, and Hartmut had visited his friend Bernd. And how was old Bernd?

But these were not people to go for an afternoon drive to a friend's for coffee, nor to ask casually about the well-being of an acquaintance. No, it wasn't like that at all, and suddenly I remembered the talk of penicillin. After a pause, the bass voice, as mellow as before, said 'Sieht noch bös' aus.'

But the news that Bernd still looked in a bad way was not the reason for the resonant timbre. I had momentarily let myself be fooled by a mere intonation. That was no Santa Claus downstairs. I was going to have to pull myself together.

Hartmut went on, 'He said the only thing the police wanted

from him was straightforward information about the truck that knocked him off. They said there was no hope of finding it, though; the driver probably hadn't even noticed the bump on that bad surface. They hardly glanced at his papers. The nastiest moment he had was when they offered to contact the Embassy in Rome for him. We're lucky he wasn't concussed when he came off, or they might have done it without asking. He said he had a sister who lives here and he had already given her telephone number to someone while he had been waiting for the ambulance. They asked nothing about his friends, so it seems nobody connected us with him. He said we were quite right to clear off, although he had felt pretty lonely and frightened for a moment, lying there on the motorway with his leg smashed, everyone driving off into the dark, and his bike wrecked.'

The kitchen noises had stopped during this long report, and the others were obviously listening to every word.

'He has a perfectly clean break and no complications,' added Hartmut as an afterthought.

'*Klasse!*' said Klaus, and there was a relieved noise from the dining room, too.

Jens's voice approached, speaking decisively.

' . . . have to get him to Roswita's apartment in Florence. She can keep her ears open at the Consulate, and her work is quite enough to keep any cop at a distance. It's our fall-back address anyway, as soon as this job's over.'

'And we could get him on to the motorway from there in three minutes,' rumbled Hartmut, 'north, south, or even over to the coast.'

'Riding pillion with his leg in a cast, I suppose,' said Jens with scorn. 'How long will he have to stay in hospital?'

'That's the good bit,' replied Hartmut. 'When he said he had used crutches before and he had a sister nearby to look after him and could come in for check-ups, they raised the roof, but eventually agreed to only two days more.'

Was it *zwei Tage* or *drei* he said? Whether two or three, it was still good news for them.

'Pity we can't get him here, but he can't ride and we can't risk using Ellis's jeep,' said Klaus.

Jens had started to reply, something about not forgetting to get the jeep to the house first thing in the morning, and the kitchen background noises had started up again, but I no longer listened. I had heard a click and felt a draught, and I opened my eyes to see the door moving.

In the dim upstairs hallway I could make out a fist with a glass sticking out of one end and a bottle out of the other, obviously to free one hand to open the door.

Shutting my eyes and breathing shallowly, I wondered what someone looked like when he had fainted. Fortunately the door striking my outstretched foot came quite expectedly, and my non-reaction to the sharp blow must have strengthened my performance.

Come to the Mike Ellis School of Drama. Personal tuition by experienced principal, speciality: crime plays.

There was silence as the newcomer froze. My right eye was near the floor, with my face turned down that way and facing towards the door. I peered between my lashes, knowing that the light was behind me and, in any case, that my nose was almost touching the floor.

Under the inverted horizon of the bridge of my nose I could make out a pair of motor-cycle boots, quite immobile. Seconds passed. One foot left the floor and the other moved slightly as it took the weight. There was a gentle nudge against my left knee-cap, enough to move my legs and hips and let them fall back sluggishly.

I calculated my chances of slipping out of the room and getting out of the top doorway. The house, like most farmhouses in the area, had originally been inhabited only on the first floor, while the ground floor was for the animals, crops and implements. There was still the outside staircase; the interior one had not existed before the renovation. The great old key was always left in the well-oiled lock of the top door, and I was sure the hinges did not squeal. I could even re-lock the door on the outside and perhaps even lock them in downstairs too, if they all went up to look for me.

No, that would be a waste of time. They would be out of the windows in a flash.

All these thoughts shot through my mind in a short moment. As the boots began to move again, I already knew what I should do if I could only get out of the room: be stealthy as far as the door, and then get as much woodland between myself and the house as I could, putting speed before silence, as they would not hear me inside the house anyway. With my intimate knowledge of the country I should have no difficulty in escaping. Always assuming I got out of the room.

The shins above the boots tilted forwards, and a black leather behind came into view as the visitor crouched down and put the bottle and glass on the floor.

I shut my eye until I heard the footsteps return to the corridor, and slitted it open again as the door was pulled to. *But not locked!*

As the footsteps faded, I was already getting to my feet and opening the door in one smooth movement. Swinging round the door-jamb like a kid round a lamp-post and thankful for my silent rubber soles, I shot into the corridor away from the stairs and towards the outside door.

And almost into the back of Ulli. Obviously before doing anything else, he was turning the upper floor into a cul-de-sac, open only towards the stairs, because he was taking the old iron key from the lock and putting it into his pocket. Not such a dumb terrorist after all, I thought bitterly, and snatched up a heavy glass ashtray from a side-table. It was too late to stop moving, he was already turning back towards me.

What happened then was all so fast that I'm not quite sure what order it took. I have a clear recollection of Ulli's short-cropped blonde head turning towards me, of the ashtray connecting from behind with a nasty crunch, of wondering just how hard you have to hit to crack a skull, and of realizing that Ulli wasn't short for just Ulrich, as anyone who had heard of Andreas Baader and Ulrike Meinhof should have known. And of thinking, this must be the first time in twenty-five years that I have hit anybody. Then I had a glass ashtray in one hand and an unconscious girl in the other, and someone was coming up the stairs.

Six

Dragging Ulli into the master bedroom, surprised at how heavy such a slender body could become, I deposited her as silently as possible on the big double bed, and put the ashtray down beside her. It was fortunate that the cassette-player downstairs was running, for it covered up any scuffling or rustling sounds this made.

There was an inarticulate grunt of surprise from the next room, and then Klaus crashed into the corridor, hesitated while my heart thumped, and then leapt down the stairs three at a time, shouting, 'Die, sind weg, die sind weg!'

The house exploded with noise as I slipped the key from Ulli's back pocket and stood in the angle of the room behind the door, which actually touched one end of the huge wardrobe when open wide. Someone dropped an empty saucepan into the sink with a ringing clang and boots clattered on the tiles. Somebody was coming up the stairs faster than Klaus had just gone down. It was Jens, calling instructions: 'Hartmut, round the back; Klaus, down the track!'

He went into Katrina's room, cursed, and then burst into the room where I hid less than two feet from him, flinging the door wide open so that it smashed heavily against the corner of the wardrobe right in front of my nose, making me flinch.

And hiding me effectively.

I heard him gasp sharply, click the light on and cross the space to the bed in two steps. There was a rustling as he examined Ulli, and muttered 'Scheisse!' which told me nothing about the extent of the damage I had inflicted. At least part of the sick tight feeling in my stomach was a result of not knowing whether I had killed the girl or not.

I had never before reflected much about the amount of thinking one can compress into a moment in time, but today I had ample opportunity. I stood in a rough square, two stone walls behind me and two wooden ones in front, about as much space as a coffin except for the headroom, and considered quite clearly that it was strange how I would have had no compunction about slugging a man in the back of the head; but a girl – that was different. I felt the stirrings of guilt.

Once again I pulled myself up with a start. First a melodious warm voice, now long blonde eyelashes, helpless open mouth and firm breasts under a tight T-shirt . . . I had to get used to the idea that if I gave them any more reason these people would kill me.

Jens ran to the top outside door, shook it, and then ran back along the corridor and down the steps. He stopped half way, came back and looked into the bathroom across the landing. Then he went down again, looked into the ground-floor lavatory and ran outside.

I moved the door two inches and looked out. Ulli was unconscious, but I could see that she was breathing. Jens had lifted her trailing leg on to the bed, shifting her up higher than I left her. There was no patch of blood where her head had been. I was glad.

A new thought crossed my mind. My best weapon, surprise, was gone, and the only one I had left was my better knowledge of the terrain in the dark. Not being by any means a violent man, I had planned a purely defensive action. But reminding myself forcibly a moment ago that these kids were dangerous had recalled the machine-gun, and there was no reason to do without such a precious advantage if it was still where Jens had put it. They would hardly want to advertise their presence with it unless *in extremis,* for the sound would carry far on the night air. But I had nothing to hide and everything to gain from attracting attention.

As I tiptoed swiftly to the top of the stairs, a motor bike roared into life and then moved off down the track, the rider revving it hard like a schoolboy on a moped.

I ran halfway down the stairs and ducked under the landing to look across at the shelf. The machine-gun was gone, but I saw something else which made me pull up short. The briefcase was still standing under the coat-rack, and its contents – fifteen pages of clear text in my neat, legible handwriting – were high explosive. In the hands of these people, my notes could be a superb weapon of extortion.

It was ironic that I had not thought of this until I had far more pressing problems on my hands, but finding myself captive at gun-point in my own house had understandably driven most other things from my mind.

There was no reason to let them know I was still in or near the house, so I darted down the stairs, opened the briefcase, and scooped up the manuscript. I left the briefcase exactly where it was and ran back up the stairs as lightly as I could. The upper floor was a cul-de-sac for them; Jens had rattled the door and found it locked. But for me it was still an open road.

As I passed the fusebox on the landing, I snatched up the heavy rubber-coated torch which always stood on top of the electricity meter. Power failures were frequent in this isolated area. I shifted it approvingly in my hand: it was quite a handy weapon, if one disobeyed the manufacturer's instructions. With a thrill of horror, I realized that I had every intention of doing so given an opportunity.

Of course, they might give me none. And then they would have the manuscript again. As I hesitated, precious seconds passed. Finally, I turned into the bathroom and knelt down beside the bathtub. Opening the service hatch in the tiled surround, I pushed the manuscript in below the S-bend of the bath drain and replaced the false tile.

Creeping along the corridor towards the outside door, I had to pass the master bedroom, and peered in cautiously. Ulli had not moved, but try as I would I was unable to see any movement of breathing. I noticed that dispensing with a bra suited her very well indeed, and then I noticed myself noticing. I had quite possibly killed this girl, and all I was thinking about . . .

I stepped across the room, intending to feel for a pulse, and she let out the breath she had been holding and opened her eyes wide. They were a cold greyish blue.

'They will kill you if you try to run away,' she said conversationally.

I stood with my mouth open foolishly, and took another step forward as she started to get up. Or so I thought at the time. My movement added considerably to the force behind the kick she aimed at my groin, and I doubled up in agony as the breath whistled between my teeth.

Lying on her back on the bed and using her arms as springs, she aimed another kick at my head, but I had bent over at an angle to the right and her feet connected with my left shoulder, just as I was beginning to straighten up again. The blow sent me staggering backwards, arms windmilling to keep my balance, out of the door and across the corridor where my shoulders slammed into the opposite wall, while it carried the girl off the edge of the bed on to the floor.

A moment ago I had been feeling bad for hitting a girl. That was gone now, knocked out of me by that vicious kick. I reeled back off the wall and jumped with both feet together towards her stomach as she lay dazed from the fall.

Not dazed enough. She twisted aside, and in mid-jump I saw that I was not going to connect. My feet hit the tiles behind the small of her back as she rolled away. Over her shoulders she saw me raising the torch and opened her mouth to scream.

It all sounds so easy in detective stories, where A hits B and puts him out for two hours. But people can take quite heavy blows on the head without even losing consciousness. So you know you have to hit pretty firmly. But if you hit too hard, you smash in the skull. So how hard *do* you hit someone on the head?

Fortunately, I was getting a certain amount of practice, and I slammed the torch, which for this purpose made an excellent rubber truncheon, on to the side of her head above the ear.

I stood up and leaned gasping against the front of the wardrobe, the pain still sending sharp surges through my abdomen. In thirty seconds I had fought more than in thirty years, and I was astonished at the thought of what I, a mild-mannered consultant more used to boardroom squabbling, had just done.

As soon as I had enough breath, I lugged Ulli back on to her bed, putting her in as nearly the same posture as I could remember. Thinking ironically of my hesitation of so short a time ago, I felt under her breast for a heartbeat. It was faint but reasonably regular. It was time to go.

As I made for the back door, I heard the motor bike coming back up the track, still revving uncertainly, and I cursed. The corridor light was not on, but there was a lot of glow from the master bedroom, too close to the back door for comfort. I pulled the bedroom door to. If I slipped out through a narrow gap, the light would not show outside. The door was at the back of the house, and I could hear Jens's voice and the sound of the bike still in the front. I guessed he would be revving the engine as he

34

moved slowly in low gear, probably swinging the lights from side to side.

I slipped the key into the lock, and as I turned it I made a plan of action for outside. The track at the front led round the left of the house, and the back stairs pointed towards the same side, so if they drove the bike around to the back to have more light I would run into them. But if I was quick enough, I could be off the steps and round to the right and in shadow before they came. And they had already searched the track, so that would be the safest place to head for right now. A pity about the jeep, but I would be safer on foot.

The door made not a sound, and I slipped out on to the stone steps which had been the main entrance when the house had still been a farm. I ran down them three at a time, and saw the glow of the bike's lights approaching from around the side of the house out of the corner of my eyes as I doubled back at the foot of the flight. The bike stopped with the motor running, and I heard a confused conference, shouted but unintelligible over the engine noise and around the whole mass of the house.

Under the staircase was an outdoor oven. Nearly every Tuscan farmhouse has one: a narrow, square entrance at the front and a domed brick vault a yard or more in diameter inside. The farmers still use them today, but they require a whole morning of heating up with brushwood before you can bake in them, so it is worth the effort only for large families. Usually ours was a convenient shelter for garden implements. I risked a flash of the torch with my hand well inside the opening.

I saw at once what I was looking for and grabbed it. As I ran around the corner of the house away from the noise and lights, I stuffed the torch into the waistband of my trousers and hefted the *roncola* in my fist instead. It was a vicious pruning-hook, the blade about a foot long, curving over to a sharp point. Down the back was an extension with a straight, razor-sharp edge for use as a hatchet, and the whole of the inside of the curve was similarly whetted for stripping twigs off branches. The *roncola* is one of the most useful and frequently carried tools of the Tuscan countryman, but I had something unusual in mind for it: fighting off terrorists armed with machine-guns.

Pausing for breath as soon as I was around the corner, I heard the bike rev up again and the gears engage. If I didn't move now

I would probably not have another chance. It was ten strides to the trees, which were fairly thin close to the house, but less than fifty yards of crashing through undergrowth under cover of the engine noise ought to see me out of range of the headlight.

I am not sure even now how I had managed to forget Hartmut. Perhaps it was because I had never seen him, and tried to erase the only image of him I had formed – as a jolly Father Christmas – as soon as I realized its danger. But perhaps that is just a pseudo-psychological cover-story and it was nothing more than downright carelessness. I saw him now, all right.

One of the trees in my path grew monstrously to one side until the growth split off, took on a life of its own, and held up an arm towards me. There was a muffled *plop* and a sharp crack above and behind me. Shooting high to scare me, I thought automatically, and ran on, lifting the *roncola*.

Between the starlight and the reflected glow from the motor bike, I could make out quite clearly how Hartmut stood in my path and had raised both arms to block me, relying on his bearlike build. What puzzles me in retrospect was that he had not seen that I was armed, as he had had longer than I to accustom his eyes to the darkness.

Something in the fact that he had deliberately aimed over my head filtered through my brain as I ran, and I knew that Ulli was wrong. They wanted me alive, even if it was only because a corpse meant problems. They had probably told Hartmut that I was slightly built, of a mild disposition and no match for him. As far as I was aware, only Jens knew that I had used violence on the girl.

Seething with fury at these ruffians who were messing up my life and fired by the success I had had up to now, I hurled myself at Hartmut and brought the *roncola* down savagely. It made a glittering arc in the starlight. At the last second he dodged aside, and that probably saved his life, although it cost him an arm. The razor edge of the inside of the curve hit his right arm on the outside, just below the shoulder, slicing through the flesh like butter and jarring into the bone at an acute angle.

I distinctly heard the bone crack. Immediately afterwards there was another *plop* below me to the left as his fingers tightened spasmodically on the trigger, but the gun was pointing way off to one side. As I cannoned into him, knocking us both breathless, he let out a high falsetto scream which ended in a sob, and fainted.

Leaning against the tree behind which he had been hiding, I drew a shuddering breath and fought down the nausea which was welling up inside me. My catharsis of violence was over. I could feel my knees trembling and threatening to let me down at any second.

The motor cycle suddenly roared as it came round the corner of the house, and the headlight wavered back and forth through the wood like a baleful, searching eye. But between it and me were several trees, and for the first critical seconds the many shifting shadows gave me cover, while Hartmut was lying in a heap on the ground. I saw quite clearly the great raw gash in his arm, which from there down was twisted at a sickening angle, and the black pool of blood spreading under it. His face was screwed into a tight grimace.

I remembered not to look into the burning eye of light so that I would not be dazzled. It was the light that saved me, I suppose. Jens and Klaus could see everything in the dazzling tunnel it cut through the night, but nothing outside it. They started their search immediately behind the house, instead of to the side where I stood trembling. The first beams had been either a quick cursory check before getting down to the methodical search, or merely the result of random movements while the bike was manoeuvred into position.

I stumbled off into the night, the noise of their search adequately covering me. I crashed painfully against trees, my face and hands lashed by vindictive brambles, and was in safety within minutes. But I kept staggering on, until the burning in my eyes made me aware that I was crying. My breath was coming in deep sobs although I was no longer making any great physical exertion. Once I fell and drew blood on my temple against a rough pine. My clothing was being shredded. I had no idea what direction I was moving in, except that it was away from that bloody wound and those cold, grey-blue eyes.

It had to be them or me, I kept repeating to myself over and over again. Perhaps I was saying it out loud, I don't know. But I can remember clearly how it became less convincing the more I repeated it. Never before had I been at such close quarters with

37

violence, and then of my own making! I had done savage, animal things, and I hated them for it.

In an open patch I stopped in the starlight, and realized that I still held the *roncola* firmly in my right hand. I held it up and saw it was covered in blood. Looking down at my shirt, I saw that it, too, was darkly smeared. I threw the weapon down, turned away from it and retched helplessly into the darkness.

Taking three heavy steps forward, I lost my footing, swayed for a moment in nothingness, and then crashed down a steep, boulder-strewn bank. Violent pain shot up my leg as my foot caught under a root, and then the night closed in on me.

Seven

I was awoken by the flies. Smeared with dry blood and vomit, I must have been an object of great attraction to them.

It was morning. The grandfather of all sick headaches was whirring like a dynamo behind my right eye. At the first, slightest movement I attempted, tears came to my eyes as icy hot flashes of agony shot up from my right ankle. I rolled over cautiously, trying unsuccessfully not to move it, and examined the damage. It was swollen to about twice its natural size, and the top of my shoe was cutting a nasty welt.

Gingerly I eased the shoe off. The pain brought sweat to my face and neck, although the day was still cool. I was soaked with dew, had a high temperature, and didn't know where I was.

The events of the previous evening forced themselves through the mental and physical sluggishness with which a full-scale migraine always afflicts me. I was sorely tempted to close my eyes again and hope the world would go away. I tried it. It didn't.

I had long before developed and practised a useful habit in times of stress – forcing myself to think of nothing (or of anything innocuous) for about a minute, and then taking stock of the situation, separating the advantages from the disadvantages, checking the apparent disadvantages for their hidden positive sides, and finally making plans. Sam always said it was this which made me good at my job. Only I didn't have the IBM here now.

Lying on my back, I looked up at the morning sun through the branches. The smell of pine-needles reminded me of bath salts. God, I could use a hot bath now. Birds were singing their morning roundelays. It was going to be a glorious day.

Gradually, reluctantly, I began stocktaking. I was sick, injured, lost and hunted. I could not think of any more disadvantages. Not that these weren't bad enough, but at least they circumscribed the periphery of the problem.

The sickness I was just going to have to master. I had survived feverish migraines before and I would again. It would not kill me. The injury, too, was not an insurmountable problem. I checked the rest of my body carefully. I was a mass of bruises, scratches and lacerations, but nothing apart from the ankle seemed to be serious. The day was going to be warm: I could tear up what was left of my shirt to make a bandage, and somewhere up yonder bank was lying the *roncola* with which I could fashion a crutch.

As for being lost, that was no enormous problem, either. I knew the area intimately, as Sophie and I often wandered for hours in the woods. If I kept heading south, sooner or later I had to hit the dirt road which led to the village.

The greatest problem, as I saw it, was going to be avoiding the hunters. But these were no trackers, no countrymen with eyes like Red Indians. They were city kids, handy enough with motor bikes and pistols, but not about to go looking in an unknown forest for broken twigs and bent blades of grass. Or drops of blood.

Come to think of it, they had enough blood of their own to worry about. I winced and flinched physically as I remembered that gaping slash in Hartmut's arm, and immediately hardened myself again to any trace of remorse. Hell, the bastard had shot at me.

Advantages? Well, I was likely to make it to a phone before they made it to me. And I was pretty sure I could persuade the *carabinieri* it was no practical joke as long as I talked about armed robbers and kept quiet for the time being about foreign terrorists.

Not having found me by now, in fact, my former captors were

almost certainly going to reckon on the worst and take off. For all they knew, I might have alerted the police during the night. They were probably already on the motorway.

I ripped the tattered remains of my shirt off without bothering to undo the buttons. My torso was covered with scratches and contusions, crusts of dry blood and a few thorns. Tearing the shirt into strips, I bound my ankle as tightly as I could bear, bringing tears to my eyes. I pulled myself upright in a series of hoists on a friendly tree-trunk, and looked around for a way to the top of the bank.

It took me more than ten minutes to get up the six yards of slope, and I collapsed at the top soaked in sweat, my head throbbing like a steam engine and the pain in my ankle excruciating. But I had to have that *roncola*, I had to have a good crutch.

It was lying propped against a bush. After I found it, things started getting easier.

I was quite handy with a *roncola* (the irony of this did not escape me) as I used it all winter long for firewood. I soon found a suitable sapling and trimmed it down until it supplied a fork for my armpit and a grip lower down for my hand. Starting the tear with the hatchet-edge, I tore strips off my trouser legs to pad the fork comfortably.

I took my bearings on the sun and set off through the forest. It was still only ten to nine, but through my distress, pain and exhaustion I was pleasantly aware of the warmth of the early sun on my skin.

Before I had been moving ten minutes, I heard the rushing of water over to my right, and veered in that direction. The stream had cut a deep groove in the mountainside, and getting down the bank was slow and painful, but the relief of that cold, clear water on my burning face was worth every moment. I held my swollen ankle in the water and felt the beneficial effects almost immediately.

I bathed all the scratches I could reach, breaking off frequently to splash water on my forehead. These makeshift ablutions cheered me up so much that I felt I would be able to tackle anything.

Some suitable stones on which I could half recline with my right leg supported under the shin provided a primitive latrine, and after I had washed myself with fresh water, Arab style, I was wet but clean. All I needed now was a toothbrush, I thought cheerfully, in a conscious effort to fight the depression with good spirits.

But the greatest advantages I had saved until last to consider. I knew that the stream was at least as good a landmark as it was a watering-place, and I sat down on a boulder in the sun to scratch my tentative sketch-maps with a pebble and try to work out where I was.

I knew of three streams which at this time of year could have about this amount of water in them and which were within reasonable distance of the house. It should not be too difficult to work out a plan of action which would cover any of the feasible alternatives.

First I scratched a cross for the house and a meandering line southwards for the eight kilometres of track down to the dirt road. This, when you hit it, ran east for about five kilometres into the village, and west for about twenty-five, past scattered homesteads until it reached the tarmac road, which in turn led to the main road from Olmo to Città di Castello.

I had been on the right side of the house, the side nearer to civilization, when I had fled the night before. But I had no means of knowing how far I had stumbled in the dark nor whether I had kept going in the right direction. Any of the three streams was, on the face of it, likely enough, although one seemed perhaps a little far away. But the other two both crossed the track to my house, and since I had not crossed it myself, I needed only to follow this one down in order to find it.

A small fish jumped in the water behind me with a gentle splash, and an enormous black bee bumbled past on iridescent wings.

I tried the hypothesis on each of the three scratches I had made for the streams, and each time it seemed to me that there was, in the words of the old joke, nothing that could go wrong. I was reluctant to leave this peaceful place, with the murmuring of the water and the welcome rest for my ankle. I would rest for ten minutes, bathe the dressing again, and then set out.

Again the fish jumped, but this time the splash was preceded by a clear clink of stone on stone. I wheeled round and squinted into the sunny morning, and Klaus said 'Good morning, Dr Ellis.' He was pointing a pistol with a silencer at me and picking up in his left hand a transceiver with a long antenna, which he had put on the ground to throw the pebble at me. He was being extremely cautious.

Despair swept over me, and I slumped back against the warm boulder.

'Ich hab' ihn,' I heard him say into the walkie-talkie.

The answer began 'Wo . . .' but turned into a squeal as another station transmitted on the same frequency.

'One at a time,' said Klaus. 'Jens, I'm at the stream about three kilometres beyond the jeep, and then three hundred metres upstream from the track. You had better come and help me.'

'Ist gut,' cracked the reply. 'Ulli, get home and keep listening.'

'Okay,' said another voice, which I would not have recognized as Ulli's.

My new-found resolution had seeped away completely before this conversation was finished. Had I been through all this, got so far, only to be defeated now? Would they simply destroy me and save all the trouble of keeping me prisoner? Would they exact vengeance for Hartmut's arm?

'You, come up here!' ordered Klaus brusquely.

'I can't,' I said. 'I think my ankle is broken. I can't walk any more.'

'Then we shall carry you,' he said brutally, 'and it will make far more pain. I saw you walking before.' He put the transceiver back up to his mouth. 'Jens, Kannst Du den Jeep bringen?'

There was a longish pause, and then the loudspeaker crackled, 'Ja, ist gut. Wartet dort auf mich.'

Before he had finished speaking, I heard the sound of a motor in first gear, grinding up the track out of sight in the trees below. Klaus and I looked at each other tensely. He must have seen the wild hope in my eyes. We were working the same thing out. The vehicle, whatever it was, would be at the jeep in five minutes' time, give or take a little, and even if Jens were standing next to it now he would not be able to find a suitable place and change the tyre in time. I also knew, and wondered whether Klaus did, that the odds were ninety-nine to one that this car was heading for my house. My mind-reading was confirmed instantly.

'There's a car on the track,' he said urgently into the radio. 'It's passing me now; perhaps five minutes to the jeep.'

Again a pause. Jens was obviously thinking this out, and the others were letting him do it in peace.

'Ulli, wo bist Du?' was all that came.

'One minute from the house.'

'Okay. Go to the house, take the machine-gun and wait with Hartmut. Unlock the back door. Watch what happens and don't let yourself be seen. Move now. Klaus, stay where you are. Put a silencer on. Okay, Ulli?'

'I'm already there.'

'Okay, Klaus?'

Klaus said tersely into the radio, 'Ja' and then sat down at the foot of the nearest tree, watching me closely from above and keeping the pistol pointed unwaveringly at my chest. I, too, made myself comfortable, and reflected that Jens had possibly made a tactical error. Now the others were waiting for word from him. If anything happened to him, they would wait on in ignorance until long after they could have helped.

'How did you find me?' I asked Klaus.

He gave me a tight, grim smile with not much amusement in it. 'The early bird catches the worm, Dr Ellis. We have been looking for you for a long time.'

My head was again beginning to throb dully, and again I wished I could close my eyes and shut out the world. I tried and it helped a little.

'Why don't you all go away?' I said after a little while. 'Now is the right moment. You can take my jeep, cut the telephone wires, and leave me in the house. There is no way I can walk to the village like this.'

'Be silent,' he replied listlessly.

'You have nothing to gain by waiting here . . .'

He did not let me finish, but cut in angrily, although not loudly.

'I have told you to be silent. You will do as I say or I shall drop a stone on your leg.'

Learning from his brother, I thought. He means it. So we sat and stared at each other until I got tired of it, leant my head back and shut my eyes again. For all I knew, he never stopped watching me, because when the sound of the car returned, perhaps ten minutes later, I opened my eyes and looked straight back into his. And up the barrel of his gun, too.

He stood up and tried to catch a glimpse of the car through the trees, but it was apparently too far away. It was returning with all due respect for the state of the track.

The sound faded unhurriedly down the road, and again I shut my eyes. We waited another ten minutes but I had to steal a glance at my watch to know it; it could have been an hour. It was still only five past ten — the day had plenty of time to find new disasters for me.

We both snapped to attention, more or less, as the radio spoke again.

'Klaus?'

'Ja?'

'All okay here. Can you get down to the road?'

'He is saying he can't walk, but I'll get him there. Otherwise I'll call you if I hear you going past. Who was it in the car?'

'Tell you later. Get moving.'

Klaus stood up. 'Either you come now, or I will hurt you badly and we shall carry you. What do you want?'

'I'll come,' I said, 'but it won't be fast.'

There was little point in slowing things down for them. My chance of outside help had just come and gone, and reason told me that there wouldn't be another. Who could it have been? And what had Jens told him? But I played it out slowly anyhow; there was no harm in their believing I was worse off than I really was. And the pain of walking was real enough.

We were not far from the road and could see it through the trees below when we heard the jeep coming down the track. Klaus behind me said in German into the walkie-talkie, 'Up to your left,' and at that moment it came into view.

Jens looked up, saw where we were, and carried on without a wave or any sign of recognition. I saw him pick up the transceiver from the passenger seat. He said into it, 'I'll turn round and come back up.'

He was waiting for us when we reached the track. He looked at me blankly and said nothing. He helped me into the back seat, not as gently as a nurse but not unnecessarily brutally, either. Klaus kept me covered, taking care not to let Jens get in his line of fire. They got into the front seats. Klaus half turned to keep me covered.

Jens took the gun by the barrel out of Klaus's hand, slowly, to give him time to take his finger off the trigger. He turned round, raised the pistol, and before I had realized what he was going to do he brought the butt down hard on my bound ankle.

I screamed with pain. My vision swam and I must have passed out for a minute. When I came to, the vehicle was already moving, but I had not felt it start; I felt nothing beyond that atrocious pain.

After a while, Jens spoke without turning around, raising his voice above the rumble of the engine.

'You thought we are soft, Dr Ellis, but you were wrong. You had a little luck, that is all. You have already had all the luck you are going to have with us. We are not soft. If you do not co-operate we shall kill you. Or somebody.'

'Piss off,' I said futilely, through teeth ground together in a mixture of hate, impotent rage and agony.

But however I felt then, it was nothing to how I felt when the jeep pulled up outside the house, and my eye caught a brightly-coloured object lying just outside the front door.

It was Katrina's favourite woollen doll.

Eight

I probably went berserk for a while, because I cannot reconstruct any coherent order of events. There are some details I can remember quite clearly, and some that are more hazy though still there. But they do not hang together in any sort of natural sequence, like a jumbled box of colour slides taken on a travelling holiday.

There was the constant pain; sometimes stronger, sometimes less so, but always there. It no longer occupied my mind to the exclusion of everything else. I was clinically, detachedly aware that there was a pain, but it might have been somebody else's for all that it mattered.

There was the struggling, the arms holding me down, a nose I drew blood from, the speechless grunts and gasps of men fighting,

45

no mind or breath wasted on discussion, taunts or warnings.

After a while there was the pinprick in my arm and an endlessly slow breaker, creaming into foam, refracting the sunlight and crashing silently over me, and then the warm peace of cotton-wool all around me, slightly stifling but otherwise calm and comforting.

I awoke completely blind.

I felt the hair at the back of my neck straining to stiffen, and goose-flesh covered my body. I was absolutely, utterly blind, and had no idea where I was, or how I had got there.

I knew that I was lying down, and tried to swing my legs off the edge of the bed into nothingness, but the slightest movement of my right leg made the ankle explode into multi-coloured sparks of pain. This, I knew, meant that something bad had happened, but I did not know what it was. And I dreaded to find out.

Cautiously I tried to hop away from the bed and again I crashed down like a felled tree, this time away from the bed on to a hard floor. Groaning, I flailed around until I found the bed, my only anchor. Was I in a tiny cell or a vast hall? My head sang with the effort to apply some sort of measurement to my surroundings, and I heard the pulse thumping in my ears.

Giving up the attempt to walk, I crawled two or three yards in a straight line until my head bumped lightly into something. It was unnerving. I gasped and fell flat. I felt it: it was a flat-sided, square-sectioned piece of wood apparently growing out of the floor. Dragging my right foot painfully, I got into a crawling position again and tried to kneel upright. My shoulders and the back of my head struck the wooden ceiling simultaneously, but it gave readily, swayed for a moment across my shoulder-blades, and then fell with a crash behind me.

A table! I had crawled under a table! So I was in a room with furniture. There must be walls, and a door. Shuffling forward on my knees, and waving my hands in front of me, I found a wall. Plaster, no wallpaper. Setting off at random to the right, I almost immediately smashed my nose into another wall at right angles to the first, and remembered to use my hands again.

A flash of light on my left startled me, because it was clearly stronger and more real than the pulsating, sombre patterns my eyes had been registering, and my brain rejecting, up till now. I moved my arm again, and the flash was repeated. I stopped my hand in mid-air, and a luminous green V hung there. It took me several seconds to realize that it was made of the hands of my watch indicating five to one.

My consciousness was a strange mixture of not knowing, wanting to know and dreading to know, because I knew it would be horrible once I remembered. I was in pitch darkness in a strange room with a badly injured ankle, and something frightful had happened, something I wanted to keep at the back of my mind for as long as I could.

I heard the sound of a door closing and of approaching footsteps. There was something familiar about these sounds, not so much the person making them, but the place where they were being made. A thin rectangle of light suddenly leapt alive to my right, foreshortened by my kneeling perspective, and I knew where the door was.

A key was put into a lock, and then turned. The rectangle spread dazzlingly, and I blinked and swayed on my knees as a tall, silent figure came towards me. I realized I had used up all the strength I possessed, and allowed myself to be hoisted under the armpits, back on to the bed, and my trailing right foot carefully but still painfully lifted after me.

A name came into my mind as I saw my helper standing looking down at me, and I said, 'Klaus, where am I?'

'At home. Just sleep now.'

His voice was neutral, with no inflection whatever. Neither friendly nor unfriendly. But why should he be unfriendly? What made me surprised at that?

With a rush a lot of it came back, and I gripped the sides of the bed and tried to sit up.

'Where are they?' I asked, 'and what have you done with them? I want to be with them.' Then my voice dried up in my throat.

'They are quite safe and unharmed. You will be with them as soon as you have slept enough.'

He righted the table, put something back on to it which had been thrown off, and went. I did not hear him lock the door; I was already asleep again, exhausted as after a day's hard work, aching all over from the effort. My mind was only too grateful to pull back from this nightmare, back into sleep.

This time I dreamt, or at least this time I remembered my

47

dreams after waking. I remembered them with an extraordinary vividness which events later pushed temporarily out of my mind, but now I can still recall scenes from that second, drugged sleep.

There was Wharton, courteous and charming as he had been all along, driving a tractor through a farmyard packed with busy, turbanned Koris. He called down to me from the driver's saddle, 'I suppose you know it all now,' just as he had done that day over lunch at the Bagh-i-Bala.

I remembered the dream so clearly because there was a lot of historical fact interwoven with the random fantasy of a sleeping mind. At that final, decisive lunch he had just nodded, looked down at his plate, and said, 'I see.' But in my dream his face crumpled and dissolved, and he clutched his hand to his biceps while blood gushed between his fingers.

And there was Tuula, his beautiful Finnish wife, running between the trees with a machine-gun, looking everywhere but at the bush behind which I stood half hidden. Her eyes had exactly the same look as they had had the evening she knew that I was going to put the evidence in my briefcase and leave, and that neither Wharton nor she could stop me.

And there was Sophie, her red-gold hair spread like storm-clouds on the pillow, and when I kissed her neck to wake her up she opened her eyes, and they were blue-grey, and Ulli said in a satisfied voice, 'Now they really will kill you.'

I have never believed in dream analysis. Nothing can persuade me that it is not the rigmarole of witch-doctors, that dreams are not the same random juxtaposition of real and fantasy images that a computer will print out if you try to run it at half voltage. But I would have provided some fascinating material for a psychoanalyst that day.

What woke me was a firm hand shaking my shoulder. There was bright sunlight coming through the drawn curtains, and I saw I was in Katrina's room on the guest bed. Jens was carrying a steaming bowl of vegetable soup and two large hunks of dry white bread. On a table from the dining room were a wine bottle and a glass, and my jeans and a roll-neck sweater.

I struggled into a sitting position and waved aside the soup impatiently, although the strong, delicious steam made my stomach growl. It was, I later realized, Sunday morning, and I had eaten nothing since Friday lunch on the plane, a skimpy affair designed more for colour than nutrition.

'Where are Sophie and Katrina? I wish to see them at once.'

'That is quite impossible; they are in Florence. They are perfectly well and unharmed, and will stay well as long as you co-operate with us.' He held the soup out again.

'If you do not eat something, you will not have the strength to go and see them,' he said, as though to a child.

'Taste it first,' I demanded.

Jens laughed pleasantly, stirred the soup thoroughly with the spoon, and ate two spoonfuls, dredging them up from the bottom. My stomach growled again from watching him. I took the bowl and ate greedily. It occurs to me only now that I did not demand that he taste the bread or the wine.

I ate in concentrated silence, and he watched me equally silently. When I had finished, he asked me if I wanted more, and I said yes. He brought it promptly, locking the door while he was away and thrusting it open wide before re-entering the room. They were taking no more chances.

'Now tell me where they are.'

'I told you,' he said patiently, 'they are in Florence and quite safe. We shall telephone with them in a moment. You had better wash and shave first. Do you drink coffee?'

'Yes, two sugars and no milk. And I want some cigarettes.'

Again he left the room with meticulous precautions, and came back in five minutes with a lot of things he had to put on the corridor floor and bring in one by one: a large mug of coffee, a pack of cigarettes and my lighter, an ashtray, a towel, a face-flannel, a nail-brush, a hair-brush and comb, my electric razor and a small shaving-mirror. Last of all he brought a plastic washing-up bowl filled with steaming water.

I was puzzled as he looked at the loaded table closely for several seconds, and then I realized he was memorizing the objects he had brought. He put the table next to the bed.

'I shall come back in ten minutes,' he said, 'and we can talk then.'

'We can talk right now,' I said, lighting a cigarette and drawing the smoke gratefully into my lungs. 'I'm not prudish.'

I decided to shave first, and took up the mirror. The sight of

49

my face did not reassure me: I saw hollow, bloodshot eyes, two days' growth of stubble and several scratches, albeit no bruises or blood. Somebody had washed my face while I was out to the world, and I wondered why. And who.

We did not talk until I had finished. I told him I wanted to clean my teeth, and he took everything away but the cigarettes, lighter and ashtray before he brought me a toothbrush and tooth-paste and a glass of water. While he was gone, I took stock of my physical condition. There were still some contusions and scratches on my chest and arms, but apart from my throbbing ankle I was feeling fit enough.

I also had time to remember something else I wanted to ask Jens.

'How is Hartmut?' I said the moment he came back.

He did not reply at once, but looked at me thoughtfully for a moment.

'He is very sick,' he said finally. 'He will probably lose his arm. I think he wants to kill you.'

'I'm not surprised. So would I.'

'You are wrong and he is wrong, too,' said Jens with un-expected vehemence. 'Your reaction was perfectly understandable and predictable. He should have been prepared for it. Eine Ueber-legenheit an Kräften ist keine echte Ueberlegenheit, wenn keine Vorbereitungen getroffen worden sind. We know that you speak fluent German, Dr Ellis.'

'A mere advantage in strength is no real advantage if adequate preparations are not made,' I translated, adding: 'A well-prepared but inferior force can often beat a stronger enemy by a surprise attack.' But my heart was sinking as I wondered how much they realized that I knew.

I think that was the only time I saw Jens look disconcerted.

'You have read Mao's works!' he said, and it sounded almost like an accusation, so astonished was he.

'Certainly. And I didn't find anything about kidnapping in-nocent women and babies, or taking people prisoner in their own homes.'

'Do not be dramatic, Dr Ellis. Your wife and child are perfectly safe. In fact, we took them to Florence for their own safety; you have been very violent and we did not want them to come to any harm.'

50

I was so furious that I would have struck him if I had been on my feet.

'So I have been violent, have I?' I shouted. 'Christ Almighty! What the hell did you expect? Was I suppose to ask you all to stay to bloody dinner?'

'I told you that we would leave as soon as possible,' Jens snapped, 'and with the minimum of inconvenience. I was also prepared to pay you adequately for your trouble. You chose to struggle against hopeless odds and cause violence, against my express warning.' His voice was now terse and strained — I had begun to crack his composure.

Although I wondered if it were not a mistake, I retorted, 'Pay me with stolen money, that's easy enough!' Then, partly in order to change the subject and partly because I genuinely wanted to know, I asked, 'Is Hartmut getting medical attention?'

Stiffly, he replied, 'He is in an intensive care unit in a hospital to which we have access, and where no questions are asked. These things are possible in Italy when you know the right people. We shall know about his arm in a few days.'

I thought of asking why they had not taken Bernd there, but decided the less they knew about what I knew the better. Besides, I could work it out for myself: Bernd had been injured in a genuine crash in a public place, and there had been neither the need nor the opportunity to use emergency procedures.

Instead, I asked, 'How did you know I spoke German?'

'I remember you once asked me how we knew your name,' he replied. 'From the same source, more or less. And there are plenty of German books in the house.'

There was something shifty about the tone of the answer, but I could not place it, so I changed tack again.

'I want to speak to Sophie now.'

Jens stood up. 'Very well. Stay there, I shall bring you the telephone.'

'You can't,' I said. 'The lead isn't long enough.'

'I have attached an extension,' he said with a strange look.

'Before you call,' he added, 'I have some instructions which you will follow perfectly, otherwise the consequences will be very unpleasant. Not only for you.'

I felt as though I had been socked in the groin again.

'If you so much as lay a finger on either of . . .'

He interrupted me brusquely and loudly.

'Dr Ellis, we have talked about this before. You are in our hands. We do not wish to hurt you or anybody else, when will you understand this? But if you oblige us to, we shall not hesitate. When will you grasp that you are causing all this ... all this deplorable violence by not following my perfectly simple instructions?'

I sat back weakly and could feel the sweat prickling on my spine. Katrina chuckling in her pram. Katrina laughing proudly the first time she crawled across the rug. Katrina swathed in bandages, eyes closed and the tears still in the corners. Katrina waving goodbye to old Giorgio, palm upwards, bending all the fingers together Italian-style, and trying to say '*Ciao Jojo.*'

'What are your instructions?' I asked slowly and clearly.

Jens looked relieved.

'You will tell your wife that there are things you have to clear up and that you will be free and back within a week or so.' I tried to interrupt, but he carried on firmly. 'You will tell her to follow our instructions promptly, and then no harm will come to anybody. You will not discuss your injured foot with her; that would only upset her unnecessarily. If at any moment you disobey my instructions, I shall cut the connection and there may be other consequences.'

I nodded weakly, but he had not finished.

'One other thing: do not talk about your work. Are we agreed?'

The question was rhetorical. I had no choice whatever.

'Of course.'

'Then we can go. If you would please get dressed, we shall go to her at once.'

I gaped at him.

'She is here,' he said. 'I told you she was in Florence so that you would eat and wash calmly. Now we can go. I have a walking-stick here for you. But remember: my instructions still apply, even though you will be seeing her personally.'

Jens showed me the stick he had bought from the hall, but made no move to give it to me until I had got dressed. Putting on my trousers was slow and painful, and I left the right shoe unlaced.

Motioning me with a movement of his gun to precede him to

the stairs, he fell in behind me. As I started the painful descent, he spoke again.

'She is here, Dr Ellis. But how long she remains here depends entirely upon you.'

SOPHIE

Nine

Mike has asked me to recount how poor Marino's death came about. That was the beginning of the worst part of the nightmare for me, because up to that moment I had not believed that these people were really prepared to kill in cold blood. But from that moment on there had been no doubt remaining about their readiness to kill, their brutality.

No, that's not the right word; brutality almost implies a kind of random, uncaring hurtfulness. But these people, just as they had said, were professionals. They dosed out pain and death as it was required for their purposes, neither too much nor too little.

I still hate going back over it now, but I agree with Mike that it should be recorded while it is fresh – all too fresh! – in our minds.

If it hadn't been for Fuessli's kindness, I would never have been in Tuscany in the first place. I had planned to spend the weekend in Geneva and go over to see him in Zurich on the Monday, and possibly spend Tuesday haggling as well.

But when I rang him from London to make an appointment, he was totally charming.

'There is no need whatever to come all this way, my dear Sophie,' he said, 'although I would love to see you. There is not a single work I would care to replace. The collection is a poem, an absolute poem. And strictly between us, the fee you suggested was considerably lower than I had been expecting. I have not shown your letter to my partner, for he has more business acumen than artistic taste. Why don't you write a new one and suggest two thousand more, and I shall drop this one into the Limmat.'

'Oh Fuessli, you are a darling,' I said, and meant it. 'But you know I have to come and see the colour proofs.'

'Ah, the impetuousness of youth. We do have other works to publish now and again, you know, my dear, and we shall not be getting around to yours for three or four weeks. Why don't you take a holiday and tell your husband that my wife is getting tired of asking me when that charming Dr Ellis is coming round again? I shall send you a cheque this afternoon for a 20 per cent advance.'

So it was that Katrina and I arrived in Arezzo, about thirty kilometres from Olmo, on that Sunday morning.

I rang the house to see if Mike was there, as I had had no word from him except a telegram from Nooriabad saying he would need a few more days. The line was engaged, and again five minutes later, but that didn't mean much in Italy, where telephoning is a kind of lottery, especially on the rural lines.

We had taken the night train via Switzerland which was one of the few that do not stop in Terontola, otherwise I would have heard from Rita in the bar whether Mike was there. As it was, there were only twelve kilometres more to the house from the Arezzo station, so we took a convenient bus to Olmo.

We might have come up in a taxi, but a voice hailed me as I got off the bus with Katrina balanced on my hip, clasping me like a Koala bear on a gum tree. A friendly hand reached for my suitcase.

'Signora Sofia, ben tornata!'

It was Marino, the son of old Giorgio who theoretically ran our village shop. But Giorgio was getting on – he was seventy-four, as he was proud to tell anybody who gave him the chance – and his wife Maria had been bedridden for three years, so that

56

most of the work fell on Marino's shoulders. Far from being depressed by it, Marino was one of the most constantly cheerful people I have ever met, despite the fact that he often worked more than sixty hours a week. He was a godsend to his parents, who had almost given up hoping for a child when he was born.

'Grazie mille, Marino! Come stai?' I had known Marino since he was a teenager – longer than I have known Mike, because I had bought the old house years before with an unexpected legacy – and still called him by the familiar *tu*. By him, however, I would always be addressed by the formal *Lei*, and there was nothing I could do about it.

Marino was, of course, very well. He always was, and the answer was not just politeness; he really meant it. He asked about Katrina's burns and spent a few moments tickling her. She loved him and played the shy lady for just about no time at all. Then he said, 'If you can wait two minutes while I pick up the bran that old robber has just sold me, I'll take you up to the house. Two American minutes, not two Italian ones!'

It had been our long-standing joke that an Italian minute might take an hour, that one of Mike's precise English minutes would need sixty seconds, and my impatient American minutes were gone in a flash. Without rancour, Marino would often spread his hands at an unexpected delay, and say 'What do you expect? Siamo in Italia – we are in Italy!' and we would laugh together at his philosophic patience.

He drove us carefully through Olmo up the narrow, winding street and out of the arch in the mediaeval walls which suddenly opened a vista to the Apennines and the ravine where Francis of Assisi spent many years in meditation, and where a diminishing company of Cappuccini monks in brown hooded habits with white rope belts still tends the monastery and its gardens.

As we climbed the mountain behind the town, Marino took the frequent hairpin curves gently, often glancing over to see that Katrina was safely held on my lap. I remembered how Mike had once told me what a reckless driver young Marino was. This countryman obviously had a tact and breeding that would shame many people who would think themselves his social superior.

'Have you seen Mike, Marino?' I asked him.

'Not since you left together last time,' he said, changing down as the gradient steepened. 'If there's anything you need from the shop, we can drop in there first. We're supposed to be closed by now, but no *carabinieri* are going to check my opening hours,' he added with a grin. 'But I'm only stopping for a moment and picking up a sandwich or two for lunch, and then I'm off hunting for the rest of the day, so if you need anything we had better call in now.'

'No, that's all right, thanks. I'm pretty sure we got everything before we left last time. Unless you have any fresh eggs?'

'Not one,' Marino replied. 'Sold out last night. But I'm going past the chicken farm anyway on my way home from hunting, so if you care to come down in the jeep this evening there will be as many as you want, and all fresh.'

'I don't know if I'll have the jeep, Marino, but if Mike's back I'll come down. It's not really that important.'

We turned up our track in the morning sunshine, and I remarked, 'It'll be a fine season for the hunters.'

'They won't bother you much up here, though,' replied Marino shrewdly, knowing that we did not have much sympathy for the annual Italian massacre of anything that flies or crawls. 'Not the right kind of country, and too far away for most folk.'

We chatted about the hunt for a while, until he exclaimed, 'Why, look! There's the jeep. But who is that with it?'

We got out, and a long-haired young man with a wheel-brace in his hand came towards us.

'You must be Mrs Ellis,' he said to me, with a slight northern European accent, and added a polite 'Buon giorno' to Marino.

I agreed that I was, and he went on with a smile, 'I'm very pleased to meet you. My name is Jens Försterling, and I met your husband in Olmo. He was kind enough to invite me to stay the night in your house, as I can't afford too many hotel bills. I've been for a ride in your jeep, but I'm afraid I've burst a tyre.'

'Is Mike there, then?' I asked superfluously.

'Oh yes, he was making coffee when I left. He said you might come any time, so I guessed who you were. And I saw your photo on the desk.'

Marino offered to help, but the young man insisted it was no trouble whatever. He spoke passable Italian, and impressed me as a pleasant person, just the kind that Mike often picked up hitch-hiking along the motorway or lunching off cold pizza under a statue in Florence. He apologized about blocking the track.

'But if you let me roll back, there is a wider bit back there,' he pointed. 'You can turn around there, too, and I can take Mrs Ellis to the house,' he added to Marino.

The two men manœuvred the vehicles, and Jens started to change the tyre on the jeep.

'I'll be off, then, signora,' said Marino. 'I'll be back up from the chicken farm by five at the latest. I'll bring you some eggs up here, if you like.'

'Good heavens, no,' I insisted. 'If I need any I'll come down to the shop at about six, as soon as I've fed Katrina. Bye now, and thanks a lot for the ride. Say hello to your parents.'

We shook hands, Jens offering Marino his wrist as his hand was black from the tyre, and we parted.

'What a nice chap,' said Jens. 'Who is he?'

'He and his parents own the village shop,' I explained, 'and he gave me a lift up from Olmo. Are you staying long?'

'I'm afraid not,' he replied. 'I'm only passing through on holiday, and I don't wish to take up room in your house now that you and the baby are back home.'

'You are welcome to sleep in my studio if you want,' I told him, getting into the jeep with Katrina on my knee. 'I shan't be doing any work until Thursday or Friday.'

We chatted together for the few moments it took to reach the house. When we stopped at the front door, however, he did an extraordinary thing. He called something in German up to one of the first-floor windows, I could not see which, before he started unloading my things on to the front doorstep.

'Who on earth were you talking to?' I asked in surprise. 'My husband?'

'Does he speak German?' he replied, equally surprised.

'Of course. Very well. I imagined you would have spoken German together.'

At that moment, the front door opened and a rather pretty girl of about twenty-three or four came out, and looked around quickly before giving me a tight smile which faded at once. 'Guten Tag,' she said. 'My name is Ulli.'

Jens looked at me soberly for a moment, and then he said, 'Mrs Ellis, we have some bad news for you.'

'Mike . . . where is Mike? Has something happened to him? Where is he?' I stammered.

59

'Dr Ellis is perfectly well,' he said carefully, 'but you are all three my prisoners.'

He stopped to let this sink in. I wanted to laugh. I looked from one to the other, but they were deadly serious. I kept turning the phrase over and over in my mind, but it made no sense at all.

'What are you talking about? Where is my husband?' was all I could say, and my voice sounded very small. An ironic thought flashed across my mind that I must be making a fine show as an adult, emancipated woman, bleating for my husband at the drop of a hat, and I added, 'Something has happened to him, hasn't it? You must tell me at once. I am not afraid to hear. Is he . . . is he alive?'

'You do not understand, Mrs Ellis,' said the young man, 'but I am not surprised. My sister and I and some friends have taken your husband prisoner. He is perfectly well, and he is sleeping now. You will see him as soon as he awakes. You are now also my prisoner, and we shall not harm you either, if you do as I say.'

I became more furious than frightened. I stepped forward and suddenly became aware of Katrina's weight in my arms. It was horrible. They knew that I was helpless, that I could not put the baby down and leave her to go and hit them, but they could see that I wanted to.

'This is preposterous,' I said. 'This is not a war, we are not your prisoners. You will tell me at once where my husband is and then go away.' But my voice betrayed me. Because I had Katrina with me, I was terrified of these pleasant, polite, horrible people. 'Who are you, anyway, Jens whatever-your-name-is?'

'Mrs Ellis, please calm yourself,' he replied. 'We are political partisans from West Germany. We are hiding for a few days because the police are looking for us. Your husband surprised us when he came home unexpectedly, and of course tried to throw us out of your house. We have given him a *Beruhigungsmittel* –' he looked enquiringly at his sister, who said promptly, 'Sedative' ' – and he will be awake again in a few hours. We shall go away very soon and we do not want to harm you. Please do not oblige us to use force.'

'Force?' I said incredulously. 'Sedatives? Are you mad? Where is Mike? What have you done to him?'

The girl spoke quietly and competently. 'I am a qualified nurse and I have given him a sedative which will not harm him at all, but instead will leave him feeling very rested after a sleep. If you do not do as we say, I shall have to give the same sedative to you.'

'But . . . but what about my daughter?' I stammered.

'I am sure you do not want me to look after her,' the girl said, in a well-trained, matter-of-fact voice, 'but if you are asleep I can do it very well.'

It was the thought of leaving Katrina in the hands of these people while I slept that made me pull myself together.

'Let me see my husband,' I demanded. 'When will he wake up?'

'In about an hour,' replied the girl, with a flickering look at her brother. If it was her brother.

'Please come this way, Mrs Ellis,' he said and stood aside for me to enter the house.

Automatically I followed him. As I advanced, the girl stepped back, so that I was between them for a few steps.

He asked her something in German, and she replied *ja* and another few words which I did not understand. I looked from one to the other helplessly, clutching the sleeping baby to my shoulder.

'I am sorry about this Mrs Ellis,' he said, in a dead, not very sorry voice, and I was still wondering what he was sorry about as he gripped my right arm just above the elbow, reached to the shelf next to the coat-rack for something small and glittering, while the girl reached out for Katrina.

'No, leave her alone!' I cried in terror, pulling back, but at that moment I felt the needle in my arm. 'No, no, don't, I won't struggle.'

But the needle was already withdrawn. The tableau froze for a moment before my eyes, the girl with her arms outstretched, a coaxing half smile on her lips, and the man looking on quietly, his hands again by his sides.

I started to back towards the door, but before I had taken three shuffling steps the room began to ripple as though seen through disturbed water. I felt Katrina sliding through my relaxed arms, and I was glad that Ulli took her as the room suddenly steadied, narrowed down to a speck of light, and went out.

Ten

Mike woke me up, and I stretched and yawned luxuriously, holding his hand and feeling rather muzzy.

I don't know how long it took me to realize that something was wrong, but thanks to Mike's thoughtfulness it didn't happen at once. I started to say several things, like have you made any coffee, and why are you dressed already, and how was Koristan, and then slowly a sense of unreality swept over me, and I looked hard at him to see if I was awake.

I was awake, and what I saw was not reassuring.

Mike was looking tired and drawn and trying not to. And I was in my studio, where I had not slept since we'd had a dreadful row two years before, which we made up after two days.

Sitting up, I looked around me, and saw the young man Jens sitting by the door. In his hand was a gun with a long, fat barrel which I presumed was a silencer. He was resting the gun in a relaxed fashion on his knees, but its general direction was plain. Next to my bed was Katrina's large old carry-cot and she was peacefully asleep in it as though nothing had happened.

'Mike, darling, are you all right?' I managed to stammer out.

'Of course, chick,' he said cheerfully. 'Nice to have you home. It's all quite all right; Katrina's okay too, and we'll sort this out in no time.'

Mike is not usually one of those husbands who organize everything and see that fragile little wifey doesn't bother her pretty head about anything. We have always tackled problems together, often not agreeing on the solution, but almost always managing to concur on which one of us was more concerned and should therefore have the last word on the subject.

He was obviously trying to set a confident, cheerful tone and I felt that he was right to do so. I looked to see what Jens was doing. He seemed to be trying not to take too much notice of us. Apart, of course, from listening to every word we said and covering us with a gun. Something about his attitude seemed awkward, however. Suddenly I realized that I was naked and sitting up in bed.

Well, if it disturbed him, so much the better. It didn't worry me, and that was a free advantage. I decided not to clutch the sheet to my heaving bosom, but it did occur to me unpleasantly that I had been drugged for some time.

'How did I get here?' I said directly to Jens.

'My sister and I carried you, and my sister undressed you and put you to bed on her own,' he replied, taking the point. 'She also changed your baby's clothes, fed her, washed her and put her to bed.'

'Very thoughtful of her,' I said. But my sarcasm was lost on him, and I knew that this was not somebody to play foolish games with.

'Not at all,' he said politely. 'I have told you and your husband many times that we do not want to hurt you and that we shall not do so unless you oblige us. I cannot leave you alone with Dr Ellis. You will understand that this is not possible. I am very sorry.' This time he really seemed to mean it.

I gripped Mike's hand firmly, and he sat on the bed. He winced as he lowered himself, and I noticed that he put a walking-stick against the wall.

'Mike, what's wrong? What has happened to you?'

'Nothing serious, chick,' he replied in a matter-of-fact voice, and I knew I could believe him. 'I sprained my ankle trying to run away, but it's a lot better already, and our uninvited lady guest is a very efficient nurse.'

'They didn't get violent with you, did they?' I was listening to Mike but watching Jens who, however, remained strictly neutral and watched the baby, the trees outside the window, in fact anything but Mike and me.

'No,' said Mike, 'they didn't need to. They pointed guns at me and so on, but you know there is nothing worth risking your neck for in this house.'

He was trying to put something over to me that Jens would not understand, but I did not get it.

We started talking about everything but the situation in hand, how the trip to England had gone, how my brother is managing. How he was satisfied that Katrina would not need any more check-ups. How Koristan was in the fall. How Rome got more confused every week.

After a time we realized that we had said everything we could think of while mentally pushing these bandits into the background, and there was now nothing left that we wanted to talk about more than them.

Mike turned directly to Jens and asked him straight out: 'What do you intend to do now?'

Jens had obviously been prepared for this, and had his answer ready.

'Dr Ellis, there is something you must do for us – in another place – and it will take you two – or, at the most, three days. You will go there tomorrow. Mrs Ellis and your daughter will remain here meanwhile and will be treated with the maximum consideration.'

Mike started to boil over and spoke angrily to Jens about women and children and filthy bastards with guns and similar things, but Jens just looked at him calmly and he stopped. He turned very white, and I saw that he was genuinely worried.

'But darling,' I said, 'you know that they will not do anything to me or to Katrina. You won't lay a finger on her, or I shall kill you,' I said to Jens as calmly and rationally as I could, imitating his manner.

A tense silence hung in the room. For a few seconds nobody moved or spoke. Then Jens raised his gun a few inches off his knee, looked down at it and then over in the general direction it was pointing, and while I screamed, 'No! Stop!' and Mike started to get up, the gun made a quiet *plop*. Jens turned it immediately back towards Mike and me.

The bullet went into the wall less than a yard above Katrina's carry-cot. Plaster crumbled away from around the hole and showered over her head, pillow and eiderdown.

I gasped but could not speak. Snatching up a dressing-gown that was lying across the chair next to the bed, I dashed over to the cot and knelt beside it. Katrina only stirred restlessly in her sleep and made brushing movements with her little hands up by her head. I cleared the plaster away, and she sighed contentedly and half turned over, still without waking.

Mike hissed something in German which sounded very rude, but when I turned around he was sitting on the bed again with a bitter, white face, and the gun was still pointing at him.

Jens stood up. 'We shall talk again together this evening,' he said. 'Dr Ellis, please come with me. There is something I have to show you. Mrs Ellis, my sister will come at once. Please think about anything you might need for yourself or your daughter.' He looked at his watch, and Mike and I automatically did the same; it was just after four. 'We intend to cook dinner at about seven, but of course if you are hungry now we can bring you something at once.'

I was too shattered to reply, but sat numbly on the bed and shook my head at him. I was trembling all over, and knew that if I spoke I would give my fear away. If I had not done so already. I fought back the tears.

Mike moved near me and put his arms round me, and my trembling slowly subsided. He hugged me hard for a long, silent time, and then took me by the shoulders and looked into my eyes. He was pale but calm, and I think I have never loved him so much as at that moment.

'Take it easy, chick,' he murmured. 'They are tough bastards, and they mean business. But they won't hurt you or her if you play along. This isn't *Clockwork Orange*.'

I nodded and hugged him wordlessly. He gave my shoulders a parting squeeze and went over to where Jens was standing at the trapdoor over the stairs.

'Where?' he asked Jens coldly.

'The house, please,' Jens replied, and his calm did not seem to be ruffled at all. He followed Mike down the stairs without a backward glance at me, closing the trapdoor behind him. I felt very lonely.

When they reached the bottom of the stairs, I did not get up to watch them cross the ground floor. My studio is in a sort of gallery running around the back and two sides of the building, with a large working space at the back and surrounded by a balustrade. The narrow arm to the right finishes in a small toilet and wash-room, and to the left is the staircase to the ground floor, which can be closed off by the trapdoor. This I normally leave open, but when it is closed, as it now was, it forms a continuation of the gallery floor.

They paused at the foot of the stairs, and I heard the plastic rattle as the receiver of the intercom telephone to the house was raised. After a moment, Jens spoke in German and hung up again, and then they left. I noticed that he did not lock the door to the studio, but guessed that he had called for Ulli to come, and knew that I would not leave Katrina alone, and had no time to flee with her.

I was right, for a few moments later Ulli arrived.

'Do you want anything now?' she asked me.

I almost said, yes, go away and leave us alone, but instead I just shook my head and tried to ignore her. Katrina would wake up soon, and I wanted to get my thoughts straightened out before she started to occupy them.

My studio had always been bare and uncluttered, and the only addition to the furniture at the moment was the carry-cot. Apart from that, there was the couch on which I had been sleeping, three sailcloth armchairs, and my painting and drawing gear on a table. My clothes were folded neatly on one of the chairs, and Ulli sat in another, the one nearest to the trapdoor, where Jens had sat. She, too, carried a gun.

Against the long wall behind the couch was a bookshelf with a few dozen books in it and a glass vase on top, an alarm clock and other odds and ends. The flowers were dead and mournful. I had picked them on a walk through the wood with Mike four weeks ago.

The light came from two enormous skylights we had installed in the roof over the well to the ground floor, which could be opened by cords looped over the balustrade rail below. On the ground floor was a large kerosene stove. Its metal chimney-pipe came up through the floor in the wash-room and then followed the short wall and two-thirds of the long back wall before disappearing out through the roof, so that the whole building was adequately warmed, even in winter.

I had always loved my studio, both before the renovation when it had been a simple outhouse still smelling strongly of the animals that had lived there and teeming with mice, and afterwards when it had been transformed into a comfortable, private world where I had produced some of my best work. But now I cannot imagine the day when I will love it again.

Ulli and I sat for perhaps twenty minutes in silence while my mind slowly stopped spinning. Finally I knew that I had no plan for escape and no intention of jeopardizing Katrina's safety in any way; at least, not as matters stood at present. I said coldly to Ulli, 'I shall need some hot milk and some biscuits soon for my daughter.'

'I have put a lot of milk in the refrigerator downstairs,' she said. 'And I have brought biscuits and some *Windeln.*' She thought for a moment. 'Nappies? – yes, nappies, and some toys. I changed her nappies when you were sleeping. But Mrs Ellis,' she looked at me directly, 'Katrina will not wake up until about eight o'clock.'

I went cold inside and felt my heart thump suddenly in my throat.

'What have you done? For Heaven's sake, she's only a baby! You can't have drugged her ... can you?'

The girl did not look contrite at all, but quietly efficient.

'Please remember that I am a trained nurse and that I have my *Diplom* in paediatry.' I looked blank, and she sought a word. 'Paedi ... you know, as a specialist for children.'

I was sceptical, and it must have shown on my face, for she added, not proudly but as an explanation, 'Not a governess or anything like that, but a medical speciality. I gave Katrina a small dose of the anaesthetic we use every day in the hospital for operations on children. It is perfectly harmless, and it will only make her sleep.'

I remembered how the plaster had fallen on her face without waking her.

The girl went on, 'I have also prepared a meal for her. It is in the refrigerator and I only need to heat it up when she is awake.'

Grudgingly I began to admire Ulli's efficiency, but I was not about to let her take over my baby.

'What have you prepared?' I asked.

'Some breast of chicken and carrots, and rice and milk. I hope that is good?'

It was indeed good, but before I could answer the intercom buzzed at the foot of the stairs. Ulli went down to it, lowering the trapdoor behind her. I heard a few words, but I did not understand them, and anyway she was doing more listening than talking. I heard her hang up, and she came back up the stairs.

'Mrs Ellis, will you please get dressed. You will go out with my brother for half an hour and then come back. I shall look after Katrina.'

'Impossible,' I said firmly. 'I shall not leave her alone with any of you for one moment.'

This reaction had obviously been foreseen.

'Then my brother will bring your husband here and hit his sick ankle with a stick until you obey us,' she said coolly, and my heart once again thumped painfully.

'You are the most despicable swine on earth,' I said bitterly, and I started to dress.

I thought things had been hard up to now, but I was wrong. It had been child's play compared with what was in store.

Eleven

As I dressed, I watched Ulli and I had to admit to myself that she would have been very pretty if she had not been so cold.

She had short blonde hair which suited her elfin face, and the thickest, longest natural eyelashes I have ever seen. Her figure was lithe and supple, her legs long and she moved with an economical ease but without a trace of coquetry. I don't believe she had the slightest idea that she was attractive, or perhaps she didn't care a damn.

As I finished dressing, I heard the jeep start up at the house, approach and then wait with the engine running outside the studio. I checked that Katrina was sound asleep and comfortable, and then went down the stairs and out of the door, ignoring Ulli, who did not follow me. Jens was sitting in the driver's seat.

'Get into the back, Mrs Ellis,' he said, looking me quickly over. For a moment I mistook this for provocative insolence, but I was wrong. When I had climbed in, he turned around and with a formal 'Excuse me, please,' put his hands into the pockets of my windcheater. I pulled away automatically, but he was only checking the empty pockets.

'Would you open your jacket, please.' It was not a question.

I unzipped the windcheater, and he glanced quickly, almost modestly over my clothing. I was wearing slacks without pockets and a roll-neck pullover. 'Thank you,' he said.

He picked up a walkie-talkie from the passenger seat and said something in German which might have meant, 'We're coming now.' The radio crackled and a voice said, 'It's good,' or near enough. I wondered how many of them there were as we set off down the track. Someone would be guarding Mike, so that made three at least.

As we went between the trees, Jens said pleasantly, 'Please hold on tightly, Mrs Ellis. Because if you should fall out, or do anything to attract attention to us,' and his eyes met mine in the driving mirror, an expressionless pair of blue eyes looking out of a mask, 'my friends have instructions to set fire to your house.'

As my stomach knotted with hate and fear, he added superfluously, 'And they will not rescue Dr Ellis from the flames.'

The hood of the jeep was up and the side flaps closed. I doubt whether anyone would have recognized us through the crumpled plastic side and back windows, although through the front windscreen any of the villagers would see that it was not Mike at the wheel.

We drove in bitter silence to the dirt road which connects the village to the asphalt road half an hour away. At the junction, Jens stopped and looked cautiously left and right before turning into the road, away from the village, and changing up through the gears.

'Where are you taking me?' I asked.

'Not far now,' he replied smoothly, and indeed we travelled only another kilometre or so.

We rounded a hairpin bend carefully at a point where the road seemed to cling in fright to the side of the mountain. To the right the trees rose up steep and thick, but to the left all was open, and if one kept away from the edge there was nothing to see but sky. I knew from many, many trips up this road how the ground fell away on the outside of the curve, almost vertically at first, dotted with huge boulders thrown there in some prehistoric upheaval of the earth.

The edge was protected and marked by a row of white concrete posts about a foot high with reflecting patches on them. I had often wondered about the story behind the broken one in the middle, but to my knowledge nobody had missed this corner as long as I had lived in Italy. The consequences would be horrible.

Just after the corner, to my surprise we stopped. A small track ran up into the forest here, and Jens reversed expertly into it, using the large wing mirrors. The track met the dirt road at an acute angle, so that we were facing back towards the village. The jeep, thirty yards or so from the road, would be invisible to any driver heading for the village, while those coming the other way would be concentrating on the tricky road and not looking up into the darkness under the trees.

'We must wait for a moment,' he said, but he left the engine running.

We waited in silence for about four or five minutes, and I was just getting fidgety and about to ask him what was happening when the walkie-talkie crackled again. I could not make out what was said, but Jens answered, 'Okay.'

He turned and looked me in the eyes, coldly and deliberately.

'Remember the fire, Mrs Ellis,' was all he said.

I could say nothing in reply, but merely looked equally coldly back at him, while the skin crawled on my back.

We set off slowly down the track, and paused again about ten yards from the dirt road. A heavy motor cycle came past, travelling far too fast, towards the village, and heeled over into the hairpin corner.

I noticed that Jens's back seemed to be very tense. He was slightly hunched at the wheel, and the jeep was making little false starts and then stopping again.

Once more the radio hissed and someone said, this time much louder, 'Okay.'

I was puzzling over what that could mean, as it had not answered any question that I had heard, when everything seemed to happen at once.

A car came into view, slowing for the bend as it passed within a few yards of us heading towards the village. The jeep lurched forwards and the gears protested as Jens crashed through from first into second, accelerating wildly. As I was thrown back in my seat I recognized the car as the one in which I had come up from Olmo only a few hours before. There were two people in it.

The jeep bounced crazily as it hit the road only a few feet

behind Marino's dark red Fiat. I screamed as I realized that Jens was not slowing down at all. For an instant I could see Marino turning his head and gaping in horror, his eyes wild, as the nose of the jeep came into his field of vision. On his right sat old Giorgio, looking innocently out into the vista which was just opening up on the right as the ground fell away and the road switched wickedly round.

This picture burned itself into my mind as I clung desperately to the handgrips along the top of the front seats, screaming to Jens to stop. It has haunted my dreams since, waking me with the sweat running from my armpits and down my back.

We smashed into the Fiat just in front of the back wheel. Marino was braking – I had seen the stop-lights flash on – and the little car was swung around by the impact, the rear-mounted engine acting like a stone on the end of a length of string. For a moment the two vehicles were nose to nose and, over the bonnet of the jeep I could see only the clear, cold sky behind the Fiat.

Suddenly the little car tilted away backwards and disappeared as Jens wrestled with the wheel and I screamed still. I had not even the presence of mind left to leave him alone with the task of fighting the cumbersome vehicle around the rest of the corner, but aimed weak, futile blows at his back with my left hand while I clung on to the handgrip with the right.

We came out of the corner slowly and stopped. At that moment, there was a rolling explosion behind us and the echoes crashed up and down the deep valley below. I looked around in horror, and saw a cloud of black smoke belch up over the precipice.

I was sobbing hysterically as Jens took a deep breath, hunched his shoulders again and started off. I clutched both forearms across my stomach and felt as if I had just been punched there.

After no more than fifty yards, we rounded a curve and saw the motor cycle halted by the roadside, the driver looking back towards the explosion. I was confusedly trying to weigh up the chances of screaming for help against the danger of Jens's threats of arson, and thought vaguely that the rider was sure to remember the jeep which had not even stopped at the scene of the accident, when he raised his gloved hand and turned back to lead the way.

Jens followed him, and both vehicles swung up the track to the house without meeting any other car at all. The whole, horribly simple plan was clear to me in a flash; how Jens had heard that Marino would be coming back about now from the chicken farm, how the motor cyclist had warned him of Marino's approach and confirmed that the road ahead was clear.

But why, *why*? Why cheerful, helpful, harmless Marino? And his ancient father?

As my brain whirled, some answers and half-answers spun off. Marino was probably the only person who knew that Jens was at our house unless he had happened to mention it to anybody, which was unlikely, given the full timetable he had had for to-day. And Giorgio, along for the ride, was just an uncalculated casualty.

A new question entered my mind: why had Jens taken *me* along for the ride? And turn it over as I would, I could find only one possible answer. He had wanted to show me in no uncertain terms that Mike was right, that they meant business and would not stop at putting bullets into plaster walls. And he had succeeded.

By the time we reached the studio I had cried all the tears I had, and my stomach was aching from the sobbing. I could not speak and could not look Jens in the face as he stopped the jeep.

I climbed feebly out of the high vehicle and almost collapsed as my knees tried to take my weight. Jens was about to get out and presumably help me as he saw this, but the thought of his touch was enough to stiffen me again, and I staggered into the studio, leaning on the wall at every pace, and almost crawled up the stairs.

Nobody was in sight as I reached the first floor, and with a cry of anguish I stumbled over to Katrina's cot. She was sleeping peacefully with an angelic smile on her lips.

With trembling hands I lifted her to my shoulder and then sat on my bed, moaning and rocking to and fro long after I had heard the jeep drive up to the house.

It wasn't long before Katrina started to wake up. As she clenched her little fists and stretched, I tried to pull myself together for her. She was not at all surprised, of course, at finding herself in the studio, and smiled contentedly to see me when she opened her eyes.

We played together on the bed, and my heart was ready to burst as she gurgled happily. I wound the alarm clock and held it to her ear, and she started a long monologue of which, despite her conviction that I was understanding every word, only the occasional 'Mama' made much sense. If anyone else is around, Katrina will hardly make a sound, but when we are alone together she chatters away gaily. She crawled to the edge of the bed.

I grabbed her. 'You little beggar,' I whispered. 'Where do you think you're off to?'

She chuckled with delight, but broke off at the sound of the downstairs door opening. I caught her up as my fear and anger surged back, and held her at my shoulder. Footsteps came up the stairs. It was Ulli.

'What do you want to eat?' she asked, as though knocking people's cars off precipices were a weekly event.

'Get out,' I said in a low voice, 'get out and keep away from me. I shall tell you by telephone if I want anything.'

She did not move, but looked genuinely puzzled at my anger. It dawned on me that she did not know what had happened. As if in answer to this thought, she asked, 'Where did Jens take you? What did you do?'

I closed my eyes and felt the tears on my face, and pressed Katrina to my breast.

'Go and ask Jens,' I finally managed to answer, and after a moment I heard her go back down the stairs and bolt the trapdoor. She did not use the intercom, but went out of the studio.

They left me alone for half an hour. Then I heard the outer door open again, and Ulli's voice called up to me, 'Mrs Ellis?'

I had not moved from the bed, but I did not have the strength to answer. She came up the stairs fast, a gun in her hand.

'Mrs Ellis, are you all right?' she said as she saw me, and put her gun away. For the first time, I saw the nurse and the terrorist's training at war in this cold, efficient girl with a pistol.

'I'm feeling better than Marino,' I muttered and I distinctly saw her pull herself together. It was a stupid thing to say, but I wanted to hurt her, hurt all of them.

'I am going to make you something to eat,' she said. 'You must eat, you know.'

She went downstairs, leaving the trapdoor open, and I heard her busying herself in the kitchenette on the ground floor. Somebody came in and up the stairs without speaking to Ulli, and I stiffened as I saw Jens's head and shoulders rising through the aperture in the floor.

I had been prepared to strike him when I saw him again, or spit in his face, but I now found that all emotion had been drained out of me, and I looked at him blankly as he sat down in one of the sailcloth armchairs, neither avoiding my eyes nor meeting them deliberately.

He was brief and to the point.

'Mrs Ellis, you now see that we do mean business.' His gaze strayed over to the bullet-hole in the wall and back to me. 'For the safety of yourself and your daughter – and your husband – you must do as I say. We do not require anything from you except that you stay here for two or three days until your husband gets back. Then you will all be free.'

I shrugged listlessly.

'There is something which we want your husband to do for us,' he carried on quietly. 'There is somebody who has to be eliminated for everybody's good. By everybody, I mean not just you and me. I mean all mankind.'

Uncomprehendingly I looked at him and tried to make sense out of his words.

'It is somebody very important, and your husband can get close to him without arousing suspicions.'

I went cold as the next words fell into the silence.

'And Dr Ellis is going to kill him for us.'

MIKE

Twelve

Sophie's amber eyes were dry and bright when I left her in the studio, and her trembling had calmed. Jens paused on the ground floor to telephone for Ulli to come to the studio before leaving, and we walked – or rather, in my case, limped – the hundred yards to the house in silence, passing Ulli without a word on the way.

'What do you want to show me? And what do you want me to do for you?' I asked Jens as we entered the house.

'What I said was not quite true,' Jens replied, indicating that we were to go into the dining room. 'I want you to show me something.'

I had often noticed discrepancies in Jens's words, and I now surmised that these were to a large extent deliberate, designed to keep up a situation of insecurity in which Sophie and I would be too confused to be able to plan anything.

The dining room was much tidier than it had been the last time I had seen it, on Friday evening. Either our arrival had prompted them to take more care, or more probably they had simply had time to settle in.

75

I went to sit in my armchair at the fireplace, but found in it the pile of newspapers I had not had time to study and which they had brought downstairs again. Turning to put them on the table, I stopped short, for I found my briefcase there, and its contents neatly stacked beside it. I turned questioningly to Jens.

'Is this all you carry about with you when you travel?' he asked.

'This and an overnight bag.'

'Where is your overnight bag?'

'I left it at Rome airport, because I intended to fly on Saturday to either Geneva or New York. There was nothing in it which I needed, just a change of clothing, some dirty linen, toilet articles and so on. And when I decided to come up here for the weekend, I did not bother to go and get it. I have to go to Rome now on Monday morning anyway. Tomorrow morning,' I added, realizing with a start that it was already Sunday afternoon. 'People are going to notice if I do not come, you know. I have an appointment at eleven with the head of a U.N. agency there. There will be inquiries if I do not keep the appointment.'

'You will keep the appointment,' said Jens calmly. 'We have already organized a car to take you there. I am to tell you that you will receive further instructions in Rome. Don't look for them or wait for them – they will know how to reach you.'

I looked at him in astonishment, and decided to say nothing.

'We were told that you are to keep your appointment,' he repeated, 'and to remind you that any attempt to warn the authorities or anyone else that we are here will have fatal results for your wife and daughter.'

I bit down several possible replies, and finally decided that not only did they have me by the short hairs, but also that there was no advantage to be gained from denying it. 'That is perfectly clear,' I said. I was coming around to Jens's viewpoint that co-operation was by far the most comfortable course to steer.

'I do not believe that either your wife or yourself really thinks we are prepared to kill anybody.' He was speaking quietly, rationally, as usual. I had come to distrust that calm tone. But it still took a moment for the meaning of his next words to sink in. 'We are arranging a demonstration. Your wife is going to watch us kill the young man who brought her here.'

'That is monstrous!' I finally gasped. 'Monstrous and quite

unnecessary. I quite believe you are capable of selling your grandmother for a frankfurter. Do not think you have to spill any more blood to prove it. Leave the young man alone. Marino is no threat whatever to you.'

'Perhaps, perhaps not,' he said dispassionately. 'I must remind you, Dr Ellis, that the only person who has spilt any blood yet is you. However, I do not have time to discuss that now. What I wanted you to show me is the result of the work you have just been carrying out. Here is no report, no notes. The tape on the dictating machine is empty. Where are your notes?'

I felt weak as I struggled to keep my face neutral. How did they know? Or did they? Were they just guessing? Or being extraordinarily thorough? Or had they instructions? From whom? I heard my own voice talking naturally as though from a long way away.

'I am in the middle of a long investigation and at this point I have had no need to make notes. I have not reached any conclusions yet, and I shall have to have some meetings in Rome or possibly New York and then go back to Koristan where I was working.'

He looked at me silently for what seemed a long time, and then said, 'I hope that what you say is true. I was told to look for a report, notes for a report, papers, anything; but there is nothing here which corresponds to my instructions.' I felt my knees trembling as he repeated thoughtfully, 'I hope what you say is true. For your sake.'

'Ridiculous,' I said. 'Nobody but myself knows what stage my investigation has reached. Your . . . your employer was wrongly informed. Who is it anyway? Has he caused all this violence and discomfort just to get something that does not exist?'

He did not answer, but instead asked me another question which made my blood run cold. 'What were you doing at the American Express in Rome?'

I struggled to sound calm.

'I had almost no cash left and withdrew some money from my account.'

'It took a long time, and you did not go to the usual counter.'

I remembered the queues of young hitch-hikers and older tourists, and tried to stop the vision from parading before my eyes. I knew it was hopeless at this stage to try to recall a suspicious figure; I had had no reason to be wary of anybody on Friday afternoon. Instead, I was going to need all my concentration now.

'My account is in Geneva,' I said, 'and it would normally take a day or two to clear the amount I needed. But I know the manager of the Rome branch, and apart from paying him a courtesy call, I asked him to clear my withdrawal by telex. I felt a little guilty at asking for a rush treatment on a Friday afternoon, so I went straight to my friend.'

Jens gave me a considering look, and then seemed to reach some conclusion and told me to go upstairs. He followed. As he was locking me into Katrina's room, I suddenly remembered his threats about Marino, and crashed my fists on the door, shouting, 'Leave Marino alone, do you hear? Leave him alone! He has done nothing , he is no threat to you !'

But Jens went off down the stairs without replying, and I sat on the bed with my head in my hands and felt on the edge of despair.

I heard the jeep start up and drive over to the studio. After a few moments it left. Then somebody came into the house, up the stairs, and tried the door of my room.

'Who is it? What do you want?' I called, but there was no reply, and the footsteps went off down the stairs again. Apart from occasional movements in the dining room and kitchen, the chink of glass, the running of water, the house was silent for almost an hour.

It was five-thirty when the jeep came back, preceded by a motor bike. There were various comings and goings for an hour or more, and then Klaus unlocked the door. He took away the bucket in which I had urinated, and brought it back clean and smelling of disinfectant.

'Dinner will be ready in about half an hour,' he said, sounding rather like a manservant. 'Do you wish to have a bath first?'

That was exactly what I needed, and I said so.

'*Gut*. Then please take all your clothes off and leave them here.'

He went into the bathroom, leaving both doors wide open, and I heard him turn the taps on. He came back with a dressing-gown. When I got to the bathroom, the door was propped open with a stool, and there was a chair in the corridor outside, on which Klaus sat down with a copy of *Der Spiegel*.

The bath improved my spirits no end. I was almost amused at the thought of the papers hidden under my feet. I told Klaus I wanted some clean clothes from the main bedroom. He said I could not go in there but should tell him what I wanted. I had him bring me some cream slacks and a khaki shirt.

I tried to ask him about Marino, but he said I must ask Jens. Since Jens was not there, I could get no information at all. I began to think it had been an empty threat.

When I had finished my bath, Klaus escorted me back to my cell, and served dinner shortly afterwards. The meal was excellent, roast chicken with mushrooms and potatoes, fresh fruit salad, and local wine. After dinner, Ulli came and changed the bandage on my ankle, and said it would not hurt much tomorrow so long as I did not put too much strain on it.

She disappeared and came back with coffee and a sheet of paper, which she handed to me without comment. I unfolded it, and my throat tightened as I recognized Sophie's writing.

Darling, they have killed poor Marino. They forced his car off the road over the cliff, with the jeep. It was terrible. I had to watch. There was nothing I could do. They are cold, terrible brutes. Do anything they say, anything. I am sure they will not hurt me or Katrina or you, if you do what they want. Come back soon, I shall be waiting for you. I love you, darling. P.S. And do not worry about me, I am all right and so is Katrina, and they are treating us well. Just come back as soon as you can.

Ulli said quietly, 'She is right, Dr Ellis. We shall not harm them as long as you do what we say. Come back soon and we will go away.' But I was not listening. I was sitting dazed and sickened by the confirmation of Jens's threat. Ulli was watching me closely. I put the note in the pocket of my shirt without replying.

Ulli stood up. 'You have had a long day, and you must get up very early tomorrow to go to Rome,' she said. 'I have put a mild sleeping draught in your coffee. It will not put you to sleep like

the injection, but if you let it, it will help you sleep well and rest.'
When she had gone, I yawned again and stretched out on top of
the bed.

The next thing I knew, Jens was shaking my shoulder to wake me
up, and saying, 'It is a quarter to five, Dr Ellis. Here is some
coffee. What do you want for breakfast?' I sat up and stretched,
and I found I had been undressed and put to bed.

'A boiled egg and some yoghourt,' I told him. 'And I shall
need some business clothes.'

'I am sorry, there is no yoghourt. We did not know that you
eat it. I will bring you the egg and some more coffee. Your clothes
are here.'

He was gone before I remembered about Marino. The suit I had
worn from Rome was freshly pressed on a hanger on the back of
the door, and a clean shirt and underclothes were on the chair. I
had not realized before that kidnappers had so much housework
to do. Or perhaps I was getting preferential treatment.

As I dressed, I remembered Sophie's note from the previous
evening, but the shirt was gone and the note nowhere to be
found. When Jens came back with my breakfast, I asked him
where it was, but he just shook his head silently.

'What about Marino?' I asked him. 'Why did you do that?
What was the point?'

'Marino unfortunately had to die,' said Jens without emotion.
'He was the only person who knew we are here. We want to stay
here without disturbance until you return, then we can go and
leave you in peace.'

I felt the anger boiling up in me, and fought down the desire
to strike at him. 'You are slimy bastards,' I told him in disgust.
'What a despicable unnecessary thing to do. I suppose you are
going to tell me you had "your orders", like they did at
Nuremberg.'

It had not the slightest effect on him, and he merely shrugged
impatiently at my last, childish insult.

'It was a necessity.'

I was numbed at the unbelievable callousness of this young
hoodlum. What kind of political persuasion can justify behaviour like that? I wondered. But I was clearly going to get
nothing more out of him. I tried to pull myself together and

tackle my breakfast, but I had little appetite and soon pushed the tray away.

But as I toyed with the egg, my mind shaking off the last wisps of sleep, I became aware that I had scored a minor victory without even trying. I had been suspecting for some time that my unwelcome house-guests were not an autonomous group, but that there was a lot in the background which I had not yet learned. Their unnatural consideration towards me, for example, especially compared with their cold-blooded extermination of Marino, was somehow significant. As so often happens, my brain had continued processing the flimsy evidence while I slept, and had reached its own conclusions.

My infantile stab about Nuremberg had been a result of this conclusion. And Jens had not denied it! He had hardly seemed to notice the implication.

I stood up. He had only been waiting for me, and now he too made ready to go.

'I shall want to say goodbye to my wife,' I said as we went down the stairs.

'That is unfortunately not possible. But you will see her again in only a few days. If you want to leave her a note, you may do it.'

I scribbled a few words of love and comfort for Sophie, promising her that I would take no risks and be back soon, and Jens and I left together in the jeep. I looked up at the studio windows, though I knew there would be nothing to see from ground level, even if she were awake.

It was a cold, misty morning, and Jens had the side lights on. We travelled in silence to the dirt road, and then turned right towards Olmo. Jens passed the place where Marino had been murdered without comment, and I did not know where it was until days later.

Jens reached behind him and took my briefcase from the back of the jeep, and gave it to me. I opened it and checked the contents as we approached the tarmac road. Everything was there, as far as I could see, except of course the draft report I had taken out myself. In addition, I found my passport and wallet and various small items taken from the pockets of my suit, like my lighter, fountain-pen, and appointments calendar. The key to the luggage locker at Fiumicino where my overnight bag was stored was still in the wallet.

When we arrived at the tarmac road, the mist had already lifted and the morning was cool but sunny. The woods were decked in autumn colours. It was the time of year I liked best, but the beloved landscape could give me little delight this morning.

A limousine with smoked-glass windows was waiting for us where the dirt road ended. Two men in chauffeur's uniform were sitting in the front, and Jens motioned me to stay in the jeep while he went over to them. The driver opened a window, and there was a short conversation, Jens leaning over with the collar of his pilot's jacket pulled up around his neck and his breath making clouds in the air.

One of the men looked over to me, and back to Jens again. Then he got out and opened the back door of the limousine. Jens beckoned for me to come, and as I reached the limousine there was an almost comical moment when we each hesitated as though about to shake hands, or say goodbye, or something equally conventional.

The man in uniform touched his cap and said, 'Buon giorno, dottore,' as I got in. Then he closed the door and went back to his place beside the driver. Jens stood back with his hands in his pockets. I pressed the switch and the window purred down.

'Don't do them any harm,' I said. He shook his head, and then gave a curt, embarrassed half-wave and turned back to the jeep as the limousine moved off.

'Where are you taking me?' I asked the chauffeur in Italian.

'Why, to Rome of course, sir,' he said in surprise. 'This is an I.D.A. car. We were told that you want to be there by eleven.'

'That's exactly right,' I said to cover my confusion. The sedative was still having an influence; I dozed in the comfortable seat until we stopped at the motorway entrance to pick up the toll ticket. The man beside the chauffeur, seeing that I was awake, asked, 'Do you want to stop for a coffee, sir?'

I didn't particularly, but they obviously did, so I said yes. He looked relieved. We pulled into the service area at Chianciano Terme and he leapt out and opened the door for me. In the bar, the two men sat discreetly at a separate table and had quite a hearty breakfast by Italian standards, where a coffee and a bun is usually enough until mid-morning. I guessed that they had driven up from Rome for me very early, and that reminded me of something.

'I'll just make a phone call and then we can be off,' I told them as I passed their table. They nodded politely and took no further notice of me as I went to the cash-desk, paid for all three orders, and asked for some *gettoni* for the pay-phone.

I rang my own number, and Jens's voice answered. I spoke in German, because Italian bar telephones are not usually designed for privacy, and this one was no exception.

'It's Ellis,' I said curtly. 'Who are these men and what do they know?'

'They know nothing at all,' he replied. 'The I.D.A. was told you had no transport and required a car, and they sent you one.'

'You might have told me. I almost let something slip.'

'Then please be more careful. You should have understood. You are now a free man, and you are not being shadowed. You know perfectly well why.'

I rang off without replying, and the drivers got up as soon as they saw me coming back. I spent the rest of the journey thinking, planning what I could say in Rome.

Despite the usual chaotic Monday-morning traffic, we arrived on time at the I.D.A. skyscraper near Monte Mario and the Observatory in north-west Rome and I limped up the steps to the glass doors of the foyer trying to decide how to play this one.

The guard on desk duty recognized me at once, for I had already done several jobs for the agency, and the original desk research for this job had occupied me in Rome for almost a week.

'The C.E. is expecting you, Dr Ellis,' he said in Americanized English, 'please go straight on up. I'll let him know you're on your way.'

I handed him my briefcase and went over to the lift, while he picked up the telephone.

The lift took a long time to reach the nineteenth floor, because it was apparently the end of the morning coffee-break. It stopped at almost every level, and the people getting in and out were as colourful and heterogenous as the pictures in a child's first geography book. There were maxi-skirted English girls with lank hair and gaudy nail-varnish, statuesque African girls and tiny, exquisite Asian girls incongruously dressed in denims, Frenchmen in blue suits and crew-cuts, Englishmen with rumpled hair, chewing unlit pipes, Italians trying to look like Americans, Americans trying to look like Italians . . .

I was the only person left on board at the nineteenth, and as the doors slid smoothly open, someone was waiting to get into the lift whom I knew but could not place.

'Why, hello Mike!' he said with a pleasant smile. 'Nice to see you back. Are you going to be in Archives again for a while?'

George Hamilton, that was it. He had been seconded from the U.N. in Geneva to supervise the co-ordination of archives between the I.D.A. and the mother organization.

'Afraid not, George,' I said, shaking his hand. 'I think I'm leaving again today.'

'You're not going back to your office, are you?' he asked. 'Because if so we might be travelling together. I'm taking the four-thirty flight to Geneva.' He held his hand in front of the photocell to hold the lift doors open.

'No,' I said slowly as an idea came into my mind, 'I'm going the other way. But maybe we could have lunch together if you have time. There's something you might be able to do for me.'

'Pleasure, Mike. See you in the restaurant at one?'

'Fine, just right, George.' The lift doors closed behind me as I turned and headed for Mkara's office.

My original appointment with Black Jack for Friday afternoon had been to inform him for courtesy's sake of the explosive material I was about to present to his masters in New York. After all the facilities he had given me, it would have been brutal to let such a scandal descend on him out of the blue.

I was no longer convinced that I should go ahead as I'd planned, however. Jens's interest in my briefcase had put the idea into my head that the extraordinary, unpleasant business in Olmo was tied up somehow with Wharton's case, and his question about my visit to Amexco had strengthened it. My intuition told me that, as long as Sophie and Katrina were hostages, there was still a lot I had to know before I took any irreversible steps in connection with the investigation.

But first and foremost, I needed to know what the 'instructions' were that I was going to receive in Rome.

Thirteen

As his secretary, a tall, gaunt Irish girl with dark brown ringlets, closed the door behind me, Cyril Mkara stood up elegantly from behind his desk and came towards me with both hands outstretched.

'My *dear* Dr Ellis! How *nice* to see you! I am so terribly sorry about Friday. I do hope you had a pleasant weekend, at least?'

His dark blue suit was impeccable, and he was wearing a quietly striped tie on a light blue shirt. His large teeth gleamed brilliantly in his highly-polished ebony face.

'My dear chap, you're limping! What on earth have you done? Do sit down.' He clasped my right hand in both of his and led me to the chair in front of his desk.

He pressed a button on the intercom. 'Coffee? Or would you prefer tea?'

His smile faded almost imperceptibly as I replied, 'I think I could use a whisky.'

'Ah, Miss O'Hara,' he said, looking over my shoulder. 'Please bring Dr Ellis a Glenfiddich . . . Soda? Ice?' I shook my head. '. . . as it comes. And I would like some tea, if you please.'

The door presumably closed, for he waited for a moment watching in that direction before swinging his smile back towards me.

'How did you get on in Koristan? I hope you found out everything you wanted. Wharton is a most helpful and charming fellow, is he not? Oh, by the way, talking of Wharton, I've had a message from him. Perhaps you know what it's about. I have it somewhere here. Unless Miss O'Hara has pigeon-holed it, of course. She is almost too efficient sometimes . . .'

He managed to fumble about among the three or four pieces of paper on the top of his pristine desk, talking until the whisky came, followed shortly by the tea. I imagined that Miss O'Hara made fresh tea at quarter-hour intervals all day in case it was required. I couldn't imagine Black Jack standing for tea-bags.

I raised my glass silently to him and drank the dainty portion that Miss O'Hara had thought proper. Mkara's eyebrows twitched slightly in the direction of his short-cropped, iron-grey hair as I poured out a rather more man-sized shot from the freshly-opened bottle that she had left on the table beside me.

Once she had gone, he got down to business. 'Now, I got your telex and I managed to keep most of Friday afternoon free. But I really had to be in Stockholm first thing on Saturday, so this was the best I could manage, I'm afraid. I understand you have a country house quite near, so I hope you weren't too inconvenienced. What was it you wanted to see me about?'

He put the tips of his long, spatulate fingers together in a tent and leaned forward with his elbows on the teak desk top, looking slightly down on me, as his chair was higher than mine.

'Perhaps you could tell me first about Wharton's message,' I suggested. 'I might be able to shed some light on it.'

'Of course, my dear fellow!' he exclaimed, and picked up a piece of paper by one corner between his thumb and forefinger. It was curled slightly, with the writing on the outside, and I thought, that has come off the telex this morning.

'He says: "Important new developments. Imperative Ellis returns immediately repeat immediately to Nooriabad." And yet,' he picked up a similar piece of paper, also with both top and bottom edges torn, but this time quite flat, 'you telexed me last week: "Investigation concluded except archive visits to Rome and Geneva. Request appointment Friday afternoon." Now, what is it all about?'

'There were one or two points which were puzzling me, and I was prepared to do some more desk research and then check the results back by telex with Wharton,' I said. 'My message was a little truncated, I'm afraid. It should have read, "*Field* investigation concluded".'

'Of course, I don't even know what you were investigating,' said Mkara suavely between sips of tea. 'New York was very difficult to pin down on that. But naturally they may conduct independent investigations of field situations if they deem it necessary. It is just that they have never made use of this facility before, and in any case it was tacitly understood, at least by us here, that we would be kept informed if such a case ever arose – fully informed. So what is it you wanted to see me about?'

His choice of the same words seemed to imply that whatever had gone between was in parentheses and we were back at the starting point. To emphasize this, he put his fingertips together again and waited with a benign smile.

'I'm afraid that as far as the subject of the investigation goes, Mr Mkara, I don't feel at liberty to discuss that even with you, with all due respect. I am in the difficult position of being a free-lance consultant employed by New York, and I would need the mandate of my immediate client before taking any such independent step.'

Mkara spread his elegant hands outward and murmured, 'Of course, of course,' but I carried on with the lie which I had thought up in the car on the way to Rome. Not that I was particularly happy with it, but I had been able to think of nothing better at short notice.

'I needed your authority to have access to the confidential personnel files of all staff in the Koristan mission, and all who have worked there since it was set up six years ago. I didn't think my telex would cause you to cancel any appointments, but I didn't want to go behind your back to Personnel with the matter.' Mkara was looking extremely disappointed. 'Perhaps I could study those dossiers this afternoon?' I suggested blandly. To my amazement and relief, he swallowed the thin story without batting an elegant eyelid.

'My *dear* Dr Ellis, of course, of course! You really didn't need my authority for that, but thank you for your courtesy. Except that, as Wharton's telex really sounded terribly urgent, I took the liberty of having Miss O'Hara book you on the one o'clock flight to Nooriabad.'

My head spun as I tried to work out this new development. Jens had said that I was to get further instructions from Rome. But if I left now, there would be no time for anybody to get instructions to me. Or was Wharton's telex to be regarded as 'instructions'? Certainly my departure would leave me no time to do anything at all. I glanced at my watch; it was ten past eleven, and I would have to leave within a quarter of an hour or so to get to the airport in time to pick up my bag and check in, even if Miss O'Hara telephoned ahead to warn the airline that I was going to be late.

'Just how important is this research in the personnel files, Dr

Ellis?' Mkara interrupted my thoughts. 'As far as I am aware, there is nothing on the files here about the mission staff that is not duplicated there.'

'In that case,' I said, stalling for time to think, 'I have probably made a journey for nothing. I suppose if Wharton is so insistent...'

Mkara stood up with a smile. 'I shall telex Wharton this afternoon and authorize you to have full access to the files there. And I shall instruct Personnel to check whether there is anything in Rome which the mission office does not have on file. If anything turns up, I have a courier going to Delhi tomorrow in any case, and I shall have him drop it off for you on the way. How is that?'

I could see no possibility of talking my way out of this. My only hope now was that I would get my new instructions on the way to the airport, or perhaps at the airport itself.

As I, too, stood up, another question occurred to me. 'Thank you for providing transport, by the way. How did you know I was in Tuscany?'

He came around the desk to usher me to the door. 'Miss O'Hara said your house-guest rang on Saturday afternoon, and she was fortunately doing some overtime. Have a good flight, my dear chap, and let me know at once if you should need anything else.' Mkara opened the door for me. 'Miss O'Hara, perhaps you could telephone the airport and say that Dr Ellis will be late for check-in?'

'Certainly, Mr Mkara,' she murmured, and Mkara gave me a parting salute as he closed the door on his own brilliant smile.

'Thank you for the car, Miss O'Hara.' I smiled at her.

She looked at me uncomprehendingly, and the ringlets bounced on her shoulders. 'The car, Dr Ellis?'

'Yes, the car to bring me down to Rome this morning.'

'Oh, of course . . . Not at all, Dr Ellis. Not at all.' The bright smile was back, but I was certain that Miss O'Hara had known nothing about the car until I mentioned it. Somebody was lying, but I couldn't work out who or why.

I went to Archives on the fourth floor and looked for George Hamilton. He was telephoning and with his free hand waved me into a chair. I thought he would never finish, and by his grimaces he obviously thought the same of his caller.

Finally he put the receiver down, and before he could speak I got in first.

'Look, George, I'm sorry but I'm not going to make it for lunch. My flight is earlier than I thought. But would you do me a favour in Geneva?'

'Two if I can, Mike. What's the problem? You look worried.'

'I'll tell you one day, George, I promise. Just see that a letter reaches my partner in Geneva, would you? Not by post.'

'I know the post is a bit slow here, old boy, but it usually gets there in the end, like the Mounties,' he said. 'But of course I will. Have you got it with you?'

'No, George. I'll need five minutes in a quiet corner with a bit of paper and an envelope.'

'Nothing easier, Mike. Use that desk over there by the window. Nobody'll disturb you there.'

After some thought and several false starts which I tore into very small pieces, I wrote:

Rome, Monday
Sam: I've had to go back to Koristan for a couple of days. I have to ask you to do something for me. Get on to John in Florence and have him find out *discreetly* where an employee of the West German Consulate there called Roswita, last name unknown, lives. Probably near the *autostrada*. I will be there in a day or so to ask him for the result. And whatever you do, don't go anywhere near my place at Olmo, or even telephone there. *Believe me, this is absolutely vital*. Sorry if that sounds odd, but I'll explain as soon as I can. Take care – Mike.

I read it over and doubled the underlining before sealing the letter in the I.D.A. envelope George Hamilton had given me and bringing it to him. As he watched, I put a small mark in a corner on the back of the envelope, so that he would recognize it at once.

'My address is in the phone book, George,' I told him, 'so I'm not putting it on the envelope. Just ring my partner Sam Greaves or my secretary Christine and they'll pick it up. Sorry about the cloak-and-dagger bit; as I said, I'll tell you all about it one day.'

I reflected that I was promising a lot of explanations to various people.

'I sincerely hope so, Mike,' he answered, and I agreed with him from the bottom of my heart. But I was never to get the chance to explain.

He stowed the envelope in his briefcase, and stood up with me. 'I'll come along with you. I was just going to the bar over the road. Have you time for a quick one before you go?'

I said I had, and we took the lift down to the foyer.

'I'll be in Geneva by seven,' said George as we crossed the red marble floor, 'and I'll see to it straight away. Nobody will know about it,' he added with a conspiratorial touch of my elbow. 'Will your partner be there?'

'Somebody will be, George. Thanks a lot.'

At that moment, I noticed that Miss O'Hara had been walking beside me, I didn't know for how long, trying politely to get my attention.

'Excuse me, Dr Ellis. I have been looking for you everywhere! The guard told me you hadn't left the building yet. I have a car waiting for you outside. You'll never make your flight if you have to wait for a taxi at this time of day.'

I turned to George and held out my hand. 'Looks as though I won't make it this time, then,' I said. 'I'll get the next round, okay?'

'Well, hard luck, Mike,' he said with a smile. 'Have a good flight.'

As he left, Miss O'Hara walked with me to the receptionist to pick up my briefcase. I glanced sidelong at the efficient – 'almost too efficient' Mkara had said – young woman who had pretended to have forgotten sending a car to pick me up, I was sure of it now. Like hell you had, I thought. Getting a car and a crew together on a weekend, persuading them to leave Rome at two in the morning and rendezvous with a jeep on a back road in Tuscany at dawn, and now you've forgotten!

I looked at Miss O'Hara, spare and efficient, with her Jane Austen ringlets and tailored red woollen dress, and thought, God, am I getting paranoid, or who else is mixed up in this?

She took my briefcase down the steps to another car with another driver in the reserved area at the kerb. This one didn't salute or jump out to open the door.

'Bon voyage, Dr Ellis,' fluted Miss O'Hara, and closed the door.

To the driver she added, 'As fast as you can to the airport, please. You have very little time.'

Fourteen

As it was, we hardly made it to the airport in time, and I reflected that whoever was planning my life for me at the moment had organized it very well. The ten minutes in Archives with George Hamilton were almost the only time I had had to myself since Klaus had found me beside the stream on Saturday morning.

I picked up my overnight bag and made my way over to the baggage check. Although Fiumicino is reputed to be one of Europe's worst airports for security, as journalists have repeatedly proven, it was my bad luck to have my baggage checked this time. The moment I opened the zip, I knew something was wrong.

When I had left the bag there on Friday, I had rummaged through it quickly to make sure there was nothing in it I would need. I remembered clearly now that I had left the contents in a pretty muddled condition, hastily stuffed back in after I had gone through it on the floor in front of the lockers. Not my usual methodical style at all. But now, everything was clean, neatly arranged and folded. It was as though somebody wanted to make me understand that it had been tampered with.

The policeman lifted up a shirt or two in a perfunctory manner and waved me on. As I hurried to the exit gate, I wondered who could have done it. And why. And, above all, how they had known in time to launder and re-pack everything, for I had told Jens only the previous afternoon where the bag was. I remembered once more his question about my visit to Amexco. Had I been followed all the way from the airport on Friday, perhaps even before that?

A ground hostess took my boarding card and escorted me with more haste than courtesy across the concrete apron. But my thoughts were still elsewhere. I was reluctantly coming to the conclusion that I was up against an organization much more powerful and far-reaching than I had thought. I wondered what would have happened if I had been able to keep my appointment with Mkara on Friday and had not gone to Olmo for the weekend. No doubt this, too, had been anticipated and a contingency plan drawn up. A phone call to Jens, for example, and the whole Olmo squad could have been on the road.

The Iran Air 707 was not crowded, and although I was the last passenger on board I found a window seat with no neighbours. The actual flying time was to be only some eight hours, but there was a stop-over during the night in Teheran and a time difference of three and a half hours, so that I would not be getting into Nooriabad until eight in the morning, local time.

A snack was served as soon as we were airborne, and I devoured it gratefully. I had not been hungry when I got up that morning, but the tension of the day, or perhaps it was the sleeping draught wearing off, had left me ravenous. The stewardess laughed prettily and asked if I would like another one. I said yes and ate it rather more sedately.

As the big jet soared above the glittering sea of cloud, carrying me back to Nooriabad and whatever awaited me there this time, I had plenty of time to think the whole thing over again from the beginning. I needed to. As long as Sophie and Katrina were hostages for my good behaviour, I wanted to be absolutely certain that I would make no foolish mistake.

Bob Harding had called me from New York almost a month earlier and asked me if I could handle a big one for him. The fact that I could was all that interested him at the time, and I had heard his sigh of relief via a satellite or two. The fact that I could, but only because I had for six months been considering, accepting and rejecting commissions with an exclusive view to keeping September free for a month's holiday with my family, was my problem not his.

But Bob and I were good friends, and when he almost pleaded with me, dismissing as unimportant my warning that it would not be cheap, the thing was clinched. He wanted me in New York the next day, and I haggled for the end of the week and won. When I got there and heard what it was he wanted, I understood his urgency.

There had been uneasy rumours for some time about big discrepancies in the U.N. programmes in developing countries. The press was not yet on to it, but there were bits of information which had come Bob's way, until finally he was putting quite a picture together. As the Asian Co-ordinator of U.N. Programmes should. And that very week a big or at least key piece of the puzzle had come into his hands, from sources he was 'not at liberty to mention', and a whole lot had fallen into place for him with a smooth click.

Everything was now pointing at the I.D.A., one of the U.N.'s most highly regarded and trouble-free programmes, and at the Koristan mission, which was run by a man with an unblemished career and excellent standing in development circles: Charles Wharton from New Zealand.

Bob Harding was frankly scared. He was a fairly good friend of Wharton and, although it shouldn't have, that tended to tie his hands, too. He wanted an independent investigation by a freelance consultant.

After lunch, he had stood with his back to me looking down on the East River traffic from thirty-two floors up, and had dictated to me from memory the meat of all the rumours he had heard. As a second course, he filled me in on everything he knew – and with his experience that was just a modest way of saying 'everything' – about how the books could be fiddled in a development agency.

We went to see a Broadway show later, but although we strictly avoided the slightest hint of business, it was preying on both our minds, and the evening was dreary. I don't even remember what show it was. The next morning, I accepted the job, outlined what I intended to do – a week or so of desk research in the I.D.A. archives in Rome and then a field investigation in Koristan, reporting back only to Bob – and he gave me a covering letter to Cyril Mkara and a letter of introduction to Charles Wharton.

As I was collecting my papers together to put into my briefcase, Bob sat drumming his fingers on the desk top, trying to get up the courage to say something. He found it as I stood up to leave.

'Don't take any chances, Mike,' he said with an embarrassed cough. 'There's a whole pile of money involved, and people can sometimes get nasty when there's that much at stake.'

'I've taken care of that, Bob,' I said. 'Have another look at my fee.' Now I come to think of it, I hadn't really taken care of it. Not seriously, anyway. It was a flippant remark to reassure Bob, but nearer to the bone than I could have guessed.

We shook hands and he watched me go all the way down the corridor. He was still standing there as I turned the corner. He raised his hands in salute, but his shoulders were drooping.

I had found out several things in Rome, but of course nothing anywhere near conclusive, or even suspicious unless you were looking for it with a very jaundiced eye. Naturally I was working under a cover, even as far as Cyril Mkara was concerned.

For Charles Wharton and everybody else with whom I had to co-operate, I was applying experience gained by other U.N. and independent programmes to I.D.A. methods in an effort to increase the efficiency and decrease the cost of early-warning and preparation mechanisms in case of nutritional or other emergencies. Which meant that I had to bone up quite a lot on that, too.

Wharton turned out to be one of the most naturally charming and efficiently helpful people I had met in my experience of working for the U.N. I was sure from the start that he had no idea what I was really investigating, and I worked on for ten days convinced that, although something was definitely wrong in the Koristan mission, Charles Wharton did not know about it.

The mission employed eighty people in the Nooriabad offices and another fifty or so in the field. About a hundred of these people were foreign experts and secretarial staff, and the rest local employees. The discrepancies, and they turned out to be on a scale which not even Bob Harding had dreamed of in his worst nightmares, could have been organized by almost anybody near the top of the tree, but not without co-operation at various levels. Or, as I realized far too late, by somebody at the very top of the tree with co-operation from outside.

Wharton looked after me very well socially, making me a welcome guest almost every evening but never phrasing his invitation so pressingly that I could not refuse. He was a big man approaching forty, witty, cultured and fond of the cinema and the theatre; we talked on these subjects for hours. He steadfastly refused to talk shop, and I never had the faintest impression that he was trying to influence my work in any way.

Tuula, his wife, was one of the most exquisite women I have ever seen, with cornflower-blue eyes and waist-length, golden-blonde hair. Although she looked petite next to Wharton's bulk, when she stood alone you noticed that she was not small at all, merely very slender, and she moved with grace. She looked equally beautiful in the formal gown of floor-length black velvet she wore when we all went together one evening to a reception at the French Embassy, and in the jeans and shirt she would wear in the house.

She spoke English with only the lightest of accents, but I loved to hear her speaking the liquid vowels and lilting music of Finnish, which she sometimes spoke with Wharton, who was reasonably fluent in that difficult tongue. She was devoted to him, and they certainly made a handsome couple. I suspected that their childlessness was a tragedy for them.

Tuula, too, was intelligent and cultured, and my evenings with the Whartons were pleasant indeed. Except that, as my work progressed and the evidence piled up, I began to feel more and more uncomfortable in the presence of these people over whose heads I was soon to hold a bombshell. I suppose, in the light of later events, that I was already beginning to suspect that such large-scale embezzlement without Wharton's active connivance was almost unthinkable, but it was not for several days that this crystallized into certainty.

Apart from this, Koristan was an agreeable enough place in which to work. It is high enough in the mountains to be protected from the worst of the summer heat, and the Koris are cheerful, hospitable people. Nooriabad, the only city of any size, has a large expatriate community with a flourishing cultural life of its own, for the discovery of mineral wealth in the mountains brought to this peaceful, fertile country an asset which larger states had not been slow to notice.

I did a three-day field trip into Afghanistan, taking an I.D.A. Beaver from Kabul airport up to the strip at Mazar-i-Sharif near the ill-defined Russian border, and then going by Land-Rover to Kunduz, visiting several small field stations on the way. I met the Beaver at Kunduz for the return flight to Nooriabad.

I was becoming progressively more convinced that there was a route up there over the border, which was in many places uncharted, but what was puzzling me was that there were signs that it was not just cash, but actually merchandise that was moving.

The Kori and Afghan governments are on excellent terms, and frontier formalities between the two states are as simple as, for instance, between member countries of the European Common Market. It became increasingly clear to me that the friendly relations between the neighbours were being abused. Whoever was diverting development funds was taking advantage of the easygoing Afghans.

Arriving back at Nooriabad, I thanked the cheerful Australian pilot and drove myself downtown. Although it was seven in the evening, there was still a lot of activity at the I.D.A. offices near the Crown Prince's palace. I was glad, because I knew Wharton was expecting me back and would be waiting for me. As usual, there was nowhere to park within blocks of the entrance, and I hurried breathlessly along the street and up the stairs.

I was going to have to stop off in a men's room and get some of the sand of the dusty northern provinces out of my hair and from under my fingernails before I sat down for the meeting we had planned. But for courtesy's sake I knocked and put my head around the door of Wharton's office on the way past, to let him know I had arrived. His secretary was not 'on guard' in the outer office, and her desk was tidied for the night.

To my dismay, Wharton barked at me in an unfriendly tone I had never heard him use with anybody before. 'I wish you wouldn't burst in like that! Perhaps you could knock and wait in future.'

'Bursting in' was a bit exaggerated, I felt; I had hardly put more than an eye around the door-jamb. But I let it go.

'Sorry, didn't mean to disturb you. I only just got in, I'm afraid, and I wanted to let you know I'd be with you as soon as I've had a wash and brush-up.'

'Well, yes. All right. But it's too late for a meeting now. Can we talk in the morning?' He was already looking contrite.

'Right-oh. Glad to go, actually, it was a tiring trip. I'll be in at nine,' I said, and withdrew thoughtfully. For in my brief glance into the room, I had seen Wharton leaning over his desk, frozen in an unnatural attitude, and it had seemed to me that he was covering some papers with his forearms. And his glance had strayed away once to an open green cash-box of the type which seemed more in place in an ironmonger's shop than on the mission chief's desk. And there was something else: the metal filing cabinet behind his desk had stood slightly askew.

Still, I needed that wash, and I went to the lavatory before leaving the building. I was wrenching a comb through my filthy hair and looking forward to a hot bath when the crash took place. I opened the window and leaned out, and saw the tail of a truck sticking out of the building below me to the right. An army vehicle, it turned out, had swerved to avoid an incautious cyclist, and the truck had piled through the line of donkey carts in front of the block and through the glass windows of the ground-floor exhibition room which was also the entrance foyer to the I.D.A. offices.

Showcases, scale models and leaflets had been scattered everywhere, but despite the incredible amount of noise the only casualties had been the driver, cut in the face by flying glass, and a donkey which was revoltingly mashed by the wheels.

The crash echoed up and down the corridors and stairways of the I.D.A., and everybody left in the building poured down to the entrance hall, jabbering in at least five languages.

As I left the lavatory to run in the direction of the hubbub, I saw Wharton turn the corner at the head of the stairs in front of me and disappear. What I did then I can explain only in terms of animal instinct – indeed, I remember noticing immediately afterwards that I had hardly reflected at all. If I had done so, I would surely have stopped in my tracks and turned back. I was hired as an investigator of sorts, but my mandate was to search among columns of figures and not play private detective.

I slipped in to Wharton's office and closed the door, leaning my back against it. There were no papers, no cash-box to be seen. The filing cabinet stood squarely against the wall as it always had done. Had I imagined it? No: the more I thought of it, the more Wharton's unusual irritability a moment ago seemed to be guilty surprise, and his contrition, regret at losing his grip. Something very odd was afoot.

I stole a glance out of the window. Wharton was talking to a police officer, his back half-turned to the building. I knew that I had a little time to act, but I did not even know where to begin to look.

I shook the cabinet, but it remained as firm as though screwed to the wall. Kneeling down, I tried to see whether there was any hidden catch or spring under the base, but the gap was so small I could see nothing but the bottom of the wheels. *Wheels!* So it did move!

The drawers were locked, but I had seen Wharton drop his key-ring into the drawer of his desk many times when we arrived together in the morning. I took the ring and found the key that fitted, but all that happened was that the drawers were free to move. I looked hastily through them, but there was nothing suspicious, and no room at all to hide anything the size of the cash-box. In feverish haste now, I felt around the edges of the drawers but could find no spring. The sweat was prickling on my back and chest despite the air-conditioning.

Almost crying aloud in frustration, I withdrew the key from the lock. I was about to put it back in the desk drawer when something caught my eye. The next key on the ring was almost identical, but it was slightly longer and had a notch filed in the circumference of the round head. I tried this key, and it made half a turn like the other, met a spring, and then went another quarter-turn. There was a click somewhere at the back of the cabinet, and it was free to move at the lightest touch.

I checked that the mechanism closed itself automatically without a turn of the key, and then left the cabinet at a slight angle and put the keys back in the desk. I stole another glance out of the window, and dodged back as I saw Wharton on the road, still talking to the police officer.

My heart was thumping in my chest, I pulled the cabinet back. On the floor underneath it was a curved, flat band of metal, out of sight normally, which was obviously a rail for a wheel in the back right corner. The pivot was in the back left corner. In the wall behind the cabinet was a niche, and in the niche was the cash-box with a steel handle on the lid and a combination lock with six figures. That was all.

I reached out to pick up the cash-box. As I took hold of the handle, the lid opened. I could not believe my luck. Wharton had obviously been so flustered by the crash that he had simply put the box back without neutralizing the combination, and hurried down to the commotion below.

Changing the last digit one figure, I picked up the box, swung the cabinet back into place and left the room, going back up to the office which had been put at my disposal on the floor above. I met nobody on the way, and slumped at my desk with the sweat now freely pouring off me.

Up till then I had acted on blind instinct, but that was over and I had to make some plans quickly. I knew that this cash-box must contain something of particular delicacy, because Wharton had access to the safe in his secretary's office, and since only he and the head cashier had the keys to that one, this box must contain more than just money.

I took a sheet of brown paper from the waste-basket where my assistant had put it after opening a parcel, to judge by the writing and stamps, and wrapped it around the cash-box, securing it with a strip of adhesive tape. Except on close scrutiny, it now looked reasonably like a postal packet. I put it under my arm, left by the back staircase, and made for my car, thanking my stars that I had not found a parking space on the busy street in front of I.D.A.

Fortunately the Kori driving habits are so undisciplined that my nervous stalls and erratic course attracted no attention, although they would have had me arrested in Geneva. I headed straight up the hill to the Nooriabad Intercontinental where I was staying, and went up to my room with hardly a pause for breath.

I spent three or four minutes calming myself down. Then I unwrapped the box and was still looking at it when the telephone next to the bed purred discreetly.

'Mike Ellis,' I said into it.

'Mike, dear, at last you are back. Tuula here. Charles and I wondered if you are coming round for dinner. We are dying to hear what you thought of north Afghanistan.'

Fifteen

'Hello? Mike? Are you there?' she asked, as the silence lengthened.

'Of course, Tuula, I'm sorry. I was ... er ... I'm still half asleep. I thought I'd have a quick nap when I got back. It was quite an exhausting trip.'

'Oh, Mike dear, I'm so sorry. Did I wake you up? Well, there will only be the two of us here this evening, anyway, so there's no need at all for a formal confirmation or anything like that. You just come over if you feel like it, and if you'd rather have an early night we'll see you another time. You know you don't need an invitation anyway, don't you.'

'You're very sweet, Tuula,' I said. I felt a particularly vile bastard saying it. 'I don't think I'll be much good for anything this evening. I'll probably have an early night, thanks all the same.'

'Of course, I know what it's like,' she said lightly. 'But are you sure nothing's the matter? You sound so ... so worried.'

'Nothing at all,' I replied as firmly as I could. 'Thanks for calling and ... tell Charles hello.'

As I hung up, something which had been nagging in the back of my mind sat down in front of me and said boo! I had been a prize fool. Instead of taking the box, I should have noted the combination and found a pretext later for using the keys. Wharton was bound to remember that he had not changed the combination, and it was only a matter of time before he went back to do so and found the box missing.

Would he do it as soon as the police had gone? If it occurred to him at home, would he drive back into town to do it? There was no way I could know; it was a time-fuse of unknown length. I had to examine the contents immediately, and if they were innocent, somehow put the box back in its hiding-place.

I turned the last digit wheel, and opened the box. It contained a lot of cash and a lot more papers. The cash was in fifty and hundred dollar notes, and they added up to about five thousand.

After half an hour of going through the papers, I knew everything I needed to know. Except for the answer to one question:

why had Wharton kept such incriminating material? Was he constantly reminding himself of his guilt? Does embezzlement require book-keeping?

I sat cross-legged on the bed where there was more room, put the cash in the box and the box out of the way on the floor, and started sorting the papers into piles. One pile for those in a language I did not understand (there was Russian in large quantities, something in Persian script, presumably Farsi, the language of Koristan, Finnish in Wharton's handwriting and a lot in code), another pile for accounts and other figures, and a third for documents I could read. They were all jumbled up as though Wharton had stuffed them into the box in a hurry when the crash disturbed him.

Putting a rubber band around those I had no hope of deciphering without help, I dropped them into the cash-box. The accounts I put in, too, for scrutiny later. I settled down to a serious study of the documents in English and French. I had been reading for an hour when there was a tap at the door.

I leapt to my feet, dropped the last pile into the box and kicked it well under the bed as I went to answer the knock.

'I have to talk to you, Mike,' Tuula said simply.

She was dressed in a sleeveless yellow Marimekko dress and had bound her hair into one thick golden plait hanging down over her right shoulder. The corridor was in shadow, and her eyes looked enormous.

I could say nothing. I stood aside for her to enter. She closed the door without turning round and leaned back against it. She was pale but composed, and devastatingly beautiful.

'I'm in a mess,' she said, and as I started to protest, she patted her head and said, 'up here.'

I still could not speak. Here was Wharton's wife needing help, and I was feeling guilty as though I had betrayed him. Perhaps in a sense I had, for had I not accepted their friendship? I held out my hand for hers, which she gave me promptly with the innocent trust of a niece. I led her over to one of the comfortable armchairs in front of the picture window, looking out on to Nooriabad. It was twilight, but I had not noticed how dark it was getting, so absorbed had I been in my task. The first lights were twinkling, but the double-glazing cut off the sounds and smells of the city. The last donkey caravans were heading for shelter now as the evening grew cooler. From a grove of silver poplars beyond the hotel lawns, a minaret soared, white as ivory before the purple, snow-capped Hindu Kush.

'You had better have a drink and tell me all about it,' I said feebly. 'What shall I order?'

'Get me a vodka and lime, please Mike.'

As I waited for room service to answer, I pulled the bedcover straight. It certainly looked as though I had been having that nap. I ordered a bottle of vodka, a bottle of lime juice, another of whisky, and a lot of ice. I turned the lamp on as I put the phone down, but Tuula said, 'Don't, Mike. Look how lovely it is out there.'

I said, 'I'll put it off when the waiter has gone,' and she gave me a rueful little smile before turning back to the view.

When the drinks arrived, I poured out both and put the rest in the little fridge with the Cokes the management provided. Then I put out the lamp again and sat on the arm of her chair. We drank for a moment in silence, and then she put her elbow on my knee and rested her forehead in the crook of her arm.

I put a hand on her shoulder and said, 'What's happened?'

'I love him very dearly, you know,' she said, so quietly that I could hardly hear her.

'I know,' I said, 'I can see that. Where is he, by the way?'

'He rang me half an hour ago to say something dreadful had happened at the office and it was going to take him a long time to sort it out.'

There was a pause, and then she added: 'So I told him I was coming over to see you. He said he didn't think you were back, and I said, oh yes, I had already telephoned about dinner. So he said, why don't you have dinner there with Mike, I'll be tied up until late.'

'And that's a problem?' I held my breath, waiting for it to come.

'No, Mike.' She spoke slowly, carefully, as though anxious not to hurt me. 'That isn't, but there is one. Or rather, there are two really. Charles is sure that you have been investigating him, and that you have found something out which might be the end of the world for him.' When the punch-line came, it knocked the breath out of me. 'And the other one is that I think I love you, too.'

She got up and went to the window, leaning her forehead against the cool glass. I saw her breath cloud it as I sat stunned and trembling like a fool. I did not know how to handle this.

I was very fond of Tuula; who would not be? But I was too old-fashioned – or perhaps just too correct, too unimaginative – to have wanted to take it any further. I am perfectly happy and contented with my wife, I told myself; I have no need and no desire for anybody else, not even this exquisite girl in an almost transparent dress silhouetted against the evening sky.

Tuula turned round and looked at me, her eyes inscrutable in the dusk. 'Do not break him, Mike,' she said. 'You would break me, too.'

I stood up and moved towards her. She almost fell into my arms, sobbing like a little girl. I folded my arms around her shoulders and pressed her to me, and she buried her face in the front of my shirt. The perfume of her hair filled my head, and the pressure of her body against mine was unbearably exciting.

'I know what you are thinking,' she said in a muffled voice.

'You can have no idea,' I said sincerely.

'You think I want you to cover up for Charles.'

I stroked her hair in silence as I searched for the right words but, although I knew what I wanted to tell her, I could not find a starting point. Gently I took her shoulders and pushed her half a pace away from me. 'I don't believe anything of the sort,' I told her as kindly as I could. 'I don't believe you would do it this way even if that were the case, and even if I could do anything for you.'

Perhaps she misunderstood me, perhaps in her desperation any straw was worth grasping for. Hope crossed her face for a moment.

'You mean there is no – what do you say? – no irregularity, there is nothing to cover up?'

'No, it's not exactly that. I have not quite finished my work here, but . . . Well, quite honestly I don't think I ought to talk about it to you – to anyone – until I have spoken to Charles.'

'But Charles has already told me.' She was on the verge of tears. 'I mean, you know he has. I wouldn't have known otherwise, would I?' Her eyes switched back and forth, seeking in both of mine a reflection of the hope she had briefly held. Slowly her composure had cracked and then crumbled away. Now I felt weak with shameful pity, like you feel when you see a wounded, dying kitten and cannot find the courage, the mercy, to break its neck. I would have done anything to wipe the hopelessness from her wide forehead, anything.

Almost anything.

'There are things I have discovered,' I answered carefully, 'which I cannot keep secret. I am going to talk to him tomorrow. I must do, urgently and give him every chance to explain.'

Her eyes screwed up with pain, and we stood for a time in silence. Finally, without opening her eyes, but relaxing her face slightly, she whispered, 'Let me kiss you once anyway. Then I'll go.'

It was a long, tender, hungry kiss; we were both trembling, and both our faces were wet with tears. Finally our mouths parted. She gave me another darting kiss on the corner of my lips before slipping out of my arms. I sat down, shattered, on the edge of the bed and stared at the floor. I did not look up as she stroked my hair once; there was a movement behind me, and then I heard the door-latch click.

I looked around with a start; the room was empty.

After that, there was little more to recall. I spent a terrible night, waking frequently with confused visions of Tuula, Charles Wharton and Sophie fading in the back of my eyes.

I was paged at breakfast. It was Wharton on the phone. He said, in a collected, not unfriendly voice, that he understood I wanted an urgent conference with him. I had said nothing of the kind to anybody except Tuula, but I let that go. He had to go over the border to Kabul in the morning; would I care to join him for lunch at the Bagh-i-Bala?

When I got to the erstwhile prince's palace on one of the many hilltops overlooking the Afghan capital, he was already waiting for me. He had obviously not slept either. We lunched almost in silence. Stirring his thick coffee afterwards he said abruptly that the fact that some of his notes were in Finnish did not involve Tuula in any way whatever. It was just a relatively little-known language which he used for confidential jottings. I stammered that I had already surmised that, and we did not mention Tuula again.

I was amazed at his calm, and at the way he took the initiative, as though we were merely continuing a discussion started on some previous occasion. I had expected anything but this. I had thought that the plunge into the icy water would be very difficult, never imagining that he would make it so easy for me. He had relieved me of any need to mention either the cash-box or Tuula's visit, tacitly admitting that he knew of one or the other. Or both.

We sat on the terrace overlooking the fabled city, and talked rationally until the *muezzin* called for prayers at sundown. It struck me that his choice of venue, over the border and away from his office, was evidence of considerable tact. As we spoke, for all the emotion involved we might have been discussing some long-past undergraduate flirtation with extremist politics on his part, not a large-scale diversion of funds. In all my professional experience – and actuarian consultants are often called in when something has gone wrong, and that 'something' frequently involves dishonesty – I have never known anybody admit his guilt so freely, in such detail, and with so little wish to stab vindictively back at me for having uncovered his wrongdoing. He made no attempt to make me feel at a disadvantage.

He had been approached quite early in his career, and after a year of hesitation he had come to share a lot of the ideals of his masters. For a long time he had passed on only information, knowing that this was harmless and only much later realizing how he had been led on from one thing to another, how a file was being set up which, if he were to be exposed, would at the absolute minimum make him seem an utter fool and smash his career. He was still convinced that a lot of this information was being put to humanitarian use. He had seen how competition and jealousy among nominally co-operating agencies had caused foul-ups and decreased efficiency, and honestly believed that he was helping the situation.

But Wharton's disillusionment grew as his career blossomed. He found he was equally disillusioned, moreover, by those who feathered their own nests while regarding their work with cynicism, and those who worked long hours in hard conditions, convinced that they were bringing the light of civilization to the brute native. He believed he saw more and more clearly the destroying effects of 'civilization' on simple, peaceful, self-sufficient rural cultures that would better have been left alone.

Soon Wharton was in the quandary of not knowing which was worse, the work he was overtly carrying out, or the deception he was practising behind the scenes. His contact at the time – it had been the cultural attaché at a Soviet embassy, but he would not tell me where – had been quick to recognize the moment of indecision and pounce on it. He had made brutally clear to Wharton that there was no going back, and the screws had been put on.

At the time, Wharton had been administrative chief of a mission in the Far East. They started asking him for money and equipment. He protested that the risk of discovery was too great, but they remained adamant. He slowly began to suspect that he was being classified as a burnt-out case, and that they were now wringing him for all they could as long as he lasted.

A week before he received the official invitation from Rome to take over the Koristan mission, his contact had told him that the promotion was being discussed in New York. He had scoffed at the idea, for he was a young man for such a delicate post, but the Russian had merely repeated that the offer was coming, and if he refused he would be exposed. By the time the invitation was made formal, Wharton had arrived at a decision: to accept, but to try to swim with the tide and pray that Nemesis would not catch up with him. For he feared that this was to be the test of his loyalty, and he had spent a terrible week imagining the outcome if he failed the test.

At this point in his story, Wharton clapped his hands for the servant, and ordered more of the thick, Arab-style coffee. He looked at me candidly, and I could see that he was trying to decide whether to tell me something or not. I lit a cigarette and nodded, 'Go on.'

'You see,' he said slowly, and for the first time that afternoon I noticed how pale he was under his tan, 'I knew something by now which I hadn't known before.'

The Soviet diplomat had told him, with no frills, that a department had been set up in Moscow which was co-ordinating and financing terrorism and subversion all over the free world, from the I.R.A. to the Baader-Meinhof gang, from the Khmer Rouge to the scattered remains of the Weathermen. Wharton's contributions had been earmarked for this pool. He did not know the vital details of the routes and methods, how building machinery became hand-grenades and fertilizer became rifles, but the outline story he did know had been enough to break his spirit.

Wharton had seen no solution. He knew now that his time was running out, and the most desperate ideas presented themselves. He rejected them one by one. He could not defect, for he had lost the infatuation with Marxist ideology which had started him on his shadow career. And besides, they would not want him. He was more use where he was. He even contemplated suicide once or twice, but never for long.

And when my visit had been announced, he had recognized the thin end of the wedge. Or perhaps the gleam on the blade of the hatchet. His only hope now, he said – there was no trace of pleading in his tone, but the meaning was clear – was that Tuula should not suffer more than necessary.

I wondered whether Tuula's visit the previous evening had been at his instigation. I could find no way to ask him. I felt goose-flesh that had nothing to do with the evening air as I wondered whether she had been playing a part to save his neck. I saw her eyes again in the dim room, searching mine for a hint of acquiescence. *Do not break him, Mike. You would break me, too.*

Shaking the ghosts out of my head, I stood up.

'It's Tuesday. I'll want a day to think about all this, and I suppose you will, too. We can talk about it again on Thursday, and I'll fly back to Rome on Friday morning.'

He got to his feet, and I saw that his composure was far less complete than it had been over lunch. It must have been a harrowing experience for him to recall the whole story in sequence, and to put it all into words.

'I've thought it over quite enough already, but you take your time,' was all he said in reply.

As he drove me back across the border, we spoke no more. There were no formalities, for the guards recognized Wharton and saluted as he passed the frontier post. Bob Harding's warnings came into my head, but I could not begin to imagine Charles Wharton trying to kill me. On the contrary, he seemed almost relieved that everything was finally in the open and out of his hands. However, I decided that it would be no more than prudent to keep to public places until I left Koristan.

I spent the next day in the hotel, studying the papers in the cash-box and noting questions I had for Wharton. I made two attempts at drafting a report, but gave it up until I had the answers I needed.

On the Thursday morning we had a dry conference. The rapport which his confession had seemed to strengthen, rather than damage, two days before was now gone. He was brusque but correct.

When I left his office at about lunch-time, many questions settled and the picture complete as far as Wharton knew it (I was convinced he was being open with me now), he shook my hand silently. It almost seemed that he was wishing me the courage I needed. I did not manage to face Tuula again, nor even, to my everlasting regret, telephone her to say goodbye. I spent a lot of the afternoon locked in the photocopy room of the I.D.A. offices, borrowing ledgers and files from departments all over the building, and getting my documentation together.

I had flown out to Teheran on the last flight of the day, and as I watched Nooriabad dropping away beneath me I had had no idea that I would ever see the place again. Now here I was, flying right back again; Sophie and Katrina were hostages, and the boot was on the other foot.

I will know the worst in half an hour, I thought, walking across the apron in the chill mountain air of a splendid morning, but I was wrong. As I approached passport control, a tall figure came towards the other side of the barrier. Despite the early hour, Wharton had come to meet me.

SOPHIE

Sixteen

I had no idea that Mike was going to be spirited away in the night, and my first thought when I awoke was to see him. But the studio was empty and silent, and the trapdoor bolted, so I started mechanically to wash and dress before Katrina awoke.

It was seven in the morning, and the day was going to be cold and clear, I could see that out of the windows. I was hungry, but I could not get at the food downstairs. I had nothing to lever the trapdoor up with. I hoped somebody would come before Katrina was awake and hungry.

She woke up very soon after, and I changed her, using a disposable nappy from the supply that Ulli had put in the washroom. There was almost no scar tissue left, only a few marks on her tummy. She had healed very well physically, but her nature, while not becoming by any means bad, had lost its original sunniness and become rather subdued.

We played for half an hour on the bed, and I coaxed several chuckles out of her. The tears came to my eyes for a moment when I thought that, after all she had gone through in her short life, she might finish up in the hands of terrorists. Then I mentally shook myself and tried to think of something practical. I considered asking them to let her at least be taken to safety while I remained in their hands, but there was obviously no way to do that, even if they had been willing.

Shortly before eight, Ulli came in. She came over to the bed and, not letting me out of her field of vision, watched Katrina for a while.

'You have a beautiful baby, Mrs Ellis,' she said, and I almost thought I caught a hint of envy in this terrorist girl with a gun in her overnight bag. 'I played with her a little when you were asleep, because she woke up. Believe me,' she added earnestly, looking at me with those cold eyes, which now surprisingly seemed to be more human, 'we don't want anything to happen to Katrina.'

'That seems to be up to you,' I retorted, being deliberately rude because I have never been able to resist overtures made via Katrina. But I added quickly, 'She will be hungry soon. Can I make her some breakfast? I could use some myself, too.'

'Of course,' the girl said.

We went downstairs to the print-shop. I carried Katrina on my arm and Ulli brought the carry-cot. Katrina was quite happy in it, gurgling loudly and playing with some soft toys, while we made three breakfasts.

The trash bucket was pretty full and beginning to smell. Ulli went upstairs for the nappies and brought them down in a plastic bag, adding them to the contents of the bucket and tying up the handles of the plastic liner-bag. She took the enormous old key to the studio door from the hip pocket of her jeans and let herself out, leaving the rubbish just outside the door. She locked us in again and returned the key to her pocket.

I watched her covertly, not so much because I was planning to escape, but merely as a general policy of piecing together as much information as I could. It is only now, talking about it all with Mike, that I have found out about the rather eerie parallel between his experience of the kidnappers and my own.

Independently of each other, and with no opportunity to compare notes, we were both puzzled by their unexpectedly considerate attitude towards us, and both looked for chances to turn it to our advantage. But while Mike never had much of a chance, mine came on the Monday after his departure.

I was surprised and, I must confess, a little piqued at first by the way Katrina took to Ulli. It took me most of the morning to realize that the little lass wasn't the victim of a confidence trick – I don't think it's possible to deceive babies like that – but that, silly as it may sound, Katrina was perhaps responding to something which she could see in Ulli and I could not. And the train of thought which this insight set off took an unexpected direction: I became aware that I had already noticed a vague difference between Ulli and the others, a slight mental distance between them, so to speak. It was one of those intuitive observations which I am usually rather wary of voicing, for fear of being laughed at.

Ulli and I had been cool, reserved, but not unfriendly with each other all day. There was a mutual unspoken agreement to avoid either friendliness or unfriendliness. The former would have been impossibly artificial anyway, and the latter would have helped nobody. But after lunch, when I saw her for the twentieth time watching Katrina with a strange look in her eyes, I made a comment without reflection which I immediately wished I could have taken back. But it was already said, and the result thoroughly surprised me.

'You get on very well with children,' I said to her. 'Is that why you studied paediatrics?'

As she hesitated, a shy expression crossed her face.

'Yes . . . it is. I had a baby of my own once. But it died before it had one year.'

'Oh, I am sorry,' I said in embarrassment. 'But . . . it? Was it a boy or a girl?'

'She – a girl. The German words are neuter, *das Baby, das Kind*. Yes, she died.'

She did not tell me why her daughter had died, and I could not ask. We both withdrew from this moment of intimacy and busied ourselves with little jobs. For the rest of the afternoon we were careful to avoid any further approaches, each aware of the other's reasons for reticence. The ice was not broken, but it had cracked.

Ulli stayed with me most of the day, cooking lunch and dinner, which she did competently, making coffee, playing with Katrina and generally being very efficient. Occasionally she telephoned the house on the intercom, and twice she let herself out and was gone for half an hour, but she offered me no explanation.

I asked her if we could have the radio here, as I was in no mental state to do any work, and she called the house. The answer, she reported, was no; they needed it themselves. But they were bringing the cassette recorder and all the cassettes. Shortly after that there was a knock at the door, and she went down and brought in the music. I did not see or hear who had brought it to the studio.

After dinner, when Katrina was already asleep, there was more telephoning, followed after a little while by a knock on the door. Klaus was there with a camp bed and Ulli's overnight bag, and she installed these in the print-shop, out of sight of anyone on the upper floor. I noticed that whenever any of the others came she closed the trapdoor before opening the door, although otherwise it stayed open. I wondered if she were overstepping her instructions by giving me this freedom.

She asked if I needed a sleeping pill, and on the spur of the moment I said yes. I had had an idea. She watched me swallow it, but I had pushed it up between my top teeth and lip first, and as soon as I had a chance, I took it out and dropped it unseen into the pocket of my shirt. It was slightly soggy but still intact.

In a few minutes, I said, 'That pill doesn't seem to be working, can I have another?'

'It's not for going to sleep,' she replied, 'but for sleeping deeply when you once get to sleep. But I will leave you another one here in case you wake up,' and she put it on the bookshelf. I put it inside a lidded brass inkpot in which I keep small trinkets.

'I think I shall go to bed now,' she said with a yawn, and I realized that she too had had a strenuous weekend.

When she went to get her towel and toothbrush from downstairs, I took the second pill out of the inkpot and put it in my pocket with the first. I took off my jeans, but kept the shirt on and put on a dressing-gown over the top, buttoning it up to the neck. Ulli came back up. She took off her jeans and pullover in my work-room because the wash-room was too small for much movement, but took them in with her. She left the door open, and I noticed that she did not leave me an opportunity to get near the key or out of her sight for long.

She certainly had an athletic body, I thought. It was trim from physical exercise, and I would not want to risk taking her on in an attempt to escape. When she had finished, she put her clothes over her arm and went down to her bed virtually naked, saying, 'Good night, Mrs Ellis,' as she closed the trapdoor. I washed and brushed my hair, while I worked on the idea I had had.

'Ulli,' I called over the balustrade when I was ready, 'I would like to make a cup of chocolate. I always drink one when I go to bed. If you want, I will make one for you, too.'

There was silence for a moment as she thought it over. Then the camp bed creaked and she came into view below me, the gun in her hand looking incongruous against her white skin. 'That would be nice,' she said, and came up the stairs far enough to open the bolt on the trapdoor, returning at once to her bed. When I came down, she had positioned an armchair for me at a safe distance from her bed, near the foot of it, and her clothes were nowhere to be seen.

I went to the kitchenette, which had no door, and where I could be observed as well as she wished. It was about ten paces from the bed where she sat up with a sheet wrapped around her, the gun on the pillow near her right hand.

'This chocolate is fairly strong,' I said over my shoulder, once I had lit the gas under the milk. 'Do you like it bitter, or do you want more sugar?'

'I like a lot of sugar, please,' she said, and I let out, very quietly, a sigh of relief. This had been the weak point in the plan; that trim body did not look as though it was used to much sugar.

As I mixed the chocolate and sugar in the cups, I dropped the pills into one of them. I had palmed them on the way down the stairs and held them down with two fingers of my left hand since then, and these were cramped and aching. The pill I had had in my mouth was gooey and left a mess on the palm of my hand, but I managed to wipe it off on my dressing-gown. I creamed the mixture with a little cold milk and frothed it up as I added the hot. With any luck she would scald her tongue, and that, too, would disguise the taste of the pills, I hoped.

She watched me narrowly as I brought the cups over, but I made slowly, unambiguous movements, putting her cup within her reach and retreating to the armchair with my own. She sipped it appreciatively. While I was stifling another sigh of relief, she was stifling a yawn.

We drank in silence, and I tried not to look too obviously for her jeans. But when she pulled the sheet closer around her, I saw for a moment the cuff of the sleeve of her pullover between the bed and the wall where she had pushed it, and guessed that the jeans were there too.

'Thank you, Mrs Ellis,' she said demurely as she finished the cup.

I put both cups on the draining board and said goodnight as I went back up the stairs, but she did not answer. She followed me closely with her eyes until I was out of sight.

As I got into bed, I heard her get up and close the bolt.

My plan had been born of three elements, and I now had to string them together to a chain. The first had been the pill, and I had started to act on that without knowing precisely what to do next. The second was the carry-cot, which had taken a while to register at all. And the third was a glimpse of one or two things in the print-shop which I had seen in passing while making breakfast. At the time I had had no particular idea of escaping, but they had stuck quite autonomously in my mind and nibbled away there all day, until I now started putting them together with the rest to form a plan.

Whatever I did, it was not going to be until shortly before dawn, because everybody would be in the deepest sleep at that time. If I did anything at all. My immediate priority was to work out whether I should try to escape. If so, how? And if that was settled, when? Next, I had to stay awake all the time. I was glad that the blinds on the enormous skylights were open, for the moon was at least two-thirds full, and it was illumining the working space where I lay, but deepening the shadows on the ground floor.

My eye fell on the alarm clock on the bookshelf, and I wound it up cautiously under the bedclothes, setting it for four o'clock and then leaving it under my pillow.

I twisted the situation back and forth in my mind. After what seemed like an hour of concentration, which took only ten minutes by my watch, I arrived at the conclusion that while I was a hostage for Mike's good behaviour, or rather Katrina and I were, he was not a hostage for mine. They would do nothing to him because we had escaped; indeed, they would not dream of letting him know, because they would have lost their hold over him.

But if I escaped with Katrina and went to the police, I might be too late; Mike was going to be forced to murder somebody. The authorities would take into consideration the fact that he did so only because the lives of his wife and daughter were threatened, and that would probably be enough for a reduced sentence because of extenuating circumstances, but it would not make him innocent. And I had no idea who was to be killed, nor where, nor when.

So if I were to escape, I would have to find Mike on my own. Had I known that he was already well on his way to Nooriabad, I might never have had the courage to start. But I was certain that I could trace him with Sam's help, and so my first decision was made. In fact, it now occurred to me with a shock, I had no choice; Ulli would be certain to notice the next morning that I had given her a double dose of sleeping pills, and even if I were still there, undecided, their vigilance would be redoubled.

The 'if' being resolved, I worked on the 'how'. Assuming that I was docile, partly because of their demonstrations of brutality, partly because of Katrina, and finally because of their plans for Mike, they had relaxed their attention considerably during the past day and I had done my best to reassure them of my tractability. If I could once get down to the ground floor without waking Ulli I thought that I would be safe.

I was certain that, if I took all my clothes off to prevent rustling and went barefoot, I could climb over the balustrade, hang from my hands, and drop silently on to the floor below. The tricky part would be getting the key out of Ulli's jeans without waking her, as I had no idea how strong the sleeping pills were.

I ran through the plan twenty times in my head, each time coming up against new problems, backtracking, amending, rejecting, improvising, until I had something which seemed plausible. By a quarter to two I was as satisfied with the plan as I would ever be in theory. Still I waited and kept looking at the time. Fortunately, after the deep, drugged rest of the past two nights, staying awake was not so difficult. In no danger of drowsing off, I put the alarm on the bookshelf to watch its hands creeping round.

Finally at three-thirty my patience could last no longer. Ulli had been snoring loudly in a most unladylike fashion for over an hour, and if four o'clock was an arbitrary hour, then so was half past three. Silently I unbuttoned and discarded my dressing-gown and shirt.

Getting to the ground floor was as easy as I had anticipated, except that I stubbed a bare toe painfully on the concrete floor we had had cast to take the weight of the presses. I froze, crouching where I had landed, to accustom my eyes to the gloom below, but the rhythm of Ulli's snores did not break. The moon had set, but the stars were bright in the sky.

Her jeans and sweater were under the camp bed; with a cautious tug I disengaged the cuff I had spotted the evening before and crept away with the bundle in my arms. The key was in her jeans pocket.

I crept up the steps to the trapdoor. It took a half a minute, while I held my breath, to slide the bolt back with delicate, jiggling movements, and then I was upstairs again. I lowered the trapdoor, just in case. Silently I dressed and transferred the key to my own jeans.

Katrina, the angel, did not even miss a breath as I picked her up. I put a spare pullover, my sandals and some nappies in the cot, which I took with me. There was now nothing left to do but go, so I did, leaving the trapdoor bolted, I'm not really sure why, but I thought it was better that way. I unlocked the outer door and in another minute I was outside, free.

But when I had put Katrina back into her cot in the starlight in front of the door, before locking it again I went back for the two things which had caught my eye in the print-shop.

One was a plastic carrier-bag containing a length of chain with a spring-clip at each end. This had been the running-chain for poor Hayo, our ancient German shepherd dog, whom we had had to put down in the spring when he got too feeble to feed himself. It was a ten-yard steel chain which we would stretch between two trees and upon which his shorter lead-chain would run, thus giving him a good area to move in when we were in the village. The chain had lain rusting in a corner of the print-shop in a plastic bag ever since. We had missed old Hayo too much to get a new dog.

The other thing was a canister of heating oil for the stove. The jeep looked like a standard Willy's Overland on the outside, but when the price of normal petrol in Italy became prohibitive Mike had fitted a Mercedes 240 motor and a diesel engine I knew would run perfectly, if illegally, on heating oil. Poor Marino had once explained the difference to me: it is only in the colour, for the same product sold for cars at the gas station is heavily taxed, and dyed red to prevent illegal use of the blue household product.

And that had reminded me of something else about the jeep, which had been the clincher to my decision to escape. Once Mike had left his keys at the village shop, and he had used a piece of twig for a key. Laughing at my amazement, he explained that diesel engines do not have spark-plugs, and therefore require no ignition circuit. The 'key' was merely a suitably shaped piece of non-conducting metal which held two spring contacts apart.

Expensive diesel private cars, he said, would have a proper lock and key to prevent theft. But trucks, and his old jeep, and often motor bikes, needed only something to open the circuit. Like a twig.

Slipping the ancient key silently out of the lock of the studio door, I reflected that my plans were going perfectly up to now. Katrina, the chain in its bag and the canister, I left by the studio door, praying that she would stay in her angel's sleep. As Mike's plane was touching down in Nooriabad, three and a half time-zones away, I crept up the last bit of track towards the house, the dew soaking my feet through the sandals I had taken from the carry-cot, the breeze fanning my hair.

To my horror, the jeep, although standing on a slope, was facing towards the house. I knew only too well from unsuccessful tries that you cannot bump-start a car in reverse gear; at least, I can't. My plan had not covered having to start the temperamental diesel motor in the pre-dawn cold, and then manœuvre around before leaving. To my chagrin I realized that I had had plenty of time to think this out, but I had automatically assumed the jeep would be facing down the track, such a habit had it become for Mike and me to leave it that way.

Standing in the shadows of a friendly tree, I frantically tried to work out what to do. Finally, I saw there was only one silent way, and it would require some accurate driving, because it would be one try and one try only. If I took the handbrake off, let the jeep roll backwards until it had enough speed, and then put the wheel hard over, it would swing right around and be facing downhill before its momentum ran out and it came to a standstill. Then I could roll off downhill, forwards.

The only problem was that there were only about twenty yards of open ground in front of the house before the track started into the trees, and that was all the run I would have. And the canvas top was still mounted, so that rearward vision was just about nil. Only the side door-flaps were missing.

Try as I might, I could see no other way. Memorizing the lie of the land, I silently snapped three twigs of likely-looking size off the tree under which I stood and, taking a deep breath, ran across the open ground to the jeep. The second twig fitted, and a pilot light glowed red. I wiped the dew off the mirrors and windscreen with a rag from the dash locker, and climbed into the driver's seat. The springs creaked slightly, and reminded me that I must stop hesitating and get on with it while my luck lasted.

I took off the handbrake and the jeep gathered speed through the starlight. It was terrifying to run backwards more or less in the dark, steering by memory alone. The jeep creaked and rattled. The noise sounded ear-splitting in the still of the night. When I could stand the tension no longer, I wrenched the wheel over to the right, and the jeep lurched on its springs. It rolled slower and slower, the trees rotating before the windscreen, until it finally stopped and I caught it on the footbrake. I was panting with tension, and the steady breeze blew cold on the sweat on my forehead.

The jeep had gone almost half a circle, just about enough. Before letting it roll again, I put the wheel hard over the other way. I could see it was not going to make the mouth of the track, but I now had no choice but to go on. The right wing crashed through a bush and I dragged at the wheel to aim the cumbersome vehicle down towards the studio. I stopped on the steep slope before the door, got out, and knelt in the dew, stroking Katrina's hair from her face with trembling fingers.

Then I picked her up in the cot and pushed it across my seat to the passenger side. I heaved the chain and the canister over on to the back seats. I had just realized that the canister wasn't heating oil at all, but an oil canister I had used to bring mineral spirits for cleaning my printing plates, when a noise in the studio made my heart leap into my throat. For a moment I could not think what it was, and then there was a muffled crash and the sound redoubled.

The alarm clock! It was four o'clock; the alarm had shaken itself off the bookshelf and was now buzzing around on the floor above Ulli's head like a bluebottle in a jam jar! What a fool I was! What a fool!

I scrambled into the seat. The jeep rumbled quietly off down the track, and as the trees closed in around me I saw in the wing mirror the ground-floor windows of the studio spring into light.

Seventeen

I am quite a competent driver, or so I'm told, but I don't know very much about the theory of diesel engines. I know they need to be warmed up before they will start, and that this uses up a lot of the battery, especially in cold weather.

But I knew that it was suicidal to try to negotiate the darkest part of the track without headlights. If my flight was discovered anyway, I had nothing to lose, so I compromised by putting on the dipped headlights and holding the starter knob at the warm-up position with one hand while trying to steer with the other.

A jeep is not as easy to steer as a car. First of all, it is designed for soldiers, or at least tough, outdoor men. The wheel is thin, functional and unpadded. And there is not a trace of assistance; the steering-wheel operates directly on to the front axle. And finally, the whole thing works in such a way that the slightest bump on the front tyres makes the wheel jump viciously in your hand, whereas the smallest movement of your hand makes the jeep try to climb the nearest bank.

I fought the unwilling vehicle down the rough track, cannoning off boulders and banks and teetering on the edge of ditches, until the warm-up coil on the dash glowed feebly.

I did not dare to strain the ancient battery any more by using the starter motor, so I forced the unsynchronized gears with a crash into second and let the clutch come. The cold engine braked the jeep violently for a moment before it started, sliding Katrina's cot to the edge of her seat before I caught it, wishing I had four hands, and then it fired, and the yellow of the headlights brightened to white as the jeep picked up speed again.

I took the well-known track at a speed I had never risked before, pushing the cot back into the bottom of the seat after every curve. All the time I was trying to decide whether the alarm clock had changed my plans at all. I had vaguely intended to put the chain across the track to hold up any pursuit; was that now more necessary than ever, or a waste of valuable time?

After thinking it backwards and forwards, I finally decided that it could do no harm and probably some good, and started looking out for a good place to work quickly. As soon as I saw that there were stout trees and no undergrowth on each side of the track, I skidded to a halt and leapt out. It took only a moment to attach each end of the chain to a suitable tree. I could put the spring-clip through any link to fasten it, so I didn't even have to find trees of the exact distance apart. The rusty chain hung at chest-height across the track, almost invisible in the dark and swaying in the wind.

In my panic to start off again, I stalled the engine, and this turned out to have a peculiar significance. For as I leaned forward to pull the starter, I heard in the silence the roar of a motor cycle starting up, and then another, carrying clearly the kilometre or two on the night air. My hand paused on the starter. Would the chain hold? If all three of them came, would at least two get through? To me and Katrina?

Before I had properly thought it all out, I jumped out of the jeep again and grabbed at the canister of mineral spirit. My teeth were chattering with chill and fear and panic, and I think I was muttering incoherently to myself. I unscrewed the cap with rebellious fingers and ran from one side of the track to the other, splashing the volatile liquid on to the ground.

I had gone a few feet up the track to pour the spirit, to keep away from the jeep and its precious cargo, and there was more undergrowth here. I was facing the jeep, in order to see faintly what I was doing in the glow from the rear lights, and the wind blew drops of the spirit on to my feet and my jeans. At that moment Katrina began to wail.

Throwing the half-empty canister in an arc to the right of the track, I pelted back to the jeep to look for a match. I knew there would be plenty in the dash locker, together with half-empty cigarette packets and all the other useful junk Mike always left in there. I scrabbled blindly in the black hole, and finally found a book of matches. Empty! Gibbering with fear as the sound of the motor bikes approached, I tore my nails on the inside of the locker, until I came up with a battered box of *cerini*, the tiny, pink-tipped wax matches that most people use in Italy.

The headlights of the motor bikes were swaying through the trees as I fumbled the box open and took out one of the short, soft matches, spilling most of the rest on the ground. I struck it and it lit, but I had lost the place where the spirit was rapidly evaporating away in the wind and it went out. There was one left in the box, and I gripped it in my fingers while I felt around with my free hand for the wet patch of bush.

As I found it and struck the match, a bike came around the last bend twenty metres away. I screamed and flung the match to the ground as the headlights dazzled me. There was a tremendous *whoosh* of flame and I staggered back, my eyebrows and hair singeing. My foot turned on a stone and I fell backwards into a shallow ditch.

It saved my life, because at this moment the motor bike appeared through the wall of flames, passing over the very spot where I had stood. I saw the driver distinctly, as he was not wearing a helmet. It was Jens, and he was screaming with horror, one forearm in front of his face.

I had forgotten the chain, such was the hellish fury of the blaze which spread in a second across the track and off to where I had thrown the canister. Jens cannoned into it at full speed, and it held. His scream was cut off short. He landed with a thud on his back in the middle of the track and lay still.

The bike careered on the few yards to the jeep, struck the back left corner, shattering the rear light, and crashed over the bank. The headlight went out with a tinkle of glass, and the bike's engine stopped abruptly. Katrina's voice came angrily through the sudden quiet.

I staggered to my feet, my hair snagging and tearing on the undergrowth where I had fallen, and heard the other motor bike skidding to a halt on the upper side of the wall of flames. Klaus's voice called out 'Jens, Jens!' and something which sounded like 'Where are you?'

As I stumbled towards the jeep, past Jens's crumpled form, I heard Katrina's voice choking from the front seat. Then, over the crackle of the angry flames, I heard the motor bike rev again, and looking back I saw the headlight bucking over the rough ground away from the track.

I was about to climb into the jeep, lit with an unearthly, flickering light, when a dazzling blaze and a second, louder *whoosh* came from the night, followed by a terrible high-pitched cry.

I had to look, nothing could have stopped me. Klaus had passed the place where I had thrown the canister. It was an inferno of flame, higher and brighter than anywhere else. As I stared, the motor bike lurched out of the thickest part, the rider outlined in fire, the headlight pale in contrast.

This bike, too, rocked and bucked like a crazy, nightmare horse through the unreal scene, touching everything it passed with fire which the wind immediately fanned and spread. I could hear Klaus's screaming above the flames as he traced a mad, incendiary course through the wood. Suddenly he hit a tree a glancing blow, and as the bike somersaulted, I saw him fly in a high trajectory out of the saddle, the flames billowing behind him like a cloak.

He landed in a gorse bush, struggling feebly and still crying out, and I held my breath. I knew what would happen. I had seen enough burning gorse when fighting forest fires. Everybody turns out here when a fire starts, but nobody goes near a gorse bush. In a moment it went up like another canister, and Klaus disappeared. He did not scream again.

The wind was fanning the flames, and they were spreading fast towards the house, perhaps a kilometre away. And I had the key to Ulli's prison in my pocket. Jens lay at my feet, out of the path of the flames but burnt and perhaps bleeding from internal injuries. As I hesitated, I heard Katrina's coughing cries again, and I knew what I must do.

I drove carefully down the track, hunched behind the wheel, and at one moment I actually put the windscreen-wipers on before I realized that the blurring of my vision was caused by tears. After a nightmare distance, I came to the dirt road and swung up towards the village.

I stopped and left the engine running, and lit the map light on the dash. Katrina was red-faced and furious, and her clothes and pillow were covered with vomit. I cleaned her as well as I could with one of the nappies I had packed, but it was a makeshift job at best. I did not have the time to give her the comfort she needed; she was still sobbing angrily as I put the light off and headed for the little group of houses.

There would be nobody at Marino's shop now that he and Giorgio were murdered. If old Maria was in any state to be moved at all she would be in the care of relatives. No, I thought, of course not! She is bedridden, they will have kept her there and moved in with her.

I slithered to a stop beside the single petrol pump and slumped over the wheel, uncertain as to what I should do. In the sleeping village, the sound of a window being banged open was like a pistol-shot.

'Che c'è Michele?' called a voice from the other side of the road, and as I got out, he corrected himself, 'Ah, è Lei, signora!'

But even as he spoke, the man, whom I did not recognize, saw over the rooftops the flickering of the flames up on the hillside.

'Are you all right, signora Sofia?' he called anxiously, and as I came around the front of the jeep I said yes, all right, but it was going to be a big fire. I leaned against the mudguard in exhaustion, and he said, 'Wait a moment and I'll call the fire brigade.'

The head disappeared and the window shut, and a moment later a downstairs light went on. My legs were against the mudguard and I felt how badly bent it was. I looked down curiously, for in the whole scene of terror which had just been enacted on the mountainside, the front right of the jeep – where Katrina was – had been away from the action.

Scrapes of dark red paint stood out vividly from the cream-coloured paintwork of the jeep, and with horror I remembered where it had come from. And I was standing right outside Marino's shop!

Nobody in the village must see this, I thought confusedly

as the man from across the road came out of his front door, pulling on a sweater as he came. He took no notice of the jeep, but said as he passed me, 'You look finished. You're sure you're all right?'

'Yes thanks,' I said. 'I'll take the baby to friends and come back and help.'

'Va bene,' he called over his shoulder as he thumped on the back door of the village shop, and I climbed stiffly back into the jeep and did a three-point turn.

The next part of my plan was the last I had been able to think out during the long, silent night in the studio. It had seemed doubtful enough then, without money, papers or spare clothes. Had I imagined what I would look like, singed and blackened from the fire and almost at the end of my tether, I don't know that I would have had the courage to think this far.

I put fifteen kilometres between myself and the village, and then had to stop and go behind a bush. I was amost wetting my pants in nervous exhaustion. With a guilty start I recalled that Katrina had not cried again all the way from the village, although the wind was whistling in where the door-flaps were missing. I found them under the back seat and fastened them into place with the twist-buttons. They were only canvas flaps with yellowed, creased plastic windows, but they would keep the worst of the draught off her cot.

She was safely asleep again. I tucked her in more securely and got on my way. I had to be gone soon before the villagers and firemen wondered where I was. I hit the asphalt road to Olmo a little after five, and headed down the hill. A few moments later, three fire engines passed me going the other way, blue lights flashing eerily, and one of them gave me a short howl of the siren which I decided to take for a good-luck greeting.

The sky was getting light in the east as I drove into sleeping Olmo, and I stopped at the telephone box in the square on the edge of town still called the *Mercato,* although the market has long been held up in the centre. There was always a supply of *gettoni* among the other trash in the dash locker. I took three or four and breathed a silent prayer as I dialled the number of Radio Annibale.

The local radio station, high on a hill overlooking the lake where Hannibal had fought, was named after the great Carthaginian general. I was pretty sure that Manfredi Ferri, whom we always called Fred, the Worst Disc-Jockey in the World, would be there all night. Fred's hours were so long at the weekend that he usually spent the night in a sleeping-bag on the floor under the worn desk in the station's single shabby office. And I knew that the telephone was on top of the desk.

The phone rang seven, eight, nine times, and then cut off to an engaged signal, because the station was just over the border in Umbria, the next province, and the call was thus long-distance. Fumbling nervously, with frozen fingertips, I dialled again, and this time after four rings a sleepy voice muttered, 'This is Radio Annibale, but if you think anyone is awake, you're wrong. That's a tape on the air.' The line went dead, and one of my *gettoni* clinked into the bottom of the box.

Despite this apparent setback, I was elated, for it had been Fred's voice, and I was within sight of a safe house. Literally, in fact, because I could make out through the trees the flashing red aircraft-warning lights on the station antenna, perhaps thirty kilometres away across the valley.

A third time I dialled the number, and Fred answered, 'All right, all right, so you think I've nothing better to do. Who are you, anyway?'

'Ciao, Freddy, sono Sofia.'

'Wow,' he shouted, making the receiver buzz in my ear, 'why didn't you say so? Such a beautiful lady at such a wonderful hour of the night!'

Despite my aches, pains and distress, I had to smile. Fred's exuberance always had a heartwarming effect on us, and this was one reason why I had thought of him to start with.

'I did try, Fred,' I said apologetically, 'but I don't think you were listening. Anyway, I'll bet you've got Bruna there, so you don't need another beautiful lady.'

'Never when I'm on duty, ma'am,' he replied sternly, and a *gettone* clicked through the gate to remind me that I had to cut this short.

'Listen,' I said, 'I'll be there in half an hour. Will you make me some coffee?'

'I'll send the porter to Rio this very instant,' he promised. 'To what do I owe the pleasure?'

'Tell you later,' I said tersely, and rang off.

I swung out of the *Mercato* and down the hill, but on an impulse decided not to take the direct road. There was too much possibility of a police road-block on that particular road in turbulent Italy, and I had no wish to run into one now. It would normally be easy enough to flirt gently with a *carabiniere* and persuade him to overlook the fact that I had neither my licence nor my log-book with me, but at five in the morning and looking as though I had been dragged through a burning bush backwards, I was certainly not an object in which the police would repose confidence.

Instead, I took the back road up the rolling foothills and then turned off on to a dirt track which soon became all but impassable, the deep ruts of last winter having been baked iron-hard by the summer sun. Only a jeep and perhaps a motor bike could have taken this track, and the only motor bikes I was worrying about had been left behind long ago.

After four kilometres or so I passed under the welcome intermittent glow of the antenna lights, and following the land-line arrived five minutes later behind the station, where the jeep could stand unseen. The main road would have brought me round to the front, where two hundred metres of gravel track joined the station to the asphalt.

I picked up the carry-cot and resisted the temptation to kiss Katrina; she deserved her sleep. I pushed through the outer door into the dimly-lit building, and headed down the corridor towards the glow at the end, where the permanently-lit 'On the air' sign was disregarded by everybody.

We had met Fred two years before when a sculptor friend of ours had decided to advertise his next exhibition on the local radio station, and we had gone with him to interpret. Fred had charmed us from the start, with his wild blond hair, his rapid slurred voice, and his encylopaedic knowledge of music. He had green eyes which gleamed with sly wit, a wit which came over in his broadcasts and had made him something of a cult figure among the young people within listening distance of the station.

He had been studying to go into accountancy when he started working part-time for Radio Annìbale. So-called 'liberated' FM stations block the air-waves in Italy, and this station claimed to be one too; but it was tucked away in the provinces, where no demos or police-and-student shootouts ever happened, so it was just frankly commercial, transmitting pop music 24 hours a day.

This didn't worry Fred one little bit, for he lived for music. And despite his freaky appearance, he didn't despise us 'straight' people either, especially after he and Mike spent a whole weekend discussing the entertainment world, and he found that Mike knew more about the cinema than he did, and very nearly as much about popular music.

He had once brought his girlfriend Bruna up to the house on one of the rare days off he allowed himself nowadays, and the four of us had remained good friends. As I pushed open the door to the studio, he waved from behind the soundproof window, headphones flattening a band of hair across his head, and he didn't miss a word as he announced the time and set the next tape spinning.

But as he took in my state, his face was sober and wide awake. He came out of the 'hot room', kissed me on both cheeks, and checked that his 'second favourite girlfriend' was serenely asleep in her carry-cot.

'What would you like first, Sofia,' he asked, 'a coffee or a wash?'

'Both Fred,' I said, and took the key to the lavatory from the hook beside the door. 'Have you got a comb for me?'

He spread his hands helplessly. 'Me? Do I look like it?' he asked.

I managed a smile. 'Put some brandy in the coffee if you have any,' I said, and went to the bathroom.

It was a primitive wash, but it was a help. In fact, I had felt better from the moment I had heard his voice on the telephone.

I went back to the studio looking something more like normal, though the corridor was waving under my feet, and the door would not stay still for me to open it.

I sank into the only chair in the room while Fred sat on the edge of the desk and handed me a coffee with an alcoholic perfume.

'Do you want to tell me now or later?' he asked.

'Now, Fred,' I said, but all I could do was cry, and I cried for ten minutes while he held my hand gently and gave me a whole box of Kleenex one by one.

Eighteen

When I was calm enough, I told Fred more or less everything. Maybe it was stupid, but future events proved that I was not mistaken to trust him. At that moment, I just had to talk to somebody, and I don't think I could have chosen anyone better.

'What you need is somebody to drive you to Rome,' he said after a long silence. I had not known what I needed, but as soon as he said that, I knew that he was right. In Rome I had access to money, I had a beginning of a trace on Mike; and if somebody drove me there, I could make it.

I nodded silently. He picked up the phone and dialled a number without looking at the dial.

'Ciao, Bruna, wake up, it's your morning sunshine,' he said into it.

The answer was obviously stormy, because he held the receiver at arm's length and let it squeak for a while, with a grimace at me that made me sniff and laugh and pull myself together.

'Listen,' he said, as soon as he could cut in, 'Sofia's here and she's in a mess and she needs someone to drive her to Rome. Now. Can you get here in ten minutes?'

I had never heard Fred so businesslike, and obviously Bruna hadn't either, because there was some rather more efficient-sounding squeaking after which Fred hung up. Turning to me, he said, 'A quarter of an hour.'

It was a quarter to seven, and I could hear the morning bird-song outside.

Fred made another call, and said, 'We've got breakfast for you in Rome, too, and somewhere to stay if you want it.'

After that, I felt almost human again. Fred was the best idea I had had; the horrors of the night were fading like a bad dream.

Bruna came in twenty minutes dressed in something like a parachutist's overalls. She ignored Fred completely and smothered me with kisses. She was a tall girl with that dark-olive Italian skin, a wide red mouth, and short, heavy black hair cut close around her face like a cap. Her eyes were sometimes brown and sometimes green, and always sparkling with good humour. She had a sumptuous figure, but like many of her friends active in the feminist movement she disdained the clothes which would have shown it at its best, preferring instead practical, shapeless and – to my eyes – thoroughly unattractive gear. She was not really pretty, seen objectively, but her vivacity and enthusiasm made her so attractive a person that you didn't notice.

'Tell me what's happening,' she demanded, but before I could speak, Fred cut in.

'Bruna, just be a sweet little lady and take Sofia to Stefano's place in a hurry. Stefano's not asking questions, and please don't you start.'

She was about to explode, but I caught her hand and looked pleading, and she stopped herself.

'Right now?' she asked, and I stood up and picked up the carry-cot.

Fred came with us to the door, and pushed something into my hand. I looked. It was five bank-notes – fifty thousand lire. We kissed on both cheeks, and he was gone.

We went back to Bruna's apartment before leaving. She found a packet of biscuits and gave it to me, and I warmed up some milk for Katrina, putting some more in a Thermos. The baby gurgled and chuckled, and Bruna went all gooey-eyed. 'I'm hoping Fred will marry me next year,' she confided, 'but I think I'll have to learn to play the drums or something first.'

She looked me up and down critically, and said with cheerful bluntness, 'You look a real mess. Why don't you go and have a real hot shower?'

'I'd love to, but I haven't got time,' I protested. 'But a hot wash and a hair-brush would help a lot.'

While I was drying my face, Bruna knocked and opened the door a few inches. She held a bundle of clothes through the door, and to my surprise they turned out to be rather smart blue slacks and a cashmere sweater, a bit large, but they would do. From both the style and the fit I saw that she had not worn these clothes for some time; they were completely contrary to the current Bruna image. Looking at myself in the mirror, I thought I looked almost passable again, at least in comparison to earlier, although the past days had left me pale and haggard.

Shoes turned out to be more of a problem, but we finally found a pair of lace-ups, flat and sensible, which fitted if I didn't tie the laces too tight. I wiped Katrina's face clean, while Bruna was convinced she had recognized her own name among the gurgles, and then we were ready to set off.

'Come on, little one,' I said as I hoisted Katrina on to my shoulder once more, 'time to go again.'

When I got into the back of Bruna's car, a new Mirafiori, it took me about two minutes to fall asleep. I later heard that she had driven most of the way to Rome with one hand and played with Katrina with the other. But her driving must have been pretty efficient for all that, because when she woke me we were parked outside an apartment house not far from the Quirinale.

Stefano and his wife Maria professed to have met me and to be delighted to see me again. But I was so exhausted, and so many students and other young people had been introduced to us during each visit to the radio station, that I could not place them at all. They asked me no questions, but offered me a bed for the night, while Maria commandeered Katrina immediately and successfully.

As I looked around their tiny, brightly-decorated apartment, I shook my head to clear it of the wispy remains of sleep, and some of the nightmares receded. Others proved to be real and remained.

'No, thanks a lot,' I said, 'but if I may leave the baby with you for a while there are one or two things I have to do. Bruna, are you going back to Olmo?'

'I have to, Sophie,' she said. 'I didn't even ask Dad if I could take his car.'

We all laughed and I said, 'Then be a dear and drop me off at the Spanish Steps on your way out.' If Mike was going anywhere, he would need cash, as indeed I did, and the Amexco office was the best place to start tracing him.

Bruna dropped me right in front of the American Express building, and we kissed on both cheeks. I put twenty thousand lire for the petrol in the glove pocket despite her protests, because, as I told her, I would have no cash problems once I had seen the Amexco branch manager. But as I turned to open the car door, she put her hand on my arm.

'I'm going over to that bar to make a phone call,' she said, pointing, 'and then I'll need a drink. Why don't you come and tell me how you get on?'

'You're a darling, Bruna,' I said gratefully. 'I'll join you there as soon as I can.'

I asked the clerk at reception to tell Jim Hawthorne I would like to speak to him personally, and was being ushered up to the second floor within minutes. He met me with a warm smile and outstretched hand, but it was clear that he was fighting to keep his expression under control. It wasn't every day that he received good customers with hair and eyebrows singed, and wearing hand-me-down clothes.

'Sophie, my dear, what can I do for you? It's a pleasure to see you in Rome again.' Something seemed to pass across his mind, and the smile slipped slightly. 'In fact, it's only a couple of days since Mike called in. Perhaps you're picking up his papers for him?' he asked hopefully.

'Sorry, Jim, but I don't know anything about that,' I said. 'I've . . . I've hardly seen him myself all weekend.'

'Well, he left some pretty high-powered stuff with me last week for safe-keeping,' said Jim, offering me an armchair and going back behind his desk. 'I guess he'll be in to pick it up in a day or so.'

'What makes you think that, Jim?' I asked, a glimmer of hope glowing in the back of my mind.

'Well, he left instructions that if he didn't pick it up by Thursday noon, I was to forward it to, uh, well, to New York, and I told him I didn't have the facilities for diplomatic mail.' Jim looked even more worried as something else occurred to him. 'Come to think of it, I don't think I could even hand it to you, Sophie, as his instructions were pretty specific. Only to him personally.'

'Listen, Jim,' I said, leaning forward urgently, 'I don't want to put you in an embarrassing position, and I don't want his papers, but could you tell me more about what he said? You see, Mike has disappeared, and I . . .'

I saw the blank look come down over his face like a shutter, and I immediately realized what it must sound like.

'No, Jim, not like that,' I added hastily. 'We're not splitting up or anything. I know this must sound incredible to you, out of the blue, but I believe he may have been kidnapped or forced to do something against his will. Please believe me, Jim; I know this doesn't happen every day, but when it does, people desperately need help until it's cleared up. I'm trying to trace Mike now.' I put all the sincerity I could into my voice and I watched Jim weighing it up.

'I truly don't want to know what's in those papers, Jim,' I coaxed. 'Just tell me when he deposited them and when he's going to pick them up.'

He seemed to come to a decision, because he took a deep breath, held it a moment, then blew it out and answered me.

'I couldn't tell you what's in them myself, Sophie, because I didn't read them. He brought them in on Friday, and said that a strike at Fiumicino had held him up so that he missed an appointment with the top man at the I.D.A., and the appointment had had to be rescheduled for Monday morning, that is, yesterday.'

I nodded encouragingly, and he carried on.

'If the papers were not picked up by Mike within five days, and by the most generous possible interpretation that would be Thursday morning, I was to send one lot to New York and the other to his partner in Geneva. Send them in a special way, I mean. I told him I didn't have the facilities for that, but he said it didn't matter, because he would pick them up Monday anyway. I think he just didn't want to carry them around all weekend with him. That's about all I know, except that he didn't turn up yesterday.'

I thought it over and over, while the air-conditioning hummed and the honking and roaring of the traffic on Piazza di Spagna came muted through the windows. Jim watched me in silence and let me get on with it.

'May I use your phone, Jim?' I asked finally, and he pushed a button on the complex gadget on the desk and turned it around to face me. 'The Rome books are on that table next to you, or do you want to call away?'

'No that's fine,' I murmured, opening the A to K volume. I rang the I.D.A. and asked for Mr Mkara's secretary. I got a fluting Irish voice on the line, and explained that I was Mike Ellis's wife and wanted a short, personal word with Mr Mkara.

'I'm not sure that he's in, Mrs Ellis, but I'll find out at once,' she said primly, and I thought, you're an efficient one, my dear.

'At once,' turned out to be less than fifteen seconds. Without warning a suave, cultured voice said in my ear, 'My *dear* Mrs

132

Ellis, how nice to hear from you! What can I have the pleasure of doing for you?'

'I'm sorry to disturb you, Mr Mkara,' I said, and watched absently as Jim Hawthorne's bushy eyebrows crept up his forehead, 'but I seem to have missed Mike at every turn this weekend. When I was here, he was there, and now I've not made it home in time to see him before he left. But I understand he had an appointment with you yesterday, so I thought you might know where he has gone to from there.'

'Yes *indeed*, Mrs Ellis,' Mkara purred, 'we had a most valuable conference yesterday. He will be in Koristan again for perhaps ten days, and then he will be finished with the present job, as far as I know.'

'Koristan!' I gasped in dismay. 'I had no idea it would take another ten days.'

'What would take that long, Mrs Ellis?' he asked. Jim was slumped at his desk. As I carried on talking, he pulled a pad towards him, scribbled something, and passed it to me.

'Er, well, to wrap up the job he was doing,' I improvised. 'Do you have another conference scheduled with him, Mr Mkara?' On Jim's pad I read: ASK HIM ABT. PAPERS IN MY SAFE, and I shook my head vehemently at him as Mkara replied, 'No, nothing was planned. But I was going to telex our man there in any case this afternoon, and if you wish I would be only too glad to add a note to ask Dr Ellis to get in touch with you. Where are you now, Mrs Ellis? In Rome?'

Although I had nothing more than intuition to go on, I said, 'No, not in Rome. But I'll be coming into Rome tomorrow.' Jim Hawthorne's face was a study.

'Where can Dr Ellis find you, then?' asked Mkara, and I answered off the cuff, 'I'll keep in touch with his partner in Geneva and he can reach me through him. I'm so sorry to have bothered you with my domestic problems, Mr Mkara. I'm sure you have much more important things to do.'

'Not at all my dear Mrs Ellis,' he said with a laugh. 'It is a great pleasure to be able to help you. Dr Ellis has one of the finest minds in his field and he is a very valued collaborator of I.D.A. Perhaps you would care to call me when you come into Rome? I would much enjoy being allowed to give you luncheon.'

'I'll certainly do that, Mr Mkara,' I said. 'Thank you again, and excuse me for troubling you.'

As soon as I had rung off, Jim Hawthorne exploded.

'Look, Sophie, I don't know what's going on and I'm sure it's none of my business, but I'm going to be left here holding the baby, I can see that! What was that about ten days?' Slowly his agitation evaporated as he saw the expression on my face. 'Why, what's wrong, Sophie? Something's really wrong, isn't it?'

'I'm afraid it is, Jim, and I can't tell you the half of it,' I said slowly, 'although I would dearly like some advice right now. But I don't want to get you involved in this any more than you are. Just bear in mind that I haven't been here, would you? And that you should spare no expense to deal with those papers as Mike wanted if he should not come and pick them up. Charge it to our account in Geneva, all of it.'

His face was a mixture of concern and relief. 'Well, I'm sure there'll be no problem with the papers, Sophie,' he said, 'but I can see that your worries are worse than mine at the moment. If there's anything at all I can do . . .?'

'As a matter of fact, there is another small problem, Jim,' I said, and I almost had to laugh as his face fell. 'I've been caught in a forest fire – no danger, just lost a few things – and I have no cash, no passport and no Amexco card.' His face cleared again comically as this problem turned out to be something he could deal with quite easily.

He helped me fill out the forms declaring my Amexco card to be lost and accepting responsibility for misuse, and suggested I open another account in Rome, so that he could issue me a card here and I could draw on that. 'We can have a telex back from Geneva by tomorrow morning and clear an account for you for as much as you want.'

'Tomorrow morning!' I exclaimed in dismay, 'Is there nothing you can do today, this morning, Jim? Please help me; it's vital that I leave Rome this morning, and I have nothing, nothing.' I could feel the tears coming, and I think Jim could see them, too.

'How much do you need, Sophie?' he asked kindly.

Oh, I don't know, three or four hundred dollars.' He laughed. 'Why, that's no problem,' he said. 'I'll give you that out of my own account, and you can transfer it to me when you are in

Geneva. No problem at all for you or for Mike. I thought you needed much more.'

He accompanied me down to the cashier's office and, while I sat in a daze and tried to work out what to do next, arranged the formalities. He came back in no time at all, it seemed; at least, I had not reached any decision. Pushing an envelope into my hands, he said, 'Here, half a million.' As I looked at him in astonishment, he added, 'Lire, of course!'

He took me right down to the door, and as we shook hands, he said jokingly, 'Don't forget to send me that back, Sophie. I may be branch manager, but I spend three months of the year trying to fight for a raise!'

I took his shoulders and kissed him on both cheeks, Italian style, while one of the clerks turned with a smile to whisper something to her neighbour.

'Jim, you're an angel,' I told him, and remembered to add, 'and don't forget, I haven't been here. Unless, of course, Mike comes in. Tell him I'm in Geneva.'

I waved again and dashed across the road in front of a horse carriage, whose driver swore half-heartedly and winked at me broadly.

I found Bruna installed comfortably in the back of the café. She had consumed two hot chocolates and had had time to re-do her make-up completely, and also to make her phone call.

'I'm dying to know what's going on,' she said, 'but Freddy told me not to ask questions. But perhaps I may ask where you are going now?'

'I have to go to Switzerland as fast as I can, Bruna,' I said, 'but I don't want to fly. I can't tell you why just now, but I don't want to go near the airport.' I wondered if I was exaggerating, but decided it was better to be on the safe side.

'Then it's settled,' she said contentedly, and as I looked at her in amazement, she said, 'I'm taking you, of course. My call was to Papà. I told him a girlfriend of mine was in trouble and I needed the car for a day or so and he could take my *Cinquecento,* and of course he assumed he knew what the 'trouble' was because of my activity in the feminist groups and so he couldn't really say no, could he?'

She smiled with delight as I found no objection, and two dimples appeared in her cheeks. 'The only problem,' she said, 'will be getting Katrina and ourselves away from Stefano and Maria. They are bound to have a six-course breakfast ready. You know what Romans are like.' She was right.

Nineteen

We made it to the *autostrada* shortly after midday, narrowly escaping a Roman lunch as well.

Stefano and Maria packed us some sandwiches and a bottle of *acqua minerale* and some wine for the journey. They also gave us an old baby-seat to clip on to the car seat. I suggested giving this to Bruna to give back to them.

'We won't be needing it again,' said Maria.

'Then give it to me anyway, Sofia,' said Bruna. 'I hope I'll need it soon!'

We all had a good laugh at that, and it was the signal to get on the road. We did not tell Stefano and Maria where we were going, nor did they ask.

While Bruna's Papà's Fiat made light work of the traffic, I was busy with the practical details of the flight for which I had had no time up to now. The main problem was going to be my passport. This, of course, was in the cottage at Olmo. However, I have dual nationality since my marriage to Mike – there was a loophole in the law which did not seem particularly important at the time, but for which I now thanked my lucky stars – and I still held a U.S. passport, which was in Geneva.

Finally I decided the best thing to do would be to call Mike's secretary Christine and arrange to meet her at the Swiss border, or as near as possible. My priorities were very clear. Firstly, I had to get little Katrina to safety, there was nothing more important than that. Then I would have to start trying to get in touch with Mike, and his partner Sam would be the only person who could help me.

We passed Olmo with barely a glance. The motorway cut up the middle of the broad, fertile Val di Chiana parallel to the hills, and the little hilltop town was clearly visible in the bright afternoon sunshine off to our right. Instinctively I cowered deeper into my seat as I saw it, and that reminded me that my red hair is rather distinctive. Bruna fished an elastic band out of the depths of her voluminous purse and even found an unexpected treasure: a headscarf which I tied babushka-style over my head.

At Bologna we stopped to call Christine. Leaving Katrina with Bruna in the car park was difficult, for I could not explain my reluctance to be seen in the restaurant of the service station. Borrowing Bruna's sunglasses, I slipped cautiously into the filling-station office and asked to use their phone, explaining that there were long lines at the public phones in the restaurant.

Christine was there, but the surge of relief I felt at the sound of her calm, efficient manner was quickly damped by some of the disturbing news she had to report. I decided to keep it short and get the news from her in detail when we met, so I gave her a list of things I would require from the apartment – she had a key, of course – and agreed to her suggestion that we meet in Aosta the next morning. This was the last large town before the border, and we were certain to get a hotel bed there. Christine would come down from Geneva in the early hours and meet us in the station buffet at nine.

'What's wrong, Sofia?' asked Bruna, her eyes gentle with compassion as I returned to the car.

I didn't know that it had shown on my face, but the conversation with Christine, while filling me with relief on many counts, had given me a lot to worry about, too. Already there had been another violent death.

'I'm not sure myself, *cara*,' I replied. 'We'll find out tomorrow. Tonight we go to Aosta and tomorrow we'll know more.'

Her eyes lit with excitement, and her regular teeth sparkled as she laughed. 'Wow! This is going to be fun!'

How could I put her down? She had no conception of the ugly business she was caught up in – no, that I had involved her in. I smiled wanly and left it at that.

I took Katrina as we swung back into the traffic and headed north again. She was being as good as gold despite all the extra attention she was getting. I was thankful that she was not a show-off by nature.

Bruna asked me if there was anything she could help me to

work out. When I replied that there was nothing I could do at all until the next day, she started to tell me anecdotes about Freddy, whom she had met at the radio station some years before. Soon her cheerful tales began to take effect, and by the time we reached Aosta shortly after seven and started looking for a hotel for the night, she had managed to make me feel almost happy again.

'Dear Bruna!' I said as we pulled up outside a decent-looking hotel on a small side-street. 'I don't know what I would have done without you!'

'Well, we've got to stick together, haven't we?' she replied in a matter-of-fact way. 'It could just as well have been me to need help, and it might be next time.'

Sisters, I thought as I collected our scattered belongings in the car, that's the word they use in the States. Bruna sure was a sister to me. I felt the tears pricking behind my eyes and pulled myself together to go into the hotel.

As long as I was feeding and changing Katrina I did not notice how tired I was, but when we went into the dining room for supper I stumbled against a chair and suddenly realized that I was all in. I cannot even remember the meal any more. As we left to go upstairs again, I barely remembered to ask for an early call before the lights started going out in my head. I fell into a long, dark tunnel and slept like the dead.

Bruna woke me with an enormous double cup of *cappuccino* and said it was a quarter past seven. I had not heard the telephone ringing for the early call, nor Bruna getting up to answer it.

The streets of Aosta were already loud under the window, and bright sunlight was pouring in between the slats of the Venetian blind. Katrina was still asleep, but I could tell that her sleep was now light and would soon be over.

Bruna sat on the edge of my bed and let me sip the coffee and pull myself together before unfolding the newspaper she had brought and showing me an article on the fifth page.

My nerves tingled when I saw the headline she pointed out to me. Wide awake in an instant, I seized the paper with impatient fingers. I still have the cutting, and the following translation is my own.

138

MYSTERIOUS FOREST FIRE IN TUSCANY

One Dead, Three Missing
140 hectares (about 350 acres) ravaged.

Local police are still not ruling out foul play in the starting
of a widespread blaze in the Apennines near Olmo, province
of Arezzo, which would probably still be spreading if it had
not been for a timely thunderstorm and downpour yesterday afternoon. A still unidentified body was found charred beyond recognition beside a crashed motor cycle with West German licence plates near the scene assumed to be the starting
point of the fire, which has put Tuscany back at the top of the
regional table of fire damage after a relatively quiet summer
season. A second motor cycle with plates from the same city,
Berlin, was found a few metres away, but there was no trace
of the rider. A steel chain was stretched across the track between two charred tree-stumps at the scene, but preliminary
investigations have not shown whether this obstacle caused
the riders to crash. The villager who alerted the local fire
brigade – which was aided by three neighbouring brigades in
a tiring and courageous battle against the flames – told police
officers that he was awoken in the early hours by a Swiss [sic]
resident of the only inhabited house in the affected area, who
was bringing her child to safety. Investigations are being
made along the hypothesis that the brave young woman returned to save her husband, who was not with her at the time
of the alarm, and perished in the inferno. Neither her vehicle
nor any further bodies have been found on the scene or nearby, and efforts are still being made to trace the foreign address
of the protagonists of this mysterious incident. A strong breeze
hampered the efforts of firemen and volunteers, and the unusual
hour of the alarm – about 4.30 a.m. – not only retarded the
intervention of the firefighters but also strengthened police
suspicion of arson.

'A hundred and forty hectares!' exclaimed Bruna. 'That's one
of the biggest fires I remember.'
'Yes,' I said absently, hardly listening, 'but I wonder what
happened to Jens and Ulli.'

I had already realized that my tongue had slipped before Bruna asked curiously. 'Who are they? The mysterious motor cyclists? Who was the dead one?'

For a while I hesitated over whether to tell her the full story, or as much of it as I knew, but then decided that the less she knew the better it would be for her. For this reason I already regretted having told Fred so much.

'They are dangerous people, Bruna,' I said, 'and they have caused me a lot of pain and heartache. Even so I'm not sure I would want anybody to die like that . . .'

Bruna waited a moment. Then, as I said nothing more, she became brisk and businesslike, and showed me her watch. I jumped out of bed in a rush.

Christine was already waiting in the station buffet when I arrived, and we embraced fondly. She had chosen quite a secluded corner where I found her only after a good look around. I walked back to the hotel with her and ordered Continental breakfast for three in the room.

Sam and Mike often tell me – and Christine – that she is the reason for the company's success. She is thirty, with a strong, serene face and dark hair as long as my own, but much more severely styled. Her husband is a journalist. Despite the odd working hours that both of them keep, she and Pierre have made a superb job of bringing up their little son. Christine always seems to be there when you need her, and yet she complains when Sam or Mike tries to persuade her to take a day off.

She had a small suitcase of mine with her, and it would not have crossed my mind to ask whether she had brought all the things I had asked for. I have never yet experienced nor heard of Christine's getting anything wrong.

I introduced Bruna, and Chris took the time for a fond greeting to Katrina before sitting down with an expectant look. I was now in a spot, for I fully intended to tell her the whole story; but even if I did so in English, which Bruna understood only very poorly, she would still know what I was doing and might be offended.

To my relief, she solved the problem with beautiful tact by getting up and saying, 'I'm sure you two have a lot to talk about. I want to get some cigarettes. Why don't you pick me up at the corner bar when you're through?'

I was pretty sure that Bruna would not be known by sight to anybody of whom I was afraid, but I still warned her not to talk to any strange men. 'That depends on how good they look,' she retorted, but she assured me she was aware of the danger of the situation, even if not what the situation was.

Jiggling Katrina on my knee, I told Christine an abbreviated version of the whole story. As it progressed, she went silent and white.

'And now you tell me,' I concluded, 'who is this man who was murdered?'

'Well,' she said in a low voice, 'he rang on Monday evening, just as I was about to go, and asked for Sam. He said his name was George Hamilton, but he wouldn't tell me what he wanted. I remember I asked because Sam was in conference with Ferrier and didn't want to be disturbed, but this Mr Hamilton said it was important.'

She lit a cigarette. 'So I put the call through, and took the opportunity to tell Sam I was ready to go. He said he didn't need anything else, and he would lock up the office himself. He came in late the next morning looking very pale and worried, and said he had just come from the police. When he had gone as arranged to Hamilton's hotel, they had rung the room, but there was no answer. As his key was not there, they looked around the hotel for him, but couldn't find him anywhere. The clerk asked if Sam was Mr Greaves. When Sam said yes, he gave him a letter Hamilton had left in the hotel safe for him. This letter.'

Christine opened her handbag and passed me a plain manilla envelope, printed 'I.D.A. for internal use only'. It had been sealed and ripped open again carelessly. On the front was written 'M. Grive'. Inside was Mike's note to Sam and my heart leapt to see his handwriting.

I put Katrina down on the bed for a moment, and read the note. I had to read it two or three times, because it made no sense to me at first.

'There are several things here that don't tie up,' I said slowly. 'For a start, I have no idea who this Roswita might be, or why he wants to know about her. But she's sure to be connected with the gang in Olmo. "John in Florence" will almost certainly be John Morris, that's clear. And that's quite right about keeping away from Olmo. But he says here he'll be in Florence in "a day or so". In Rome they told me more like ten days.'

I went over to the window and pushed the curtain aside a little, and watched the traffic while I turned things over in my mind. Christine waited in silence.

When Katrina called me, 'Mama, mam!' I went back to the bed and picked her up.

'I'm going to have to get to Florence as fast as I can. As soon as Katrina is in safety ... What happened then, Chris?'

'Well, Sam went back to the office to finish off dictating his agreement with Ferrier on to tape for me,' she continued. 'At about seven-thirty the police rang and asked if he was the Mr Greaves who had been to the hotel, and of course he said yes. They told him Hamilton had been found murdered in his room and he was to wait there and they would come at once.

'Sam said he remembered how Hamilton had said on the phone that Mike had seemed very worried about something in Rome. Sam didn't know why, he just felt intuitively that Mike wouldn't want the police to see the note, so on the spur of the moment he typed another one – just something innocent.'

'Good old Sam!' I interjected. 'That's exactly right! And what about these strange people you mentioned, asking for him?'

'They had just gone when you called.'

'And then my phone call! You had quite an afternoon, poor Chris!'

'Yes, one way and another. They weren't unpleasant at all.' She frowned in perplexity. 'Just ... odd, somehow. They spoke good French, but they were dark-skinned. Arabs, maybe. There were two of them, in jeans and black leather jackets.'

I interrupted her hastily: 'Motor -bike jackets?'

'Oh, no, Sophie, nothing like that. Quite smart jackets, but who of our clients or of Sam's friends would wear black leather jackets? And they were just too – too pleasant, I don't know ... odd,' she repeated. She caught sight of Mike's envelope which I had put on the bed, and picked it up thoughtfully. 'They asked for "Monsieur Grive", not "Greaves" in the English way. That's probably why I felt sure they didn't know him personally. When I asked them what they wanted, they said it wasn't important, they would come back. They didn't even say when.'

'Did you tell the police about them, Chris?'

'Well, no, I couldn't, really. I mean, what did I have to go on? They would have thought I was a hysterical old bitch.'

The thought of anyone taking Christine for a hysterical old bitch made me smile. 'There was no trouble for Sam, was there?'

'Good heavens, no. The police just hoped he might be able to tell them something useful. After all, Sam hadn't left the reception desk all the time he was in the hotel. He told the whole story exactly as it happened, except for substituting the note.'

'Where can I reach him today?'

'You can't. He took the overnight train to Florence. He was so worried about Mike's note that he decided to go down personally and check it out. He didn't even get me to book a hotel room for him – said he'd have time to see to that today, or perhaps even take the overnight train back up tonight.' At that moment there was a knock on the door. Bruna put her head around it and said, 'May I come in?'

I jumped up in embarrassment and looked at my watch. It was already a quarter to ten. 'Of course, silly,' I told her, 'this is your room too. I'm sorry we kept you waiting.'

Christine, like most Swiss I know, speaks passable Italian, so we continued in that language.

'What happens now?' asked Bruna, obviously excited but trying to take her cue from Christine's calm efficiency.

'We go to Florence, *cara*,' I told her, 'if Christine can take Katrina for me.' I turned to Chris. 'The problem is the passport. I know it's a lot to ask, but would you be prepared to take Katrina to Guy and Jacqueline's place in Lausanne on my passport? I'm sorry to ask you to take on such a responsibility, but I want her out of harm's way while I chase up Sam and get a lead on Mike again.'

Christine and I looked at each other for a moment. We both knew that the 'responsibility' was not just a matter of false passports. The crash had left invisible scars on all of us. Although Katrina knows Christine very well, and although I have enormous confidence in her capability, it was still not easy to entrust the baby to anybody, for any reason.

She came over and kissed me. 'Of course, Sophie dear,' she said. 'There's no problem at all. They're doing only very superficial checks at the border now with all the tourists going back. Let's ask Bruna what she thinks.' She took my passport out of her handbag, looked at the photo, and handed it across the bed to Bruna.

Bruna looked critically from her to the passport photo and back again, and said, 'You could just about get away with it, if they're not checking too carefully. You'll have to say you've dyed your hair if they ask, that's all.'

Christine took it back, hesitated, and then said, 'Why can't I take Katrina to my apartment, Sophie?' and I sensed that she was the tiniest bit hurt.

'Because you live too near the office, Chris,' I told her, 'and they might be watching it. People looking for Sam or Mike or me will possibly check on you too. I don't believe there's any danger for you, but if they saw Katrina there they would know you have seen me, and then the balloon would go up. Nobody but a close friend would connect us with Guy and Jacqueline, and in Lausanne they're a good safe distance away.'

Chris approved of this argument.

'I'd prefer to take her to my family in England,' I went on, 'but there's no time, and I don't think we could get you in there on the wrong passport.'

'You wanted this, too,' said Chris, and handed me the American Express form. I signed it and handed it back to her.

'Would you have them transfer half a million lire into Jim Hawthorne's private account at the Rome branch as soon as possible, Chris, please. He was such a dear – I turned up looking like a tramp and didn't even have my card with me, so he lent me some money out of his own pocket.'

She nodded, and then said, 'All right. Is that everything? Can we go?'

'Sure,' said Bruna, and picked up a carrier bag. She had already packed all our gear, and there was nothing left to do but pay the hotel bill and leave. I paused with my hand on the door-knob.

'Chris, when we get downstairs, show Bruna on the street-plan at reception where your car is, without letting anyone else see. Then take off while we are paying the check. We'll meet you there.'

This time nobody was self-conscious about security precautions.

We found the parking garage without difficulty. Christine's

Renault was on the third level in a quiet corner. Bruna pulled in next to it, and watched the entry with the aid of a make-up mirror while we waited for Chris to arrive. She came on foot within five minutes, and I took the suitcase while the others transferred the baby-seat to the Renault.

Suddenly there was nothing left to do but go. I felt a lump in my throat at the thought of leaving Katrina. I hugged her to me. She looked at me with wide blue eyes, and I imagined she was wishing me luck.

'Good luck, yourself, little one,' I whispered, and installed her in the baby-seat. We all tried to be businesslike about it, because we realized more or less simultaneously that we would have to get moving quickly, but the tears were near the surface.

I hugged Christine and murmured, 'Thank you, pet,' in her ear. Bruna and Chris embraced warmly, and we got into our respective cars. Again, Christine left first. With a wave she was gone, and as I watched her disappearing down the ramp, with Katrina's fine fluff of hair just visible over the back seat, I felt cold in the autumn sunshine.

Bruna said cheerfully, as she tidied up the interior of the car to give Christine time to get away, 'She's super, isn't she? You're lucky to have her, Sophie.' She was trying to make me feel better, I knew, but she really meant it.

I put my arms around her neck and said, 'I'm lucky to have you too, Bruna,' and she glowed.

We headed out past the sports stadium and Augustus's Arch and crossed the river. The Matterhorn and Monte Rosa were ahead of us and Monte Paradiso on our right. As we flew down the picturesque Dora Baltea Valley, with its mountain views and beautiful castles and ruins, I had no wish to focus my mind on what lay ahead of us, but just wanted to enjoy the ride.

We would not be in Florence until past lunch-time, and at the first petrol-stop I told Bruna I could do a shift at the wheel.

'You've got enough to think about,' she replied firmly. 'Let me be your chauffeur, and relax.' So I did, but it didn't help much.

Because the more I thought about it, the more certain I was that there was terrifyingly little I could do in Florence to help Mike.

MIKE

Twenty

One of life's most fascinating, and most useless, puzzles must be the retrospective planning of alternative courses of action, assuming that just one little detail had turned out differently.

If you had said this, if A had done that, if B had known C . . . There are many respected scientists who hold that every moment of every life is the branching point for hundreds of alternative consequences, which in turn branch a moment later. The fact that we happen to be on one particular 'time-line', which could be traced back through billions upon infinite billions of such junctions, is pure chance; all the others are equally valid, and on one of them another 'I' might be a butcher, a baker, a candle-stick-maker . . . or might have been the inhabitant of a coffin for twenty years.

I have never followed the mathematical reasoning behind such arguments, and even the popular versions written by serious science-fiction authors have made my head spin. Mine is not the kind of mind that revels in toying with such ideas. But I have had ample opportunity to daydream about what I would have done if, as I walked that morning in stiff silence with Wharton from the passport control at Nooriabad airport to his car outside the terminal building, I had known that Sophie was at that very moment starting out on her successful bid for freedom.

Wharton himself was driving, and I sneaked a sidelong glance at him as he pulled out of the airport car park into the main road towards the city. He was looking ill and drawn, and had obviously missed a lot of sleep. I was feeling the way he looked after a bad night at the stop-over hotel in Teheran. We had said nothing but 'hello' at the airport, as though by mutual agreement. I now felt that the ball was in his court, and had no intention of making things any easier for him, so I lit a cigarette and said nothing.

'My con . . .' he began, but his voice was out of control, and he had to clear his throat and start again. 'My contact got in touch with me on Saturday and said you would be coming back. Apparently you have instructions to help me cover this whole thing up again.'

I closed my eyes as the wave of relief swept over me, and I felt goose-flesh prickle on my arms. So I was doing the right thing to keep Sophie and Katrina safe! Someone, somehow, had managed to feed my 'instructions' into the I.D.A. communications system in such a way as to render them innocuous, unsuspicious even to Mkara. It was an insolent master-stroke, using the Chief Executive himself to pass on the message. I wondered whether the telex he had shown me had really come from Wharton.

Wharton looked over at me nervously as I continued musing.

'I have no instructions whatever,' I said dryly, 'except to report to you. And I had those from the C.E.'

'Ah, yes. I see.' He drove on for a moment in silence, concentrating on the traffic. We were overtaking a mule caravan, the turbanned nomads wielding their sticks with much gusto and little effect. They gave us a friendly laugh as we passed, their white teeth gleaming in brown, weather-beaten faces.

'Well,' he said flatly, '*I* have instructions to cover it up, and I was told that you were going to help me. You are the only person who can, you know.' He turned to me with an earnest look. 'You are the only person who managed to find it all out, and even then only when you discovered that cash-box. If you and I bury it all again, nobody will know.'

And then, casually, he dropped the question I had been waiting for all along. 'Where are those papers, by the way?'

I opened the window a little, and carefully flicked the ash off my cigarette, watching that the airstream did not blow it back into the car. I drew again and inhaled slowly before answering, watching his fingers tighten on the wheel as I spoke.

'They are in a very safe place in Europe, from which they will be sent to the Secretary-General if I do not pick them up personally.'

Finally it came, almost a whisper: 'When?'

'Thursday morning, Wharton.'

The traffic had thickened as we passed the souk and approached downtown Nooriabad. As we crossed the traffic-lights at the Koh-i-Noor Hotel, our pace was being set by a three-decker truck hogging the middle of the road before us, fat-tailed mountain sheep on the bottom deck, cartons and bales in the middle, and a group of peasants hanging on to the rails at the top.

'Good God, man,' he said finally, 'do you realize what that means? They might kill your wife and child!'

'So you know all about that, do you.'

Wharton braked sharply and stopped at the side of the tree-lined road just before the Crown Prince's palace. The I.D.A. building was visible half a mile ahead on the other side of the road. He turned and looked at me, leaving the engine running.

'Yes, Ellis, they told me about that,' he said. 'And I told them they were bastards. Please believe me, I had no idea that they would do that to you. No idea.' His voice was breaking again. 'I'm . . . I'm sorry, Ellis. What else can I say?'

In the wing mirror on my own side I saw that the grey Opel Kadett which had followed us from the airport had also pulled over to the side, two hundred metres behind. I thought there were two men in it, but I could not be sure, as the image was small and distorted by the curved glass, and they were due east of us in front of the morning sun.

'Why didn't you tell them you've hidden the papers?' he said hoarsely. 'Why didn't you do something?'

'Whom should I tell? The kids who picked me up were competent at their job, but they were only obeying orders and didn't know anything, that was evident. I never had an opportunity to speak to anyone else. You've got to tell them, Wharton. You are the first contact I have had.'

He drummed his fists on the wheel as he thought this out. 'Are the papers somewhere where you can send a telex?' he asked finally.

'They are,' I said doubtfully, 'but that would leave traces that a Boy Scout could pick up. I don't think your people would be very pleased at that. There's another thing,' I added. 'Why should we go to all the trouble of covering this up, when the moment we have done it they will shoot us down like rabbits?'

'Oh no, Ellis!' He looked shocked. 'They could do that at any time, anyway. My contact more or less told me they would not be using me again. At least, he said that if ever the slightest hint of this came out, I would need police protection for myself and my wife for twenty-four hours a day for the rest of my life. And even that isn't enough; look at Schleyer in Germany. Four armed bodyguards. And Buback, shot dead on the street. And Moro. Anyway, they've given me a taste of the whip too.'

I looked at him curiously.

'I think they've got Tuula,' he muttered.

I closed my eyes and leaned my head on the window.

He went on in a dead voice, 'She went shopping on Saturday afternoon and hasn't come back. I'm going crazy, Ellis. And I can't reach my contact until later this morning.'

I thought of her visit to my hotel room, and my doubts about her motives. 'Did she know everything?' I asked him.

'No, but I think she knew enough,' he said. 'They'll have told her now, anyway. They enjoy that kind of thing,' he added bitterly.

He put the car into gear and pulled out behind a bus. The Opel tagged along. 'Let's think this over in my office,' he said, and we made a U-turn in front of the I.D.A. block. The Opel went on to the next corner and disappeared.

There were respectful and friendly 'Good mornings' all the way up to Wharton's office. He was an efficient and popular mission chief. His American secretary brought coffee without asking, gave me a 'Hi, Dr Ellis, nice to see you back', and left us in peace. We both took our jackets off, and Wharton poured out the coffee.

'They won't need to touch us,' he said after a while, 'because it is not in their interests and not their policy, either, despite popular conception to the contrary.' (You poor fool, I thought.) 'Killing us or . . . or anybody else at this stage would only attract attention and make people start probing again where everything was quiet. And they have no guarantee that there isn't another stash of information somewhere for publication in the event of anybody's untimely death.'

'That is exactly what I have, Wharton, although I didn't put it that way when I deposited it. The way I see it, I'm threatening their rook, but they have replied by attacking my queen, and I'll have to back down. But I need some guarantee that they won't take my queen anyway. Not to mention Tuula.

'And another thing,' I added with emphasis, 'don't make any mistake about this. I agree that they don't kill *wantonly*. But if they see the need for it, they will not stop at murder. I know. Three days ago they killed someone whose only crime was that he saw one of their least important people in the wrong place at the wrong time. And an innocent passer-by with him.'

Wharton's voice was almost a whisper. 'Who was it? Where?'

'Never you mind. Nobody you know. Just a poor pawn that got taken. But on the whole, I think you're right. If we cover it all up again – thoroughly, so that it won't come back up later – we might have a chance that they'll leave us in peace. I just can't weigh up whether these documents I have could be turned to my advantage. Or yours, if you want.'

It was the nearest I could get to admitting that I saw him now as being to some extent in the same boat that I was, and was prepared to join forces.

He got up and went over to the window, idly pushing apart the plastic slats of the Venetian blinds and looking up to the corner where the grey Opel had turned out of sight. I wondered if he had seen it too, or if he was just used to it.

'And if I were to tell them that the papers will be released Thursday morning if I don't pick them up? And I won't pick them up until Sophie and Katrina are free?'

He turned round with his eyes wide, and spoke urgently. 'For God's sake don't do that, Ellis! If what you say is true, they'll bring you her head on a plate.'

'Yes,' I said slowly. 'Don't think that thought hasn't been with me all the way here. And will be all the way back. I suppose there's nothing for it, then; I'll have to go. It's just a damn nuisance they couldn't have let me discuss this with some-body before now. All this inter-continental commuting is going to leave me in no state to do my best work.'

'There is one thing I am to clear up with you before we lift a finger.' He came back to the seat behind his desk and sat down heavily, the tiredness showing again around his eyes as he looked at me intensely. 'Have you told anyone anything at all about the . . . the progress you made in your investigations here? Bob Harding, for instance, or Black Jack? If we cover up the written evidence, is anybody going to get suspicious?'

Was he – were they – asking me to put the finger on anyone else? Fortunately, there was nobody; but the thought that I might have had to endanger someone else's life by naming him now made my blood run cold. Angrily, I said, 'Look here, Wharton, I can't give you a cast-iron guarantee that this will never come out. I'm not a bloody prophet. No, I haven't told anybody, to answer your question. But don't assume you're in the clear for another twenty years yet.'

He was looking abashed now and playing nervously with his lighter, not meeting my eyes. Less unkindly, I continued, 'I can guarantee only my own intentions: to do the best possible job now. It's in my own interests. If it all comes out later, I will at the very least be ruined professionally, quite apart from anything your people threaten me with. Just make it clear to your contact that somebody was already suspicious, otherwise I wouldn't be here at all. When can you contact him?'

Wharton looked at his gold Rolex. 'Later this morning,' he said evasively. 'What do you want to do?'

I reviewed the facts one last time, and found only No Exit signs everywhere. I was in a corner, and the only way out was over the dead bodies of Katrina and Sophie. I took a deep breath.

'All right. I'll need a return ticket waiting for me at the air-port tomorrow morning. I'll be back here by the weekend, and I'll need five days in peace with you, and nobody breathing down our necks.'

'But I'm supposed to be in Rome on Sunday night until Wednesday,' Wharton interrupted. 'What am I going to do about Tuula?'

'Hell, I'd forgotten that conference.' I thought for a minute.

'All right, I'll meet you here Saturday, we'll plan it together bit by bit, and I'll start doing what I can. You'll have to point out to your contact that you can't just no-show in Rome. We can finish it off together in a day, and I can leave on Thursday next week. Tell your contact that that is my proposal. I don't see any other way to do it, and anything faster than that would risk exciting attention. If he agrees, the signal will be the return ticket at the airport in the morning.'

'How do you intend to do it?' he asked.

'Why do you ask? You'll see soon enough. Anyway, I'm not even sure yet.'

'I have instructions to append details of what you plan to do when I make contact this morning,' Wharton said.

'*Append?* So you contact in writing?' I almost jumped down his throat.

'Yes,' he said after a shade of a pause. 'I contact via a special delivery letter to a post office box at a particular time, and I get a reply by phone within the day.'

'My God, Wharton, they've really got you sewn up,' I said pityingly. 'All that stuff in your writing, if you should ever change your mind.'

'It's typed,' he said defensively, 'not that I suppose it makes much difference.'

'Sure as hell it doesn't,' I agreed. 'They'll have a sample of every typeface in the building and a few letters written by you at home, if you have a machine there.'

'How do you intend to do it?' he repeated, as much to get me off the subject as anything else.

'I've thought a bit about it,' I told him, 'but I can't work out the details until I've had another look at the archives. The entries in the books are the easiest, because it just means calling in the books for a fictitious check by Head Office and making the changes. No clerk is going to carry figures of that kind around in his head. The problem is going to be cross-referencing every bit of correspondence, internal memos, field reports and so on, in which these figures crop up. When we've done that, we can probably invent two or three extra field units to account for the missing material over the years, and start building up a retro-active file on their activities.'

I poured another cup of coffee and put in some sugar.

'These fictitious field units will have to have been run directly by you as observational experiments, so that they crop up as little as possible in other offices. Where cross-reference to other departments is unavoidable, we shall reduce that to a minimum, concentrating on one or at most two departments, and prepare the paperwork. Then you will have to arrange for promotion or transfer or removal somehow of the clerical staff involved and work the substitution in the department files before the new clerk gets the feel of them. Fortunately, your department heads move around so much from country to country that none of them is going to remember exactly what was going on two years or more ago.'

Wharton looked at me in admiration. 'I imagine you could make a mint of money applying those principles to big companies in Europe or the States,' he said.

'My job is tracing that kind of thing, not perpetrating it,' I snapped. 'There are enough people taking money out of other people's pockets behind their backs; I don't intend to join them. This is an exception. Nobody ever fired a pistol at my daughter before.'

Wharton busied himself with the papers on his desk. His hands were shaking. Finally he pulled himself together with a visible physical effort.

'I have arranged for the same cars as you had before,' he said. 'My secretary will give you the keys. You also have the same room at the Intercontinental. They're not very busy at this time of year. If you want to go and unpack, I'll be in touch with you in the course of the day . . . as soon as I know something,' he corrected himself, as he saw me about to object. Tossing his key-ring across the desk, he said, 'Please ask the porter to lock up my car and bring me the keys when you have taken your case. They steal everything around here.'

I picked up the key-ring and singled out the key with the notch in the head. 'Yes,' I agreed, 'they do, don't they?'

Wharton was going bright red as I left the room.

I kept an eye on the rear-view mirror all the way through the Old City and the residential area behind the hospital and up the hill to the Intercontinental, but if there was a tail, I didn't see it.

The reception clerk gave me a bright smile. 'Very pleased to have you back, Dr Ellis, sir,' he said, and handed me my key with

154

a flourish. 'There is a message for you, sir,' he added, producing an envelope.

It was addressed in an unfamiliar handwriting to 'Dr Ellis, to await arrival'.

The letter inside was in the same handwriting.

I meant it, Mike, all of it. I love him, and I love you, too. What can I do? And now he says you're coming back and it will be all right. Will it? Will it ever be all right again? I don't believe it. There was a look on his face when he said it, I don't know it in English, hunted? cornered? like almost captured? And now that I know what he has done, and you must tell what you must tell, I cannot stand it any more. Forgive me.

T.

I went back to the desk, my head full of dark thoughts.

'When was my room reserved?' I asked the clerk.

'Saturday morning, sir, Mr Wharton rang and reserved your room. The same room as before, if possible, he said. He reserved it for yesterday, too, but the management will not charge you for last night because we are not short of accommodation right now, Dr Ellis.'

Thanks a lot,' I said absently, and headed for the lift.

'You're welcome, sir,' he replied promptly, and snapped his fingers for the boy with my bag.

I lay on my bed with my hands behind my head and thought it over. *Forgive me.* What had I to forgive her? *I know what he has done.* How much did she know? *How* did she know? Where was she? What danger did that mean for her? *I don't believe it.* She was right. It didn't matter what we covered up, it would never be all right again. I groaned aloud as I saw her ghost against the window, leaning her forehead on the glass as the lights sprang up in the evening city below.

Whatever happened now, there was nothing I could do until Wharton's contact gave his approval of my proposal. I dozed fitfully until one, tired out after the poor night I had spent in Teheran, and went down for lunch. Still no word from Wharton. I was sitting in the bar in a corner, keeping a low profile and avoiding any approach which might lead to idle conversation by looking surly – not a difficult rôle to act – when a page came and said there was a call for me.

I took it in the cabin off the bar. It was Wharton, and his voice was tense and urgent.

'Ellis, Mike, thank God – listen, they've found the Range Rover. Up at Bamiyan. But there's no trace of her. I'm going to fly up there this afternoon. Will you come with me?'

'Whoa, steady,' I said. 'Where's Bamiyan? And what Range Rover? And when did it disappear?

'I told you,' he said impatiently, 'she went shopping in our Range Rover on Saturday and didn't come back. The police have been looking for it. Discreetly, of course. They rang me just now. It's been standing at Bamiyan since Sunday evening.'

'Okay,' I interrupted, 'now tell me: where's Bamiyan?'

'In the Valley of the Buddhas,' he said, 'over the border in Afghanistan. Up towards the Salang and off along a dirt road for about 180 kilometres or so into the mountains. It's an easy day's drive in the Range Rover if the weather's good. I could fly there and back in the Beaver this afternoon. As soon as I've had, er, a phone call.'

'How long will that take?' I demanded.

'It's two-thirty now, and they were supposed to call at two,' he said, 'but the phone has been occupied a lot since then. I'll keep it clear now until they ring. Will you meet me at the airport?'

'Right,' I said, and rang off.

I drove down to the airport and looked around for Wharton's black I.D.A. Mercedes. It was not in sight, so I headed for the crew rooms. There were several crewmen in there, smoking and chatting or working at the tables with maps and pocket calculators, but nobody paid me the slightest attention. Suddenly I saw Russell, the Australian pilot who had flown me to Mazar-i-Sharif the previous week. He was sitting in front of a map of Koristan and eastern Afghanistan and copying readings off it on to an old-fashioned pocket calculator with a wipe-clean plastic screen and a revolving frame calibrated in degrees.

'Hello, sport!' he called cheerfully when he looked up and saw me. 'Are you coming along too, then?'

'Not this time, I'm afraid. Have you any idea where I can find Mr Wharton?'

'Sure. He's in the lounge, out that door and first on the right.

I'm picking him up there as soon as I've got our course worked out.'

I thanked him and followed his directions. Wharton was sitting in the corner of a large but spartan lounge, his briefcase on the floor beside him. He had an unhealthy yellowish colour and was staring absently out of the window which overlooked the apron. When I came in he started to get up, but I motioned him to stay where he was and pulled a chair over to sit facing him.

'Well?' I said briefly. He looked around before answering, but the only other people in the room were well out of earshot. He leaned forward just the same.

'I've had the call. They've approved everything. You take the eight forty-five via Teheran from Kabul tomorrow morning, you'll be in Rome at sixteen oh-five. They told me to spend the afternoon starting the work, but I told them I'm still mission chief here and I can't just break certain routine appointments.'

'But they'll know you're here, man, and they can get Russell's flight-plan from the tower,' I objected.

'How will they know that?' he said, startled, and looked around again.

'Do you mean to say you don't know they tail you?' I asked incredulously. 'That grey Opel Kadett this morning, for example.'

Wharton laughed shortly. 'That's not my lot. Those are local boys. They tail everybody who's anybody around here. Of course,' he added soberly, 'there's no knowing where their reports end up. But that takes quite a while, I think, and anyway' – the tension began to show again around his eyes – 'I don't care. We're going to do what they say, but first I have to know about Tupu.'

It was the first time he had ever used Tuula's pet name when speaking to me, and I remembered that he had called me Mike on the phone for the first time, too. As thick as thieves, I thought bitterly.

'Now listen, Ellis,' he interrupted my thoughts, 'I'll be back as soon as I can. I've told Jean to let you have full access to anything you need. If you want to start today . . . ?'

'I don't see any point,' I said flatly. 'I would only have to break off tomorrow morning anyway. I'd rather get my plan together and do it all in one go. Let's stick to the original plan. Call me when you get back, will you?'

He stood up and stooped for his briefcase. At that moment

Russell called out from the doorway, 'Ready when you are, Chief.'

As Wharton turned to go, his shoulders slumped and the lines scored deeply down from his nose to the corners of his mouth, I reached on an impulse for his hand.

'Good luck, Wharton.' I hesitated for a moment, feeling indescribably foolish. Then I just muttered again, 'Good luck. Give Tuula my love.'

He nodded briefly, returned the grip on my hand, and was gone.

I went straight back to the hotel and spent a lot of money getting tight in the bar. The scotch was good, and it dulled my tongue to the point where the bottle of atrocious wine which I had with the dinner was just about bearable. I had a large brandy in my room before turning in, but despite it all I still had a poor night, dreaming of both Tuula and Sophie.

I was awoken by the telephone. I had the impression it was still dark, although it was difficult to tell with the curtains drawn. I knocked a glass of water over fumbling for the bedside lamp and grunted something into the phone.

'Yes. Who's that?'

'It's Russell, the pilot. Sorry to disturb you so early. I'm at the airfield. Mr Wharton has just gone home, but I thought maybe you ought to check him out. He's not in very good shape.'

I was wide awake now. I struggled to a sitting position and squinted at my watch: it was ten past five.

'I'm afraid I've got some bad news, Mr Ellis. Mrs Wharton is dead.'

I closed my eyes and sat in silence for a moment, until Russell called, 'Hello? Are you there?'

'Yes. I'm sorry, Russell. God, how terrible! How did it happen?'

'They found her in the lake at Band-i-Amir. Seems to have been there all weekend; at Band-i-Amir, I mean.' He hesitated, and lowered his voice a little. 'It's not at all clear how she fell in, but it just might have been suicide. She left a note for Mr Wharton in the Range Rover, and he was pretty cut up when he read it.'

'Do you know what it said?'

'No. I saw it, it was written in Finnish. Just two words. He's gone home now – perhaps you'd care to see that he's okay, seeing as you're good friends.'

'Yes, of course. Thank you for thinking of it. What about . . . about Mrs Wharton? Where is she?'

'In the hospital, I suppose. I radioed the tower on my way in and they met us with an ambulance. The local police at Bamiyan took Mr Wharton's statement, kept us up all night, so they didn't make us any trouble here.'

'All right. Thanks again, Russell. I'll see what I can do.'

But I had to collect myself for ten minutes before I could ring Wharton. I looked around the room where I had last seen Tuula. My stomach was tight and aching, but my eyes were dry. I think I was more angry than anything else. Why, I thought, why did she have to suffer? It was so brutally unnecessary.

Wharton answered the phone at once. It was an agonizing conversation, of which I can remember practically nothing but the dry, distant tone. Wharton was very together but somehow infinitely far removed from me. I offered to come round, but he refused politely, and added that there was no need for me to watch over him, he wasn't about to take his own life or anything like that.

I asked him about the note Tuula had left him, and he answered so swiftly that I did not even hear him and had to ask him to repeat it.

'It said, "Forgive me". I still don't know what I have to forgive her for. Rather the other way round, really.'

We agreed that this new development should change nothing in our plans, and that I would leave for Rome that morning. He thanked me formally for my call and rang off abruptly.

So distressed was I at the news that it wasn't until I had almost finished my breakfast that it occurred to me to think about the consequences for myself. I had spent a miserable hour dressing and packing, reflecting on what Tuula had wanted Wharton to forgive her for, what she had had to forgive, and even whether she had anything to forgive me. I saw visions of her lying in the water, the weeds tangled in her long, golden hair, her cornflower-blue eyes wide and reproachful. My movements had been mechanical and detached, so that when the thought flashed across my mind that her death might be neither accident nor suicide, I dropped a teaspoon with a ringing clatter.

On the whole, I decided it was unlikely that Sophie, Katrina or I were in any more danger than before. Until I had finished my task, they needed me, and similarly they needed Sophie and the baby to keep me to my task. It even seemed unlikely to me that Tuula had been murdered. If so, the timing could hardly have been worse.

I checked out of the hotel, leaving the bill for the I.D.A. to settle, and reserving a room for Saturday night. I drove to the airport with the intention of calling Wharton's secretary and having the car picked up there, but to my astonishment Wharton was in the departure hall waiting for me.

He looked tired but collected. He was impeccably dressed and wore a black tie. I gripped his hand silently and thought of the last time I had shaken it.

'I just wanted to see you off,' he said calmly. 'I was on my way in to the office anyway. You have no baggage to check in, have you? Then come this way. Your ticket will be at immigration, and we can avoid the queues. I've already spoken to the Iran Air people.'

He led me through a side door into a service corridor which bypassed the narrow hall where the check-in counters stood. I touched his elbow as he walked ahead of me, and he half turned.

'I don't know what to say, Wharton,' I blurted. 'It's a terrible tragedy.'

His eyes dropped. 'Thanks. You're right, a tragedy, yes. I don't know what to say either.' He turned and walked on ahead.

The corridor ended at the Customs bench, and Wharton raised his hand to the officer who sat picking his teeth behind it. Taken by surprise at seeing such an important person coming from an unexpected quarter, he jumped to his feet with a salute. Wharton pointed to the right and said to me, 'You go that way.' With a final wave he turned left towards the main hall, but stopped short after three paces, while I was still watching his back.

Fortunately he was out of sight of the Customs man, because his behaviour was odd. He stopped in the middle of a stride, took a step backwards, and then backed to the wall and looked towards me. Seeing me watching him, he beckoned with his arm. I went over to him.

'Look round the corner carefully,' he said. There was a row of five check-in desks, seen from the back, and passengers who had completed formalities would pass down the corridor where we stood to go to Customs. 'The second from the left is Iran Air,' he said into my ear. 'Do you see the two men there?'

There were two men with heavy, unmistakably Slavic features arguing earnestly with the ground steward at the check-in.

'Those are two people who work for my contact,' he said. I wondered why he was telling me. 'They won't hurt you, I'm sure, but they seem to have been waiting for you. You had better get on board.'

He drew himself up straight and walked out of the corridor and into the hall. I did not wait to see, because I knew he would not be contacted in such a public place, but strode past the Customs counter, where I got a salute, and went to the immigration desk. I produced my passport for stamping and was given my ticket with a flourish and another salute.

There were no passengers left in the building, but a stewardess was waiting for me at the exit and shepherded me to the 727. I was getting into the habit of having airliners wait for me, I thought.

The first-class cabin was almost empty. I took a window seat and started to fasten my seat-belt. My eyes wandered to the apron I had just crossed, and my fingers stopped moving as I saw the two Russians from the Iran Air desk hurrying across towards the tourist-class entrance in the tail of the aircraft. Well, they had their tickets from the same place, so I guessed they got the same extra service. At that moment, the first-class entrance closed with a heavy thud.

As I sat biting my lip and wondering what this meant for me, there was another thud from the tail of the airliner. A few moments later, the music went off and the cabin lights dimmed as the first engine started up.

There's nothing much they can do to me in the air, I thought, as I started to drift towards sleep.

Twenty-one

I slept through until eleven-thirty, when we landed at Teheran with a gentle bump. Looking around me in the first bewilderment of waking, I recognized the Elburz Mountains and relaxed, until I remembered my tail. Then I relaxed again. It was to be expected, after all; and if they were flying only tourist class, I couldn't be that high a risk, I told myself ironically, in an attempt to stay cheerful. For I knew that this was no economy-class espionage; if they travelled tourist, they had a reason.

I looked over my shoulder on the way into the terminal building and saw them at the head of the passengers emerging from the rear exit. Last on, first off. I went through to the first-class transit lounge and asked the ground steward there for the telephone. I dialled International and placed calls for my home number and American Express in Rome in that order, and then sat and read the Iranian Chamber of Commerce's Illustrated Monthly Bulletin until twenty past one.

The first call had already gone out for my onward flight before I was called to the phone, and my shadows had started nervously taking things off the table and putting them into their pockets and waving at the waiter. They didn't fly much, I thought with grim amusement. For all they knew, of course, I might be intending to stay there and not take the thirteen thirty-five at all.

My home number was unobtainable and Amexco engaged. I had the operator try again, and a third time. But the ground steward was now anxiously looking my way, too, and trying to decide whether to come and get me.

'Still no reply, sir.'

It was one twenty-nine. There was nothing more I could do now. 'That's okay,' I said, 'I'll try later. Is there any charge?'

'No charge at all, sir. Thank you, sir.'

I arrived at the boarding gate simultaneously with the two tails; we all studiously ignored one another. 'Thanks a lot,' I said to the ground steward in passing, and he beamed at me. 'Have a good flight, sir.'

Two hours and twenty minutes by DC8 to Rome. The Alitalia stewardess came to check my seat-belt, and found it fastened.

'Ciao,' I said and got back an icy smile. So much for your friendly advertising, I thought.

I ate a plastic lunch and watched Mount Ararat pass on the starboard quarter until the tray was taken away, and then I knew I would be free to doze until Rome. I closed my eyes and stretched my legs, but the turbulence off the Taurus Mountains kept my snooze near the surface, so that I heard the captain's anouncement from the beginning.

'Ladies and gentlemen, this is Captain Passavanti speaking. My navigator has been in touch with Rome, and it seems that the ground staff there may have begun a strike before we arrive. If this is the case, there is a risk that other Italian airfields may be involved. We shall have a fresh report in about thirty minutes' time and I shall keep you informed. If the strike takes place, we shall divert to Munich at abcut seventeen-fifteen hours local time, and we shall arrange transport for you to Rome at once. Thank you.'

By the end of it I was wide awake. I listened to the Italian version to hear whether there was anything to be gleaned from that, but it corresponded word for word. If I sent a telex from Munich, that would do until the next morning. I snoozed again, and vaguely registered the captain's voice confirming the detour half an hour later.

Munich was grey and drizzly, and as we turned into final approach and I heard the undercarriage rumbling out, we were coming in parallel to the *Autobahn* to Salzburg. I watched the double lines of white and red lights in the early gloom and wondered which my fastest route to Rome would be.

'Auf Wiedersehn,' I said to the icy smile on the way out, and got into the almost empty first-class bus. In the arrival lounge, I waited until my tails had caught up with me before making for the Alitalia desk, and gave them a chance to get into hearing distance before waving for attention.

'Is it certain that the Rome strike will be over tomorrow?' I asked the harassed ground steward on duty.

'Pretty certain, sir.'

'That's not enough, I'm afraid. I have to be in Rome tomorrow. If there is any doubt about flying there, I'll take the night train.'

'We'll get you to Rome all right, sir.' But the smile was

wavering. 'If we can't land, we'll put you on a T.E.E. at our expense.'

'Expense is not the point,' I said. 'Can you guarantee me a landing in Rome tomorrow morning?'

'Well, sir, there is always a chance . . .'

I felt quite sorry for him. 'Can you send a telex to Rome for me?' I said.

He pushed a pad and pen across. I wrote:

Telex to American Express Head Office, Rome, Piazza di Spagna
For Jim Hawthorne personally
Hold dispatches flight rerouted Munich because of strike arriving tomorrow to pick up
Mike

While I had been composing the telex, he had taken a time-table out from under the counter. 'There is the Brenner Express at twenty thirty-five, sir, that will be in Rome at eleven-fifty tomorrow. Will that do you?'

'It will indeed,' I reassured him. 'Thanks a lot.'

I noticed that one of my fellow-travellers had worked his way forward to my elbow, so I carefully copied out:

Brenner Express
dep. Munich 20:35
arr. Rome 11:50

pressing deeply into the pad with the biro, and wondering whether agents still tore off the next sheet and sprinkled it with graphite as they used to do in novels.

I went to the exchange counter before leaving and asked for a supply of one-mark pieces among the change. I tried dialling through to Olmo from a public box in the lounge, but there was still a 'number unobtainable' signal. Either the line's faulty again, I thought, or they have cut it themselves.

I tried the office number in Geneva and was surprised to hear Christine's voice answering on the tape, because she would nor-mally still have been working at that hour. While I listened to her finishing the familiar announcement, I was working out what to say, but my thoughts were interrupted when I heard her say that calls would be answered the next week. That threw me so much that I missed the chance to record a message; I was still wondering what it meant and what to say when the automatic cut-off was triggered by the long silence.

I hung up thoughtfully and turned the message over and over, but I could make no sense out of it, so I dialled again. When Chris's voice said, 'Please speak now,' I replied at once.

'Hi Chris, this is Mike. It is Wednesday evening, I am calling from Munich and travelling to Rome tonight and back out to Koristan tomorrow. I sent a message to Sam, please see that he gets it. The instructions in it are of vital importance. If anybody should be worrying about me for any reason, I am okay and will be back by the second half of next week.'

I left the terminal building and took the shuttle bus to the Bayrischer Hof, next to the station, and booked a sleeper to Rome.

There were still almost two hours to kill, but there was nothing I could do in Munich which would not look like trying to shake off my tail. There were several bars in Schwabing I liked, but to get there and back would be a rush-hour trip in the tube, and they would almost certainly think I was trying to throw them. I rubbed my chin in thought as I waited for the clerk to finish filling out my sleeper ticket, and the stubble reminded me I had forgotten to shave on board the DC8.

I went to the 24-hour barber's shop in the station and read a magazine for a quarter of an hour, and then it was my turn. I ordered the lot: trim, shampoo, shave and facial massage. It took an hour, and I felt like a new man afterwards. When it was finished, I still had time for a plate of *Würst und Sauerkraut* washed down by a *Hofbräu* before boarding the Brenner Express.

With German precision, the train tooted once and pulled smoothly out of the station into the misty drizzle at 'five past half to nine', the improbable local expression for 8:35. Perhaps I shouldn't have dozed so much over Turkey, I thought. Now I wished I had a sleeping pill.

I had pushed ten marks into the conductor's pocket on the way past his compartment, and he knew exactly what it was for. I had the sleeper to myself all night. When he came around to lock up and warn me about thieves, he brought me a tot of brandy from his own stock.

He shut the door and I locked it behind him. Sophie, I'm coming, I thought as the train whistled its way into a tunnel. For a few moments I toyed with the idea of getting off at Terontola, but not very seriously. My business was to get to Rome, pick up those letters, then do what I could about Sophie and Katrina and get back to Nooriabad.

Put in those terms, it seemed very reassuring. To my surprise, I didn't need the sleeping pill. I awoke only once during the night, and even that might have been a dream. From behind a corner of the blind I saw an anonymous but definitely Italian platform, with a sheet of newspaper trying to catch its tail under a bench in the chill night wind, and the pool of light spilling up and down the wall as the dim lamp swayed. Then the platform started to roll away and was gone, awakening a low rumble from under my compartment floor. I woke up again just past Florence.

'We're a bit behind time, but we'll make it up before Rome,' said the conductor cheerily. He didn't seem to have spent a wakeful night at all. Breakfast was a ridiculously expensive puzzle of little cellophane packets. The rich German butter and fresh black bread was worth struggling for, but the coffee was instant and tasted strongly of the plastic cup it came in.

I knew this bit of railway, and the road parallel to it, so well, and my heart was aching as we left Arezzo and passed Olmo serene on its hill in the morning sun. Just an hour's drive, I mused, and then forced myself to sit down and tear my eyes away from that too familiar view. I pulled the blinds down at Terontola, as I didn't want to be recognized, in one of those chances which can upturn lives, and as the Trasimene Lake slipped away on the left I opened the *Spiegel* I had bought in Munich.

Der Spiegel is published on Mondays, so there was ample, excellently researched coverage of the abortive attempt to capture the judge, Hans Siebert, in Berlin the week before, but virtually nothing on the manhunt. The plan had obviously been to hold him in some 'people's prison', and ransom him either for cash or for the freedom of whatever top-rank terrorists were still behind bars after the mass suicide at Stammheim. The captors – five men and a woman – had not known about an alarm connected with the nearest police station, for they had made no attempt to tamper with it. They had been leaving the building when the police arrived, and in the shootout a police officer, a terrorist and Judge Siebert had died and another terrorist was wounded.

The gang had been unusually well armed, and had held the police at bay with machine-guns while they made their getaway, one of them standing up and firing out of the sunshine roof of their Mercedes. I turned a page, and there were *Spiegel* and police photos of the terrorists assumed to have taken part. None of them resembled Jens, Klaus, Hartmut or Ulli.

Word was going around ultra-left-wing circles that the bullet taken out of the judge's heart had been of police calibre, but there was still no official word on the result of the autopsy. The island city had been sealed off, but as the *Spiegel* went to press the dragnet had trawled up nothing but small fish.

As my conductor friend passed, I asked him if there was any news on the progress of the manhunt.

'Not a sign of the Commie buggers,' he said. But pointing to the pictures on the open page of my *Spiegel*, he added: 'There's not much chance of them getting on my train, but if they do, I'll know them!'

We arrived in Rome only one minute late, and I waved to the conductor on the way past his window. I could not see my friends from Kabul, but I went slowly through the crowd, giving way rather than barging, and crossed the foyer to the glass doors on to the chaos of the Piazza Cinquecento, main terminus of all the Rome bus-lines and crowded with the ancient green monsters breathing diesel fumes and racing at unwary pedestrians from every angle. I knew I would catch a cruising taxi faster here than by queueing at the ranks at either side of the station.

I let two go past until I had discreetly made sure that I was not alone, and then flagged one down.

'Piazza di Spagna,' I told him, and he hardly acknowledged me, except to hoist his superb moustache and spit the remains of a toothpick out of the window.

At the American Express office I asked for Jim Hawthorne. He was not there.

'Is he expected back?' I asked. There was a prolonged telephone conversation, and I was invited to go upstairs and speak to his secretary, Miss Wallace.

Miss Wallace had silver fingernails and hair to match. 'Mr

Hawthorne is feeling very poorly today and is not coming in,' she said with a dazzling smile. 'Can I help you, Mr . . . ?'

'My name's Ellis. Did Mr Hawthorne get my telex from Munich yesterday?'

'We get perhaps five hundred telexes a day,' Miss Wallace said. 'What was it about, Mr Ellis?'

I told her word for word and she rifled through a pile of papers on her desk. 'Here we are,' she cried triumphantly. 'It came in overnight – see, there's the time 20:42 – and was sent up to me this morning. I must say I don't really understand what it might mean.'

'You weren't meant to,' I said bluntly, as my heart plummeted downwards. 'Then Mr Hawthorne hasn't seen it yet?'

'No, sir, it will be waiting for him when he comes in, possibly this afternoon.'

My God, Jim, why today, I thought, and gestured at the phone. 'May I speak to the chief cashier?'

'Of course,' she said dialling an internal number. 'Mr Hawthorne just had a long connection with him, too.' I'll bet he did.

Miss Wallace tried another number. 'Mamie dear, is Bernard in the building?' She cupped a hand over the phone, and said in a confidential voice, 'He's just taking some papers to the Embassy.' She started talking to Mamie again, 'And when will he be . . .' ignoring her outraged squeak I pulled the phone out of her hand and asked, 'Are those the papers a Dr Ellis left?'

'That's right,' chirped Mamie. 'He was talking to Mr Hawthorne for ten minutes on the . . .'

'I am Ellis,' I interrupted. 'How did he go, on foot?'

'Yes, sir.' Miss Wallace's round blue eyes showed that she was beginning to guess something unusual was happening. I pushed the phone back into her hand and went down the stairs at a run. I slowed to cross the ground-floor entrance hall, as I didn't want to be stopped by the armed guard, and saw two burly backs, Tweedledum and Tweedledee, turned towards me at the 'Airline Reservations' counter. I tapped one of them at random on the shoulder, and said tersely 'The American Embassy', and left them gaping after me.

I set off at a steady jog and turned into Via Sistina. It was only ten minutes on foot to the U.S. Embassy in Via Veneto, and I tried all the way to remember the chief cashier's face. All I could remember, however, was the back view I had had as he stood in front of the safe. So when I saw it again, bobbing along the pavement in front of me, I recognized it immediately.

Catching him by the elbow as he turned off the pavement into the Embassy gateway, I said, 'Excuse me, but may I withdraw those papers here or must we do it in the bank?

He gaped at me for a moment, and then his face went through several shades of annoyance and relief. 'Good morning, Dr Ellis,' he managed finally. 'I rather thought you weren't coming. I went to great trouble with Mr Hawthorne . . .'

'I know,' I interrupted apologetically. 'I sent him a telex yesterday, but the fools I left it with didn't send it off until after you were closed. My flight was diverted to Germany because of a strike here. Would you like a coffee or should we go back to your office? I suppose you would like me to sign a receipt.'

'No, that's not necessary, Dr Ellis,' he replied, 'if you could just give me back the receipt I gave you. If you have lost it, that's no problem; I would just ask you to endorse my copy in the office.'

'I have it somewhere,' I said vaguely. 'Let's have that coffee while I'm looking.' I steered him over to a plastic and neon bar and ordered two *espressi* while I hunted through my wallet.

My fingers were getting more and more clumsy as I turned the contents over for the third time. A nasty sinking feeling hit me as I remembered finding the wallet in my briefcase during the dawn drive in the jeep with Jens. The wallet they had taken from my pocket and presumably rifled.

'You're quite sure that's my packet?' I asked, and the head cashier's eyebrows indicated clearly that he felt he had gone quite far enough already, handing over confidential papers in a coffee bar, without having his efficiency questioned to boot.

'Certainly, Dr Ellis. Don't you recognize it? You will find the numbers on these seals correspond to those on your receipt.'

'Oh, I'm sure . . . Look, perhaps we had better go back to your office. I can't seem to find my receipt.'

I peeled a thousand lire from the fold of Italian bank-notes and gave it to the barman. The cashier stooped and picked up a slip of yellow paper which fluttered to the floor. 'I think this is what you were looking for,' he said blandly.

I pulled out a handkerchief and wiped my forehead and the

back of my neck. I had not taken much notice of that receipt when Jim Hawthorne had given it to me, because I had been expecting to pick up the papers again from his own hands within three days. Probably I had just stuffed it in among the bank-notes, I could not remember at all. Thanks to that carelessness, Jens had perhaps not found it in my wallet. 'Two envelopes, bearing seals number 228 and 229, marked (1) For immediate, personal and confidential delivery ...' *Two envelopes.* Had Jens read that, and only pretended to believe my story about withdrawing cash from my account?

The cashier took the packet with the bright Amexco seals on it from his briefcase once more, and we ceremoniously exchanged it for the receipt. The coffee arrived on the counter. The door opened and Tweedledee came in.

Of course, it could have been Tweedledum; I didn't know which had come in and which had stayed outside. The chief cashier finished his coffee, thanked me, and promised to give my very best regards and apologies to Jim Hawthorne. He turned to go and bumped into Tweedledee, who was standing as close as he could to us in the half-empty bar without actually walking on my feet.

'E l'altra busta dov'è?' I asked the cashier. Somehow I had to find out about that other envelope. It was a hundred to one that a Russian agent working in the Middle East would not understand Italian.

Fortunately, the reply came in Italian too, accompanied by a quizzical look; I felt the cashier thought he was getting the measure of this eccentric Englishman. 'Already posted.'

'Benone,' I said, satisfied, 'that's exactly right. Thanks again.'

My shadow could hardly wait until the cashier was out of the door before opening his mouth to speak. I cut him off before he could start. 'Let's sit down,' I said, and went over to a wall table without looking back. He sat down heavily beside me, and I held out the little packet. As he reached out to take it, I tweaked it out of his fingers. A look of anger came over his face.

The waiter came around flicking the tabletops with a glass-cloth and we waited until he had wandered over to the TV from which he immediately produced a lot of noise, before continuing simultaneously.

As Tweedledum said, 'The papers . . .' I said 'Here you are,' and put them back on the table. Fortunately the waiter turned the sound down, otherwise I would have had to shout. 'Just one favour you could do me for them. Ask your bosses if I can see my wife and child before I go back to Koristan tomorrow morning. I will be in this bar again at three o'clock.'

He snatched up the packet without replying and ripped it open with a coffee-spoon. A glance inside satisfied him. I don't imagine he even knew what the documents were; he was probably just supposed to check that they weren't blank pages, or folded newsprint, or perhaps photocopies.

'I can ask,' he said. 'But of course, I cannot...'

'I know you can't decide. Just go and ask somebody who can. Three o'clock here.'

He left without a backward glance, and I wondered how good my chances were of seeing Sophie before I left. They were better than I imagined. As I got up to leave, my glance fell on the TV, and I sat down again with a bump.

Sophie was talking straight into the camera.

SOPHIE

Twenty-two

Bruna drove all the way to Florence. We were getting hungry as we left the broad, well-irrigated plain that is the valley of the Po at Bologna and started climbing into the rugged Apennines, and we stopped at the highest point to have lunch. The service area was called Aglio, which means garlic, and the chef seemed to have taken the hint.

After that it was a long, twisting drop down to Prato and Florence. Prato is probably the biggest misnomer in Italy. The name means meadow, but all you see are power stations, factories, and dozens of gaudy, tasteless advertising billboards. Florence is green and attractive after this 'meadow'. We left the *auto-strada* at the Florence North exit and at about three o'clock stopped at a bar in Perètola to look up an address.

I was pretty sure that 'John in Florence', as Mike had written to Sam, would be John Morris of the United Press Agency, whom I had met briefly once in Rome. If he wasn't, it was going to be a long search.

Somebody with a strong American accent answered the U.P.A.

number, so I asked in English for Mr Morris. 'He has a visitor, ma'am. They went to lunch about an hour ago and John said he wouldn't be back in today. Can I help you?'

'Yes,' I said, screwing up my eyes and hoping hard. 'You could tell me if the visitor was an American from Geneva called Sam Greaves. I have to get in touch with him. It's urgent.'

'Why, yes, ma'am.' I gave Bruna a thumbs-up sign through the glass. 'I believe they went to the Trattoria Pitti, just off the Ponte Vecchio, and I wouldn't be surprised if they're still there now.'

'Thanks a lot,' I said sincerely. 'I'll check there, and if they've gone I'll ring you again. If you should see or hear from them, would you mind telling them that Sophie Ellis is looking for them and it's urgent as hell? And please to leave a message where I can find them at once.'

'Sure, Miss Ellis, it'll be a pleasure.'

As I hung up, I pressed the return button as I always do. My *gettone* sometimes comes back. This time eight came back, and everybody in the bar looked round as I hit the jackpot. I felt it was a good omen, and used them to pay for our two coffees. The barman grinned. 'Courtesy of the Telephone Company,' he said, and waved as we left.

'Come on, kid,' I called to Bruna as we ran down the street towards the Mirafiori parked round the corner. I was feeling more cheerful than I could remember. 'The Trattoria Pitti, do you know it?'

'No,' said Bruna, 'but you seem to. Give me directions. What's happening there, anyway?'

I told her we were chasing two fascinating Americans. One was my husband's partner, and that wasn't much use because he was madly in love with their secretary (which may or may not have been true, I had no idea). But the other was tall, lean and dark, a reporter and an art history major, and might be fun.

Her eyes sparkled as she threw her head back to laugh, as she often did, and I thought, Bruna baby, am I glad I have you along! Or rather, you have me along, since I've done nothing at all yet.

She dropped me right outside the trattoria, and set off again looking for a parking space. Sam and John were sitting against the wall right opposite the entrance. They looked up together in annoyance as I stopped next to their table, then gratifyingly pleased surprise came over their faces as they recognized me. They were sitting at a place in a row of alcoves, with back-to-back benches fixed to the floor. Both tried to push the table away to stand up, and they knocked each other back on to their seats.

I laughed with them until something snapped inside and Sam was standing up and holding me in his arms and I was crying on to his shoulder. I thought absurdly how understandable these women are who leave things to their menfolk. All I wanted to do was to turn the whole thing over to Sam and go and cry somewhere. . . .

It was comforting to be held by dear Sam. He is a large, chunky bear who looks something like Spencer Tracy. He has big, gentle brown eyes and big, gentle hands and a deceptively ponderous manner with a very fast brain behind it. He is so large that he appears to move awkwardly; but I remember Mike once showing me over breakfast a newspaper article about a military tattoo, during which the manœuvrability of a tank was demonstrated by having it crack fresh eggs with the tip of the gun-barrel, and he said, 'That reminds me of Sam!'. It was an indescribable relief to find him, and after a moment of crying into his jacket, which smelt pleasantly of tobacco, I felt much more myself.

He sat me down with an arm around my shoulder and gave me a handkerchief, murmuring something soothing. John obviously wanted to disappear through the floor. Then Bruna was standing there and, taking everything in at a glance, she said, 'She's been through a lot, you know. It's the first chance she's had for a real cry.'

John stood up again politely, and when I had introduced them to Bruna we all had a large brandy, I for medicinal purposes and the others to keep me company.

I sniffed my tears to a halt and managed a wry smile at Sam. 'Sorry to interrupt you two, but has anyone here heard from Mike lately?'

'Yes,' said Sam promptly. 'I had this weird note. . . .'

'The one Christine showed me, from the man in the hotel?' I interrupted.

'Yes. Nothing more since that one, though,' said Sam.

'We were just discussing it,' put in John. 'I may have an idea about tracing this. . . .'

Again I interrupted and stopped him just in time. 'Yes, okay. Let's talk about this somewhere else. Have you been discussing it here?'

'Yes,' said Sam, somewhat shamefacedly, 'but we were speaking in English until Bruna came along.'

John looked at his watch. 'If I'm going to find out anything today about the lady in question, it'll have to be soon,' he objected. 'The Consulate closes in half an hour.'

'Could Sam and I use your office, John, and wait for you there?'

'Sure, of course, good idea,' he said. Turning to Bruna, he asked, 'Are you busy now? I have an idea. Maybe you could help me.' Then he looked embarrassed and turned to me. 'If that's all right, of course.'

'Sure,' I said, 'Bruna's our mainstay right now. Do you want to play detective, Bruna?'

She kicked me under the table and said, 'Depends who's going with me. I think it'll be okay. I might even enjoy it.'

'Right,' I said, 'let's move.' And as we all had our heads close together over the table to stand up, I added hurriedly in a low voice, 'And don't take any chances whatever. Nobody must know who is trying to find out what. I'm not being melodramatic, and I'm not kidding.'

My expression must have convinced them, because John gave me a sharp look. 'You got yourself together again quickly,' he said seriously.

'She always does,' said Bruna, and put the tip of her tongue out at me for a second.

We went over to the cash-desk, where Sam paid. Good old Sam, I thought in relief, watching his familiar, reassuring face again. Nobody knew how Sam acquired clients, with his lack of push, his slow ways, and his baggy suits always in need of an iron. But anybody who read his reports knew how he kept them.

John Morris was a contrast. Ten years younger than Sam – about my age – and with a rather gaunt, sardonic face, he had the quick, economic movements of an athlete. I hoped we were going to have him on our side, and catching Bruna's eye I realized that she was thinking something similar. I hoped she wasn't under-estimating Sam; people often did at first sight, and usually regretted it bitterly later.

Bruna's Mirafiori was right outside the door. 'Someone drove off as you went inside,' she said. The sight of a traffic warden twenty metres away got things moving.

'Sophie, let's walk,' said Sam. 'John's office is five minutes away.'

'See you there,' said John and Sam and I set off through the tightly-packed throng of late-season tourists on the narrow sidewalk. It was impossible to talk on the street, as we were often obliged to go single file between the cars and the walls of the ancient *palazzi*. We crossed Ponte Vecchio past the jewellers' shops and passed under the Vasarian Corridor, the sixteenth century passageway built by the Medici. Sam led the way to the right into Via Lambertesca, and suddenly turned into an art gallery. The entrance to the U.P.A. office was at the back of the showroom.

I greeted the young man who had answered the phone, and he showed us into John's office, which had a splendid view of the Uffizi Gallery and the Palazzo Vecchio with its soaring tower. Sam sat on the windowsill and looked at me quizzically.

'Now tell me what the hell is going on,' he said.

I brought him up to date in about twenty minutes, while his face became progressively grimmer. He hardly interrupted, except for an occasional 'How?' or 'When?', and when I had finished and added by the way that Bruna knew virtually nothing, he nodded agreement. 'I told John as little as possible,' he said.

Sam didn't waste time on commiseration. Sam wouldn't, although I saw on his face that he suffered vicariously as he heard my story. He thought for a moment, and then came and sat down opposite me at John's desk.

'The way I see it,' he said slowly, drawing indecipherable box-and-arrow plans on a notepad as he spoke, 'is that you and Katrina are safe as long as you keep away from Olmo and from me, and that I am safe as long as I keep away from you. That just leaves Mike,' he added ironically. I nodded.

'But our only lead on Mike at the moment is through this Roswita character,' he went on. 'Today is Wednesday. Mike is probably in Koristan. But who the hell do they want him to kill in Koristan? There's nobody there so big they couldn't tackle him themselves. I just don't get it. It doesn't tie up at all. Either he's not in Koristan, or' and he looked up at me, 'they're not getting him to kill anybody. That was just a story to keep you quiet.'

I felt zonked by this idea. It had never occurred to me. 'Can we risk going on that assumption?' I asked Sam. 'If it turns out to be true after all, Mike might already be deep in trouble.'

'Oh, sure,' he said, 'I'm not suggesting we make any rash assumptions. Let's cover ourselves both ways.' He thought in silence for a moment, and then his face cleared and he started writing. I heard the phone ring in the outer office, and then the squawkbox on the desk said, 'It's for you, just pick up the receiver.'

As Sam carried on writing, I took up the phone and said, 'Hello?'

'It's John here. We've got . . . er, Madame R, and Bruna was marvellous. Do you want pix as well?'

'Sure, if you can.'

'Okay,' John replied. 'I'm going to our processing lab. It's two blocks from where you are. I'll be there in, say, forty minutes.'

The phone clicked and he was gone. As Sam pushed over the pad, I told him, 'They'll be here in forty minutes with Roswita's address and pictures.'

'Fine,' said Sam. 'That's a real lead! Now listen: Mike left me the telex number of the Koristan mission. We'll send them this message. And then we'll get out and have a look at the lie of the land.'

I read his untidy scribble:

Telex to I.D.A. Mission Nooriabad Koristan
Attention Dr Michael Ellis visiting from Geneva
Please ring your office immediately before taking any further action. K. is very well and has gone abroad to friends. S. is with me now and sends love.
Sam.

'Maybe they could trace us to Florence via the telex number,' I said doubtfully.

'Hell, you're right,' said Sam, and crossed out the last sentence, substituting:

I saw S. in Rome and she sends love.

'That'll put them off the trail,' he said.

'In that case put them right off it and make it Paris.'

'No,' he objected, 'Mike might try to find a message hidden that isn't there – fly to Paris to look for you, or something else. Rome means "safe" as far as Mike is concerned. There's another thing,' he added, 'we don't need to push the button on the telex that sends our call sign. It's very bad form – rather like sending an anonymous letter – but if we're quick enough and switch off before they notice and press their button, we're okay.'

'I don't follow,' I said, frowning.

He led the way to the machine. 'When you press the button to request the other party's call sign, it comes with this symbol, look.' He picked up a telex at random from a spike and pointed out the sign. 'Now, if you send a fictitious call sign by hand at the same point in the message that the genuine one would normally occupy, it would take an experienced or suspicious operator to notice that that little symbol is missing.'

I nodded in agreement. We had sent the telex, giving the number of Mike and Sam's office in Geneva as the sender, by the time John and Bruna burst in the door. John was holding some dripping prints in his hand. He waved to his assistant, who seemed to be more interested in Bruna, and led the way through to his office.

'Semplicissimo,' he said proudly, spreading the wet prints on a glass table-top. They're not very well fixed and will be yellowed in two days or so, but I still have the negatives.'

There was an extremely attractive shot of Bruna posing like a tourist in front of the eighteenth-century Holy Apostles' Church with its thirteenth-century Romanesque belfry just coming into view at the top, and also a close-up of her laughing at the camera. 'Not those, *cretina*,' she said, snatching them away just as I wanted to pick them up. 'I'm having those!'

'If you leave me your telephone number,' said John slyly, 'you can have them properly fixed and framed.'

'Have you two been out playing tourists or detectives?' I said in exasperation.

'Both,' said John proudly. 'While I pretended to shoot Bruna, look who happened to walk down the street.' He gestured back at the table-top, and Sam and I bent over the prints. John was looking particularly disingenuous, but I didn't want to give him the satisfaction of being asked how he had done it.

There were six prints of a dark-haired, snub-nosed woman of about thirty-five, wearing a disapproving look. They had the flat perspective and shallow depth of field of very high focal-length tele-shots. They showed her from several angles. She had clearly not noticed that she was being photographed.

'Excellent, John!' I cried in approval.

'How did you get them so fast?' wondered Sam.

'We have a lab set up for that kind of thing, complete with wire transmitter. It's amazing what you can do if you have working tables for high-temperature development. We got her name and address, too.'

By this time I could contain my curiosity no longer. 'All right, Sherlock: how did you do it?'

'I hoped you'd ask me that. We just walked straight into the Consulate and I said I had been told to ask for a Roswita somebody, but I couldn't remember the surname. So this guy on the door said they had only one called Roswita, that was Fräulein Reiners, and was it about holiday bookings? We went in and asked for her, and now there's just about nothing we don't know about skiing in Bavaria. I tried to get her talking, but all I could find out is that she comes from Hanover.'

'The Consulate was closing soon, added Bruna, 'so we waited for her on the street. And I got her address out of the phone book while we were waiting.'

Roswita Reiners lived in Badia a Ripoli, and we saw Mike's point about being near the *autostrada*; this is a residential suburb near the Florence South exit.

'So what now?' asked Bruna impatiently, when we had all examined the prints.

'Nothing at all for you,' I said firmly, knowing the moment had come when I would have to extricate her. 'You have been just incredible, and I don't know how to thank you, but it's certainly not going to be by dragging you into danger.'

I hadn't reckoned with Bruna. 'You're not dragging me at all,' she said equally firmly, 'Non mi trascini del tutto. I am going, and I am going of my own accord. You are going to need somebody they will not recognize.'

'That's me,' said John quickly.

'And me too,' said Bruna emphatically.

I looked at Sam helplessly, and he shrugged. 'I can't see what the danger is,' he said judiciously. 'At this stage we're going to do no more than check on the lie of the land. And anyway, it's on Bruna's way home, right next to her motorway entrance.' Poor Sam. He will not forgive himself for that decision for the rest of his life.

So we picked up Bruna's car at the Piazza Signoria and headed out for the suburbs. It was the rush-hour, and it was difficult in that indisciplined traffic to rendezvous with John and Sam, driving the office *Cinquecento*, in the square across the Ponte San Niccolò. Finally we saw them pull in in front of us. Sam in the passenger seat waved a streetmap at us, so we followed them out to Badia a Ripoli.

After two wrong turnings, involving U-turns and wild gesturing (he had not lived in Italy for donkey's years for nothing), John flashed the brake-lights twice and the right turning-indicator once, and we saw on the right-hand side of the street an apartment block of some six storeys with a tired garden in front of it. We carried on in convoy until we had rounded the next corner, and then the men came and sat in the back of the more spacious Mirafiori for a conference.

The street had been residential, with a sprinkling of shops and a supermarket. There was plenty of traffic, both motor and pedestrian, at this hour, so there was no great danger of attracting undue attention.

'Just what exactly are we looking for?' asked John, and suddenly everybody seemed to want an answer from me.

'Nothing at this stage, really,' I said uncertainly. 'We just have no information at all, and anything we can find out is useful. Bruna, you and John can go inside the block, because they don't know you, and find out what floor she lives on, how big the apartment is, and so on. If you can get invited into another apartment on the same side on some pretext, we can assume theirs will have the same basic layout. And Sam and I can check the area around. We'll meet up in the supermarket.'

'Okay,' said Bruna with a gay smile, 'let's go, then. I'll bet this is more exciting than art history, anyway.'

John looked from one to another of us. 'Somebody around here has been gossiping. All right, then – come on, Watson.'

Sam and I gave them two minutes' start and then started to explore the area. There was absolutely nothing of interest to us, no foreign-registered cars or motor bikes, nothing. After a while, I said to Sam, 'Let's have a last look at that apartment block and then go to the rendezvous.' I didn't dare to say it, but I had begun to suspect that we were wasting our time.

The apartment block was tall and narrow. Its six storeys were topped by a flat roof, and inside there would certainly be only one small apartment on either side of a central staircase. Through the glass entrance doors, we could see no sign of a lift at the foot of the stairs. The outside walls were sheer and unadorned, with flaking yellow plaster unbroken by balconies.

It was the only building on the street which was not built right next to the sidewalk; instead, it was set about twenty-five metres back. What might once have been – or had perhaps never become–a garden between the front face and the sidewalk extended around both sides into unashamedly waste ground littered with paper, coloured plastic bags, and old baby-carriages and bicycles.

Finally we made for the supermarket, picked up a trolley and walked off down the aisles and compared notes as we sauntered. After ten minutes of buying nothing but a carton of milk, I said to Sam, 'This is ridiculous. Let's pick them up outside.'

'Okay,' he said, and we turned back to stand in line at the cash-desk. I put the milk carton in a plastic bag and Sam held the door open for me. A young woman outside loaded down with shopping thought he was holding it for her, and she and I collided in the doorway. I dropped the shopping, but it wasn't because of the collision.

I looked into her grey-blue eyes, hypnotized, and whispered, 'Ulli!'

Twenty-three

Ulli was sprinting down the street and I was standing there shaking from head to foot while the pool of milk spread slowly from the mouth of the bright blue plastic bag. Sam was asking me something and the shops, the street and the pavement were going round and round.

After what seemed like an hour I raised my face with a great effort and said to Sam, 'That was Ulli. The girl in Olmo.'

At once he grabbed my hand and pulled me along down the street. Incredibly Ulli was still in sight, running like a rabbit for the apartment building. In retrospect, I don't think it was panic; she was always too controlled for that. I think she reckoned on losing us in that building that she knew and we didn't, and escaping out of the rear entrance. But this is all hindsight. At the time my initial shock gave way to an exultant feeling that her nerve had broken.

We raced down the sidewalk, cannoning off people and walls, and as though in slow motion Bruna and John appeared on the path which led from the entrance of the block to the street and I screamed '*Fermatela!* Stop her!' and Bruna spread her arms to block Ulli's path and Ulli dropped a bag of vegetables and took a gun out of her pocket and Bruna didn't budge so Ulli shot her and then she was gone, inside the building, and John and Sam and I were kneeling around Bruna and looking at each other, dazed.

Bruna was already dead when she hit the ground. Her eyes were open wide in surprise, and a thin trickle of blood ran from the corner of her mouth and stopped on her chin. A dark patch was spreading across her breast. I unzipped the front of her parachute suit and tried to feel her heart beating but I found only a warm, sticky mess, and jerked my hand away in horror.

People were screaming and running away from us; others were running towards us and looking around to see what the commotion was. I thought stupidly, poor Bruna, you're not ever going to need that baby-seat after all, I'll give it back to Stefano and Maria. And other silly things you think when the world is collapsing around your ears.

A crowd had gathered, and somebody held out a jacket to cover

Bruna's face. In a little while I heard the sirens wailing nearer and nearer. Sam said, 'We've got to stop them getting away.'

'Damn right,' said John grimly. The world gradually stopped whirling and my tears were drying on my face.

The crowd parted and there was a *carabiniere* with a pistol in his hand. At the end of the corridor through the people I glimpsed for a moment the other one – they always came in pairs, like bricklayers – leaning watchfully on his blue and white Alfa Romeo and covering the scene with a submachine-gun, and at that moment I was in command of myself again.

'There are German terrorists in that apartment block,' I told the policeman, pointing, and the crowd looked up with open mouths. 'They may be the ones that killed the judge in Germany last week. They have killed my friend because she tried to stop them. You have to see that they don't get away.'

'Third floor on the right,' added John authoritatively.

There were more sirens, and one of the *carabinieri* cleared the crowd away while the other spoke into his radio. John and Sam pulled me into the shelter of a doorway and suddenly the street was deserted except for the two police cars with their blue lights revolving. The siren of the second one was dying on the evening air.

There was a hurried conference among the four policemen, and then two of them approached the doorway in which we were sheltering while the other two drove the cars in opposite directions down the middle of the street and stopped the traffic. The emptiness of the scene was deceptive; as a little old lady with grey hair walked out of a laundry with a bulky paper packet under her arm, before the policemen had even noticed her twenty voices called from all directions and she scuttled back under cover like a beetle.

I could hear more sirens approaching as one of the policemen said to me, 'How do you know they are German terrorists? And how do you know which apartment they are in?'

'They were hiding in my house in Olmo,' I improvised, 'but then I got away. I even heard them mention Badia a Ripoli, so I came to see if I could find out anything more substantial before I went to the police. One of them – the girl who shot my friend – saw me in the street.'

It was a thin enough story and would not hold together long, but it would have to do for the moment. John produced his press credentials and said, 'It's true. They may have captured this lady's husband as a hostage.' I looked at him sharply and wondered where he had got that from, and then I remembered that Bruna had been overhearing this and that and putting things together.

Bruna. She was still lying on the concrete path to the apartment block. Two squads of police in battledress, carrying machine-guns and shields, came running down the street from opposite directions and stopped, out of sight of the apartment, against the house-fronts to the left and right of the block.

'Christ, they're fast,' Sam blurted.

Another police car came down the street and stopped in front of our doorway, rocking on its springs. A captain in impeccable uniform with highly-polished black riding-boots leapt out and came over to us, a walkie-talkie in his hand. His car moved on out of sight of the block.

Up to that moment, I had been able to carry on the automatic motions of life without much difficulty; everything seemed a little out of focus, and my voice was coming from a long way away, but I don't think anybody else would have noticed the difference. I registered the police captain asking questions, but it all seemed so detached, so far distant.

Then I realized that John was holding my arm and asking me something, that people had been asking me things for some time, in fact, and it was still all right until I tried to speak, but then the film broke. I wanted to cry, but I couldn't do that either, and then John and Sam were half carrying me into an apartment and that was all I knew for a while.

When I came to, I was lying on a strange bed in a strange room, and Sam was sitting next to it watching over me. I felt a warm flood of relief on seeing his familiar figure and reached for his hand.

'Oh Sam!' I said. 'What's happened? Where are we? Oh, I'm so glad you're here! What time is it?'

Sam squeezed my hand and smiled. 'One question at a time!' he said, but he didn't answer any of them. 'A police doctor has had a look at you and reckons you're about all in. They wanted to ask you all sorts of questions, but he said you were in no fit state to answer them. He wanted to put you in hospital, but I had a word with him and he agreed to a hotel, as long as somebody keeps an eye on you. How do you feel now?'

I sat up and pushed the eiderdown away, for the room was hot and stuffy. 'Not too bad, really. I have a muzzy sort of head, but I'll be all right. Where are we, Sam?'

'We're in an apartment the police have occupied, right across the street from Roswita's house. They have set up a sort of command post here, and they are in telephone contact with the gang and with several other families in the block.'

I looked at my watch. It was eight o'clock and I was feeling dreadful, but I wasn't going to say that to Sam. 'Where's John?' I asked him.

'They've sort of blackmailed him into respecting the news blackout by making him a collective press representative. He knew such a lot about the beginning that they decided to keep him where they could watch him. Right now that means he can't file a story, but when the curtain is lifted he will have an on-the-spot report.'

'And . . . them? What are they doing?'

Sam's face was grave. 'It's bad, I'm afraid. They've got two hostages in the apartment with them, a kid and his mother, and they're holding the stairs. Everybody below them has been evacuated, but on their level and the floors above they are holding about fifteen people. They say they are going to blow the top off the building, with everybody inside, if they don't get a 707 out of the country by midnight. They are calling themselves the "Commando Gudrun Ensslin" now. That's the name of one of the Baader-Meinhof people who killed herself in jail, or who was killed in jail; nobody seems to be able to prove it one way or the other.'

'Are they going to give them the aeroplane, Sam?'

'I don't know. I heard that the Foreign Minister is looking for countries prepared to accept them, and they have been told on the phone that helicopters are being prepared for them – I overheard the call myself. But the major who has taken over command here says the Minister of Defence is holding out for a hard-line approach. I just can't think what the Defence Ministry has to do with it.'

'That's easy,' I told him. 'The *carabinieri* are an arm of the military. But what am I going to tell them?'

'What do you mean?'

'Well, why were we here in the first place? Why didn't we go to the police in Olmo at once? I can't possibly tell them about Mike until I know where he is and what he has done.'

'I don't think that's much problem, Sophie. Mike you can leave out of it altogether. You can account for yesterday and today more or less with the truth: that you panicked and wanted to get Katrina to safety first. Anyway, the doctor has said that he doesn't want you to be interrogated before tomorrow. It's just that . . .' Sam stopped and looked worried.

'What is it, Sam?'

'The police major wants you at least to talk to their psychologist first. I mean tonight. You see, you mentioned that they were in your house in Olmo, and they think you are the person who can help them get the feel of their psychology, so that they know what to expect and how to prevent any more bloodshed.'

I thought it over, and it didn't seem too bad. I was just so terribly tired. 'It'll be okay, Sam. Especially if you can come with me.'

He stood up. 'I'll tell the major you're awake and we would like to go,' he said and left the room.

I looked out cautiously between the curtains, but the room was at the back of the house. There was a dismal courtyard and the back of the building opposite. A cordon of police was keeping a crowd of sightseers at bay.

The door behind me opened, and somebody murmured a polite 'Permesso?'

Sam had come back, and with him was a police officer. John followed them in and gave me a reassuring smile, but otherwise kept out of the conversation altogether.

The major was in his middle fifties, short and plump, with greying hair and darting eyes which seemed to take in everything. But his most outstanding feature was his considerate manner; he actually introduced himself formally by name, the first time I had known a policeman to do so.

'Buona sera, signora. I am Major Salti, commander of the Florence anti-terrorism squad. I hope you are feeling a little better.'

'Thank you, Major,' I stammered. 'I'm not too well at all, but of course I want to help you in any way I can.'

Salti went over to the window and looked out before replying. As I remembered that I had been standing there when he came in, I thought: this man doesn't miss much. And I hoped he was going to follow the doctor's orders.

'Signora, I have heard some of what you have been through, and at our doctor's suggestion I think we can leave any formal interrogation until tomorrow. These signori have given me all the personal details that police reports always require,' he gave a wry smile, 'but I do have a request for this evening, if you can possibly manage it.'

'Mr Greaves has already mentioned something, Major.'

He shot a slightly displeased look at Sam, but carried on, 'As you probably realize, signora, police methods have become quite refined in recent years. Especially in my field, we make a lot of use of psychological expertise. In fact, in this kind of situation it is about all we have to go on. It would be of immense help to me in handling this business if you would be prepared to talk to our psychologist about these people.'

Courteous as he was, his direct look made it clear that it would be very difficult to refuse. Indeed, I could see how valuable my contribution would seem to him. It was just that I had not yet got my story together. Again, that was quite possibly one reason why he was pushing so hard.

'I would be glad if I could be of any help at all, Major,' I said, and I caught a flicker of relief on his face.

'That is very good of you, signora. I shall send you in a car to meet my assistant at the police headquarters. If you would not object, I would suggest you talk over dinner in our officer's canteen. The food is good, and you will not be disturbed. To be quite honest, Dr Biffi – that is my assistant – is working very hard and will be awake all night, and you would be doing us all a service if you would meet him on the spot.'

We left the room together. John murmured, 'Chin up!' as I passed him. Several policemen or soldiers in combat overalls were in the hallway, and weapons, riot-shields, helmets and other bits of equipment were scattered in orderly heaps. Through an open doorway, I saw three more men in a bedroom relaxing but fully dressed and ready for action.

The sitting room of the apartment seemed to be the command post. Lines from three field telephones were strung up through the doorway, and a policeman with headphones sat in front of a radio set on the table. A large-scale plan of the street was spread out next to it. Grey-painted metal screens stood across the window, cutting off the light from the street outside.

For a moment I thought how ridiculous it was that the television had been switched on, but then something about the picture made me look at it again. I recognized on the screen the house opposite, into which Ulli had fled. A video-tape deck was standing on top of the set, and following the cables I saw a TV camera on a mount screwed to the windowframe near the top, just nudging the curtains aside.

'Those are bullet-proof screens,' said Sam at my shoulder. 'That way they can watch the house without being seen or shot at.'

While Major Salti was telephoning, I watched the TV screen, but the street was completely deserted. The picture might have been a still. The place where Bruna's body had lain was clearly visible, but there was nothing there now. I turned away, feeling desolate, and was about to ask Sam what they had done with her, when Salti hung up and said, 'Dr Biffi is ready and waiting for you, signora.' To Sam he added, 'I believe you have a car. When you have arranged your hotel, perhaps you would pick Signora Ellis up at the headquarters.'

'I have the keys to Bruna's car,' explained Sam to me. 'I took them before ... when the ambulance came. I'll get my bag from John's apartment. I was going to stay there tonight. I'll pick you up in an hour or so.'

We took our leave of John, and made for the rear exit to the apartment, where a police driver was waiting for me. As we approached the door, John called after us, 'Watch out for the photographers out there!'

He was right. As we left the building, there was a blaze of flash-bulbs but, because we were prepared for them, I don't imagine they got a single picture they could use, or at least one in which I was recognizable. I picked up my bag from the Mirafiori and got into the police car which was right behind it.

Fortunately, the driver was uncommunicative, and as we sped back towards the centre of Florence I was glad to have a chance to think over my story and decide how to edit it. The driver used his siren to herd the traffic like a flock of sheep, and it was not more than ten minutes later that I was being asked to sit down and wait in a grey room decorated with 'Wanted' posters.

Within another three minutes, a *carabiniere* opened the door and stood aside to let somebody come in. He was an unusually tall man for an Italian, with shaggy, jet-black hair, a Fidel Castro beard to match, and big gentle eyes. He wore jeans and a denim jacket over a khaki, military-style shirt such as communist demonstrators often favour. A brilliant red scarf was knotted, cowboy-style, around his neck.

This can only be one of Major Salti's plain-clothes agents, who watches the developments in student unrest, I thought. But he came straight to me with his hand outstretched.

'Mrs Ellis?' He spoke excellent English, with a trace of American accent. 'Very pleased to meet you. My name is Carlo Biffi. Major Salti suggested we chat together over dinner.'

I got to my feet and hoped as I followed him that my surprise had not been too marked.

Carlo Biffi led me through the high, echoing corridors of the *questura,* across a courtyard where half a dozen squad cars were parked, and into a warm well-lit room where several officers were eating singly or in small groups. Some waved greetings at him, and there was no trace among his fellow-officers of any feeling against this unconventional policeman. This surprised me, as the Italian police are purported to be right-wing, and the more so the higher up they are in the hierarchy. I concluded that Biffi must enjoy an impeccable professional reputation.

We took a table away from the other diners, in a corner of the room. He limited our conversation to small talk until the *pastasciutta* was served, and I learned that he had spent four years at Harvard.

Finally he got down to business.

'Mrs Ellis,' he said, 'I know you have been through a harrowing time and you need rest. But we are badly in need of information, and some of it might be stored in your memory. Sooner or later you would realize it and say, I wish I had thought of that in time. Other pieces might not even be recognizable as useful, because you have not had to cope with terrorists before. Maybe I can help you fit some of it together.'

'I'll try anything you suggest, doctor,' I said.

'Right. Well I'd like you to tell me the whole story again, and we'll see what we can make of it.'

So I went over the past four days once again. Biffi asked me few questions and seldom interrupted. When I got close to anything to do with Mike, I gained time to think by concentrating on my food. I had said at the start that he had been abroad on business, and that I had not seen him for two weeks. When recounting my escape, I remained silent about my role in starting the fire, for after Klaus's death I was afraid I might be held on a homicide charge. Instead, I told Biffi I had seen the blaze break out behind me.

Most of the questions he did ask me were concerned with the murder of Marino and Giorgio. I was guiltily aware that I was probably withholding a key piece of information when I did not tell him of my certainty that part of the motive had been to convince me that the terrorists meant business. He was also very interested in my impression that Ulli had not seemed to fit in with the others.

The implication of my story – and Biffi seized the inference at once and put it into words – was that they had been expecting Mike and had wanted to capture him for some reason connected with his work.

Finally my tale was over. He pushed away his empty coffee-cup and took out a paper pack of stumpy, twisted *Toscano* cigarillos. He lit one and blew out a dense cloud of evil-smelling smoke.

'The way I see it,' he said, 'we are confronted here with exponents of the typical West German breed of terrorist that we have been watching very closely ever since the R.A.F. started making headlines.'

'I don't see what the Air Force has to do with it.'

Biffi smiled grimly. 'The R.A.F.,' he explained, 'is the correct name for what the press calls the "Baader-Meinhof Gang"; they called themselves the "Red Army Faction", and this is what police the world over still call them. We are now fighting the third or fourth generation, and there has been a steady, strong development in their ideologies since those early days. So much so, in fact, that Andreas Baader offered to work with the State against some of the younger terrorists, shortly before his suicide in jail.'

'I had no idea,' I said, surprised.

'Oh yes,' replied Biffi. 'He claimed, and said he was speaking for the whole cadre of first-generation terrorists, that they had never approved of brutal actions against innocent civilians. For what it is worth, this is true. In all their actions and publications, including the important book *On Armed Struggle in Western Europe,* they always advocated avoiding civilian casualties. They are fighting *for* the people, after all. Instead, they strike at the police and army, whom they see as state organs for upholding the domination of the establishment.'

'But these people are doing just that, I mean, involving innocent civilians,' I objected.

'Exactly! If you remember, I said there has been a change in their ideologies. We have been studying them closely, because the Italian terrorist has always been keen to integrate fashionable foreign developments into the Italian pattern of struggle. And I am afraid that this particular group, even if they have chosen the name of one of the terror movement's "martyrs", is more typical of the latest development in this ideological shift than of the earlier terrorists. In fact, the choice of a title at all, calling themselves the "Commando Gudrun Ensslin", came so late in the day that I suspect that it has very little political significance. It is no more than just a bit of packaging, advertising, call it what you will; an expression of their search for romanticism and flamboyant headlines that brought them into the terrorist environment in the first place.'

He paused. 'My impressions, formed on the information I had before, have been confirmed by our talk, I'm afraid,' he said. 'I am going to tell Major Salti that my recommendation is to treat these people seriously. We should do everything possible to avoid wounding their sense of dignity, because that might have spontaneous and terrible results. We should work on the lines of fighting force with force, because I see little hope in extensive negotiations.' ·

'You mean you will recommend an attack?'

'No, no, please do not misunderstand me,' said Biffi. 'At this stage I am stumbling about in the dark myself. I shall have to go out there now and stay on the scene until the final denouement, whatever it may be, and continue to analyse the development of the situation and advise Major Salti accordingly. At the moment I can give nothing more than general guidelines based on the way these terrorists' behaviour patterns mesh with those we have been studying. But in principle I think it will be a hard-line situation.'

He called for another coffee.

'There is one factor in our favour,' he said, 'and we must make use of it, because it is the only one we have at the moment.'

'What is that?' I asked.

'Terrorists are almost never prepared to carry out their ultimatums if these involve killing themselves too,' he said. 'They will let themselves be talked into deadline after deadline. But, and especially in this case, they should never get the impression that we are aware of this and playing it that way. They are often not aware of it themselves.

'Even the Palestinians who did that raid at the Munich Olympics and captured and killed the Israeli athletes – they seemed to be determined to die if necessary, walking around with hand-grenades with the pin out and so on. But it wasn't until they were perfectly sure that the Germans had betrayed them and were shooting them down, that they had no more than five minutes to live anyway, that they actually killed the hostages and went down fighting at the airfield where a plane was waiting for them.'

'You sound almost as though you were taking their part, Dr Biffi,' I said quietly.

'Not at all.' He was not in the least offended, just surprised that I had misunderstood him. 'There was every reason to believe that they didn't want to shed blood. There were also enough precedents at that time for them to believe that they would succeed in their aim, which was to trade back live hostages for live political prisoners. Once they felt betrayed, their reaction at the airfield was perfectly understandable. Indeed, it should have been predicted. In my profession many people were talking about incredible bungling by the authorities, and the blame for the deaths lying at least partly with the police.'

'Is that what you think too, doctor?'

'I think that's putting it too hard. Let us say that with the experience we have nowadays, it would be criminal to make the same mistake again.'

Biffi called the waiter over and signed the check for dinner.

'I must go now,' he said, 'and I must thank you for your help and patience. I am sorry I'm not in a position to tell you much more at present. A lot of it would require a psychological schooling, or it would take too long to explain; and some of it is classified. But if you ever wish to talk about your experiences again, Mrs Ellis, please look me up.'

'I can't imagine anything I would want to forget faster!'

'You feel that way now,' he said, 'but recent therapeutical experiments in the United States in which I was privileged to take part proved something different. Under certain circumstances, controlled discussion of the trauma has helped to cope with the depression that plagues many people after going through an experience like yours.'

At that moment, I caught sight of Sam heading for our table. Biffi stood up as I introduced the two men, and he didn't sit down again. 'I have to get out to Badia a Ripoli and report to Major Salti. Now that the worst part of your experience is over, I hope you will rest well tonight. I shall probably see you in the morning when you make your formal statements.'

He accompanied Sam and me to a side door opening on to a cobbled street and shook our hands again. 'Ring before you come tomorrow. There's no way of saying at present how the situation could develop. But I think Major Salti wants to take your statements personally as soon as he is free.'

When we were alone, Sam looked at me questioningly. 'Well?'

'No problem, Sam,' I said, and took his arm as we set off towards the car. I hoped I would make it to the hotel without having to sit down and rest. 'As far as I could tell, I didn't put my foot in it. He was awfully nice. I felt rotten about misleading him. I wish we knew something about Mike!'

Sam closed the car door for me and went round to the driver's seat. 'We'll chase that up tomorrow,' he said comfortingly. 'Right now you need some rest. I've taken a hotel out towards Fièsole, it's quieter there. Salti has had someone call them and say we're coming.'

As Sam swung round a tight corner, Bruna's sunglasses skittered across the top of the dashboard and fell off into my lap.

'Oh, Sam, stop,' I said in dismay. 'I haven't rung Bruna's parents yet.'

'The police did,' said Sam without slowing, 'and anyway it's past ten-thirty and you're tired out. Ring them in the morning. I telephoned Christine while you were talking to Biffi. There's nothing new, but I told her we're okay. She was very upset about Bruna.'

'Sam,' I said as he negotiated the light late-evening traffic, 'there's something I want to ask you, but it's rather difficult, so please bear with me a little.'

'What on earth is the matter?' he said, surprised by my tone, and he tried to see my face in the light of the street lamps.

'Well,' I said in embarrassment, 'don't misunderstand me . . . but I don't think I could bear to sleep alone in a room tonight. Would you mind very much if we took a double room? I don't want to put you in an awkward position. . . .'

Sam squeezed my hand gently and laughed. 'Don't be silly, Sophie. I was wondering about that myself. I've taken adjoining rooms with a communicating door, and you can leave it open if you feel better like that.'

'Dear Sam!' I said past a yawn. 'That is very sweet of you.'

'But there are two other things before we arrive,' he said. 'One is your passport. Before Salti arrived, when they were noting names and addresses and so on, I told them you had left your passport in Olmo, which is true. I said there would be no problem having you identified by the Olmo police if necessary. He accepted that and cleared it with the hotel, too. And the other is that he has had the hotel put under surveillance. Just in case,' he added hurriedly, seeing my look of alarm. 'He doesn't imagine there's any danger, but I'm personally very glad that he's taking no chances.'

For the second night in succession, I hardly managed to stagger up the stairs. We went straight to our rooms, and Sam appeared at once in the doorway between them.

'There we are,' he said cheerfully. 'We'll leave it open, but I suspect you'll sleep like a log. If I don't snore, that is!'

If he did, I didn't hear him.

Twenty-four

When I awoke, it was half past nine and the sun was streaming in between the slats of the blinds I had not thought of closing the night before.

Sam was not there, but he had left a note propped up prominently against his overnight bag saying, 'I'm downstairs having breakfast.'

I washed and dressed, wishing I had a change of clothes, and went to find him. In most Italian hotels, breakfast is no more than a cup of coffee and a bun in the bar, so I was pleased to find a small dining room where Sam was sitting surrounded by newspapers.

'Morning,' he grunted. 'Nothing new here. The news blackout seems to be pretty effective. They can't keep the whole thing secret, of course, but there's little enough meat to the stories.'

He had heard a bulletin on the local radio station. The apartment block was still under siege, so it seemed that Salti and his men had succeeded in increasing the ultimatum deadline beyond midnight.

While my order was being prepared, I took out a pen and started making notes on the paper napkin.

'I'm going to ring Bruna's parents and then Christine,' I said. 'Will you ring the police and see when they want us?'

'Your Italian's better than mine,' Sam said. 'Why don't you?'

'Let's just go out there anyway,' I suggested. 'To Badia, I mean.' I didn't know how to explain it to Sam – I hardly knew how to explain it to myself – but I felt a need to see the scene of Bruna's death again, to make my peace with that street I had left the day before without a backward glance.

'All right. If they'll let us through the cordon.'

'They will all right, if we tell them to take our names to Salti.'

While Sam was ringing Christine, I called Bruna's father. He had pulled himself together, but in spite of his dignity and control, it was a painful conversation for both of us. I was grateful that he made me no reproaches. I promised to see that his car was returned as soon as possible, and as I was about to ring off, he said, 'I hope you will have some good news about those murderers when you come, signora. I am a peaceable man, but justice must be done. If it is not, I fear for the lives of so many other people, too.'

I was still composing myself after this call when Sam returned.

'Sorry I was so grumpy,' he said. 'Didn't sleep too well. How did it go with you?'

'It was pretty tough,' I said, and left it at that. 'What did Chris say?'

'She didn't answer either number. It's probably a good sign. She'll be lying low for a while.'

I wasn't so sure of that. I thought it would be more like Chris to be in the firing-line, but I didn't say so to Sam. 'Why don't we go out to Badia and get it over with?' I suggested instead. 'After the dress rehearsal yesterday I think I'm up to it now.'

As we headed down the viale Giovane Italia towards the San Niccolò bridge, I remembered the police surveillance we had been promised.

'Did you see the police anywhere near the hotel, Sam?'

'Yes,' he replied, swinging left along the Arno embankment. 'And don't look around just now; they're still behind us.'

I didn't know whether that was a good sign or a bad one, but decided that on the whole it was reassuring.

Mike had already passed through Florence, asleep on the Brenner Express, and was speeding away to the south as Sam and I crossed the river.

Traffic was chaotic near the scene of the siege, as a cordon had been set up for several blocks around. The scope of the detour was limited by the river to the south, and by the narrowness of the streets on every other side. Twice we were overtaken by police cars rushing pell-mell through the confusion, with sirens screaming. On one occasion we were forced aside by motor-cycle escorts coming towards us, followed by a convoy of shiny black government limousines, squad-cars and a troop-carrier. Two or three helicopters were hovering at a discreet distance; we caught occasional glimpses of them between the buildings.

We were lucky enough to pass just at the moment when a car pulled out of a parking slot into the sluggish mass of metal, otherwise we could have been circling for hours. The police were letting nobody stop or hold up the flow.

'It's going to be a problem talking our way in,' said Sam

doubtfully as we set off on foot. He was wrong. It was going to be quite easy, although for reasons I would not have wished for. But then, if it hadn't happened like that, Mike might not have stayed in Italy.

By demanding to speak urgently with Major Salti we managed to pass a preliminary cordon keeping everybody who did not live in the area out of the outer security ring. But we saw a tighter cordon ahead, with road-blocks and *carabinieri* with machine-guns and radios, a hundred yards from the eye of the storm.

As we approached it, I took hardly any notice of a newsreel crew coming towards us on the other side of the street. They actually passed us, but a minute later somebody came up from behind and called after me, 'Scusi, signora! One moment please!'

I did not recognize the dapper young man at first. It was not until about half way through the interview that I remembered where I had seen him before: on one of the more penetrating and critical TV news programmes.

'I'm Massimo Lazzeri of the third network,' he said confidently. 'Would you tell us how you recognized the girl terrorist who ran away from you last night?'

Behind him a man with a big Bell and Howell was moving in. The lens turret stared at me like a malignant eye. Lazzeri was holding a microphone under my chin.

'I have instructions from the police not to discuss the matter with anybody. I'm sorry, there's nothing I can tell you.'

'Very well.' He turned back to the camera, and spoke directly into the lens. 'Signora Ellis, a citizen of Switzerland, whose role in the discovery of the terrorists' hideout was reported in our broadcast earlier today, is observing the official news blackout as any responsible citizen should at this moment. We hope to give you more details about yesterday's dramatic events as soon as the situation in via Marconi is resolved one way or another.'

I was wondering how responsible a citizen *he* would have been if I had been prepared to talk, when to my dismay he suddenly turned back to me.

'But as far as I know, the police have not imposed any secrecy on the story of the fire at your property near Olmo on Monday night and your sudden disappearance after it. There is obviously a connection.'

'Is there?' I said rudely, playing for time, and trying desperately to think of a convincing reply.

'Certainly!' said Lazzeri positively. 'And the mystery of your missing husband.'

My knees suddenly felt weak and I felt the blood drain from my face and then return with a hot rush. Sam took my hand and pressed it lightly. He understood a lot more Italian than he spoke, and had gathered what was happening. 'What are you talking about, young man?'

'It's okay, Sam,' I said aside. 'What mystery do you mean?' I said to Lazzeri.

'Your husband was not found at the scene of the fire, nor was he seen again after it. But the owner of a bar at Terontola, the main-line station nearest your propery, told the press this morning that she saw him arrive on Friday evening and spoke to him there.'

Seen like that, I thought, I suppose he could make a mystery out of it. I was relieved that he had meant nothing more sinister, and was perhaps careless now.

'You and your husband,' he was saying, 'own the land where one of Tuscany's worst fires for years raged on Monday, and now you turn up here, at the Siege of Via Marconi' – the capitals were audible – 'as one of the protagonists. Could you tell us where you were on Tuesday?'

'No, I'm afraid I can't,' I said directly into the big lens, holding down my anger.

'How did the fire start, signora?' Trying to build me up for something, I thought; he wouldn't be as formal otherwise.

'I'm sorry but I can't add anything to what I told the police, and which they have passed on to the press.'

'Good girl,' I heard Sam whisper.

'You can't, or you're not allowed to?' Handing it to me on a plate, I thought, and fell into the trap with both feet.

'The police have instructed me not to discuss the matter,' I said firmly, and turned to leave.

'Then there *is* a connection between the fire and the dramatic events just two blocks away from here,' he said triumphantly. He was drawing a breath for another question when a captain of police stepped between us.

'What's going on here?' he asked Lazzeri brusquely. 'You know that the Minister has imposed a blackout.'

The two of them argued, but the camera had been lowered and the reporter was obviously putting up no more than a formal front to save his face. The captain warned him severely and turned to us. I recognized him as the first officer to arrive at the scene the previous evening.

'I think you had better come inside,' he said, and there was more than just an offer of protection in his voice; it was almost an order. He escorted us into the back of the block through the same door by which we had left the day before.

The command post was filled with a haze of tobacco smoke. The occupants looked worn out. Salti was telephoning, and raised an eyebrow in surprise at our entrance. John was snoozing in an armchair in a corner, with photographic equipment scattered on the floor around his feet. The TV screen was showing the same deserted scene; it might have been a 'technical interruption' still, except that there was none of the familiar, soft harp music with which the R.A.I. soothes irritated viewers.

Salti banged the receiver down. 'Occupato,' he grunted. 'I can't think who they could be talking to, but we'll soon know.'

Something about the way he said 'they' made me start. 'You mean them?' I asked, nodding towards the bullet-proof screen at the window.

'Yes. We have their line tapped, of course. Good morning, signora. It's a pity you did not call me first. This is . . . uh, about the worst moment you could have chosen.' He shook our hands anyway.

'I saw them in the street,' put in the captain. 'They were being pestered by Massimo Lazzeri.' Major Salti turned back to me with a forbidding expression, but the captain added hurriedly, 'I overheard much of the interview and Signora Ellis told him nothing, sir. She told him she was respecting the police blackout.'

Salti's face cleared. 'Still,' he said, 'it's a damn nuisance having the TV people under our feet. Things are about to start moving here. We have already started to clear the decks for action.' I remembered the cavalcade of government cars leaving the scene. No doubt a minister would not wish to be present if bullets were flying. 'You will now please wait out of the way until we leave here. In about quarter of an hour.'

He indicated two camp chairs next to John's collapsed form, and turned away from us. I looked at Sam. Only another fifteen minutes.

The telephone rang and a *carabiniere* answered, passing the call to Salti. John awoke and stretched. He looked at his watch and swore. 'The bastards didn't wake me. The balloon must be going up any minute.'

'They said a quarter of an hour,' I told him. 'What do they plan to do?'

He put us in the picture in a few words, while he reloaded both his camera and checked that the flash was charged. The Minister had agreed to offer the terrorists an aircraft, but to see that they never reached it. They had released seven women and children, and from the reports of these people it was now known that there were four terrorists, one of them badly hurt but nevertheless able to walk and handle a gun. Would that be Jens? I speculated.

Both the apartment block here and the airport were covered by squads of expert marksmen, eight in each squad. The terrorists would be picked off while boarding the bus here or when leaving it at the aircraft.

While John was still speaking, Biffi arrived looking haggard and crumpled. He had been taking a brief rest. He overheard the end of John's account and added a comment.

'Similar to the Munich scene we were talking about yesterday, signora. Only this time nobody will shoot until we are sure of hitting them all simultaneously. Otherwise not a shot. They have no grenades with them, and they can't set off plastic explosives just like that, even if they really have any, which I doubt.'

When he moved to confer with Salti, John explained in low tones, 'They had quite an argument about that. Biffi isn't for it at all. But the others said the mistake at Munich was to open fire before all the terrorists were in the open, so that some were left alive to kill the hostages.'

'But surely there's a risk of hitting a hostage,' said Sam, aghast.

'There are two sharpshooters to each bandit, two for the first to come out, two for the second, and so on. They are spread out so that one of them is sure to have a clear line of fire at any given moment. A spotter is going to give them a radio signal at the right second to open fire. If he doesn't like the look of the grouping, no signal.'

The telephone was ringing again as John concluded, 'The bus will be here to pick them up any moment now.' Everything was building up to a climax in the operation centre. The men operating the civilian telephone, the field telephones and the radio had hardly a moment of respite, while the TV screen remained deceptively still. John pointed out a smaller set, a portable showing a concert orchestra but with the volume off, and was telling us something about Biffi having had it installed so that he could follow the news bulletins and thus know what the terrorists were presumably following too, but I was not listening.

I was slumped in my chair in the corner, holding Sam's big paw like a lost child, and the hectic activity in the room blurred to an unfocused background. Images were flying around in my mind, fragments occasionally slowing and then spinning off again, like linen seen through the glass door of a washing-machine. I saw Ulli giving a brown velvet bear to Katrina, Ulli dropping a bag of vegetables and pulling out a pistol, Bruna at the wheel of her Mirafiori, throwing back her head and laughing, Mike holding my shoulders and saying *Take it easy, chick* . . . .

Suddenly something brought me back to the present. It might have been the tense silence in the room, or the involuntary tightening of Sam's fingers on mine. Then we heard the sound of heavy vehicles approaching in the street outside.

Every eye in the room was on the TV screen. From left to right, an armoured troop-carrier slowly crossed it, bulging in the distortion of the wide-angle lens, and stopped with its tail just at the right-hand edge. A police bus followed, stopping as half of its length filled the left side of the picture. The door to the apartment block was visible in the gap.

Again the telephone rang. Salti snarled '*Madonna!*' and snatched it up without turning his head. '*Chi è?*' Then he handed it across the table to Biffi.

'*Sì?* Yes, this is Biffi.' He switched into English. 'The troop-carriers are absolutely necessary. There is a mob prepared to lynch you. There will be a lot of other police vehicles too, as soon as you leave this area to go on to the *autostrada*. There is nothing we can do to you. You have the hostages. The police are there to protect their lives, and in this case that means protecting yours too. Do not panic. We are keeping our word. You keep yours.'

The receiver squeaked again into the still room. 'Just get into the bus and on to the plane and go,' said Biffi. 'You will have your freedom, we will have our hostages back.' '

The click as he was cut off was loud and clear. He started reporting the phone conversation to Salti in a low voice. I felt sick.

For one and a half, perhaps two, tense minutes, nothing happened. Then the door to the apartment block opened cautiously, and a group of three people came out. Two middle-aged men and a woman with their hands behind their backs were followed by a hooded figure with a machine-gun. He was so close to them that a burst from his weapon would have cut them in two. A kind of growl went up around the room, and Salti snapped, *'Silenzio!'*

His voice covered mine as I involuntarily gasped, 'Jens!' I was sure I recognized the tall figure in spite of his hood. As they crossed to the bus and out of sight of the camera, I saw that he was limping and that his left arm was in a sling.

Then we saw the hostages through the windows of the bus, stumbling into seats near the front. The hooded head and shoulders were visible as Jens – if it was he – stayed on the step. He possibly called something we could not hear, because the door opened again and more people came out, first a hooded woman who must have been Roswita with three hostages; then a hooded man with two young women; and finally Ulli, bareheaded and clearly recognizable despite the small, unclear image. She was pushing before her somebody who had been hurt, a young man, possibly in his twenties, who was having great difficulty in walking. Beside her she was dragging another male figure with her free hand.

Salti gestured impatiently at the radio operator without looking round, and the loudspeaker broke the brittle silence in the room as the operator turned it on and took off his headphones. '. . . too close together. Hold your fire. As long as they're bunched up together like that we can't shoot.'

Slowly the second group made its way across the scrap of 'garden'. They were getting in each other's way, stumbling over one another's feet, the hostages handicapped by their tied hands and the Germans keeping in close for cover. The terrorists were dragging their prisoners about brutally.

Suddenly the wounded hostage tripped and fell. Ulli started to drag him to his feet, the group fanned out as she knocked into another prisoner and sent him staggering into the middle of the group, and Jens moved in the bus. Then the loudspeaker crackled, 'Now!' and all hell broke loose.

There was a hail of shots. Salti jumped to his feet, and several of the men present cried out inarticulately. After the shooting there was utter silence for two or three seconds. Then there was a short burst of machine-gun fire, interrupted and silenced by a second, ragged fusillade of single shots.

Everybody in sight on the screen was prostrate and motionless. From inside the room we clearly heard the tinkle as a loosened piece of glass fell from a broken window of the bus. The doors at the rear of the troop-carrier were flung open and a stream of men jumped out two by two.

'We got them all, but I can't see from here whether any civilians were hit,' said the voice over the radio, and then Sam and I were left alone as everybody else squeezed out through the door. Salti was shouting orders, there was a confusion of voices everywhere, and the *choppachoppachoppa* of an approaching helicopter rose deafeningly.

I sat down in Salti's place and wearily lowered my head on to my arms on the table. After a moment I felt Sam's hand on my shoulder, and I took it and held it tightly.

MIKE

Twenty-five

Sophie's face vanished from the screen. The newscaster looked at me dead-pan, put aside a sheet of paper and started to read from the next.

I sat dazed for a few seconds, wondering if I was hallucinating, and then scrambled over to the set and turned up the volume.

'... for our next bulletin.

'The President of the Republic, with still three days of his State Visit left to go, was received today at the White House...'

'What was that last item about?' I demanded of the barman.

He continued to polish glasses and shrugged without looking up; 'More bloody terrorists,' he grunted. 'They were holed up in an apartment in Florence all night. Demanding a free flight out of the country. Good riddance, I say. Don't know why they don't fly them out over the Mediterranean and push them out of the door.'

I left a thousand lire on the bar and ran out into the autumn sunshine without waiting for the change. The sky was a brilliant blue, the best-looking people in the world were strolling up and down the elegant via Veneto, and my heart was singing as I passed through the crowd with a new spring in my step.

Somehow, it didn't matter how, Sophie was free and safe and distinctly in command of the situation. And I believed I had recognized that solid, tweed-clad shoulder glimpsed for a moment next to hers. I had, after all, asked Sam to do some detective work in Florence for me, and it was not unreasonable to assume that he had gone there personally.

One of the first taxis I waved at stopped for me. Must have been having a bad day. I went straight to the main *carabinieri* station on viale Romania, because there would be little point in going to a local station and being passed from office to office.

As the taxi crawled through the canyons of the city, my mind was shoving pieces of the puzzle around and around. Every way they landed, they left questions open. There was no doubt that Sophie's speech had been connected with the siege. But how free was she? And Katrina? One thing was reassuring: that TV shot had been against an open street background and obviously professional, not an amateur video-tape job done by kidnappers.

After jumping a queue of angry citizens waiting for their turn at the information desk, I was left sitting in a second-floor office for three-quarters of an hour before being led to a colonel with a sceptical look on his fat, dyspeptic face.

'You are the husband of Sofia Ellis. From Olmo,' he repeated carefully. 'Then where have you been, Mr Ellis, because we have been looking for you everywhere? Where did you go after the fire?'

'Fire?' I stammered. 'What fire? When?'

'Your house and property were swept by fire in the small hours of Tuesday morning. Your wife disappeared, and you too, and she turned up last night in Florence, where she discovered a group of terrorists. They took a number of hostages in an apartment block.'

'How is she? How is my daughter?'

'As far as I am aware, they are perfectly well. They were not injured or burned, but escaped to raise the alarm. And where were you, Mr Ellis? You had better sit down.'

'Thank you. I had gone abroad on business. To Rome first, and then on to Koristan on Monday,' I said truthfully. I began to wonder why I was still lying, or at least telling only half-truths. I would at this moment have given a year of my life to know whether all the terrorists had been captured or killed. But even if they were, wouldn't there be another gang, and another after that? They already had the documents back, but I was still at large with my perilous knowledge.

'Listen,' I said urgently, 'I have heard nothing of a fire or terrorists or anything. I got back into Rome less than two hours ago. Could you please tell me what is going on, and let me speak to my wife. I just saw her face on TV; that's why I'm here.'

He gave me a long, calculating look, and seemed to believe me.

'I was informed ten minutes ago that the siege is over,' he said finally. 'All four terrorists were killed and one hostage wounded. Your wife met and recognized one of the terrorists in the street yesterday, and a girl who was with your wife was killed, too.' As he saw my expression, he added, 'Not a baby. A young woman from a small village in the province of Perugia, I think.'

He put a call through to the anti-terrorism unit in Florence and I was astounded at the rapidity of the connection. I wondered if they had special police lines.

'Is Salti back? How long then? And what about the American lady, Signora Ellis? Good. We have found her husband. Tell Salti to ring me as soon as they arrive. My name is Colonel Carloni.'

As Carloni hung up, I hid a smile at his claim to have found me. It seemed to me that I was not the only one telling half-truths.

'They are expected back in a quarter of an hour,' he told me. While he waited for the call, he went to a side table and looked through a pile of newspapers. Giving me three of them, Carloni pointed out an article in each. 'They have got the bones of the story right. I hope your property was insured. There's nothing on the siege, because it was too late for today's morning editions, and we've had a news blackout. I don't even know if that has now been lifted, that's Florence's decision.'

There were two other calls before the one which caused him to look up at me and nod. When he handed me the receiver, a male voice asked, 'Dr Ellis? Un momento, prego.'

'Pronto. Chi è?' asked Sophie, and I just managed to reply, 'It's me – Mike. How are you?'

The police were very patient and understanding. They let us

talk for a long time at the taxpayer's expense. We spoke in English, but I did not doubt that a tape was winding somewhere. Sophie, too, seemed to be talking guardedly. When she found an opportunity to say, 'I seem to have just missed you at the weekend,' I knew there was still a lot to sort out.

The worst part, of course, was Bruna's death. Sophie was reproaching herself bitterly for having involved Bruna in the affair. She was crying when she told me, but I just sat stunned in my chair.

Then Major Salti took the line and said the Minister's helicopter was returning empty to Rome within an hour and he was sure he could arrange for my wife and partner to have a ride down, and that was about it.

The dyspeptic-looking colonel was almost friendly with me after that. He took me to the officers' canteen, bought me a coffee and filled me in on the official side of the story. He seemed to assume that I had gone to Rome on Saturday, so I did nothing to correct this impression. Finally he took me out on to the interior courtyard where the squad-cars were parked and shook my hand. I was to be back by three-thirty. I had a lot to get on with in the meantime; there were one or two decisions I had to make before Sophie and Sam arrived, and a whole weekend to account for.

I crossed Piazza Ungheria and was heading slowly down viale Rossini towards the Borghese Gardens when I stopped in my tracks so suddenly that somebody walked into me from behind. I walked back a few paces to a restaurant I had just passed and went inside.

In the euphoria of an imminent reunion with Sophie it had slipped my mind that we were not out of the wood by a long way. I had handed over the documentary evidence on Wharton, it was true, but this was only part of the bargain. Sophie had been free for over forty-eight hours and had had a good deal of press coverage. It would be reasonable for 'them' – I was still thinking in vague terms of my adversaries – to assume that I knew she was at liberty.

My dash to the police station and the hour I had spent in there might easily be construed as the beginning of flight, backing out of the other half of my bargain, now that Sophie and Katrina were no longer hostages for my good behaviour. I myself had suggested to Wharton that they shadow me in Rome: were the two bunglers from Kabul for whom I had kept having to wait intended to dull my sense of security, to keep my attention from the more expert shadowers?

Not only that, but I was leading Sophie directly into their hands! They needed only to follow one of us, and they knew they would have the other within the day. Two birds with one stone.

It was a quarter to two. Sophie would be safe enough on the Minister's helicopter and during the transfer to the police headquarters. But how could I possibly make sure she did not leave the building and walk unsuspectingly right back into captivity?

I ate a plate of *tortellini alla panna,* but if they had brought me fish ice-cream I don't think I would have noticed. The only reason I remember it now is because, when I told the waiter I would like some, he said, 'What, again? Were they so good?'

By two-thirty, I had half a bottle of Capena wine under my belt, and I also had the beginnings of a plan. Sophie and Sam were going to have to gò into hiding, like Katrina and Christine, but preferably not all together. I could still fly back to Koristan tomorrow. There was no connection worth taking for the rest of the day, and besides, there was something I had to clear up in Rome first.

But most pressing of all was the story I would have to tell to the police. I took my cue from Sophie's remark on the phone, that she had apparently just missed me in Olmo. Rita at the bar in Terontola was bound to remember sooner or later that she had seen me the Friday before and tell somebody; even the most discreet person is glad of an opportunity to talk about personal connections with people in the headlines and on TV. Yet I could not tell the police about the terrorists at the house, for they would immediately want to know why I had not gone to them on Monday. Which meant I had to account for the period from Friday evening to Monday morning.

Working on the lines that the best lie is as near as possible to the truth, could I not say I had been blackmailed into leaving the country until today by threats against the lives of my wife and daughter? No, for the police would again want to know why, and also why I had not told Colonel Carloni the 'truth' once I knew that Sophie was free.

The answer, I decided, was a long journey: it would account

for a lot of time and require few corroborative witnesses. I had borrowed my secretary's car two weeks before, I would say, and left it in Olmo. On Friday I had flown in to Rome and, knowing I required papers from the office in Geneva, had decided to drive the car up to Switzerland and pick them up there. Tiring? Well, I was feeling quite fresh and knew she would appreciate having the car back for the weekend. Besides, I would be able to catch up on office correspondence on the Sunday and take the night train down to Rome. The I.D.A. car which had picked me up in Olmo? Somehow I was suspicious of that car. I didn't believe the police would know about it. I was beginning to wonder whether it had been an I.D.A. car at all.

I sat for a while over coffee running the story backwards and forwards until I felt I had ironed out all the wrinkles. Once that was sorted out, my main problem was to see Sophie and Sam safely out of Rome. And I had an idea for that, too.

I settled the bill and asked the waiter where the telephone was, and looked up the number of the nearest Hertz office.

Yes, they did have a minivan available immediately, a Simca. Yes, they did accept American Express cards. Yes, they could bring it out to me at viale Romania right away. I felt things were looking a bit better as I left the restaurant, but the prickling on my spine reminded me that there was no way I could know whether I was still being followed. They say you don't hear the shot that kills you, I thought grimly.

Walking through the police headquarters like a man with a job to do, I was stopped by nobody. I went straight out of the back door on to the courtyard where Carloni had left me. I remembered that it was out of sight of the street, and this had been the germ from which my idea had been born. I had been waiting only two minutes when two Hertz cars arrived, my minivan and another to take the delivery driver back.

A *carabiniere* came out of his office waving angrily, but I went to meet him.

'One car is leaving at once, and the other is mine. Colonel Carloni said I could leave it here for a little,' I lied, and enjoyed the effect my name-dropping had. 'I have a conference with him at three-thirty, and then I'll take it away.'

'Very good, sir; just don't block the yellow lines, if you please.'

I produced my American Express card and signed for the

minivan. Once the Hertz drivers had left, I parked the van with its nose to the wall, in a quiet corner near the exit gate, and went back into the building. It was three-twenty as I knocked at Colonel Carloni's door.

'Ah, Dr Ellis! They left the military airfield ten minutes ago and should be here at any moment. Take a seat, please.' You've been checking on me, I thought; I was Mr Ellis before lunch.

He put me into the picture on the denouement of the siege in Florence. The hostage wounded in the shootout was in hospital, but it appeared that his condition was not serious. It seemed to me that the police had accepted Sophie's story about panicking and taking Katrina to safety first of all.

'I suspect my own wife would have done something similar,' said Carloni. 'It's very understandable that she should not slow down to think until her child was safe. It was certainly a stroke of luck that she recognized the woman terrorist in Florence and raised the alarm.'

Not for Bruna, though, I was thinking as a knock came at the door, and then there was a long time during which Sophie and Sam and I didn't pay him very much attention. He didn't seem put out. I won't attempt to describe what it felt like to hold Sophie again. But she was trembling, and I was trembling, too. I hugged her close for a very long time.

Finally I promised Carloni I would ring him that evening to let him know what hotel we would be staying in, and again the next morning.

'You may be required to go back to Florence before you leave Italy again. They are still not very happy about that fire. I tried to get in touch with Salti before you came, but he was still out at the scene of the shooting this morning. Can you stay here for a while?'

It was not really a question. I said, 'Of course, Colonel. Might we wait in the canteen, or is that against regulations?'

'Not at all. I'll have you called there when I hear something new.'

As soon as we were in the corridor, Sophie grabbed my hand and whispered, 'Mike, did you have to kill anybody?'

I stopped, thunderstruck, and looked at her in amazement.

'Are you crazy? I hurt one of them getting away from the

house, but I'm damn sure I didn't kill him. Why on earth do you ask?'

Once she had explained, the whole trick became clear.

'Then there's nothing to stop us from telling the police the whole truth,' said Sam, and I realized that I had some explaining to do myself.

'Listen,' I said urgently, 'I hate to tell you this, but we're still in a lot of danger, all of us. Let's get down to that canteen and sort it out as soon as we can. Carloni may call us back up at any minute.'

Leaving out the details of the proof I had found of Wharton's misappropriations, I told them the rest of the story as briefly as I could. Except for the one bit of business I still had to clear up in Rome. My story about Christine's car would hold water if Sam would corroborate it and put Chris in the picture.

'But you don't mean to say you still intend to go back to Nooriabad and cover this up, Mike?' said Sam incredulously.

'Sam, I don't see what else I can do. If I refuse, it's only a matter of time before they get me. Or Sophie, or Katrina. Or maybe even you. You are the one I'm worrying about now that my family is safe. They know I'll never talk, for their sake, but they have no such hold over you. Except maybe by killing you.'

There was a sombre look on Sam's face, and he didn't say anything for a long time. I spoke urgently, persuasively, and he just nodded slowly in dazed agreement.

'Sam, you and Sophie have to get into hiding and stay there with your heads down for about a week. Let Guy and Jacqueline in Lausanne know where you are, and I'll trace you through them. I've got to go back out there and keep my bargain, or our lives won't be worth a used fifty-lire stamp. In fact, I'm on the spot already, because I was supposed to fly out today and didn't, but instead have been spending a suspicious amount of time in police stations.'

Sophie's hand flew to her mouth. 'What if they're waiting for us outside?'

'I've thought of that. Listen,' I put the keys of the minivan on the table, 'these are for a Hertz van in the courtyard here. When we leave, go down and take it. It's a red Simca with Milan plates in a corner near the gate. When you get in, Sam take your glasses off, put a hat on, do anything you can to change your appearance radically. As far as we know, they haven't had a good look at you yet.'

'And what about Sophie. She's pretty distinctive, you know.'

'That's why I took a van. Sophie, get into the back and stay there until you're on the *autostrada*. Just go straight up to Switzerland and get out of sight.'

Sophie's eyes were brimming with tears. 'What about you, darling?'

'They're not going to do anything to me on the steps of a police station,' I said, with far more confidence than I felt. 'I'll stay in the doorway, in case anybody is watching, until you've left. I can take care of myself until I leave for Koristan.'

'There's one thing I don't understand,' put in Sam thought-fully. 'If they all died in Florence, who is going to be chasing you now?'

This was just what I had been afraid of. It needed only a little carelessness and there would be another tragedy.

'Get this straight, Sam,' I said quietly. 'This is far bigger than I ever thought. Remember George Hamilton? Remember the characters in black leather jackets looking for you, the ones Chris told Sophie about? It was Monday or Tuesday last week when Wharton knew the game was up. By Friday they already had a gang organized and in the house in Olmo, including a children's nurse for Katrina. They had access to my luggage at Fiumicino airport. They got an I.D.A. car to take me from Tuscany to Rome. Or so they said; it never occurred to me until today to question it. They had access to heavy weapons. These are no small-time hoodlums, Sam! It's the big time, chum, and we're just beetles in their path.'

The silence lengthened, and Sophie toyed with her coffee-spoon while Sam and I both lit cigarettes.

'I know what you're thinking, Sam,' I said more gently, 'or at least I think I do. But I'm not going to put my life or yours or Sophie's or Katrina's on the line for this. Wharton is burnt out anyway; they as much as told him so. Whether we finger him or not, they are going to have to start again somewhere else, have probably already done so, in fact. If I do break the story, I probably sign Wharton's death warrant at that moment too. After the way they've handled us, do you imagine they would let him be recalled and interrogated, maybe put on trial?'

'What about stashing the story somewhere for publication if anything happens to any of us?' said Sam after a moment.

'I've been thinking about that too.' I told them about the report I had hidden under the bath in the cottage. 'It's all there. All except the figures, and those are in the post on their way to you at the office address. Assuming the house is still safe, of course. But I don't think the fire will have reached it. Those old stone walls are tough. I shall just have to go and see.'

I lit a cigarette before going on. 'I'm going to pick it up in a day or so. Otherwise I can reconstruct a lot from memory. Before I leave, I'm going to post it to you at the office address. So that and the other documents will be waiting for you in the post-office box by, say, Monday morning. I'll address it to you personally. Ring Chris today and tell her to pick up the envelope and another which will have arrived by then from Amexco Rome and to hold them for you.'

'The papers Jim Hawthorne was so worried about,' put in Sophie.

'Right,' I said. 'You have until Monday to work out the details of a foolproof way of stashing them, with a bank or a lawyer or somebody. And of wording the instructions so that nothing can go wrong.'

A young *carabiniere* suddenly stood at the table. 'Signori, would you come up to Colonel Carloni's office at once, please.'

As we stood up, Sam scooped up the keys to the van from the table. He gave me a long, hard look, and then murmured, 'Okay, Mike,' as I put my arm around Sophie's shoulders and we headed towards the door.

Carloni was already less friendly. 'Major Salti wants to meet you both at your property to discuss the fire. Since the whole thing seems to have terrorism as a common denominator, his unit has taken over the inquiries.'

'How long would that tie us up?' I asked cautiously.

'Maybe just tomorrow morning, if you could travel up tonight.'

'Well, I could go, I suppose, although there's not overmuch I could say as I wasn't there. But my wife is exhausted. She has been through a kidnapping, a forest fire, a flight to safety, a street-shooting and the massacre in Florence. And the police psychologist and Salti have already interrogated her. Look, Colonel, can't you let her rest for a couple of days? I'll gladly go up there tonight and meet the major in the morning and make arrangements with him.'

'The police doctor in Florence said she was in no condition for further interrogation,' put in Sam. 'Now that the excitement is over and you are only piecing the story together for the record, it seems unnecessary to harry Mrs Ellis like this.'

'I'm sure I would feel well enough to talk to Major Salti in a few days,' said Sophie meekly, with just exactly the right dose of feeble but winsome smile. 'He was very kind to me, but I'm just about all in.'

'That seems reasonable,' said Carloni slowly, but he was clearly still doubtful about something. I thought a gentle push might just make up his mind for him.

'May I suggest you let her leave, Colonel? I shall go up to Olmo right away. Tell me, you don't just happen to have a vehicle going up that way today, do you? I must confess I'm feeling pretty tired myself, too.'

Carloni's face was a study. My shot in the dark had apparently found its mark. He had been wondering how to keep an eye on a key witness whose story had certain discrepancies in it, but who was not under enough suspicion to be arrested, and here was her husband practically offering himself as a hostage.

'As a matter of fact, I do,' he said. 'I have to send some material to Salti, and my men can meet him in Olmo and give it to him there. It will save them the extra mileage to Florence.'

Sure, I thought, all of a hundred kilometres. 'That's fine, then,' I said, turning to Sam and Sophie; 'I'll make an appointment for Monday or so.' Sophie nodded, and Sam's guarded wink told me he had shared my view.

Carloni telephoned for a car and two men, and we went down the stairs together. I held Sophie tightly, and promised to keep in touch with her as closely as the situation permitted. She seemed to sag against me; she had not just been acting – she really was at the end of her tether. Sam gripped my hand firmly, and said, 'That's clear, then, Mike. See you soon. Good luck.'

At the door opening on to the courtyard, I stopped suddenly and turned to Colonel Carloni.

'I almost forgot: I must make a phone call to my client here in Rome. May I use a phone?'

I walked back with him to the main foyer and stood just inside the glass doors, clearly visible from the street.

'I hope I can be back in Rome by midday tomorrow,' I said to Carloni. 'I may have lost a house and property already, and if this business goes on much longer, I am going to lose an important client, too.'

Carloni assured me it was to be no more at this stage than a *sopraluogo,* an investigation on the spot, to try to determine the cause of the blaze.

When I could find nothing more to say on the subject, I turned from the door and went to the phone. By now, Sam and Sophie would be well on their way.

I called the I.D.A. offices and asked for Miss O'Hara. There was a long silence on the line when I told her who was calling.

'Why, Dr Ellis,' she said finally, and I pictured her gaunt face framed by bobbing ringlets, 'to be sure, I thought you were going back to Nooriabad!'

Now, that couldn't refer to last Monday, could it, I thought, but I let it go.

'I got held up, I'm afraid. There was a fire at my property, and the police think it might have been deliberate. They are asking a lot of questions, but I think I can be free by tomorrow. It's just that Mr Wharton was supposed to leave for Rome on Saturday, and that's the day after tomorrow, I don't know now whether it's worthwhile going this week. Perhaps we could travel back together.'

I left a pause, but all she said was, 'I read about the fire. I do hope nobody was hurt?' Nothing about the fire being after I had left, or why did the police inquiries take three and a half days. Nothing about Klaus's death. Nothing.

'There was a lot of damage,' I stalled. 'Could you send a telex to Mr Wharton for me asking him what he thinks? I'll call in for the reply as soon as I'm free tomorrow.'

'Why, of course, Dr Ellis. If I send it now, the answer will be in tonight.'

'Fine, thank you very much. Is Mr Mkara there?'

'No, sir. He'll be back by tomorrow lunch-time. Were you wanting an appointment, Dr Ellis?'

As a matter of fact I had been, but for some reason I now decided to say no. I didn't want to be tied down to appointments just now. I thanked her and rang off before she could say any more, and went back to the entrance.

There were two *carabinieri* to protect me as we set off through the late-afternoon traffic for Tuscany, but I did not feel very safe. In fact, I had more questions to answer now than ever before.

Twenty-six

It was after dark when we reached Olmo. We stopped at the Hotel Garibaldi, which had the advantage of being at the end of a small alley, just off the main square, so that I was able to reach the entrance without much risk of a chance meeting with some acquaintance.

My two travelling companions took the room opposite mine. They checked at once with the local police station, and reported that Carloni had already called to set up an appointment for us there with Salti at seven-thirty the next morning.

They never made it obvious that they were guarding me, but they hardly left me alone for an instant, either. At their request, I showed them a restaurant and joined them for dinner, but I chose one where I was not known, and was glad that I met no friends. I turned in early and slept very well.

Salti was waiting for us when we arrived at the police station next morning. I thanked him for being so considerate with Sophie, and he asked, apparently sincerely, about her health. He hoped that she would get over her shock soon. In order that he might question her again, I suggested.

'Dio mio, no! I hope that won't be necessary at all. She gave my assistant a very detailed account. But we would like her to sign the transcript as soon as he has prepared it.'

We made an appointment, which we were never to keep, for Monday afternoon at his office in Florence, and to my surprise he seemed completely uninterested in my plans until then. Either he was a much more relaxed investigator than his colleague in Rome, I reflected, or he had something up his sleeve. He suggested that I might like to inspect the extent of the damage. I agreed readily, and we set off at once.

The sun was well up as we climbed the familiar mountain road. It was a splendid morning, but bitterly cold. White plumes of smoke were rising on the still air where the corn stubble was being burned off. I pretended to study the view out of the back window once or twice. As the road wound laboriously up the hill, there were many opportunities to survey the stretch behind us. The only other vehicle in sight was a bright yellow school bus. Not that anyone would have any trouble in tracking us, I thought; there would be no doubt in any adversary's mind as to where we were heading.

As we drove up the mountain, Salti went over my story again. But Sophie and Sam and I had knocked all the corners off it in Rome, and it now fitted snugly to Sophie's version.

At a point on the dirt track only a short distance from the turn-off to the house, Salti pointed out the place where a local shopkeeper and his son had been killed in a car crash on the previous Saturday afternoon. 'But of course you had left by then,' he added.

'I knew them,' I said. 'My wife told me about it.' It was a jolt to realize that, in the mounting horror of the week's death-toll, I had almost forgotten the cold-blooded elimination of Marino and Giorgio. There was no reason for Salti to connect the 'accident' with the events at my house and in Florence, but I hoped he would not be over-conscientious. I hated to think what a forensic science lab. would deduce from the scratches there were bound to be on the jeep.

Soon we reached the edge of the burnt area. I gazed in dismay at the devastated scene. Not just because it was our land; it was also infinitely sad to see so much destruction where pastoral serenity had reigned. Most of the thick undergrowth was gone, and many trees were no more than macabre, blackened stumps.

A few feet into the area I saw several white pickets marking various points near the track, but we passed these without comment and drove on to the studio and the house. To my relief, the buildings were almost unscathed. Some wooden shutters were scorched, and a few panes cracked by the heat where the fire had approached quite close, but otherwise the thick old stone walls had suffered nothing worse than patches of blackening.

'There's really nothing more here that concerns me in any case,' said Salti, watching me with his hands in his overcoat pockets. 'We have been over the house thoroughly already. If the terrorists were still alive, it might have been worthwhile making a formal estimate of the damage they caused, but you have nobody to claim against now. When you are ready, perhaps we can go back down the track. There is something I would like to show you.'

There was no point in going inside, I said. No, perhaps I might just go quickly to the bathroom, since we were here?

I took the reserve key we always leave in a certain crack in the wall behind the ivy and let myself in. The police certainly had been thorough; they had left the place rather more chaotic than Jens and his gang had done when I last saw it. I locked myself into the bathroom and retrieved the draft report, still safe in its hiding-place, and thought in triumph, not thorough enough, major! For a moment I was nonplussed, and wondered what to do with it. Finally I folded it in two and pushed it into the back of my underpants. With trousers, shirt and jacket over it, the outline would not show.

Pulling the chain, I washed my hands and left, pausing only to shake my head in sorrow at the mess we would have to clear up. As I replaced the emergency key in its cache, a question occurred to me. 'How did you get in to the house?'

'We . . . ah, have our methods, dottore,' said Salti, unable to suppress a smile.

We returned to the edge of the burnt area and stopped at the pickets. Salti pointed out to me where the motor cycles and one body had been found. Then he signalled to the driver, who opened the boot of his car and took out a clear plastic bag with a label and a broken seal on it, and handed it to Salti. The officer pulled out a short length of steel chain with a clip on the end and showed it to me.

'Do you recognize that?'

'I believe I do. It used to be the chain for our dog, but we haven't used it since the old chap died months ago.'

Salti pointed at an oak which had been less damaged than most of the trees around. 'It was looped around this tree,' he said, 'and stretched across the track. It is long enough for the other end to have been attached to the tree that left that stump over there.' I nodded and waited.

'What I want to know is, how did it get there? If your wife put it there after passing with the jeep, why didn't she tell us? And if the terrorists put it there, why did they drive into it themselves?'

'I can't help you, I'm afraid,' I said after a moment. 'The only suggestion I have is that perhaps it wasn't stretched up at all, but merely prepared beforehand for putting up in case of danger. Perhaps they discovered my wife had escaped and came here to put the chain up in case she was still near the house. Then a motor cycle fell over, petrol leaked from the tank, and somehow the fire was started. I don't know – I'm just hypothesizing.'

'No, Dr Ellis. I think I know how the fire was started.' Salti went over to the open boot and took out another plastic bag. In it was a twisted yellow and blue glob of plastic. I looked at it in silence for five seconds or more before the distinctive colours and the remains of a spout on the tortured shape rang a bell, and I exclaimed, 'Agip! That was an Agip canister!'

He nodded. 'Over there, near the other motor cycle. But we've not been able to get any prints off it.'

'Off *that*? You tried?' I said incredulously.

'Oh yes,' said Salti. 'We can get prints off all sorts of things nowadays. Prints from just such a source caught an arsonist a few years back. But it's not easy, of course.'

'I can imagine!'

He asked me various questions, all easy to field, until I was sure he was just poking around in the ashes in case anything turned up. It wasn't until we were bumping back along the track that he pulled out a pipe and started stuffing it, and I sensed as strongly as I have ever felt an intuition that he was doing it to lull me into incautiousness as he spoke without looking at me, concentrating on his hands.

'What were you doing in . . . Pakistan? Kurdistan?'

'Koristan,' I corrected him. 'It's a small Moslem state which borders on Afghanistan. I was doing a consultant job for the U.N. there.'

'I see.' A pause. 'What sort of job?'

'Oh, checking their accounts, preparing their annual financial report. Book-keeping, really.'

'You don't suppose it could have anything to do with this business, do you?'

You cunning old fox, I thought. I'll bet a year's earnings that's no more than a shot in the dark, but even those sometimes hit the mark. I felt a new respect for the experienced investigator, and not for the first time in my career I noticed the similarity between our two professions.

'Good heavens, no!' I laughed. 'Other side of the world, almost. Just black-and-white uninteresting figures. Sorry, I can't give you a lead there.'

He was puffing on his pipe, and the foul smell of the fumes it produced made the driver clear his throat cautiously.

'It's just something that was on the telex this morning. I called into the office before I left Florence.'

'Lord,' I said, 'you certainly start work early!'

'A lot on right now,' he said between puffs. 'It was something about a United Nations man from out that way being murdered in Zurich last night. There was a general call to all anti-terrorist units, because it was a typical R.A.F. job. Telephone call to a news agency afterwards, enemy of the people eliminated, you know the kind of thing. Now I come to think of it, I think it was Koristan he was from. A New Zealand citizen.'

I suddenly felt icy cold. 'You don't remember his name, do you, Major?' There were perhaps a hundred non-locals in Wharton's mission, and some of them might be Kiwis. But how many of those would be likely to be in Zurich?

'I don't recall. It was a foreign name for me, of course. There was plenty on the people who might have killed him, though.'

I laughed, and although it sounded like a hoarse croak in my ears, it produced no visible reaction from Salti. 'Just might have been somebody I met there, that's all.'

We travelled in silence to Olmo, and stopped at the police station.

'There's nothing more I need from you at present, Dr Ellis,' said Salti. 'Thank you for your time.' He knocked his pipe out on the heel of his boot. 'Please call me in Florence on Monday morning.'

We shook hands and parted. I went to the pastry shop with the telephone cabins in the back and took the Florence book in with me. The first thing I did was to transfer the uncomfortable wad of paper in the seat of my pants to the inside pocket of my jacket.

John Morris was in his office, and pleased as Punch at the exclusive inside story he had got from the siege.

I asked him to get on to his Zurich office and find out the name of the U.N. man murdered there the night before and call me back as soon as he could. Then, while I was waiting for his call, I dialled the I.D.A. number in Rome and asked for Miss O'Hara.

'We've had no reply from Koristan, Dr Ellis,' she fluted, 'but Mr Mkara would very much appreciate it if you could make a conference here this afternoon. It's very urgent indeed.'

'No reply? But that's unbelievable! They must have replied something? Are the lines disturbed?'

'That could be the case, Dr Ellis, I don't know. I'll gladly try again for you. I could have an answer by the time you come, I dare say. What time could you make it this afternoon?'

On an impulse, I said, 'Not before five, five-thirty. I'm in Milan right now and still have some things to do.'

'Very good, Dr Ellis. Mr Mkara will be waiting for you.'

I hung up. Would he, by George! It must be really urgent for a top-level U.N. official to wait outside working time, on a Friday, of all days. And no reply from Nooriabad in almost twenty-four hours?

I drifted back to the front bar and ordered a *caffè corretto,* but it was not even ready before the phone rang and the lady behind the bar said, 'It's for you, dottore.'

'John Morris here, Mike. Got a pencil?'

'Go ahead John, I don't need one.'

'His name is, or rather was, Charles Wharton, a New Zealand citizen of the . . .'

'Thanks John. I've got it.' And yet Miss O'Hara hadn't mentioned it at all!

'What's wrong, Mike? You sound strange.'

'Nothing, it's okay. I just thought it might be somebody I knew, but it's not. I'll tell you about it later. What was this chap doing there?'

'He was in transit to New York. Strange route; I thought the Pole route is the fastest nowadays.'

My instinct was still to keep everybody I could out of this as long as possible. It may have been giving me a clear field, but it was leaving me alone against ... against whom? Alone in the dark, that's all. It was fortunate that Sam and Sophie seemed to have been so discreet about what they had told John, otherwise that experienced newshound would have been battering me with questions.

I promised him I would keep in touch and went out of the cabin. I was glad the coffee was ready; I needed it, and the brandy in it. A hell of a lot of coffee I'm getting through, I thought wryly.

It was now eleven-thirty. Thanks to my instinctive lying – what a habit that was becoming nowadays! – the only trace anybody apart from the police had on me at the moment was Milan, much further away than Rome and in the opposite direction, and the telephone number of the bar I was about to leave.

There was no car-hire company this side of Florence, and I couldn't take the jeep. I would have to go to the radio station to collect it, and apart from being slow and uncomfortable, it was quite a distinctive vehicle. But I could take a taxi to Terontola and, barring strikes and other acts of God, be in Rome by three, before anybody was expecting me. Then I snapped my fingers and exclaimed. I paid and hurried out of the bar, striding down the main street and across the square. I was back at the police station within three minutes.

The desk-sergeant said the Rome crew was still there, and Major Salti too. It was no difficulty at all getting a lift back to Rome. The crew had been taking their lunch-break early in order not to have to interrupt the journey. I slipped out and bought two cheese-and-ham 'sandwiches', each consisting of a jaw-breaking half a loaf cut in two and liberally filled, to eat in the car, and was on the road within a quarter of an hour.

The police crew dropped me off obligingly at Piazza del Popolo shortly before three, and I went into a bar and drummed my fingers on the table next to a cold beer, forcing myself to wait until a quarter past. By a quarter past nine in New York, I reckoned, Bob Harding would be at his desk.

At exactly three-fifteen, I got up and told the barman I wanted

223

an inter-continental call and would have the exchange ring back and tell him the charge. He looked suspiciously after me as I went into the cabin, but I left the door open, fanning it to and fro to disperse some of the stale smoke, sweat and perfume, until the inter-continental operator answered.

I told him the number and said loudly and clearly to ring back with the charge. He told me to wait on the line, and when the phone said 'United Nations' in my ear, I clicked the door shut and asked for Bob Harding.

'Who is calling Mr Harding, sir?'

'Tell him Mike Ellis and please hurry; I am in a call-booth in Italy.'

'Yes, Mr Ellis,' said the voice without a trace of surprise. It took the receptionist twelve seconds to locate Bob, and then he came straight on with, 'Jesus Christ, Mike, where the hell are you?'

'In Rome. Listen, Bob,' I said, 'I've got a real blaster.'

'I know, I know,' he interrupted. 'I've got a copy on my desk now, and the original is with the Secretary-General. The Old Man's going crazy.'

'What are you talking about, Bob?'

'You're not ringing me about Charles Wharton?'

'Sure. But a copy of what?'

'His confession, Mike – the lot! It came in his suitcase from Zurich an hour ago. You know he got killed last night?'

'Yes,' I said, feeling weak. 'That's what I was ringing about, mainly. But tell me about this confession.'

'Well, he told us you found out about his working for the Reds. And he appended a four-page chronological table of information, money and material he . . . uh, passed on – names, places, everything. It's terrible! The scale of it is just unbelievable. He also names his first three principals, not that there's much we can do about that except watch out in case they ever resurface in the West. But that takes him up to only two years ago. We don't know who's been running him since then. Do you?'

'Hell, no. I've got far less than that. By the sound of it, we'd have had to work over the material I've got for a couple of months just in order to arrive at a rough approximation of this appendix. I did no more than turn the key; he's opened the door wide now. How did it get to you?'

'His suitcase came on automatically, because he was only in transit, but when he didn't pick it up they opened it to check for bombs. There was a full, hand-written confession addressed to us, and they sent it on at once.'

The hair prickled on the nape of my neck. 'Unopened?'

'Yes. It was sitting on top of his underclothes addressed to the Secretary-General personally and still sealed when it arrived.'

'Thank the Lord for that!' I started to relax, a second too soon.

'Yes, except that there was another copy, and some dumb bastard at the airport sent that on, too. It was addressed to CBS news, and it'll be on the air in about a quarter of an hour. I just spoke to the programming director, and there's no way I can stop it.'

'Bob,' I said calmly, 'tell me one thing. You said a full confession. Did he mention me?'

'As a matter of fact he did, but only in our copy, and only obliquely. He said he was confessing because . . . just a moment . . . he says: "I have decided to confess for personal reasons, and because a first check of my accounts has been made. This has turned up nothing, but it seems to me that it will be only a matter of time before the discrepancies begin to show. I beg you to see that the consultant concerned with this investigation is not brought into it, *even among top-level staff*, for I fear for his life." In the CBS version he just says "for personal reasons", and leaves it at that. What do you make of that, Mike?'

'Did you know his wife died last weekend?'

'Yes, we heard about that. Weird, wasn't it?'

'Yes, it was. It looked like suicide, but there's no way to be sure.'

'What!'

'Listen, Bob: tell CBS about his wife – it'll be enough to account for his last actions for the moment. And for God's sake follow his instructions and keep me out of this at every level. They've already had a try at me.'

'We can see the need for taking care, Mike,' said Bob earnestly. 'The Old Man wants my photocopy back by ten this morning, and is going to destroy it personally. Maybe you had better come over and talk to him.'

'I'll do that as soon as I can. In the meantime, see that the story about his wife's death is publicized, in the house as well as out of it.' I was fumbling for a cigarette. 'Is that all he wrote?'

'There's just one other point, something about the king-pin being a very high official, higher than we can imagine, and that he cannot name him because he is not totally sure and doesn't want to foul up the career of somebody who might be innocent. He may have intended to name him verbally to the Old Man; I guess we'll never know now.'

I gave up trying to strike a match one-handed. 'Okay, Bob. I'll be over as soon as I can.'

'Make it soon, Mike. And keep your head down.'

'I'll do that. See you.'

But as I left the phone booth, I knew that I was going to have to hold my head right up and out and put it into the noose before I flew out of Rome. If I ever flew out of Rome.

Twenty-seven

There were some things I had to work out very quickly, and I needed a quiet place to do it. I crossed the Piazzale Flaminio, turned into the Borghese Gardens and wandered aimlessly across the sparse grass, absently kicking aside the litter. Despite the cool of the season, there were still a few courting couples on the ground under the enormous old conifers. It was quite pleasant in the sun as long as you were protected from the wind.

I finally sat down on a bank overlooking a little paddling pool. In summer, the kids hired pedal-driven go-karts here and raced around the concrete edge while mounted police patrolled in pairs, occasionally asking a daring sunbather to put his shirt back on and not to make an indecent impression on the tourists. But now the karts were gone and the couples wore coats. I tossed pebbles into the water and ran the evidence through my mind.

Charles Wharton had wanted to take me off the hook. He knew that I knew, and 'they' knew that I knew; but if the world thought I didn't know and I professed surprise and shock, 'they' just might leave me alone. And yet it wasn't as simple as that. There were too many possible permutations, some of them certainly booby-trapped if I misjudged my footing.

If I assumed they knew nothing of Wharton's written confession, I felt safe. Having killed him, they would only be setting signposts by killing me too: at least until I had kept my bargain and gone back to Nooriabad to re-inter the evidence I had dug up. Yet within a very short time, after the CBS broadcast, they would know that the cat was out of the bag and miaowing loudly. Did that improve or impair my chances? I decided on the whole that it improved them. If I could hold out until the news broke. I looked around me for the twentieth time, but could see nobody who might be watching me.

Wharton knew that 'they' knew what I knew (this was beginning to make me dizzy), because he himself had told them. So what point was there in his statement that I knew nothing? If I followed his cue and told the world I had found nothing suspicious on his books, was I then in the clear? Very probably, I thought, although my professional reputation would be shot. But his hint seemed to me more pointed than that. Once the story was out, it would matter very little what I knew or did not know, because his confession was so much more comprehensive than my discoveries.

Unless Wharton was assuming that I possessed some key piece of evidence, something which would pull their whole structure down around their ears, something compared with which even his shattering confession paled. Did I? Was it there, and I had not seen it?

I tossed another pebble. *A very high official, higher than we can imagine.* That was the only omission in his confession. That and the fact that we didn't know who had been running him for the past two years. *I guess we'll never know now.*

I took my draft report out of the pocket of my jacket and smoothed the crumpled pages, while a breeze fluttered the corners and shook an enormous cone out of the tree under which I was sitting, so that it landed with a thump on the grass a yard away. As I leafed through the pages, familiar phrases here and there caught my eye but refused to yield new clues.

. . . *on a scale possible only with the connivance of top-level government officials,* I read, and then I reached into my jacket for my fountain-pen. Even as I wrote, the whole picture becoming clear in my mind, I wondered what point there was in amending the report I would now never deliver. *Or indeed superbly well-placed accomplices within the I.D.A. or U.N. structure,* I added, and screwed the top back on to my pen. I put it back in my pocket, folded the summary and put that away too, and stood up and brushed the pine-needles and dust from my trousers.

I walked past the riding track and out of the park at Porta Pinciona. As I passed Doney's and the Excelsior my steps were gradually slowing. Finally, outside the American Embassy, on the very spot where I had caught up with Jim Hawthorne's cashier the day before, I came to a halt.

For two or three minutes I wondered whether I was prepared to go through with it. I was possibly about to put my life on the line, certainly my professional reputation at least. But it had to be true, it had to. There was only one person who could have known in advance and for certain that Wharton was going to be offered the top slot in the Koristan mission. And only one person capable of lifting a young head of administration out of a junior post and making him head of a politically delicate mission like the one in Nooriabad, where the Americans and Russians had veen vying for influence ever since the mineral resources had been discovered.

I had been supposed to get further instructions in Rome once I was out of Jens's care. But I had been shuttled from the mountain track to the airport, and thus ultimately back to Wharton, with hardly a pause for breath. The only 'instructions' I had received had been my airline ticket to Nooriabad.

Even the little things started falling into place; the only person, to my knowledge, who had known that George Hamilton was going to take a message to Geneva for me had been Miss O'Hara, who overheard him in the foyer. And less than twelve hours later, George was dead and my office under surveillance. Even the fact that I had not been able to get into Rome in time for the meeting the previous Friday and had decided to spend the weekend at Olmo semed now to have been predicted. Had Black Jack missed me *on purpose* last Friday?

I made up my mind. Taking a deep breath, I walked into the Embassy through the metal detector, and gave the guard my card through the slot in the bullet-proof glass.

'I need an urgent appointment with Mr Bullock,' I told him.

'I don't know if the Ambassador is in, sir, but I'll gladly check for you.'

I studied the poster of the Golden Gate, and then walked over to the one of the Grand Canyon. If I were going to New York next week, I decided, I would have Sophie and Katrina come too and take at least a fortnight's holiday out of town.

The Ambassador was in.

All the way up the curved staircase and along the noble corridor of Palazzo Margherita, the United States Embassy, I was wondering if I was going to be taken for a fool. But then, that would be the least of my problems if Cyrus C. Bullock would not or could not help me.

The Ambassador stood up to greet me with a dry, firm handshake. Now I recalled how his stoop emphasized his height, so that he always seemed to be trying not to look taller than his guest – or his host, as I had been on two occasions. His old-fashioned rimless glasses reflected the light from the lamp on his desk top, and I could not see the expression in his deep-set black eyes.

'Glad to see you again, Mike. Have a seat. How are you keeping? And how is Mrs Ellis?'

Cyrus Bullock had attended two or three openings of Sophie's exhibitions in Rome, and had once bought a highly priced print. His son had studied in the same class as Sophie in New York. Although he was not an acknowledged collector, Sophie told me after coming back from a cocktail party in the Embassy residence the year before that he had some of the finest prints she had ever seen.

The Ambassador did not really know either of us well, but we had a foot in the door, so to speak. That at least made the beginning easier, though I didn't imagine it would help much later. He pushed an open silver cigarette-box across his desk and leaned back, waiting. As politely as he could, he was telling me he was a busy man.

'Mr Ambassador,' I began, but he interrupted me.

'It was Cyrus last time, Mike. No need to change, is there. I think the staff here call me C.C., but they don't tell me.'

'Fine, Cyrus. Thank you.' Now it came with a rush, because I had to get it over with. 'I have a very strange request, one which you will probably instinctively want to refuse. Please just hear me out.'

As I lit a cigarette he said nothing, but watched me from behind his glasses.

'You have probably heard the news from New York. Charles Wharton's confession about large-scale theft of development material and funds. And the news from Zurich about his murder.'

I paused, and Bullock merely nodded faintly.

'I was the consultant called in by the U.N. to investigate Wharton, and the discrepancies I discovered played a large part in making up his mind to confess. I don't know what particulars you have heard, but the whole operation was on an unbelievably large scale.'

'Go on.'

'Well, I can't give you all the details right now, but it was financing terrorists just about everywhere. Including the U.S. They were going to considerable lengths to keep the operation going, and if Wharton had had his papers with him instead of in his through-luggage, they would have succeeded. They tried to stop me, too. They took me and Sophie and our daughter prisoner. I was . . . on the end of a leash when it broke and I managed to slip away, and Sophie escaped. The big forest fire in Olmo last Monday was her getaway.'

'Hellfire, Mike! I had no idea.' He was leaning forward now. 'The press said it was a Swiss family.'

'No, Cyrus, that was us. We are Swiss residents. And those were the same people involved in the shootout in Florence yesterday morning. You can check that with Major Salti of the anti-terrorist unit in Florence.'

I had shown the queen and the king, and was getting the jack between my finger and thumb. But I was going to have to keep it face-down for a little while yet.

'There was an important omission in Wharton's confession. He didn't name the top man. He may have intended to do it verbally; he was on his way to the Secretary-General when they got him. The point is, Cyrus, that I believe I know who that top man is. And I think they know I know. So it's a bit of a race to the finishing line.'

Bullock pulled the little American flag across the top of his desk and ruffled the silk, rearranging the folds.

'You're a British citizen, aren't you, Mike? Why are you coming to me?'

'I need help in a hurry from somebody who is prepared to accept my story. Firstly, I don't know our Ambassador, and he doesn't know me. Secondly, the only man who can corroborate my story is an American. I would not expect you to take my word for it – I wouldn't expect anybody to – in a case like this, but you might take his. It's going to require immediate, swift action and you, if you will help me, will have to justify yourself afterwards. It will be quicker and cleaner if it's all between you, me, and an American in New York. And finally, it may require some movement here in Rome which the Italian police would not like.'

He was still stroking the Stars and Stripes now, but his attention was firmly on my face. 'What makes you think I'd be more prepared to countenance that than anybody else?'

'It was a very delicate decision whom to approach, believe me. I had to base my judgment on the most tenuous of ... well, almost emotional grounds.'

There was one reason stronger than any other for my choice of Cyrus Bullock as the diplomat who might listen to my case. I had read in *Time* magazine the week before that he was on the President's short-list of candidates for the directorship of the C.I.A. when the present Director retired at the end of the year. But this was a reason I did not think politic to mention now.

'What do you want me to do, Mike?'

'The tracks are so well hidden that they would never be discovered by a normal process of investigation. So I want to beard the lion in his den. I might make a prize fool of myself; if I did that would remain between him and me. But I want to take a bug with me, and I want somebody close by monitoring and recording the conversation. If I am right, I intend to force his hand by promising immediate exposure. Risk all, win all. If I'm right, my guess is that he will head for the Soviet Embassy immediately and claim asylum. He'll know that if there is any kind of stink he'd no longer be in the game, he'd be finished.'

'Why the Russian Embassy?'

'Because the operation was co-ordinated by them.'

He was silent. I gave him a moment to think about it, and then went on, 'The agents monitoring me will have to be of sufficient rank to implement an immediate decision to pick him up and bring him in. If I am wrong, I would like to have the tape destroyed before I go and hide my arse somewhere a long way away.'

Bullock sat back again. Five, six, seven seconds passed by. Ten. I looked at my watch. It was five to five.

'Who is the American who will corroborate this for me, Mike?'

'Do you know Bob Harding at the U.N.?' He shook his head. 'He is Asian Co-ordinator of U.N. Programmes and reports directly to the Secretary-General. My suggestion is that you call him, and the Secretary-General if you want, and clear my story with them. Just don't say that I think my man is in Rome: I don't want anybody but you putting two and two together. If they back me, I'll want a bug and two men within half an hour. It's five on Friday afternoon, Cyrus. I've got to move fast.'

He pushed the flag back to its place behind the photos of his wife and children and the lump of dully glittering pyrites crystals from Elba.

'What if your man makes trouble?'

'He won't. Not where I'm meeting him. But if he does, you'll have it on tape.'

'All right.' He stood up and looked at his watch. 'Would you care to wait across the corridor? I'll be with you in a quarter of an hour.'

'Right. And thank you.' At the door I turned back. 'There's no risk involved for you, you know. You can back out any time. Or just do nothing.'

'That's the way I see it too,' he said, and steered me out of the door with a firm hand on my shoulder.

In fact, it took him twenty minutes. I sat in the ante-room and the air-conditioning dried the sweat as soon as it started. If he had required an hour I would have caught pneumonia. Then the door opened and a short, stocky man came in whom I would have taken for a Sicilian fisherman if his accent had not been from L.A.

'I'm Wallace,' he grunted, and shook my hand briefly. He took a metal object about the size and shape of a cigarette-lighter out of his pocket and handed it to me. I took it gingerly, but it did not explode. One broad side was perforated with several tiny holes. On one of the narrow sides was a flat, sliding thumb-switch. That was all.

'Push the switch down and it's operational. Try it.'

I did. The exposed area of the casing was red. I pushed it back.

'It will pick up conversation clearly at up to fifteen feet if the perforated side is towards the audio source and it's covered by no more than a layer of fabric. Operational life of the battery is about two and a half hours. Don't keep turning to face the guy you're bugging: he'll notice at once. It'll pick up peripheral signals too at about nine feet to the side and six feet behind you, more if there are reflecting surfaces like windows to the front. Is the place you are working in debugged?'

'I have absolutely no idea, I'm afraid. It's possible, but not likely.'

'Would you be able to hear a car horn on the street outside?'

'I expect so,' I said doubtfully. 'If it's persistent.'

'All right, listen. When you get there, find an opportunity to switch it on and off briefly, half a second will do it. Detectors often get screwed up and blip, for example when aircraft pass and reflect TV transmissions. People only start worrying when the signal stays on. Three seconds after you do that, I'll make beep-de-beep on the horn. If you don't hear me, or you're not sure, do it again within the next two minutes. If you still don't hear me, give it up and get the hell out. That means either you're in a debugged space and I'm not reading you, or I'm picking up a detector monitoring your signal. Uh, there's just one problem.'

'What's that?'

'I can't guarantee to pick up a detector. If I don't, and give you the clear signal, and you switch on, you may still be transmitting right into somebody else's ears too.'

'That's nice to know,' I said. 'Maybe I can get screen rights if it's good enough.'

He looked at me blankly and went to the door. A serious man.

'Do you want a ride?

'Do you recommend it?'

He shrugged. 'Nobody knows me or my sidekick in Rome.'

I went with them to Monte Mario. They sat in the car when I got out, and nobody said good luck or happy landings. Wallace just nodded. I didn't once see his partner's face. As I was about to close the door, Wallace looked up at the I.D.A. block, where one or two overtimers were still trickling out.

'In there?' he said. I nodded. 'I can read you up to twenty-eight, thirty storeys on this side, twenty in back.'

'That's all right,' I said. 'I'm going all the way to the top, here on the front side, but there are only nineteen floors.'

Twenty-eight

The guard was busy sorting out keys and hanging them on hooks when I entered the foyer, so I didn't bother to have myself announced. I stood aside as the elevator doors opened and let out three twittering Malaysian girls, and then got into the lift which they had left filled with musky perfume.

Now I stood watching the digital indicator going 12 ... 13 ... 14 ... Once I touched the bug in the breast pocket of my jacket and fought down the temptation to switch it on and off. The fire extinguisher in the corner of the lift warned me. I am always tempted to try fire extinguishers, because I don't trust them to work when they are needed. But there are some which squirt and then stop when you let go of the handle, and others which keep on going until they are empty.

I felt an urgent need to go to the bathroom, but I suppressed it because I knew it was only in my mind. It suddenly occurred to me where the expression 'shit-scared' came from.

... 17 ... 18 ... This was it.

Miss O'Hara was not in her office. I closed the outer door quietly behind me and could not resist sniffing around. Her desk was not tidied up for the weekend; she was obviously still in the building somewhere. Probably behind the inner door with Mkara. I tiptoed over to listen, but could hear nothing. Then I remembered it was a double door.

I reached nervously again for the bug in my breast pocket, and noticed what a suspicious gesture that was. I palmed it and slipped it into the bottom pocket of my jacket instead.

The papers on the desk were innocuous. A Swissair ticket-stub Rome–Geneva–Rome, Mr Mkara. A telex about renewing Mkara's

multiple-entry visa for the U.S.A. A couple of letters . . .
Ellis . . . my heart pounding, I picked up the sheet torn from a
telephone notepad, where my name had caught the corner of an
eye, but all it said was Ellis – 5 p.m. – MI (the Italian two-letter
abbreviation for Milano).

Then I heard Mkara's voice and jumped. It was muffled but
close by. I raced for a visitor's chair and sat down, crossing
my legs. The inner door opened, Miss O'Hara said, 'Right away,
Mr Mkara,' and as she closed the door and turned towards me I
was slowly preparing to stand up and greet her. She was wearing
a shapeless sack of a dress which made her look even less feminine
than usual. Her eyes were sunken and tired, and the well-
kept ringlets did little to relieve the hatchet narrowness of her
face.

'Why, Dr Ellis,' she said in a low voice. 'I didn't know you had
arrived. I'm sure I'm sorry if you had to wait.'

'Good evening, Miss O'Hara. The receptionist wasn't at his
desk, so I came on up. I arrived just this moment.'

Her eyes were sweeping the room, and kept returning to the
drawers of her desk. She reached for the intercom.

'Yes.'

'Dr Ellis is here, sir.'

'Good. Send him in. And some tea, please, Miss O'Hara. Ask
Dr Ellis what he would like.'

She looked at me questioningly. I shook my head and walked
into the inner sanctum with a perfunctory rap of the knuckles on
the green baize of the door.

'Come in, Dr Ellis, come in. Sit down. We have a lot to talk
about.'

He shook my hand over the desk top and waited for me to sit
down before doing so himself. For the first time I noticed that
Cyril Mkara's smile never got as far as his eyes. 'You have heard
about poor Wharton, of course.'

'Yes. As a matter of fact it was the police who told me.'

I thought in dismay, damn he's launching straight in and I
haven't even got the bug going yet. And I can't hear the traffic in
the street. I put my hand in my pocket and blipped the switch
on and off, then reached into the other pocket for my cigarettes,
my mouth was dry and uncomfortable. Had I heard something?
I could not be sure.

Lighting the cigarette as I went, I got up and walked over to the window looking on to the broad *viale* below. It was one of those pivot windows which open horizontally in the middle, the bottom half outwards and the top half inwards. The low sill just reached my knees. There was hardly a whisper of traffic to be heard. Leaning forward slightly, I could make out Wallace's car by the kerb.

'A sad business, very sad,' I mumbled, playing for time.

The door clicked, and I heard the thin rattle of a teacup in a saucer. It was still far too light outside to watch Mkara reflected in the window. Miss O'Hara spoke.

'There's just one thing, Mr Mkara . . .' As I turned around, he was getting up and following her to the door.

'Only one second, my dear chap. There are some dispatches which have to go out tonight.'

'Please. I am not at all short of time.' And you go out to your secretary's office to sign papers do you, I thought as he pulled the door to behind him. With my left hand I turned the grip on the window and opened it a fraction, while with my right hand in my pocket I flipped the switch again. Nothing. Then, *beep-de-beep*. I was on the air. I started to pull the window to, but before I could close it completely Mkara's voice swelled again and I dropped my hand guiltily from the handle and peered out at the view.

He closed the door behind him and we sat at the desk again. The reflections ran down his highly-polished cheeks as he tilted his head to drain the cup, his little finger decorously crooked. Suddenly I was no longer nervous but boiling with hate. Take it easy, son, I told myself; keep it objective.

'So our poor friend Charles Wharton was killed,' he resumed, and put the cup delicately back on its saucer. 'But not before he had sung his little swan song, I understand.'

'So Bob Harding told me, Mr Mkara,' I said clearly, putting his name on record right at the beginning of the tape.

'I expect that puts you out of a job for the moment, Dr Ellis? After all, the wealth of detail our deceased friend supplied was far more than you had discovered, was it not?'

'If you remember, I had discovered nothing at all concrete. Wharton confirmed that specifically in his confession.'

'That is so.' His smile was thin and formal. 'There was nothing in writing? No documents in your possession, no photocopies, not even a preliminary report?'

'As a matter of fact, there was.' He was tense now, the fingers of his left hand drumming ever so quietly on the teak. 'There was one thing he didn't put into writing, but we had a long talk about it in Koristan this week. In fact, I was on my way to see you about it when I heard that my wife had escaped from Olmo, and of course I wanted to see her to safety first.'

'I take it you have done that by now.' Not a trace of surprise at the word 'escaped'. It was mounting up, but was it enough? How the hell was I going to put it on the line?

As I nodded, he went on, 'What was it you and Wharton talked about? As I understand it, he ... er ... "spilled the beans". Everything, of course, except who the top man is. Perhaps he didn't know – I believe these clandestine operations work on the "need-to-know" principle.'

'Oh, he knew all right.' I was watching him closely, but there was no guilty start, no sweat beading on his forehead, nothing. He was taut but cool. Was he going to laugh me down and drag me through the mud? Was he going to have every right to do so? I suddenly felt drained and tired and slightly light-headed. I put my hand in my pocket and felt the bug. *Push harder, get closer.*

'Naturally, once you have the solution it's relatively easy to work backwards and reconstruct the proof,' I said.

'From what I have heard of your adventures last weekend, Dr Ellis, I would have thought you would be the last person to want to take the matter any further, to attract any, shall we say, unwelcome attention to yourself. Or to your wife and baby daughter – Katrina isn't it? You can't live under police surveillance for the rest of your life, can you now?'

I closed my eyes and saw the tree-lined avenue leading into Nooriabad, and a grey Opel Kadett distorted in a rear-view mirror. Wharton's voice echoed in my ears. Almost the same words ... Had Wharton and Mkara spoken together?

'Did Wharton also ring you from Zurich?' I asked.

'What do you mean, "also"? Did he ring you?' he said softly.

'That hardly answers my question, does it? Let us say he rang me to confirm various suspicions he had voiced. What did he tell you?' I did not know how long I could keep this up without saying it outright.

'He said he was on his way to New York, Dr Ellis. And he told me why.' Mkara got up and stood looking out of the window at the roofs of the city, his hands clasped behind his back, not with the fingers twisting together but perfectly calm.

'And that is why you had to dash to Geneva?'

He wheeled around, and I saw that his hands had lied. His face was tight with fury, and I fought down the instinct to press further back into my chair.

'There were certain things I had to warn him about, Dr Ellis, which I could have warned you about too, if you had been prepared to listen. In point of fact, I had a conference in Geneva.' There was a glint of triumph in his eyes. *Break that cover if you can*, he was telling me.

To overcome my fear of him, I stood up to face him. Wallace must have been getting it loud and clear: I was standing four feet from Mkara, right in front of the window on to the street.

'Your wife Sophie is very precious to you, Dr Ellis.' His voice was a vicious, hypnotic hiss. 'I do not think they will content themselves with locking her up next time. I think they will find her, and when they do you will probably wish first that she had never been born, and then that you had never been. And you would not believe some of the things they do to babies . . .'

I hit him in the face as hard as I could. I think I broke his nose – there was no way of telling afterwards. His hands flew up as he staggered backwards, and as the sill caught him behind the knees his shoulders crashed against the window. It flew up violently and the heavy pane shattered. For an instant he lay balanced half out of the frame, then the·window smashed back down across his chest and he was gone without a sound.

As I stood there trembling, unable to move, a pandemonium of hooting and shouts broke out below and I heard the crash and tinkle of vehicles colliding, but I did not look out. Dimly I thought, he didn't confess. He always avoided the point. I've lost. I'm sure now, but it's too late. He didn't say anything that would stand up in a court of law.

The door flew open and Miss O'Hara stood there gaping at the window and the slivers of glass on the floor.

'Holy Mother of God,' she said, 'what have you done?' She darted across the room and gripped me by the arm. I was shocked at her strength. She looked at me with staring eyes.

'You drove him to it, didn't you?' Her voice was raucous, a harsh croak. 'You told him you knew it all.' Suddenly she screeched 'They'll get you, Ellis! They'll get you, and they'll get your family too, you bastard! Bastard!'

I tugged dully at her clutching fingers. They were like iron clamps on my wrist. God Almighty, I thought. I've killed him.

'I saw you throw him out,' she shrieked in my ear. 'We have friends in the police, you know. I watched you throw him out! They'll believe me. What do you think he was about in Geneva, you fool? We sewed Wharton up, and we'll sew you up too!' Her gorgon's face was grotesque, the ringlets writhing like snakes. Flecks of saliva rained on my face.

I twisted my arm free with a wrench, and stepped back. She came at me with her fingers crooked like claws, scratching for my eyes. Finally I found my voice.

'Stop it!' I shouted, grabbing her wrists. 'It's all over, it's wrapped up, you're finished!'

'Bloody finished, are we now?' she gasped, and spat in my face. 'We're only starting! I'll come and watch you fry!' I bent one of her wrists out and up, ducking under her arm. She doubled over with a gasp and I forced her wrist up in the small of her back.

Two men in I.D.A. security-guard uniform burst into the room. I let her go. They came straight at me and fell on me like thieves. I struggled wildly, panting. 'No, no! It's her! She's a . . . a spy!' What was she? I could find no other word. I saw in a flash how it must look, the chief executive's secretary being beaten up by a wild-eyed stranger in a room with a shattered window, and the C.E. himself staining the pavement beneath it.

Sirens were wailing and dying outside, and the hooting was coming from much further away as the traffic jam grew. We fought for a moment longer in silence, and then I relaxed and let them hold me. Miss O'Hara almost danced in front of me, the beads of saliva flying.

'We've got you, Ellis! Nobody will listen to a word you say! I saw it all!' The guards stood like oxen, understanding nothing. And then a voice from behind me said, 'You're wrong, lady,' and Wallace was standing in the open doorway with a pistol in his hand. 'We've got it all on tape. Right from the start. There's nothing they can do to you, Ellis.' He said to the guards in perfect Italian, 'Let him go. You've got the wrong one.'

Slowly her gorgon's face smoothed out. Miss O'Hara stood with her shoulders drooping, her head down, and peered at me through her ringlets. The two I.D.A. men let go of me cautiously, as though I might leap on them if unleashed. For a moment, the tableau froze.

Then, casually, Miss O'Hara bent over and picked up a long sliver of glass lying on the thick yellow carpet. Before anybody had realized what she was doing, without straightening up she jabbed at my groin. I leapt backwards with a cry, and the glass slashed across the front of my thigh, cutting through my trousers and deep into the flesh. I felt nothing.

She straightened up slowly and dropped the glass. Gouts of blood were rushing between her fingers as she clenched her fist and threw back her shoulders. Without a backward glance she walked out of the door. Wallace stepped aside, then fell in beside her. I took a step towards them and an excruciating pain made me catch my breath; tears spurted from my eyes and my leg crumpled beneath me.

Twenty-nine

Well, as far as everybody else was concerned it was just mopping-up operations after that. Wallace, too, it seemed, had friends among the police. Or perhaps it was Cyrus Bullock; I learned afterwards that he had been following the whole operation on a radio link from Wallace's car.

I was put under police surveillance in a private clinic on the outskirts of Rome, where Colonel Carloni came within an hour. He sent up a message to say it could wait until the morning if I wanted, but before putting fifteen stitches in my thigh they had shot me full of painkillers, so I wasn't feeling much. There was nothing they could do about my trembling hands, though, or the way I jumped every time the door opened.

Carloni looked sharply at the overflowing ashtray on top of the bedside cupboard. He didn't miss a thing. He took my statement on a dictating machine and said he would send me the transcript the next morning to sign. It took over an hour and a half, and when it was finished he was considerably more cordial. He put the dictaphone away in his briefcase and filled me in on what the police had done so far.

I was amazed at the rapidity with which they had moved. Roswita Reiners's address book had been providing them with a lot of useful information, of course. But as he spoke on, I gradually realized that I was not as interested as I had thought. I broke in as soon as I could and asked him to tell me the rest the next day. For a policeman, he managed to look positively understanding and stood up to go.

'Is there anything you need?'

'Yes,' I said. 'Send me a carton of cigarettes in, would you?'

As soon as he had gone, I rang to have the telephone brought and plugged in and called Guy and Jacqueline in Lausanne. Sophie and Sam had not yet arrived, but I left very precise instructions for them. Then I rang Bob Harding, who had already been put in the picture by Cyrus Bullock, and told him abruptly I would be in touch the next week.

Suddenly I was very tired indeed and it was all I could do to replace the receiver.

The next morning my leg began to hurt like hell, but I knew I had to get out of Rome as soon as possible. As if in answer to the thought, Carloni rang to tell me there would be no objection to my leaving Italy if I wanted. It wasn't until he offered to take over my travel arrangements personally that I realized he would be only too glad to have me out of the country. Until I had proved, by dint of sheer survival, that nobody was still out to get me.

He also told me they had already traced and arrested Hartmut. They had done a lightning check of all hospital admissions for serious arm injuries over the previous weekend, and found him in a clinic in Bologna. They had also arrested the young intern who had suddenly volunteered for the unpopular weekend shift and insisted on handling Hartmut's admission personally. He turned out to be somebody they were already looking for in connection with the intimidatory street-shootings of journalists.

I had hardly put the phone down, forgetting to thank him for the cigarettes which had been by my bedside when I had woken up, when a dour-faced official from the British Embassy was shown in. He told me his name, but he was reticent about his position on the Embassy staff, apart from saying that he was representing H.E. in this matter.

I frowned. 'High Explosive?'

He didn't seem to think it was funny, but he gave me the bunch of grapes in a brown paper bag anyway, and sat down. He talked for about ten minutes. His 'American friends' had called with the details. For a long time I wasn't sure whether the Brits were piqued because I had gone to the Yanks, or whether they were relieved that I hadn't come to them. Finally I hit on the answer: they wanted it both ways.

I sat in silence, not helping him at all, and by the time he had eaten the fifth grape he was saying for the third time, each time in a different way, that H.M.G. (I fought down the temptation to ask whether that meant Home-Made Gravy) hoped I would be taciturn about my role in the events. I couldn't take any more.

'Don't be such a bloody fool,' I said, and he looked at me with interest as though I had just crawled out from under the strawberry plants, while I tried to keep my cigarette still long enough to light it. 'Do you really imagine that I want anybody in the world to know that I know anything at all about all this? Can you imagine why I'm going to be in hiding for the next few weeks? Do you want to know why . . .' I just stopped and shrugged. What was the point? 'I'll be travelling on to-morrow.'

'I'm very glad we see eye to eye, Dr Ellis. The Ambassador will be very pleased that you see his point of view. Now I really must be going. I hope they're looking after you all right. Let us know if you need anything, anything at all.'

He stood up, and then a thought struck him. 'Oh, by the way – the Americans wondered if they might have their little toy back. I'll take it for you, if you like.'

'That's all right, thanks. Somebody's coming any moment

now to pick it up.' That was pure invention, as it happened. I somehow couldn't imagine an embassy official playing messenger-boy for the Yanks, but I could imagine Cyrus Bullock's face if his 'little toy' came back to him from that quarter. After a detour.

'Ah yes. I see. Well, good luck, Ellis. Get well soon.'

He settled his hat and left. When the door burst open again I almost leapt under the bed, but it was only the nurse with coffee. I lit the twenty-fifth cigarette of the morning and tried to stop wondering whether the coffee was poisoned.

I travelled to Switzerland that night, in fact. I have developed quite a talent for lying about my movements. Carloni had me taken from the clinic to the yard of an anonymous police station by ambulance, and from there to the airport by a civilian van. He also arranged a reception for me at the other end.

Circuitously I rejoined Sophie and Katrina in the place where I am writing now. I don't know where Sam is, but I expect he'll be getting in touch soon. Perhaps he, too, thinks I'm better avoided until things quieten down.

I've just re-read that last remark. What a bitter thing to say about old Sam. I didn't really mean it, of course. Or perhaps I did at the time, but I admit now that it was unkind and poorly thought through. I've caught Sophie looking at me in an odd way once or twice when I've made some particularly caustic remark, more often than not uncalled-for. I'm going to have to get a grip on myself, but just now it seems so much effort. . . .

There's no indication whether the stolid young Swiss plain-clothes inspector, the one who calls in twice a day, knows the full story. He mentioned yesterday, in passing, that the guards we can occasionally see out of the bathroom window are being changed three times a day, and will be left there as long as we need them.

I just can't help wondering how long that will be.